Echoes of Like Souls

A Julie Madigan Thriller #5

Val Conrad

Black Rose Writing | Texas

©2020 by Val Conrad
All rights reserved. No part of this book may be reproduced, stored in a retrieval system or transmitted in any form or by any means without the prior written permission of the publishers, except by a reviewer who may quote brief passages in a review to be printed in a newspaper, magazine or journal.

The author grants the final approval for this literary material.

First printing

This is a work of fiction. Names, characters, businesses, places, events, and incidents are either the products of the author's imagination or used in a fictitious manner. Any resemblance to actual persons, living or dead, or actual events is purely coincidental.

ISBN: 978-1-68433-567-1
PUBLISHED BY BLACK ROSE WRITING
www.blackrosewriting.com

Printed in the United States of America
Suggested Retail Price (SRP) $20.95

Echoes of Like Souls is printed in Garamond

*As a planet-friendly publisher, Black Rose Writing does its best to eliminate unnecesscry waste to reduce paper usage and energy costs, while never compromising the reading experience. As a result, the final word count vs. page count may not meet common expectations.

DEDICATION

I can never thank my readers enough for their loyalty and perseverant encouragement. My excuses for not writing had worn out, so I cleaned out my office, charged my laptop, and sat down to write. Sure, there's much more to that story than I'll share, but the objective was achieved, along with the beginnings of the next book. Thanks for the push.

Special endless thanks go to my husband Bill. My world is enriched with our discussions and speculations of all sorts. You make me want to be a better person, to push harder, dig deeper, and reach higher in everything I do. Without your support, I'd have given up this pleasure decades ago, never having offered any of my writing to others for their criticism or compliment. You have given as much to creating these stories with your support as I have in my putting the words on a page.

To my sister K.D., who is embarking on her own writing journey. We've shared much more than genetics in our writing, but I'm still sending you a bill for the medical advice. We attended the San Antonio AWP 2020 convention together (despite the Coronavirus panic), and although attendance was severely reduced, we had an interesting time discussing our writing, meeting others with the same quirky habits, and enjoying the city. I encourage fans to keep up with my webpage or Facebook page for a shout about her publication.

And my thanks to many others: Tonie Bolin, who offered her services as first-draft editor, though I suspect it's just because she wanted to be the first to read it; Katrina Evans and Margo Hoffer, who were rocks for me while I wasn't writing but remained friends anyway. Each of them has shared a facet of medicine with me I will always cherish.

Thanks for the encouragement I absorbed from the Police Academy for Writers, 2019, in Raleigh-Durham, NC, last fall. Though I didn't find the scientific answer to my one writing question for this book, I took away other great ideas. Thanks to Sirchie, manufacturer of forensic products ranging from gloves to fingerprint powder to drug testing kits to body cams and more. Sirchie welcomed writers to its beautiful North Carolina campus to learn from its enthusiastic staff.

And to Lisa Wheelan, certified forensic & composite artist, Waupaca County Sheriff's Office in Wisconsin; I hope you picked up a writer's bug, and I look forward to running into you again soon because I have questions.

To Reagan Rothe and all the staff at Black Rose Writing, thank you for allowing me to take this step a fifth time. I love the second printing new covers and appreciate all your efforts to put my work into more hands.

Maybe you've thought that you want to write, here's my advice. Write. Be a writer. No one can take that away. Write what moves you. What you know, what you dream. What you want to learn more about. Write history, write future. Write fact or fiction. But write because you enjoy it.

Remember: None of us is ever THE best writer. Be YOUR best, whatever you do.

Echoes of Like Souls

FOREWORD

Writing this novel was different from its predecessors. Readers asked, some politely demanding, that I write another book. Initially, I thought the *Like Souls* series ended with four books, and I was sure Julie Madigan had lived enough, but Amber Samualson had the potential to carry on. As her story blossomed in my head, I intended to write this story from her point of view; but after several chapters, I couldn't get Julie's voice out of my head, so I allowed them both to speak. Then on a drive one afternoon, my husband was naming items of interest from a tool and freight sales brochure, sealing the characters and a new plot together. Figuratively, of course. Or perhaps literally. It's hard to tell yet.

PROLOGUE

July 16, 2001
The smell of blood amplified the odors of a man who had been dying cell by cell for the last few months. Cancer had raged through the body as if it had a map of the organs in order of increasing importance of function – colon, liver, lungs, brain, bones. Seventy-three years of outstanding good health seemed to evaporate after the man's wife had died a year ago, leaving a crumpled mass of what had once been a hard-working family man. Now he was dead, and it wouldn't be soon that anyone might miss him.

Neighbors might presume his family moved him to a nursing home across the state, based on seeing his recent visitor. He had no other family. Until someone came asking why utilities had gone unpaid, no one cared.

A blessing, truly. At least he didn't die at home alone and in pain.

The killer, who was cutting the body into small pieces, didn't believe the old man would have lived more than a few more weeks nor would he have wanted to endure the pains of living much longer.

While killing him might have been an act of mercy, dismembering the body was an experiment of sorts. As easy as following a recipe from a prior generation.

July 16, 2001
"Brandan Callaghan, line three," the voice on the phone speaker announced.

Detective Captain Brandan Callaghan reached for his receiver. His chair and his right knee made similar crunching noises as he moved, causing him to wince. Healing from a recent injury he'd suffered while wresting a suspect in the jail was taking longer than he hoped. Despite weeks of physical therapy after orthoscopic surgery, he still limped, which aggravated him more than the pain itself.

"Callaghan," he barked into the phone.

"Hello, Sir. My name is Ethan Wenzler. I'm told you met my biological mother six years ago during a murder investigation. Her name was Penny Tucker. I mean it's Daniels now. Well, it was," the voice stammered.

"I don't recall," Brandan said.

But he did.

The name conjured memories of a farmhouse, pieces of the barn blown a hundred yards away in a field of debris following an explosion. Oh, he recalled plenty.

"I was adopted at birth, so when I found out that Penny Tucker was my birth mother, I wanted to find her. I tracked her to Arizona, but her husband told me she died after coming home from Michigan. Mr. Daniels didn't say so, but I read that after she got home, she was a victim of the same killer as my uncle. I'm just hoping to find out what happened."

"I remember the investigation vaguely. I don't know much about her," Brandan replied in a carefully worded partially-true response, a flashback blasting in his mind. He started to tell the caller he could not discuss the local case, but then decided it was more that he would not.

"I understand, sir. Mr. Daniels mentioned a deputy named Matthew, so that's who I'm looking for, but the person who answered transferred me to you instead."

"Matt Shannaker." Now he understood why this phone call had come to him, and not the deputy who'd begun that investigation.

Matthew Shannaker was dead, now, too. Same killer.

A lot of people were dead because of the man responsible for Matt's death, even if it had been someone else who actually killed him.

"Or a lady named Julie?" the caller asked when the previous name hadn't earned a helpful response.

"Julie Madigan," Brandan supplied, her married name just out of reach of his swirling thoughts. "She hasn't lived in Michigan for several years. She moved to Washington."

"D.C.?" the caller asked with audible hope.

"No, Washington State."

"Oh. I can't afford to go there."

"She might be able to help answer your questions. Give me your phone number, Ethan," Brandan stated. "I'll see if I can put her in touch with you."

Yeah, I can do that. Finding her is no problem. She'll probably be getting on an airplane bound for Michigan for a retirement party soon.

CHAPTER 1
JULIE

July 3, 2001

"I'm trying to get packed for college, Dad. Do I really have to go?" Amber Samualson argued, standing tall, hands on her hips, looking back and forth at her father and me. This was her latest plea for release from the trip to Michigan later in the month. She had exhausted rationales about not knowing anyone there and needing to stay to take care of the animals, and an irrelevant argument that she did not want to miss so much of the last summer with her friends.

I looked at my husband with the same frustration and expectation as his daughter, who had graduated high school the previous month, still at least six weeks away from moving to Seattle for her first year of college.

Zach didn't bother looking up from the halter he was repairing. Nor did he answer her.

"Amber, there's no reason you can't go with us for ten days," I replied, hoping to kickstart Zach's support. "You'll have plenty of time to pack for college, to get moved and settled, all long before classes start."

When Amber turned her argument back to Zach, I went back to grooming the horse standing patiently next to me. I anticipated the next argument she might make to get out of going, and whether it was up to me to quash it or not.

The trip was to Michigan, encompassing the wedding of Kayleigh Katz, the younger daughter of my previous boss, Dr. Gerald Katz, who was also retiring. He assured me he had carefully vetted the groom-to-be, a young physician himself, testing for integrity using minimal power tools from the medical examiner's office.

"Although I may lose my mind beforehand if the wedding chaos doesn't calm down. However, Kim's poor decisions have trumped that, including when she moved out several months ago," he'd told me.

I knew Zach would go, even if he didn't want to attend either, so I expected Amber could give up the compulsive rearranging and sorting of her belongings long enough to spend time somewhere besides her bedroom and the barn.

Returning my attention to the mud-caked haunches of the Trakehner/Quarter Horse mix named Denali, I left my husband to deal with the next phase of the debate.

"You just want me to miss the party that weekend!" Amber's voice echoed through the barn, causing birds in the rafters to take flight and one of the horses to neigh in agreement, or disagreement.

Who could tell?

"Missing one party will not end your life," Zach replied, not looking up, I could tell from his voice.

"But," she continued, "it's my going-away bash." Seeing that argument didn't sway him, she continued. "I also need to shop for a car and pack it –"

He interrupted her with an expression I couldn't see. "No, damn it. First, you do not get to shop and select a car unless you intend to pay for it. Otherwise, you will drive what I choose for you. And second, we all hope you do not need six extra weeks to pack what you need to live in a dorm room, which means leaving space for your roommate."

Five bucks in our vacation save-jar for the cuss word, Samualson.

"I *told* you I wanted a private room if I can't live off-campus. I really want a quiet space to study." Amber puffed herself taller, which worked with most people because she towered over them at five feet eleven inches, which she'd inherited from her father.

Zach put down the finished halter he'd been repairing and stood to face her, barely disguising the smirk as he straightened up to a full six feet six inches plus his boots, yanking away her size advantage. "And we told *you* the limits of what we will pay for your housing at college. As with the car, if you have the money to pay for it, you may live wherever you wish."

"But –" she started again, only to be silenced when he crossed his arms. She crinkled her face in defeat and stomped out the door, leaving puffs in the loose dirt beneath the straw on the barn floor.

The flustered sound Zach made was echoed from the stall next to me by the slick black Friesian mare he had bought me before we were married.

I remember how he explained that when the breeder told him the mare's name, it was a done deal. Julaquinte, an antique musical reference, was too much of a coincidence to my own name to pass up, he told me.

Zach bent to grab his tools, muttering something about stubborn women, not caring if I heard. He'd used the description to describe me more than once, but dealing with his daughter usually included less rational discussion and more adolescent emotional temper.

Parenthood for us had begun with a teenager instead of an infant. Zach had complained to me how much her tantrums seemed more like a toddler's, though he lacked experience regarding children as did I. He was Amber's biological father, but he hadn't known of her existence until her mother was kidnapped, when her grandmother sought his help with the case and with the girl. After her mother was murdered, we had invited Amber into our home five years ago.

Amber had taken to our life with occasional hiccups, missing her friends from Albuquerque, and then having to adjust to her lifetime of diabetes. After retiring from the DEA, Zach had taught her to ride, rope, barrel race, and all things horse. She chose to take Zach's last name but asked that we not pursue legal adoption by me, even after the complicated legalities we faced when Zach was supposed to be dead. She had learned the importance of evidence investigation in law enforcement from me after finding a duffle bag in the forest and investigating its contents to what ended with the fatal shooting of a deputy.

Now, she chose to go to college and become a forensic scientist, having absorbed law enforcement from both our careers. "It's not like I have any real choice, do I?" she'd said with a laugh when she announced her plans at dinner one evening. "You do what you know best."

Growing up between two oak trees, one is apt to be a little nut.

While neither Zach nor I had discouraged her career choice, he was open and honest about the demands that a badge had made on him and his family. Although it had made a similar impact on me, I chose not to share so much regarding my past.

Having picked a university and being accepted, Amber was ready to pack and move away to college the day she graduated high school, and she insisted that a trip back to Michigan would ruin her plans.

"Are we being fair about this trip?" Zach's voice broke into my thoughts. "Should we let her stay?"

As much as I wanted to sneer at him and retort that Amber was *his* daughter, I decided to be supportive. "Life isn't fair. I'd like her to go," I said, arching my back in a stretch. "Besides, I already bought the tickets. And you owe the swear-jar five dollars for your little outburst."

He came into the stall and stood behind me, leaning to kiss my neck. "It was worth it. You aren't having empty-nest feelings, are you?" he asked.

I couldn't tell if he was kidding, or if he meant he was, too.

CHAPTER 2
JULIE

July 17, 2001

During the next two weeks, Amber attended one of several going-away parties, and she had accompanied Zach to pick out a car, a gray two-year-old Honda Civic. He had relented from his original choice of a Buick in trade for her going with us to Michigan without further debate.

By the time we arrived in Michigan, they both probably felt their deal had been a dreadful bargain.

The flight to Traverse City had been awful, starting with the bustle of getting everything packed into the truck when Amber lugged three suitcases down the stairs, sending her father into a diatribe on efficiency. She compacted the mass to two and a backpack to carry on the plane.

Then, after standing in line behind a dozen people in Portland, a tall blond-headed ticket agent named Michelle took too much time looking up our reservations before reluctantly telling Zach there had been "a little mix-up on the seating," so that only one first-class seat was available. She smiled at him. "It's only logical that you have it, with your height. But," she offered with gooey but fake politeness, "I can put the ladies in seats together in business class."

Zach blinked hard then shook his head and turned away so I edged in front of him to the counter and explained in a forced courtesy that I had paid for three first-class tickets weeks ago, had my confirmation in hand, and if there had been an error by the airline, I expected a supervisor to explain it and refund my money immediately.

"Oh, we can't do that," the young lady explained, but when Zach turned back and leaned over the counter to be eye to eye with her, far past unhappy and teetering on angry, she relented. "Let me see what I can do."

In the end, first-class tickets really were available. Or perhaps Michelle simply decided to disappoint two different passengers instead of facing off with Zach again.

From Portland to Chicago, the first part of the flight was smooth, but turbulence during the last hour bounced drinks and pretzels and a few stomachs, ending in a rough landing. With a tight connection and a near-jog around the terminal to our departure gate to Michigan, we learned the inbound aircraft from Minneapolis had been delayed by the same thunderstorms that had rocked our flight into O'Hare. Two dozen other disgruntled passengers sat at the gate. A few had already been waiting on the plane to arrive for more than an hour.

I heard a woman say she was headed to the bar.

It sounded like a reasonable plan of action, except Amber wasn't old enough to drink.

However, by the fourth time she had blabbed "I told you so" followed by the whiny "I'm starving," I was ready to leave her in the corridor and have a drink anyway.

Zach had interceded with recommendations for dinner in a restaurant with a bar, where dinner included two beers costing seven bucks apiece.

I thought it was a bargain.

After another two-hour delay, we finally boarded, without the luxury of first-class seats because there were no classes on the propjet. Zach had pretzeled himself into the single seat on the left side of the aisle, so he could have shoulder room even if his knees touched the seat in front of him.

Having inherited her father's similar ability, Amber was asleep against the window before the plane pulled away from the gate.

The flight, although late, was uneventful, and Amber didn't know we'd arrived until the plane was on the ground, taxiing to the terminal. "We there already?" she asked, pulling off her headphones.

"Welcome to Cherry Capital Airport in Traverse City, Michigan," Zach mouthed as the flight attendant spoke an announcement he'd heard many times.

Although we were late arriving, it was only a bit after 6 p.m. local time.

The car rental agents at two counters faced the harried and frustrated customers. In front of us waiting on ground transportation were three families. While we waited, Amber wandered around the terminal.

"Did you know the address for this airport is 727 Fly Don't Drive?" Zach asked me while I dug in my shoulder bag for the car reservation confirmation.

"You know this *how?*" I asked, aggravated both at the trivia and lack of success.

"How many times have I flown in and out of here?"

My response was a low grumble in escalating frustration that I couldn't find the notecard I'd written the reservation information on, so he sighed and pulled it from his hip pocket where he'd put it when I asked him to hold it before we left the house that morning.

I snatched it from his grip. "Really? You couldn't have produced this instead of telling me the post office listing for the – ahh, Fly, Don't Drive. I get it. Cute." I sighed. "Sorry, it's been a long day."

Zach's turn came to exchange credit card and driver's license for documents to rent a car when Amber strolled up.

"Ooh, get a Mustang convertible, Dad!"

"I'm not getting a sports car, and you wouldn't want to sit in the back with the luggage if I did."

"I could drive!" Amber said, her enthusiasm sparking.

The clerk's antenna ears perked. I bit my lip, waiting on the explosive response Zach might actually make this time.

"All of you, she's *not* going to drive, regardless of what I rent!"

I was relieved. The clerk was skeptical. Amber was fuming.

"How will I ever learn to drive in a new place if – "

Zach put his hand up between them to end the discussion. The vehicle he'd reserved was a plain full-size sedan in someone's description of green.

The ride to the hotel was quick and quiet with Amber sulking. I checked us in while they unloaded the luggage from the trunk to a cart. Back inside, I led them to the elevator, up three floors, and toward the end of the hall, stopping to slide the plastic card in the lock to open the door.

"I still think I should, like, get my own room," Amber complained, dragging her backpack as she moped behind us.

"Not happening. Welcome instead to our suite," I announced as Zach muscled the cart into the room.

"Like when you and Nolan and me checked into a hotel together in Colorado?" she asked, emotional gears changing in a neck-breaking acceleration. "Awesome!"

Zach didn't bother to correct her grammar.

"Amber slept in my room," I explained to him.

"It never entered my mind otherwise," he replied over his shoulder as he went into the bathroom.

"Rules: You do not leave your room except through this door," I told her, "And you do not lock the door between the rooms."

Amber shrieked with joy, grabbed her backpack and suitcases, almost twice the size of Zach's, and danced through the door joining the rooms.

The plan had been to unpack, wash up, then go out to eat, though dinner in O'Hare had lessened our appetites.

"Let's go to Matilda's Bakery," Zach suggested, coming back out of the bathroom, drying his face with a bleached white towel that looked fluffy but stiff. "They have the best …"

Amber's head popped around the door jam. "Dad! I can't eat dessert and you know that!" Hands on her hips, she marched into the room, "I've been eating transportation food all day, and I'm tired of walking." Punctuating her refusal, she plopped down on the room's sofa and kicked off her shoes.

"…appetizers," Zach finished, shaking his head. "Can we bring you anything then?"

Amber rolled her eyes then grinned. "I'll order room service."

"Only if you pay for it," Zach growled. "Julie told the clerk not to take orders."

"Dad!" The expression took three pitches and four seconds.

"Order a pizza," I said, tossing a flyer from the desk to the sofa. "I don't recommend the anchovies."

CHAPTER 3
AMBER

July 17, 2001

Dad and Julie had been gone over half an hour, and I had ordered as soon as the elevator doors had closed.

When I heard a knock, thinking the pizza had arrived, I peeked and saw a single male who I assumed had my meal. I opened the hotel door to a tall, wavy-haired man about my age, with deep blue eyes set just a smidgen wide. Without pizza.

We stood at the threshold, facing each other, both of us expecting someone else.

"I'm looking for Julie Madigan," he said, taking a step back.

"Samualson, not Madigan," I replied, hoping I hadn't opened the door to a kidnapper or something. He didn't *look* like a criminal, I thought. *He is kinda handsome.* "Married name – Samualson. She's not here right now."

"I didn't know," he said, his whole introductory speech seemed to be a jumble in his head. "I mean her new name. Um, okay. Can I leave her my number, please?" he asked, pulling a piece of paper from his pants. "I'd like to speak with her."

Not blue jeans, I noted. Red polo and black slacks. Black loafers. Then I realized I had just made an obvious size-up of him head to toe, and he was well aware of it. My face turned bright pink.

"Yeah, I can tell her," I said, taking the note, hesitant to step away from the door. "Does she know who you are?"

"No, but she met my mother once, so I was hoping she could give me some information."

"Does your mom, you know, live here in Michigan?"

"She grew up south of Traverse City."

Hearing the elevator ding and open, we both turned to look down the hallway.

"I hope that's mine," I said, holding out a twenty-dollar bill to flag over the delivery woman, who looked older than my grandmother. I paid and took the box, but then I didn't know whether to shut the door on this guy or to be polite and ask him in to share my food.

Well, he could have already killed me if he'd wanted. Plus, the delivery woman could identify him. And there are cameras everywhere.

I invited him in to join me for pizza to wait for Julie, although he was reluctant until I told him I wanted to hear more of how Julie knew his mother. Inside, I waved him to the desk and pulled a chair over to the other side, so we had a table of sorts.

I pulled out the napkins and dried red peppers from a paper bag, explaining my choice. "I call this a fungal fiery Hawaiian pizza – ham, pineapple, jalapenos, and mushrooms." I flipped open the box. "You might need a drink." I turned and pulled two bottles of water from the small refrigerator, and we sat facing each other across a desk. "Eat up!"

He nodded and chose a slice, taking a bite and chewing eagerly. "Thanks, this is excellent!" he announced before stuffing another bite into his mouth, trying not to look like a starving orphan.

"Tell me about your mom," I said.

He nodded to acknowledge her question but kept chewing, frowning that he'd have to interrupt eating to answer.

"Between slices is fine," I said, assessing his pause, and taking another bite, too.

He finished the slice, wiped his mouth again, then sat back. "Thank you. That is a great topping combination," he said, picking up a second slice and nibbling off a piece of ham. "Okay. Most everything I've learned about my biological mother is at least secondhand. She had me when she was a teenager and unmarried, and I was adopted by a family who didn't know her. I grew up in Ann Arbor. Once I learned I was adopted, I knew I wanted to learn more about her, but by the time I found the records, she was already dead."

"What's that got to do with Julie?" I asked, also taking a second slice.

"Penny, my birth mother, came here from Arizona to help the police after her brother was murdered, and then when she returned home, both she and my half-sister were poisoned or something. By the same man."

"How awful!" I said, leaning forward and forgetting the pizza. A dozen questions whirled in my head.

The lock whirred and the door opened, leaving the four of us staring at each other.

I jumped to my feet, feeling guilty and not knowing why. "This is..." I turned to introduce the guy I'd shared my meal with, stammering in disbelief when I couldn't remember his name, then that I didn't *know* his name.

He had scrambled to his feet, too, looking every bit as guilty as I felt when his face blotched red.

"Sir," he said, hoping to appeal to another male for support, "I stopped by to meet Julie Madigan, but she, I mean, she," he said, pointing to me, realizing he didn't know my name either, "asked why and I was telling her about my real mother, and then the pizz – "

Dad made a motion for the stranger in the room to stop speaking. Or to stop breathing.

Hard to tell as angry as he appeared.

Appealing to him had been a mistake.

Julie stepped forward, with a cooler head.

"I'm Julie Samualson. I believe you've had dinner with Amber. This is Zach."

He swallowed hard and said, "My name is Ethan Wenzler. My mother, my birth mother, was Penny Tucker."

"Nice to meet you, Ethan," Julie said, stepping forward to shake hands. "Brandan called me a few days ago about you. I told him I'd contact you, but I don't think he knew where we were staying."

Ethan's face flushed an even deeper red. "No ma'am, he didn't say anything about which hotel, just that he expected you to be in town for a celebration this week, which I guessed to be this weekend. I started calling around to the hotels today to find you."

Dad's voice could have cut glass. "The clerk just *told you* we had checked in?"

"Well, Sir, no. I . . ." he stammered. "I called dozens of places and told them it was urgent."

Dad tilted his head to look over his imaginary glasses. "You lied?"

"Not exactly, Sir. I have to get back to Lansing. My granddad has Alzheimer's. I've been staying with him while my mom – my adopted mother – works during the summer. I only have a few days."

"So, you lied to her, too?" Zach snarked, nodding his head toward the heavens.

Julie backhanded him in the chest. "Why do you want to see me?"

Ethan took a deep breath. "I want to find out what you remember about my biological mother. She gave me up for adoption when I was born. She was fifteen,

I figure." He hesitated. When Zach's eyebrows rose, Ethan realized his story was incomplete because he'd told part of it to me. "I understand from Mr. Daniels that you'd met her not long before she died."

"Yes, I did," she said. "The detectives asked her to come provide information about her brother."

"I couldn't find out anything about her or her family from Mr. Daniels, and he wouldn't talk to me about her death." He leaned forward. "I'd like to hear anything you remember."

"It's a long story to start this late."

His expression melted with disappointment.

She sighed. "Please, let's all sit," waving to the suite's living room area and taking a seat on the couch that faced the desk.

He pulled the chair closer to face her, careful not to turn his back on Dad, who continued to pace as though his goal were to keep the young man from running.

"My parents are great people, don't get me wrong," Ethan said, "but I've wanted to learn more about my biological mother since I found out I was adopted. From what I've learned, I have no living blood relatives except my half-siblings, no adults. No one who knew her."

"I didn't know a lot," Julie said, "and I'm not sure how much I remember."

CHAPTER 4
JULIE

July 17, 2001

"I read in the newspaper archives that the farm where she grew up is where my uncle died, that the barn exploded," Ethan told me. "I haven't looked for it yet, but I'd like to see it."

"That's not up to me," I said, though I remembered it in stunning detail.

Not a detail I could ever forget, I thought, feeling a chill on my neck.

"Mr. Daniels says he still owns it, but he rents it and the land. He said his son wants to live there someday."

"Ethan, the part of the story I know is much longer and complicated than I can explain tonight," I said, "but your uncle's death left a lot of questions, so investigators asked Penny to come to help fill in the information. She was a kind woman although I didn't get the impression she and your uncle were close."

Ethan shook his head. "Was my mother killed by the same man who killed my uncle?"

"I believe so, but I wasn't involved in the case from Arizona. The whole ordeal is so much more complicated than that. I haven't thought of it in a few years, so I've forgotten a lot of details," I said. "It's late and –"

"Tell us a bit about you, Ethan. Are you in college?" Zach interrupted, having settled into the other chair.

Feeling he had escaped slaughter for the earlier situation, Ethan's answer was more relaxed. "I did one year at a community college, but this fall I'm starting at Michigan State, majoring in criminal justice. Learning about my birth mother's murder, I'm interested in law enforcement."

Amber's eyes brightened. "I'm starting at Seattle University for the same thing! I love collecting and processing evidence. I've been interning at the sheriff's department where Julie works. A few years ago, we were on a search and rescue on horseback, but on the way back, I found this bag, so we dug it up and took it to the sheriff's department to . . ."

As the two young adults began comparing their own experiences, Zach looked at me with one eyebrow cocked.

I took his hand, leaning toward him, and whispered, "Were we ever like that?"

"Us? No way." He leaned even closer. "We went straight to sex. And I'll kill him if that happens." Followed by a forced smile.

"There were a few threats first, I recall," I said. "But the sex was consensual." I smiled. "And fabulous."

Ten minutes later, we were not only excluded from the conversation but had become invisible to the pair, who had discovered their shared motivation of personal criminal death and excitement for their choices despite two years' difference in age, I guessed. We gave up and left them to discuss the future of forensic law enforcement.

I doubt they noticed our departure.

"Is that weird?" Zach asked as we walked down the hallway to the elevator, on our way to the bar.

"Amber's met someone with similar interests on this trip. Maybe she won't be so pissed we made her come."

He shrugged. "Yeah, sure. That's not what I meant. Is it weird that a victim's grown kid comes looking for you to ask about his mother?"

"Can't say it's ever happened to me."

Downstairs, we turned into the bar, a dark room with loud music and lots of neon designs on the walls, booths around the sides toward the back, where Zach headed. We sat in a booth across from each other and ordered before continuing the conversation.

"Was he was satisfied with what you told him, or do you have more to reveal to him?"

"Seems determined to learn everything, but I'll need to think about it before I can elaborate. If he went to all this trouble, I guess he deserves answers."

A server with a broad pink stripe in her hair brought our drinks, and I toasted a good night.

"What makes it so good?" he asked.

"We landed safely, despite the airline's reservation and delay issues. We had a fabulous dessert tonight instead of appetizers, which we didn't have to tell her. Amber made a new friend. What's not good?"

"Oh, I thought you meant it was good, just being with me," he replied with a smug grin.

"No, Z'. Being with you makes it a great night."

Ethan was gone when we returned half an hour later, and Amber was already asleep on the sofa instead of her bed. Zach pulled a blanket out of the closet to cover her. Despite being zonked on the couch across the room, she'd wake in an hour or so and go to her own bed, so we left her there.

I peeked at her blood sugar and insulin logs to make sure she had taken her night dose, which she had recorded.

Exhausted, I pulled the covers back on the king-sized bed and melted into the crisp sheets.

The next morning, no one had any reason to wake up early, given the three-hour time zone difference. Regardless, Zach got out of bed and showered first, then made coffee, then I heard Amber's shower through the wall.

I suppose the day has begun.

When the barely-cup-sized brewer finished spewing hot water, Zach took his paper cup and went out onto the balcony to watch the sunrise highlight the bay, something I doubted he'd confess he found appealing about this part of Michigan. After a few minutes, the door opened behind him, and Amber joined him.

I stayed in bed, pretending to be asleep, eavesdropping.

"Hey, Dad, you're awake early," she said, snuggling under his arm.

"I'm always up this early, but you aren't."

She must have reached for his coffee, but he pulled it away. "Go make your own."

"Can we talk, without you getting mad?"

"No promises, but I'll try."

"It's about Ethan, you know, from last night. I really like him."

Zach nodded, probably trying to stay out of the father-mode, though her incessant misuse of the word 'like' was getting on his nerves, so he mocked her. "He seemed to be, you know, like, a nice guy, like he has his stuff together and like, you know, a direction in life. What's not to like?"

"But you know what I mean, that I like him."

"No, I don't, Amber. You've just met him. Get acquainted, so *you* really know what you mean," he replied.

"I can spend more time with him?" she asked, brightening. "Like, maybe this afternoon instead of going to the rehearsal dinner? Julie still has to tell him more about his mother."

"No. And stop saying 'like' when it's not a verb. It makes you sound uneducated. Maybe you should start at a community college first."

"Sorry," she said regarding her language. "But, Dad," she said with a pouty whine capable of making most any father wilt, "Ethan has to leave in a few days. Then he goes back to college and so will I."

"First, Ethan leaves or we leave, it's inevitable. Being in different time zones does not stop you from becoming friends. Second, we are not going to the rehearsal dinner. Third, we will make time for Julie to talk to him."

"But I hope we can become – "

"If you say 'more than friends,' the father-monster will appear." Zach took a sip of his coffee. "If it's meant to be more, it will happen. In time. Don't ruin a budding friendship by hoping to be something more too soon. Friendship is the best part of any relationship, so don't skip it."

"Even yours and Julie's?"

"Absolutely. We have things in common, which is great. But we each have likes or dislikes the other doesn't, and that's all right, too. Julie makes me want to be better a better person."

"What about when you pretended to be dead?"

"You were with me part of that time, remember? I knew how much it hurt her. And you. I hated it."

"I didn't like keeping it a secret, either. See, verb," Amber said, "but I'm glad I got to spend the time with you. I'm glad things worked out this way."

"Me, too." He pulled her close again. "We've had rough spots but look at us shine now."

I feel the same way, Zach. We are all so good for each other.

From inside, I crawled out of bed and dug around in the suitcase for Zach's worn denim shirt, then started my own cup of coffee. Zach left me what little creamer and sugar there was. I like my creamer with a little coffee, which offends his sensibilities of plain, strong, and black.

I joined them on the balcony.

"What a fabulous morning!" I said, stifling a yawn. "It's supposed to be lovely weather all week."

"Let the celebrations begin," he said, wrapping his other arm around me. "I've got beautiful women to accompany me, so let's go take in the sunshine."

Within an hour's drive of Traverse City are hundreds of spectacular sites. After breakfast, Zach drove us west toward Empire, then north around the Leelanau peninsula. We stopped at the Sleeping Bear Dunes, but Amber shook her head when she saw others taking the sandy run down the sandy hill, only to have to climb back up. I agreed it looked like more work than fun. Just watching the kids slide on cardboard or snow dishes exhausted me.

Sleeping Bear Dunes, she read us from the plaque explaining how the national lakeshore got its name from a legend that a mother bear and her two cubs were forced to swim away from a raging forest fire in Wisconsin, across Lake Michigan. Eventually, the cubs fell behind in exhaustion, and the mother bear climbed the high bluff to watch and wait for them. But they were too tired to reach the shore and drowned as she watched. The Great Spirit Manitou created two islands to represent the cubs and the sandy dune to represent the faithful but broken-hearted mother bear.

"Gosh, why are so many legends depressing?" she asked.

"Maybe because humans are sympathetic to grief," I offered.

I wonder if she understands that yet. If not, she will.

Heading on north through Glen Arbor, Amber pointed out occasional views of Lake Michigan.

"It's kinda like being in Washington, with the trees and stuff," Amber said, admiring the views. "Is the water really cold like the Pacific Ocean?"

She was referring to a trip she had gone with Savannah Fordham's family the previous summer out to Newport, Oregon. Swimming in the ocean had been high on Amber's list until she waded out into the water that was about 50 degrees, changing her wish to dive in to look for seashells.

"It's usually warmer over in the bay," I replied. "Maybe we can find a beach closer to the hotel."

In comparison, the Columbia River temperature averaged over 60 degrees, but she didn't swim in it, either.

"You'd love the Gulf waters in Florida," Zach added. "Neither of us will set foot there again in this lifetime."

That's for sure! The best memory of Florida I have is leaving.

As we drove Highway M-22 along the shoreline of Lake Michigan, I didn't mention or point out where Kimberley Katz and I had been held captive by the murderer who seemed to have wrecked everyone's lives, and I wondered if I should tell Ethan everything – or anything – about the man who had killed so many others than his mother.

No, neither of them is mature enough to understand survival against such evil or the grief I've felt since.

Zach drove past the property where the cabin had stood, not looking in its direction, and although he knew the story, I wondered if he recognized the actual location.

Through the trees, I glimpsed a new house sitting back from the road, in a perfect sunshine yellow with white trim.

Watching as Zach drove past where so much of my life had exploded with the same force as the cabin, I decided I couldn't share with Ethan how Anthony Bock had become entangled in my life. I'd skip the part where I killed Matt Shannaker in hopes of saving Kim.

Or that Anthony Bock was my half-brother.

I never told anyone but Zach that sometimes I still had horrible dreams of holding the knife to Matt's neck. Or his last words before I pulled it across his throat.

Zach, however, knew all those things from my past. He never disturbed the memories because he had held me while the nightmares shook me to tears at night, especially during the first few months after it had happened. Bock had caused a lot of scars for us both, and Zach was the second happiest person in the world that the monster was dead.

As we drove north, Amber pointed to glimpses of Lake Michigan to the left between trees and hills everywhere, the villages with brightly colored shops, all the way to Northport on the east side of the Leelanau Peninsula, where Zach parked.

I wanted to visit shops on the main street, so Zach and Amber followed me, lagging a bit, but close enough I heard most of their banter.

"I don't get it," she said. "Why would people want to live here?"

"Why not?" Zach replied. "It's beautiful."

"Maybe during the summer, but the winter is nasty."

"You mean the snow?"

"That, and like, the wind and crazy sub-zero temperatures."

I turned in time to see Zach roll his eyes at her use of "like" again. I knew it was getting on his nerves.

They turned to watch a small sailboat motor out of the harbor.

"Snow they have, by the foot, but they deal with it efficiently," he replied. "Like New Mexicans handle the heat. It's not like Siberia."

"How do you know? Have you ever been to Siberia?"

"Michigan is an acquired taste. Julie liked it, and I did, too. We could stay for the winter," he kidded. "Let you see for yourself."

She play-punched his arm. "No, thanks, I'll stay where it's warmer, even if it does rain a lot. I don't rust, but I very well could become an icicle."

"The main difference between Michigan and Washington? I don't have to shovel the stuff that falls from the sky there," he said. "That's a plus, I agree."

They gave up the weather debate and headed to the marina, leaving me to stroll alone along the shops for a while. Solitude lasted four minutes before my phone rang.

"Julie? It's Callaghan," the familiar voice boomed when I answered.

"Hey, Brandan," I replied. "How are you?"

"Same as usual, eat, work, sleep. You?"

"We got in yesterday, so we're doing the touristy thing now," I said.

"Too bad you missed the Cherry Festival this year."

"Yeah," I said, remembering thousands of people added to the normal summer residents and tourists. "Maybe next year. Going to Gerald's retirement reception? I'm looking forward to seeing you." I found a bench outside a restaurant.

"Planning on it, but you might think you're wrong about seeing me by the time I explain this. I have a question regarding something peculiar on a case."

"Brandan, you *know* I don't work here anymore, right?" I kidded. "I came back for Dr. Katz's retirement reception and Kayleigh's wedding, but perhaps I can work out a consultation fee scale to suit your curiosity."

"Dr. Katz's other daughter is where the bad news begins. Kimberly and her boyfriend were arrested in a parking lot a few nights ago. One of the beach parks out around on East Bay. Kim was taken in for minor in possession. He was just given a ticket for contributing to the delinquency of a minor and public intox. Dr. Katz came and picked up Kim. The guy was ticketed and released."

"Gerald said that boy was trouble," I fumed.

"That issue aside, they were sitting on the hood of a car, drinking beer, when the officer came by. After detaining the pair for public intox, he ran the plates, which came back to a stolen vehicle belonging to a person reported missing two months ago." He waited a beat. "Both of them denied having anything to do with the car. It had been parked there a couple of days, the kid said. She doesn't have a car, and his license is suspended. But because it was stolen, the officer searched the car."

I took a deep breath, certain he had worse news.

"The key was on, the tank was empty and battery dead, like it had been left running. The doors weren't locked. But that isn't what I wanted to ask you."

"How can that not be a problem?" I retorted.

"Oh, it's a problem, just not *the* problem. There was also," he said, drawing out "also" as an unnecessary three-second effect for drama, "a body in the trunk. Well, most of one. Human, dismembered and packed. Vacuum-sealed maybe. No smell, slowed decomposition."

"Bizarre. The owner of the car?" I guessed.

"Nope, wrong gender, from what we could tell in the packages." Another teasing pause. "One, um, package in particular."

"Someone the owner killed?"

"The woman who owns the car couldn't have done this. Brainiac woman, it sounded like."

The description created an image in my head that it shouldn't have.

"She was reported missing in a probable drowning several months ago. During the search, her car was stolen from the lake," he continued.

"Anyone else in her family missing?"

"Ah, an interesting question. Nope." He chuckled. "Like old times."

"You're having too much fun, Brandan. What is it you want me to help you with?"

"Tell me what happens when pieces of a body are shrink-wrapped. Wait, is that the same as vacuum packing?"

"Not something I have any experience with, either way."

"Seriously. Does a body decompose when sealed up like that? Could it be buried without fear of being dug up by animals? Dropped in the lake without floating? I know what I have, but I don't know what it means."

"Neither do I," I confessed. "I'll do a little research and get back to you if I find any answers, but I have no clue where to look. Dr. Katz doesn't know about this, does he?"

"We already have a new medical examiner working, so he's doing all the autopsies now. Gerald has been showing him the office stuff, finishing a few cases. He probably doesn't know about any of this yet except Kimberley's arrest."

Yet.

"I'll see what I can find out," I said, my mind already digging. "See you tomorrow night?"

"I hope to be there."

I disconnected and dropped the phone back in my bag, looking around to see Zach and Amber walking toward me.

"Dad said I could ask you if I could invite Ethan to the retirement reception tomorrow night," Amber said, skipping ahead of Zach.

"It's short notice for everyone involved," I replied, standing to meet them. "What if Ethan doesn't have suitable clothing for such an event?"

Zach joined us and offered me his drink cup.

"That's root beer, isn't it?" I said, pulling down my sunglasses to glare at him.

He withdrew the cup and made an innocent face, softly whistling.

"If I can't skip it," Amber continued, "I'd at least like to have someone to talk to."

"You can ask him if he wishes to attend the retirement reception with you tomorrow night. If so, he may meet you there, or we can pick him up, but he may not take you, nor are you to leave with him or anyone else."

"Julie!" The whine was much louder than necessary.

"Look, abundant caution of the big bad world is an unfortunate and painful consequence of having parents in law enforcement. I can't help it," I replied. "You may also invite him to dinner tonight with us, and I'll do what I can to answer his questions."

CHAPTER 5
JULIE

July 18, 2001

When we returned to the hotel before five, Amber called and invited Ethan to meet us at the hotel in an hour then go out to eat and to discuss things I recalled about Penny Tucker Daniels.

"He said yes!" she said, dancing around the room. "I've got to shower and get ready." She whirled around the doorway to her side of the suite.

"That could take hours," he said, pulling a bottle of water from the tiny refrigerator. "Take a walk on the beach?"

"Only if you promise not to bleed," I mumbled under my breath.

He raised an eyebrow, and I shrugged.

"You're the last one to get shot. Three times, including once on a beach," I offered, then turned to Amber's room to tell her we were going for a walk, but she was already in the shower. I scribbled her a note.

"Fair enough, but please don't try to even the score."

Strolling along the beach in front of the hotel, I thought of our trip to Hawaii, and how long ago it seemed.

"So much has changed," I reflected.

"The water wasn't this low when you lived here," he answered.

"Yes, but that's not what I meant." I shook my head and took his hand. "With us. We've been through so much in the last, what, six or seven years?"

"You don't know for sure? I'm baffled."

I scrunched my nose. "Life between when my dad was murdered and when David Wesley almost killed me seems ancient. From the time I met you, right up till we got married and moved out to Washington, that part of my life seems surreal, like a dream with no sense of time. Since then, being together feels like it's been most of my life when really it hasn't. I just enjoy living with you in a million moments."

"Yet sometimes it seems to have gone by in days," he replied. "A lot of your dreams didn't come true."

"What I have is better than what I dreamed, Cowboy." I stopped and tugged him around to face me. "I wouldn't trade any day of it that you weren't pretending to be dead."

"I'll make those days up to you for the rest of my life."

"You're doing a good job so far."

"Good. What is a dream I can help make come true?" he asked.

"I don't know, Zach. I have you. I have a daughter for whom I did not have to go through morning sickness, labor pains, or terrible twos. I love my job. We have an incredible home." I turned and looked out over the water. "What's left to dream?"

We resumed walking in silence.

"After Amber goes to college, would you like to go back to Europe and spend a few weeks?" he asked. "Maybe a river cruise through to Germany from the –"

A voice calling to us interrupted his suggestion. Zach turned to see Ethan walking toward us. "So much for seducing you to Europe…" he grunted and waved.

I waved, too, and we waited for him to reach us.

"I'm sorry, I know I'm early," Ethan said, extending a hand to Zach, who shook without crunching the poor kid's hand too hard. "I have a few questions about Penny that I can't get off my mind, but I didn't want to discuss in a crowded restaurant."

I nodded and waved toward a bench in the shade.

"Mr. Daniels told me she had died, but he didn't explain how." He twisted his mouth. "How could the Phoenix police not have a case of her murder?"

I have no way or reason to defend them.

"As I told you, Penny came to give the police information after J.P. died," I said. "Her family had been on vacation to the Grand Canyon. I understood the police believed that, while they were gone, the killer broke into the house and contaminated a new bottle of allergy nasal spray. When she got back to Phoenix, or maybe before, it's presumed that her daughter had already opened the bottle and used it, then so did Penny."

"So, he did poison her," he concluded. "But why wasn't there an investigation?"

"By the time her death was identified as a murder, the suspect was already dead, so there was nothing more to investigate," I suggested, "but I couldn't say."

"What kind of poison did he use?"

Certain he'd ask, I'd struggled to recall the name of the amoeba Jeremy McNeeley had told me. He had come to Michigan to help us solve a crime in which a waterborne parasite had been used to make a young woman ill, then a poisoning by another unusual substance. While he was in Michigan, the CDC asked him to consult on a case in Arizona, which turned out to the Penny Daniels and her daughter, who both died after their exposure to this microorganism.

An image of Jeremy's face flooded my mind, but not the name of the bugs.

"I don't remember, but an amoeba, I was told."

Zach's arm around my shoulder squeezed enough I felt it, making me think he'd seen what was in my head as clearly as I did.

I didn't recall its name, but I understood how it worked by entering through a person's nose and traveling along the olfactory nerve to the brain, causing a bacterial meningitis-like infection. Symptoms included fever, headache, stiff neck, nausea and vomiting, sensitivity to light. The amoebae, Jeremy told me, lived in higher temperature water, such as warm springs, stagnant lakes, or poorly chlorinated water sources such as pools or even drinking water pipes.

Which gives me heebie-jeebies about bodies of water, but Naegleria fowleri does not cause human infection from swallowing, only getting the water in your nose. Like diving, dunking, drowning . . .

" . . . police even try to find the man who killed her?" Ethan was saying, and I was aware I'd missed part of what he'd said.

"Ethan, I had nothing to do with the law enforcement portions of the investigation, but I imagine the deputies in Michigan and Florida were in contact with those in Arizona after Anthony's death," I explained.

He turned to Zach. "I understand you were at the hospital when Anthony Bock was killed in Florida, right? That you were one of the men who shot him?"

I felt Zach bristle, but he nodded.

"I guess I'm just frustrated that no one would tell me the case was even closed."

"Might have been closed because they couldn't prosecute anyone for the crime."

"What do you mean? That the guy who killed –" he said.

"That's crap!" Ethan barked loud enough I cringed. "The cops didn't do their jobs!"

"Either way, I don't know why no one completed an investigation into a homicide. Nor can I change it."

Zach broke into the conversation. "Amber ought to be ready by now. Let's go back to the hotel."

Ethan nodded.

I sensed it wouldn't take much to set him off again on this angry discourse.

Zach took my hand, and we led the way.

Approaching the hotel, we looked up to see Amber standing on the balcony, waving to us.

Zach leaned over to me and whispered, "That girl's wearing something that shows her legs."

"I didn't know she had legs," I replied.

"Who is she? She's in our room, probably stealing makeup and hairspray."

I laughed, then called to her, "We'll be up in a minute, Amber. I need to grab my bag and change shirts."

"You look fine, Julie," my husband told me.

"Should I yell that I need to go pee so everyone on the beach can hear?"

"Oh, sorry." He squeezed my hand as we rounded the hotel toward the doors. "Ethan and I will wait for you."

I excused myself and left the two of them outside, pondering how angry Ethan seemed to be over something he'd only recently discovered.

When I got to the room, Amber was waiting at the door, dressed in a short gray skirt and bright pink camisole with a denim jacket over it. She was wearing hiking boots with it. Somehow, she made it all cute, even if her legs were pale.

Not white like mine, true.

"That hot pink is a great color on you," I told her as I really did change shirts. "Just so you know, Ethan's kinda wound up about his biological mother questions. Maybe we could let it go for a bit till he cools off?"

She nodded.

We met them by the rental car, and Zach didn't give Ethan a chance to sit in the front when he opened the car door for me.

I didn't mind, of course, but his action left Ethan no choice but to open Amber's door for her, then sit in the back seat beside her.

"So, Ethan, what are you doing for the summer while you're out of school?" Zach asked, looking into the rearview mirror.

"My grandfather has Alzheimer's and can't stay alone. He wanders. I've been staying with him during the day this summer. My mother stays with him at night, although she sleeps a few hours."

"What does she do when you're in school?" I asked.

"She hires a nurse to work during the weekdays, but she stays the rest of the time, Ma'am."

"Alzheimer's makes caring for a loved one difficult," I replied. "I'm sorry."

"My mother thinks I'm helping a friend move home from college," he said. "It's not honest, but she didn't want me to dig any more about Penny."

"Why not?" Amber asked. "It only makes sense that an adopted kid would want to know, right?"

"Once I found out Penny was murdered, my mother freaked out about it."

So much for cooling off.

Zach parked at a chain restaurant, and we got out.

"I've thought of more questions," Ethan said as we walked around the building's sidewalk toward the front. "Even made a list so I don't forget any."

"They can wait until we've ordered," Zach stated. "Plenty of time this evening."

"Yes, Sir," he answered, but I couldn't tell from his body language if this disappointed him or maybe made him a little angry.

Inside, we did the usual things millions of customers did every day – took our seats, browsed the menu, chatted about choices, and then ordered.

Zach might not have, but I noticed that Ethan seemed to act a bit too common with the server. As if they knew each other but didn't want to let on. Perhaps they'd dated, and the split-up was mutual. Not friendly, not antagonistic, but a concentrated neutral.

I ordered a glass of wine, but we all munched on the bread she brought as an appetizer.

"Can I ask more now?" Ethan requested.

Zach blew out air through his nose and nodded.

And off he went again with more questions.

CHAPTER 6
JULIE

July 19, 2001

Zach sat on the couch in our room, waiting on his female escorts to dress for the retirement party, probably wishing for any other sporting event on television than golf. At the rate things were moving, he could watch all eighteen holes.

He came to the bathroom, startling me while I was blow-drying my hair.

Under my breath I cursed him sneaking up on me, something he'd been doing for years, sometimes unintentionally.

Sometimes not.

When I finished, Zach asked about the phone call I'd received from Brandan.

"A week ago, Kimberly and her boyfriend were caught drinking. They were sitting on the hood of a stolen car at a beach parking lot," I stated, wiggling into a dress and turning my back to him.

Zach stepped behind me and pulled the zipper from my waist to my neck, then kissed the skin where his fingers had stopped. "I know you don't like him, but –"

"Oh, no, I'm sure I don't like him, but that's just a sidebar," I said, dabbing at my makeup and spritzing a perfume down my lack of significant cleavage. "There was a body in the trunk. Not the owner, who is also a missing person several months prior. But the body, ever how much of it there was, had been packed in some sort of shrink wrap, Brandan said."

"Shrink wrap?" both Zach's and Amber's voices chimed in unison.

I scowled at Zach for not stopping me when Amber came into our room.

"Yes, or maybe vacuum-sealed, he wasn't clear on it."

"Cool!" Amber added. "That could be an extraordinary topic for one of my classes, I bet! I wonder if Ethan's ever heard of it?"

"It might be cool, but you are not to discuss it with him or anyone else. This is an active investigation," Zach announced.

Amber deflated a little.

"What does that do to a body? Sealing it like that," he clarified.

"Beats me. I've never seen it."

"You should, like, call one of the body farms," Amber suggested. "They might have something set up for this."

"I may do just that," I replied, putting on the diamond earrings Zach had given me several years ago. "But not tonight."

"How can you leave such a substantial question hanging? Thinking about it's gonna drive me crazy!" Amber stomped back to her room.

"Such a short trip, she won't even need a seatbelt," Zach mumbled when she shut the door.

"She's right. It's an interesting puzzle, but it's not my case."

"Knowing you and Brandan, it will be before we leave." Zach smiled in the mirror with exaggerated pacification. "You can't help yourself."

He ducked the pillow I threw his direction.

In another twenty minutes, we were ready, except for the last-minute panic while Amber looked for her necklace, then a short car ride to the convention center.

Amber promised she'd stay by the door without going outside, to wait for Ethan, who said he'd meet her there. Zach and I went on inside.

The reception wasn't a formal event, but the crowd was thick with police officers in dress uniform.

Zach fit in fine, I thought, although he could have worn a wild Hawaiian shirt with cutoff plaid shorts and flipflops and somehow still fit into a black and white ball. However, he was in his perfectly natural attire of pressed dark jeans, brown boots and belt, and a long-sleeve blue and white pinstriped shirt. His Stetson would have made it perfect, but gentlemen do not wear hats indoors, he'd once informed me.

"You look fabulous tonight," he whispered. "That is the perfect little black dress, as they say."

"I should have worn it to your last funeral," I quipped. "Maybe your next."

"No, you owe me the slutty red dress the next time I die," he whispered, guiding me with a hand on my low back through the crowd toward Gerald Katz, who shook hands with people as they passed by in a line, offering well wishes and congratulations.

When we reached him, Gerald broke out of the formality and hugged me. "I'm so glad to see you." He released me and shook hands with Zach. "Thanks for coming."

"Of course! I wouldn't miss this," I said. "Now that you aren't working seven days a week, I expect you to come visit us."

"That sounds splendid. We have so much to catch up on. We'll talk later," he said, nodding to the crowd.

"Absolutely," I replied, patting his shoulder.

We moved on to the refreshments, and Zach poured us each a cup of punch. He took a slice of the marbled cake with thick white icing with neon blue letters that now only read BE WISH YOUR RETIR now, missing servings from the right side.

Looking around the large room, I saw familiar faces I wanted to go chat with, but from my left, Kayleigh headed toward me like a charging bull.

"Julie, I'm glad you're here," she started even before we hugged. "You've heard about Kim?"

"A little bit," I answered.

Kayleigh took me by the hand and pulled me toward the corridor. "She's lost her freaking mind," she whispered with a growl, walking two steps ahead. "It's ruining my wedding and killing my father."

Struggling to stay upright on my heels, I followed her into a restroom with a powder room area including a pair of formal chairs. Intending to answer, I inhaled, but Kayleigh kept venting.

"I understand being kidnapped and all could frizzle your brain," she said, wiggling her fingers around her head but hardly taking a breath for the next minute's overdrive tirade as she paced the room. "Like, she seemed to be okay for a while. I mean, you are, right? Then Mom died, and Kim took charge of keeping things going for the rest of us, remember? After you left, she just became a lump of mud. She wouldn't even bathe!"

I opened my mouth to speak, but she kept going.

"Dad finally asked her to move out if she couldn't help keep the household running, so she did. But now? This, this drinking and th-that-" she stuttered in anger, trying to be civil, "that *idiot* she's hanging around with. I don't get where this came from. She doesn't care how much her behavior is affecting the rest of this family, but it is. Being arrested for minor in possession and public intoxication? Really? She's not old enough to drink. And this guy she's with is a druggie low-life criminal!"

Again, I wanted to speak, but Kayleigh kept going.

"He doesn't have the brains to hold a job long enough to own a car. He's dragging her down." With that, she turned to me, expecting an answer.

"Kim is in a bad situation," I summed up.

"Bad? Just bad?" Kayleigh exclaimed, going back to pacing. "No, this is way past bad. It's – I don't know, disgusting, creepy, stupid."

"Have you tried talking to her?"

She made a *Pfffth* sound. "Either she's high or drunk or …" The anger peaked and gave way to tears. "I don't know what to say to her anymore."

"I'm hoping I can talk with her while I'm here," I said, wrapping Kayleigh into a hug. "But honestly, I'm not sure what to say either."

Kayleigh touched up her makeup, and we went back into the conference hall where we found her fiancé.

Reese Connor, the groom-to-be, she said when she introduced him, was her doctor in shining armor.

He dressed like a rich kid, I thought, but he seemed warm and casual, and he doted on Kayleigh as our conversation continued over less dramatic topics.

The reception transitioned to more casual over the next hour, and I finally had a chance to speak with Gerald.

"Kim has rebelled against everything good we ever taught her," he said with a groan. "I promised Mary Anne I would take care of our girls, but I can't seem to do anything to help her. I failed."

"Gerald, what Kim chooses in her life is not a fault of her upbringing or a reflection of your failure as a parent. You no longer get to decide between right and wrong for her, and although the consequences affect you, you can't change her choices. When someone we love strays from what is right, no amount of grief or promises or wishes can make that person change."

"I'm her father," he argued.

"Failure to meet your expectations is her choice, not yours, Gerald. Little you or Mary Anne could have done to change Kim's direction if she's set on self-destruction. No amount of wishing or regrets will change the past, for any of us." I took his hand in mine. "Hopefully nothing she does will make you love her less as her father. Be there to catch her when she falls – and she will – and love her no matter what."

His eyes shifted from me to something beyond my shoulder. "Speaking of…" He offered a weak smile.

I turned around to see Kimberley making her way toward the snack table, paying little attention to anything around her.

"Please, see what you can do," he whispered. "You saved her once. Help her."

With a nod, I left him and walked toward a young woman I used to know well. Tonight, I saw a too-thin, disheveled shell of someone I barely recognized.

"Kimberley!" I exclaimed as I approached. "I'm happy to see you!"

Without a greeting, Kim shrugged and mumbled, "I doubt it."

I stopped a foot away and waited.

Kimberley sighed and stepped forward into a reluctant hug.

"I really am glad to see you, Kim."

"Why? So you can see what a loser I am now? Compare me to Miss I'm-Getting-Married-Look-At-Me-Isn't-My-Fiancé-Fabulous?"

"No, I don't think you're a loser. I'm here to see all of you."

"You shouldn't bother with me."

"Kim, why have you given up on yourself and everyone who loves you," I asked, not letting go of her hands.

The young woman shrugged, looking at the floor.

At a retirement reception for her father, Kimberley wore faded worn jeans, a dingy green hoodie, and looked and smelled like she hadn't had a bath in weeks.

"I want to help," I told the girl who had once saved my life. "I want to see you smile again. What can I do?"

"Nobody can fix the mess I'm in."

"I've helped fix plenty of messes worse than yours, if you'll let me try," I said. "Let's go outside and talk. Take some food, I'll grab you a cup of punch."

Zach nodded when he caught my eye as I escorted Kimberley to the door leading to the balcony.

CHAPTER 7
AMBER

July 19, 2001

"What's that about?" I asked my dad when we met at the punch bowl. "Who is the woman Julie's talking to?"

"That is Kimberley, Dr. Katz's older daughter."

"Geez, she looks, like, homeless."

He peered at me over imaginary glasses. "Uncrinkle your nose, Amber. Since Julie left Michigan, Kim has made some poor choices in her life."

"No kidding," I said, thinking how disrespectful it was to show up at her father's retirement in dirty clothes.

I went back and sat with Ethan at a corner table away from the older people.

Talking about family and law enforcement and forensics – it was great. Even though I wanted to discuss the case of the shrink wrap, I knew better.

By nine, the crowd had dwindled, but Julie hadn't returned yet. Ethan had left, and I was getting restless. Dad came over and sat at the table beside me.

"What's taking her so long?"

"Sweetie," Dad said, reaching across the table to put his hand on mine, "saving someone takes time."

CHAPTER 8
JULIE

July 19, 2001

"What did you think of the groom-to-be?" Zach asked as he relaxed into a chair in the corner when we got back to the hotel. His question might have sounded like casual conversation, but I knew from his expression the comment was anything but offhand.

Amber had gone to her room. I could hear a movie through the wall.

"He seems to be a reasonable, educated guy who dotes on Kayleigh," I started. "I'm a little suspect that his dreams of being a doctor in Africa, hoping to save the world, are a bit exorbitant. And I have to wonder whether Gerald is really enthusiastic that Kayleigh wants to go."

Zach had to reach to unzip my dress, and I twisted to kiss him before letting it slide to my hips, then looked at him over my shoulder seductively.

"At least the kid has a dream." Zach smiled, then reached for a cup from the afternoon drive, took a sip and made a sour face at the warm watered-down root beer. "What's Kimberley's story?"

I stepped into the bathroom to finish changing out of the dress. "Warning flags all over the place. She looks terrible, like she's drinking or maybe using drugs. Breaks my heart. She's also pregnant."

His eyebrows rose, I saw in the mirror.

"She told me. Her dad doesn't know, neither does Kayleigh," I finished pulling a loose t-shirt on and returned to the sofa next to him. "She went nuts over the fact that the officer called her dad to get her."

Zach shook his head.

"I don't know how to help her."

"Introduce her to Ethan," he suggested.

"We're too late for that to work. Amber's got her sights on him."

"Did she tell you?" he asked.

"No, sweetie, I can see it painted all over her face."

Zach sighed. "Comparatively speaking, I guess that's okay for now." He went to the refrigerator to get us each a bottle of water.

"I missed several people I wanted to talk to tonight," I said. "Did you see Brandan?"

"Yeah," he said, handing me the water. "We chatted for a while. He's focused on that investigation and waiting for your answer about how 'packaging changes decomposition,' he said. You should call him tomorrow."

"Swell, how packaging changes decomp," I muttered, the problem sidetracking my thoughts but leaving the monologue going. "Never had a reason to research such a process. Logically speaking, the gut has the greatest concentration of bacteria, which would spread when the body was dismembered, so the other tissue would need to be separated quickly. Unless it's dressed like a deer."

Zach made a gagging noise coupled with a smirk.

"What?" I blurted, my concentration broken.

"Sounds gross," he said, wrinkling his nose. "But I haven't seen that look in a long time. You know, when your brain changes gears, makes a left turn, then speeds away with a new challenge. Like Laser when he'd chase a tennis ball."

"He loved those balls, didn't he?" I said, my brain coasting from its focus. "I wish we could have brought him back one more time."

Laser, the law enforcement dog I'd adopted out of service from the Grand Traverse County sheriff, had died in his sleep early in the year.

Amber had been heartbroken. Then she'd wanted another puppy the next week, which Zach had refused with the rationale that she would go away to college within the year and couldn't take it with her, and he didn't want to raise a dog she had wanted.

I dug my laptop out of a carryon bag and powered it up, hoping I could find the answers regarding decomposition in pieces. In vacuum bags.

Next time I looked over at him, Zach was asleep in the chair, and it was almost 1:30.

When I closed my laptop, he woke, stretched and stood, then helped me to my feet and led me to the bed.

July 20, 2001

The next morning while Zach was gone to exercise, I was skimming documents from dozens of websites when the hotel room phone buzzed. As anticipated, I heard a rapid thud of feet in the adjoining room, accompanied by the also predictable yell, "I'll get it!" from Amber.

Hearing no disappointed follow-up statement of "It's for you," from our teenage answering system, I returned to reading.

"Julie," she said, peeking around the doorway, "it's Ethan. He said he thought of another question for you."

I picked up the receiver on the desk and said hello.

"Mrs. Samualson," he said, "I was wondering. Mr. Daniels mentioned that Penny had kept a journal. Did she say anything about it?"

"I don't recall her mentioning she had, but she went back to the attic in the house and looked for her mother's journals."

"Did *she* write anything about my mother being pregnant? Who my father is?"

"No, Penny only pointed out information pertinent to our investigation, but she didn't mention that she'd been pregnant," I said.

"I found my birth certificate, but it doesn't give a father's name. Do you have any ideas where else I can look to find out?"

"Doesn't Mark Daniels have Penny's mom's journals?" I asked. We had intended to ship her the books after the ME's office made copies.

"He told me that after his wife's death, he threw away a lot of that stuff."

I found that a little odd: surely one of Penny's kids would have wanted diaries of their grandmother. Names I hadn't thought of in several years popped into my head: Marissa, Colby, and Jaralyn. I couldn't remember which girl had also died when Penny did.

"Okay, thanks anyways. It was worth asking, I thought," he said. "Can I talk to Amber again?"

I nodded at her, and she went back into her room. When I heard her pick up, I returned the receiver to its cradle.

Stumped on both problems, I put the computer down and took my cup of coffee out on the balcony.

While I wasn't surprised Penny hadn't mentioned her illegitimate teenage pregnancy to me, if it had been in her mother's journals, I'd only seen what she showed me.

In the distance, I could see Zach, running on the paved trail along the beach. Running wasn't something I saw him do often. At home, he might stop throwing around hay and do fifty pull-ups on a beam or pushups with his feet up on a bale, but if he went running, it was when I wasn't around to see it.

Although I had run when I was in high school after my dad died and continued until my forced rehab, now I made lame excuses why I couldn't find the motivation, the location, or like any exercise routine avoider, the time.

I changed into a pair of shorts and put on my sneakers.

I might have to chase him, but the view alone would be worth the exertion.

When I caught up to him, Zach was merciful and slowed for me to jog alongside him, letting me set a pace I could maintain. The slowdown was easy for him, and he probably could have maintained this speed for another five miles and still held a conversation without being winded. The asphalt trail turned, so we stayed on the beach.

I envied how easy he made running look, but I eased into a rhythm, feeling the cool on-shore breeze in my face.

We finally reached a place where we would either have to divert to the paved path or turn around. I nodded we should go back.

"Is Amber awake yet?" he asked as we slowed a little more.

"Yeah, and Ethan's already called this morning," I said in a broken cadence. "He asked me if Penny's mom's journals indicated who his real father was."

"And?"

"She didn't show me, and I didn't read them all." I hesitated and stopped running. "Ethan said Daniel told him he threw them away. I had them copied and was going ship the books to her, but Jeremy saw that the name on the label was the same as the one on a medical case he had conferred on from Arizona. She was already sick. We intended to ship them to her, but I don't know if that happened."

Zach had gone a few steps past me before he stopped, turning around to face me. "Maybe Mr. Daniels didn't want Ethan to have them," he suggested. "Or he didn't want to deal with the kid anymore about his dead wife and her past. Race you to the room."

• • • • •

When we got back to the room after breakfast, Amber asked if we could walk the downtown area and shop a little, and I thought it was a great idea, but Zach asked to be excused.

"You can call me when you're done, and I'll pick you up for lunch. Then you two can spend the next four hours getting dressed for the wedding," he said, ducking as Amber and I both chunked pillows his direction.

"At least five," she said with a pretend frown.

Even after our morning jog and showers and breakfast in the hotel, it was still only nine. That left a lot of time for shopping.

Zach drove to the east end of the downtown area on Front Street to let us out, having selected a storefront on the west end where we would meet at noon unless I called and delayed.

I looked forward to browsing several stores, including the candy shop where I'd always bought the white chocolate-covered caramels. Amber had mentioned seeing a pair of boots at Dr. Katz's reception that she wanted to find, making for an easy agenda and plenty of time.

"Do you like Ethan?" she asked as we browsed along the storefronts.

"I don't dislike him, but I don't know him very well," I answered.

"He's easier to talk to than Cody or other guys I hang around with."

"Ethan is several years older than most of your male friends, and he has a career direction similar to yours. Boys don't mature as fast as girls."

"You mean Cody will catch up?" she asked, surprised.

"Yes, he'll begin to catch up with you in the next few years, but you both have a few years to go."

"You're saying I'm not mature?"

I turned toward her. "I'm not saying you are immature, but you have more experience to gain in life."

She put her hands on her hips in what I recognized as the start of an argument.

"Amber, you are eighteen. You will never stop learning, I hope, how to be better at whatever you do, whether it's being a forensic scientist, a model, or a stay-at-home mom. Continuing to learn and improve yourself and your skills is a sign of maturity."

She frowned.

"Experience is what you have, right after you really need it," I quoted for her, although I'd long forgotten where I'd read it.

She rolled her eyes and returned to browsing windows. "All right. Oh, look! There's those boots!"

Crisis averted, we went inside and tried on boots. And a cute sweater. And a bright multicolored summer shirt for me.

"You have to get these ankle boots," she told me in her attempt at a very stern mature voice. "They'll look outstanding together with your gray skirt and white blouse for the wedding. And this silver belt, too."

Turns out, she was almost as good at designing my wardrobe as she is at handling evidence.

We wandered on, hitting a bookstore and several local shops, and I called Zach early to come pick us up for brunch, which was at another of my favorites in Traverse City, where the soups were fantastic.

I noted that throughout our meal, Amber seemed to be more reserved.

She had a brief conversation with our server about a beautiful silver sand dollar necklace pendant, and then offered to leave the tip for the meal. Back in our room, she separated our purchases on the bed and took hers on to her side of the suite.

"Who did you bring back and which shop takes trades on women?" Zach asked me in a low tone, nodding toward the door where Amber had passed.

"Why? Did you want to trade me in, too?" I asked with a sweet smile.

"No, darlin'," he said, returning the smile, "but I thought I should give whoever buys the other model of her a warning that she's prone to backfiring."

"She's just high maintenance." I started folding the clothes I'd bought.

"Wonder where she learned that?" he said, wrinkling his nose at me.

"Are you insinuating I taught her?"

He came to me and wrapped his arms around my waist from behind. "Not insinuating. You are extremely high maintenance, but I wouldn't want you to be anything less. I like all the tuning up and expensive attention you require." He snuggled his face into my neck.

Amber must have stuck her head around the doorway, saw us, and made a gagging sound that broke her streak of perfect maturity.

CHAPTER 9
JULIE

July 21, 2001

Though it surprised us both, we were all ready for the wedding half an hour early, so Zach drove out to the lighthouse on the peninsula and back so we wouldn't be too early. We reached the church in time to be seated on the bride's side.

The ceremony was perfect.

Kim, the maid of honor, still looked unhealthy and underweight, despite the baby bump hidden in the dark blue dress. But she was present, which was something she and I had discussed at Gerald's reception.

She had been homeless on and off since she'd left the Katz's house months before, staying with friends or sleeping in their cars sometimes. Or with the boyfriend, I presumed, which had led to the pregnancy.

At my behest, she had agreed to check into a hotel to clean up and eat well for a few days at my expense, and to come to her sister's wedding.

"Kayleigh very much wants you to be there with her," I said. "And so does your father. He would do anything to help you if you would let him."

"You think so?" She sounded desperate.

"I promise. All of us want to help you."

She had agreed, and I'd put her in a hotel with a kitchenette and a daily breakfast, money for a little grocery shopping. Gerald had picked her up for the rehearsal dinner. Someone else had brought her to the wedding. Everything she'd needed in between had been taken care of.

She'd looked better, but as she stood in the wedding party, her appearance was a significant improvement over the weeks prior, Gerald told me in gratitude after the ceremony.

The wedding was beautiful, as I'd have expected from Kayleigh. Simple but elegant. The reception was aimed at a younger generation but was also enjoyable.

Although I hadn't brought my phone, Zach had his tucked in his jacket. An hour into the party, I saw him reach for it then duck out of the ballroom to hear better.

I excused myself from the groom's parents to follow him, knowing he wouldn't have answered a call from just anyone.

Zach was still talking, heading outside, and I kept following.

"I'll tell her and let you know what arrangements we can make, Mom. Thanks for calling." Zach turned to me as he hung up.

"Oh, that expression doesn't look good on you," I said. "What is it?"

He led me over to sit on a bench before speaking. "It's Dagmar," he said, taking my hands. "Mom said she had a stroke at work tonight, which means they got her treatment immediately. Mom asked me to put you on a plane as soon as possible."

"How is she? When did – ?" I had a dozen frantic questions.

"You call and talk to Mom; she can tell you that stuff. I'll call the airlines, but it might be morning before you can fly out. I'll check flights from Grand Rapids, too." He handed me his phone.

I started to dial but hesitated. "See if you can find Kim and send her out here. I have an idea."

He nodded and went back inside.

Before I finished placing the call to Vera, I took a moment to get my head together, then hit the send button.

Vera answered on the first ring, expecting my call. She explained all the answers I needed. "She's awake and alert, able to speak but it's a little difficult for her. There is lateral paralysis, but they don't know the extent yet," she explained. "She won't be able to live alone for a while. But honestly, Julie, she might not ever be that independent."

"One step at a time," I said, trying to remain hopeful. "I'll be there as soon as I can. We'll let you know the itinerary."

I disconnected and sat alone, holding my world together by sheer will, unsure how long before Kim came to join me.

"Zach said something has happened to your mother," she said, sitting next to me.

"She had a stroke, so she's paralyzed on one side of her body," I explained. "I need to go to Albuquerque, and I may be there for several months. My question is, would you like to go with me and stay until your baby is born? You can live at my mom's house with me. I'll pay for whatever medical costs are necessary for you."

I saw tears in her eyes. "You'd do that? For me?" she said, resting her hand on her belly.

"Of course I would. You are as important to me as Amber and Kayleigh. I want you to be healthy and be able to make good decisions because it's what you choose, not because you don't have any choices."

"You aren't afraid I'll get into more trouble?"

"Trouble found you when you didn't have choices, Kim. I want you to come with me. That's your first choice."

With that, Zach came back and informed me he'd borrowed a phone from Amber to book two seats on the first flight out to make Albuquerque early the next morning.

Kim went to find her father to let him know, with a smile I hadn't seen this trip.

"Two first-class tickets, 7 a.m. tomorrow, change planes in Chicago.

"How did you know to book two?"

"Because you asked me to find Kim, not Amber," he said, shrugging. "I also know you are sure about this or you wouldn't ask her."

"She's a good kid who needs a hand from people who care about her. I never thought she'd walk away from that cabin without scars and without the maturity to see what it might do to her life. I don't think anyone else in the world can help her see how to escape that except me."

"I seem to recall a woman in a similar predicament, on the verge of self-destruction, and she turned out fabulous." Zach wrapped his jacket around my shoulders. "I'm proud of you. Just know that I'll miss you."

We gathered both girls, and I explained again what had happened and my plans.

Amber loaned Kim one of her oversized suitcases, and we drove to the Katz home so Kim could pack. Before we left, Gerald sat and talked to Kim after I'd excused Zach, Amber, and myself to the car to wait.

"Why are you taking her to Albuquerque with you? I don't get it," Amber said.

"Did you want to go instead? Julie may be there for three months or more," Zach offered.

"No! I have to go back so I can move to Seattle!" she huffed.

"Then taking Kim and getting her away from an unhealthy environment is a decent choice," I explained. "We invited you into our home to be part of our family forever, because we wanted to, not just because it was the right thing to do. Offering to help Kim isn't permanent, but it is the right thing, too."

"Will she come live in Washington when you come home?"

"Maybe. She isn't due for another four or five months," I replied, thinking the scenario probable.

"She's pregnant?" Amber exclaimed. "You guys would have grounded me till I'm 45."

"And that's a possibility if you don't get your head straight about dating," Zach mumbled.

"Dad!"

"You have a much better living situation than Kim's had recently, Amber. The expectation remains," he said, turning around to address her. "I have a beautiful, intelligent daughter, but I also have a gun, a shovel, and a solid alibi."

CHAPTER 10
JULIE

July 22, 2001

Getting the two of us to the airport for the early morning flight took a little practical magic that Zach conjured, a practiced wizard at getting to and outbound from the Cherry Capital Airport in the wee hours of the morning when I'd lived in Traverse City.

The flights were smooth and uneventful, and better yet, uncrowded from Chicago to Albuquerque, allowing us to stretch out into all three seats.

Vera picked us up at Sunport International just after lunchtime, giving me the good news, that Mom was doing better. We stopped at the hospital so I could see for myself.

Kim elected not to go into Mom's cubicle, staying with Vera in the waiting room for me instead. No doubt, they would be chummy in no time because Vera exuded the motherly warmth Kim needed.

My mother's brain damage had been on the right side, leaving her with a strong tendency to deny there was any problem, although she had a significant left-sided paralysis.

After I left her, I ran into Dr. Morgan outside the unit in a meeting I suspected Vera had arranged.

He explained the prognosis and the other deficits they expected could present themselves as she regained her strength.

"She's a stubborn, formidable woman," he declared. "While I doubt she can ever work again, she may recover enough to live with minimal assistance, given time and focus."

That seemed a good enough place to start.

Vera drove Kim and me to Mom's house, helped us settle in, and offered to take us to lunch, which we accepted.

"Kim, have you ever had authentic Mexican food?" she asked.

"Sure," she said, naming a few restaurants in Traverse City she'd been to.

I held back a laugh.

"But I don't like spicy food since I got pregnant," she explained. "I have horrible heartburn now."

We opted for an all-day breakfast place although I explained I'd been craving enchiladas with eggs.

"That sounds gross," Kim told me, so I had a Denver omelet, bacon, hash browns, and toast.

She ordered oatmeal and fresh fruit, which I found admirable though lacking in protein, so I gave her my bacon.

I let her and Vera continue chatting while we waited for our food.

Kim was open, explaining how she'd left home a few months ago, living with friends here and there, even living a few months with the father of her baby until she found out she was pregnant. He'd kicked her out then, but in the last few weeks, they'd begun seeing each other again.

"He's not interested in having a family," she told us. "I don't want to push that on him. It's not his fault."

"Um, I beg to differ. He had a choice, just like you did," I said, though I wasn't trying to accuse her of making a poor one, I realized that's how it sounded. "I just meant he was involved, too."

"I know, but if he doesn't want to be a parent, I'd rather him not be."

That makes sense.

She also told Vera how happy she was I'd offered her the opportunity to get away from those bad choices she wanted to leave behind.

"Have you decided about your baby?" Vera asked a question I hadn't had the guts to verbalize yet.

Feels horrible to keep referring to it as "the" baby.

"Not yet. I wanted to clear my head a little and discuss my options and make the best decision for her I can."

"You're sure it's a girl?" I asked.

She smiled. "No, but I don't want to call it 'it' until I find out. And I come from a long line of girls."

Vera dropped us off at Mom's house then went to catch a nap before having to go to work that night.

I scheduled Kim with one of my mother's favorite obstetricians for prenatal care and ultrasound, then we kicked back in Mom's house for a nap.

The house where I grew up was an average three-bedroom, one-and-a-half bath home, but over the last few years, it had been just my mother and me and then Zach. Or maybe an occasional guest I didn't want to remember.

She'd converted one bedroom into a hobby room, using several long tables to hold hundreds of photographs, a light table to view negatives, and dozens of three-ring binders holding negative sleeves. While the mess looked out of control, I realized she had a very precise organization system, which made sweeping everything haphazardly into a box seem a little rude. Hopefully, this hobby could be a part of her stroke rehab when she came home, so I didn't disturb it more than necessary as I dug my way to a daybed in the corner.

"Wow, your mom took all these?" Kim marveled, staring at prints on the walls as I worked.

"After my dad died, Mom took up two new hobbies that surprised everyone she knew – photography and horsemanship," I said. "And her biggest joy came from putting the two together."

"All Dad did was work more after Mom died," she said, meaning Mary Anne. "He needs to take up fishing or something now."

We laughed.

"I can't see Gerald sitting in a bass boat or standing in a creek in waders to fish."

"Maybe he could learn photography, but I doubt he'd spend time around horses," she said.

I helped Kim get settled into the other bedroom, leaving the master for Mom, though I figured I'd sleep in her bed until she came home.

Finished with making space for everyone to sleep, we sat in the living room, each with a glass of apple juice.

"I wanted to thank you again for everything," she said. "I'd really dug myself into a hole."

"The first thing one should do when he finds himself in a hole is to stop digging and figure out how to climb out. I'm tossing you a rope, Kim. The hard part is up to you."

She nodded. "Because you believed I could, I feel like a whole new person, like the last year's bad stuff has vanished. Thank you."

"You are welcome."

• • • • •

My mother remained the same stubborn woman she'd always been, insisting I not sit all day in her hospital room.

"I've sat with you enough to know it's cruel and unusual punishment, wishing and praying, yet knowing there's nothing you can do to help," she said in her broken and still slurred speech. "Go do something fun."

She had sat many days and nights with me in the hospital, starting from when David almost killed me. And she was right, nothing she could do improved the medical recovery, but her presence was appreciated during my emotional disasters. While I was still in the halo with a broken neck, she helped me by washing and drying my hair, rubbing in lotion on places I couldn't reach, and holding my hand while I cried a few times. Sometimes, though, I just wanted to be alone.

She'd been happy to find out I'd brought Kim to New Mexico and the reasons. She called me altruistic though she had to try the word three or four times until it came out right.

Most of her speech came out with the words she intended, but occasionally, she either said a wrong word for the context or knew what she wanted to say was wrong and stumbled on finding and speaking the right one. And she could tell it was frustrating to me, too.

So, Kim and I went in search of fun things in Albuquerque.

"Have you ever been to the zoo and aquarium here?" she asked, flipping through a local tourist magazine for ideas.

"Not since I was a kid, I guess. But I've always loved zoos."

"Could we go?" she asked, as if she needed to beg.

She did not. It was a special excursion for us both.

I had taken Amber to several zoos when I first met her, but I hadn't been back to one since. Kim's reactions were a mix of kid-wonder and adult appreciation, which I enjoyed. She liked the African and Australian animals most.

Who doesn't love koalas?

While we didn't go to the events requiring entry costs every day, we agreed to walk a park each morning after a healthy breakfast. A new park each morning wasn't hard – Albuquerque had several hundred parks.

Our breakfasts, however, became magnificent events. What began as basic eggs and toast or pancakes morphed into feasts worthy of Zach's jealousy. Kim and I learned to make Eggs Benedict. We spent hours picking and cutting up veggies for omelets. One morning, we made cinnamon rolls from scratch, which were fabulous alone, but the next day she cooked four apiece in the waffle iron. The experiments made our days.

Evenings, we often rented movies, sharing what we found appealing before we watched and interesting or disgusting after. After the first week of randomness, Kim devised a daily schedule of themes we had to choose a movie to fit – new releases on Monday, remade movies on two-for-Tuesday, science fiction on Wednesday, released before 1970 on Thursday, and so on.

Lunch at a local restaurant the week after we'd been through this regime had led to a discussion about choices.

"Do you think," I asked, "that a person's top ten favorite movies can be a good profile of their personality?"

She chewed a moment before answering. "Maybe in their social personality, but not their underlying psyche, you know, like criminal profiling."

I asked her to continue, intrigued.

"Socially, for example, I love deep suspense movies with the riddle of who the bad guy is. I won't watch horror movies with overkill blood and guts. I prefer space stories to water stories. I don't like military war movies, but I like history," she said. "What can you conclude based on that?"

"To be clear, I wasn't looking to profile you," I stated, "but those criteria lead me to believe you have a clear sense of right and wrong and don't like gratuitous violence."

"So that information could be used to describe someone," she said, nodding. "How about food choices?"

"Average dietary choices probably don't indicate psychologic suppositions. However, someone who has rigid and uncommon dietary beliefs might also have an underlying event that triggered it or an exaggerated response to variance."

"I won't try snails or octopus. Is that weird?"

"No, I don't eat them either. For example, if you didn't like eggs, it's not a big deal. It's not unusual someone is a strict vegan or vegetarian. If one believes he can only eat beans and bananas or foods beginning with the letter B, that's kinda weird and not terribly healthy, but not pathological. But if someone purports to require drinking blood or the need to eat human flesh, those choices could be specific enough to profile."

"Yuck!"

"Shall we go somewhere with escargot or calamari on the menu and try them?" I asked, grinning.

She shook her head. "Nope, not interested!"

"Whew, me either."

"Can I ask you a question?"

"Of course."

"Does what happened to us, to you, ever bother you now? You know, in the cabin?"

I leaned back in my chair. "Not a day goes by I don't remember that damned mess. Whether it's the people Bock killed or him kidnapping us. Yes. It still bothers me a lot." I took a drink of iced tea. "You?"

"My folks sent me to the psychiatrist for a year, right?" She played with a French fry. "I hated it."

I nodded, having gone with her on her first visit.

"He was such an ass. I told him the story, but then he told me I should just feel better because my parents were trying to help me. He wanted to know if my friends ever asked what happened or that he was seeing me. He even asked me if I'd gone back to the cabin, things like that. Nothing he told me made me better. I wanted him to help me deal with how it made me feel." She frowned. "It was like it was more about him than me."

I'll ask. I hate the question, but it's what she wants to discuss.

"So how *does* it make you feel?"

"Angry," she said without missing a beat. "Infuriated that one man could destroy so many people's lives, even people he didn't kill. Or especially them. I was – no, I still am furious because I wanted him to be dead, but I wanted to be the one who killed him. To make him suffer. Torture him. Make him bleed and gasp for air like the deputy did."

"I'm the one who killed Matt, not him," I said in a low voice.

"But he made you do it, Julie. I don't know how, but he made you do it. Why?"

Time for the whole truth.

"Matt had told me to do whatever it took to get us out because he knew he wouldn't survive. Bock told me what he would do to you if I didn't comply; but if I did, he said he wouldn't hurt you."

"But he did, Julie," she said, tears puddling in her eyes. "Maybe not physically, but he screwed up everything in my head. He told me he wanted me to watch you kill that deputy, to see how much you would like it. I didn't believe him, but then when you did, I was horrified. I didn't know how to tell anyone, even the stupid shrink."

I hesitated, unsure if what I would say to her would make her feel better or worse. "Do you understand that I killed Matthew in the hope Bock would let you go?"

She gasped and slapped her hands over her mouth. Tears rolled down her cheeks. "You did that," she sniffed, "for me?"

I could only nod, afraid I'd cry, too.

CHAPTER 11
JULIE

August 2, 2001

Routines were easy while Mom was in the hospital, and even the four weeks she was in rehab, getting stronger. When we were arranging the house for her return, I cautioned Kim that although our breakfasts were still on, we should curtail our wilder experiments with food until Mom was settled.

"You'll need help with your mother, too," she said. "And I want to be there to help you both."

I'd took Kim to her sonogram a few days before we got my mother home. We were both thrilled when the physician told us the baby appeared to be healthy and let us hear its heartbeat.

Because of her history of drug use, he ordered a urine drug screen, but on the way home, Kim assured me she was clean.

"I trust you. And I'm proud of you."

Mom had been in the hospital for over two weeks for inpatient physical, speech and occupational therapies. I'm sure they kept her for so long because she had been an employee for twenty-two years. Then she was admitted for four weeks in a rehabilitation facility to work on her speech, mobility, and independence.

In the same rehab facility where I'd stayed, a lifetime ago.

Her homecoming was both similar to and wildly different from my own when she brought me home after David's attack. She was excited to come back to her home; I'd had no home to go to because I'd asked her to empty and sell my place in Alamogordo. She was in pleasant spirits; I had been under a nearly suicidal black cloud. She still had both unresolved and permanent physical ability losses; mine, while severe, had been improving as I healed.

Still, I remembered the black cloud and watched her for signs of depression. If she had any, I couldn't see them.

Her speech had improved. Her physical deficits were still significant, but she still hoped these would decrease as she worked on recovery.

I woke the second morning she was home to find my mother and Kim were in the den, doing Mom's PT exercises. On the third morning, I joined them.

They had found a park with suitable wheelchair access, and plans were to walk. With her chair available, Mom could walk as her ability and tolerance allowed, then have a safe option to ride when she tired.

Although I was skeptical at first, Kim assured me it would work, and Mom was anxious to get outside.

The park idea worked great, and we did this several days a week.

Vera called during the second week and asked if we thought a trip to the ranch was feasible and whether Dagmar was ready to see the horses.

Mom declined. "It's too much work to load everything for a trip like that," she insisted. "I would love to see Kalimar, but I don't feel up to it yet."

Vera did the next best thing. She loaded Kalimar into a trailer and brought him into town.

Now having a horse in the backyard of an Albuquerque Heights home is anything but normal, and it brought noses to the windows of a few neighbors, I noticed.

Kalimar behaved like a gentleman, nuzzling Mom, and delicately nibbling the carrots and apple she fed him.

We spent the afternoon in the backyard, with the horse wandering away from Mom to sample the flowers or graze, coming near where he folded his legs and seemed to sit and chat with the ladies.

I caught my mother wiping away tears.

"You didn't have to do this, you know," she admonished Vera, who was having none of it.

"If you won't come to the mountain, I'll bring the mountain to you, my friend," Vera told her. "This was a fun thing to do. The neighbors will gossip about this for weeks! We'll have you out to the ranch when you're ready."

Before being led out of the gate, Kalimar stopped and waited for Mom to get to her feet and take a few steps toward him, Kim and me by her side. Once there, I snapped a photo, showing her arms wrapped around the gelding's neck, his head turned to return the hug.

I called Zach before I went to bed that night.

He'd helped Amber complete all the paperwork for college.

"She seems to have settled down a bit," he said. "But she's already packed stuff and ready to load."

"Has she met her roommate yet?"

"About that," he said. "I gave in and paid for a private dorm room for her. She made a rational argument for it and offered to pay half of it from her savings."

"I understand."

"She'll be on her way next week. I may explode in the peace and quiet." He paused. "Speaking of quiet, you haven't said much. Is everything okay there?"

"Yeah, it's fine. Mom's home, and we've planned walks and activities," I replied. "She's made a lot of progress. Your mother even brought Kalimar to town this afternoon. Made Mom's year."

"I wouldn't have thought of it," he admitted. "How'd the horse take it?"

"Like he'd been trained to be around sick people. What are they called, a therapy animal?"

"Wouldn't surprise me. He has always been a peaceful soul."

"Kim needs to spend more time with him, then." I wrestled with my pillow, now relegated to a daybed in Mom's hobby room. "She told me the other day how much she thought Bock had screwed up her life as well as everyone else's. He'd told her she would watch me kill Matthew because I liked doing it."

"Pretty fucked up."

"Ten buck's worth of freebie," I said, referring to our swear-jar collecting money for the transgressions of using profanity. "She said she's glad he is dead, but she still has a lot of anger that she didn't kill him."

"Does she know what happened in Florida?"

"I told her, and maybe it helped, knowing that you killed him. She feels like no one else has listened to her and tried to help her. It's festered inside her all this time." I wiped away a tear running toward my pillow. "She was afraid to talk about it with me, too, and that makes *me* angry."

CHAPTER 12
AMBER

September 11, 2001
0846 Eastern Daylight Time – Impact #1

0858 Eastern Daylight Time –
"Daddy… oh please answer, Dad… Oh my God," I panted into the cell phone as it rang, lucky to have gotten a cell signal on the fourth try.
 "You've reached Zach Samual –" the voice was saying when I punched the button to end the call.
 I punched in a different number, heard another message that the system was busy. In stomping frustration, I paced the window of the hotel, watching, hitting the redial button again and again until a connection was made.
 One ring. Two rings. Three rings.
 A familiar voice answered, "Hello, Amber."

0859 Eastern Daylight Time –
"Oh my God, Julie! I'm here by myself, and I don't know what to do, and the jet crashed into – !"
 "Amber, slow down."
 "The jet! Aren't you watching the news?"
 "No, I'm getting ready to take Mom to her physical therapy. What news?" Julie asked, perplexed at the hysteria in Amber's voice.
 "Television news! A jet hit the building, and the news says it's on fire and –"
 "What building?"
 "The World Trade Center!" I was so freaked out I couldn't stand still. "Ethan went to meet an attorney this morning, but he didn't take his phone and –"
 "Amber, stop!" Julie yelled to interrupt me. "I don't know what you are talking about. First, are you safe?"
 "I guess so," I said, trying to catch my breath.
 "Where are you?"

"Don't be mad, but I'm in New York City. I came here yesterday to see Ethan. He went to —"

"You're in New York?" Julie said, her voice rose. I could hear when she turned on the TV.

"I was just looking out our hotel window at the city —"

"*Our* hotel window?"

I kept talking, not taking time to answer her question. " — and I saw this jet fly into the side of one of the Twin Tower buildings! There's fire and —"

"And what about Ethan?" Julie asked, changing channels to find the morning news, it sounded like.

"He went to meet with a lawyer. I don't know where exactly, but he showed me the Twin Towers from the room and said that when he came back, we were going back there for brunch at the top of one. He forgot his phone so I can't reach him, and I don't know what to do!"

"Amber, don't —"

0903 Eastern Daylight Time —
The call went dead as the second jet struck the other building.

I screamed, watching the terrifying scene happen again, less than a mile from the hotel, with the same thing showing live on the television.

Newscasters seemed to stumble on words to fill the space, needing none.

Words failed to describe the enormity of such an accident.

It's an accident, right? Has to be. Maybe a glitch in air traffic control directed the planes into the buildings. But twice?

Listening to the news broadcasters discussing stupid theories why helicopters didn't just land on the roofs to rescue people trapped above the impact. Then when the media began describing all the debris in the air, and how, *Oh My God!* people were jumping, I couldn't stand to watch the television.

I couldn't bear to watch out the window, either.

I hit redial over and over.

When I couldn't get through after dozens of tries, I slumped to the floor of the 14th story hotel room and squeezed my eyes closed against the repeating memory, unable to stop it. Unable to connect.

Unable to understand what was happening.

Slowly realizing that what I'd seen couldn't be an accident. Wondering what would happen next.

CHAPTER 13
JULIE

September 11, 2001
0703 Mountain Daylight Time –

The call disconnected moments after I found a channel showing a live feed from New York City.

I saw the jet strike the skyscraper in a huge ball of flames and debris, and for a few seconds, I thought this was a repeat of the video showing what Amber had already described to me. Within just dumbfounded seconds, I realized the impact had happened a second time.

Both Towers of the World Trade Center had been hit by airliners.

I tried calling Amber back, but the voice mail answered immediately. I tried sending a text, a recent technology to cell phones. *"Where are you?"* There was no way of knowing if the message had been received. When I realized the cellular service was disrupted or overloaded and there was no way to get in touch with Amber, I dialed Zach.

0706 Mountain Daylight Time –

"Hey," he answered on the second ring. "I just came in from the barn and saw that Amber had called. Everyone's up early today."

"Go turn on the TV," I said, trying to keep my voice calm. "Turn on the news and watch for a few minutes, then I'll tell you the rest of this story." I waited while he went to the den and heard the volume increase, followed by a long pause while he watched a similar version of what I kept seeing, over and over.

"No way! An airliner hit each of the Towers? That's no accident, Julie. Oh, shit," he exclaimed, his voice trailing off to a whisper as he watched the footage for several minutes. Finally, he inhaled, held it, steeling himself for news worse than what he'd seen on television, exhaled. "Okay. Tell me."

"Amber's there," I said, feeling my stomach clench.

"Here?"

"No, Zach. She's *in* New York City, watching this mess live out a hotel window, alone," I explained. "She had trouble getting a connection after the first building was hit, but we were talking, and the call dropped again when the second plane hit."

"What the hell is she doing in New York?"

"Ethan," she said, knowing one name would fill in a lot of details for him.

"Then she's not alone, however much I don't want to think about that," Zach replied. "Why are *they* there?"

"No, Ethan went to a meeting with an attorney this morning, then he was coming back to take her to eat. In the World Trade Center," I said, realizing how close Amber had been to being in one of those buildings. "She is alone."

If she'd been killed in New York City in that catastrophe, we wouldn't have known for days she was there.

I shivered as the TV station repeated the same footage, already seared into my memory. "She said Ethan forgot his cell, so even if the phones worked, she can't reach him."

"What are you going to do?" Zach asked.

"Me?" I gritted my teeth. "Zach, I can't very well leave New Mexico right now, so what are you going to do?" I retorted.

"Was Ethan's meeting supposed to be in the World Trade Center?" he asked. "I mean, you don't think he was there, do you?"

"I don't know. We only talked a minute."

We discussed that, unless Ethan returned to the hotel, it would be up to Zach to find Amber.

Adrenaline-laced fear surged through my body, causing my hands and feet to ache with cold. My heart galloped in my chest, and my stomach burned like I'd swallowed a white-hot branding iron.

0945 Eastern Daylight Time –

Americans are told that airspace within and inbound to the United States is shut down. No further civilian air traffic is allowed to take off, and all aircraft already in flight are ordered to land at the nearest airport as soon as possible. This is the first time in US history that airspace has been closed in response to an event. Other countries assist with landing aircraft.

0953 Eastern Daylight Time –
CNN confirms a plane crash at or into the Pentagon, including a video of a gaping hole in the building and raging fire.

The loop of media footage increased to include these two events.

0803 Mountain Daylight Time –
Behind me, Mom's wheelchair creaked as she pushed herself into the hall, rolling into the living room, her attention glued to the television.

Each minute, the repeating footage and the next piece of breaking news all felt. . . well, I had no words to describe the nauseating breathless sensation.

Helpless.

Angry.

Frightened.

Only when I didn't hear Zach's voice did I realize I'd let my hand drop to my shoulder. It didn't matter, neither of us had been speaking, though similar muttered words of shock passed unanswered as we watched different news programs.

"Mom's awake, Z'. I gotta go."

"Give her a kiss for me," he said.

We said goodbye and disconnected.

I texted again to Amber, *"Keep trying to call or text."*

0959 Eastern Daylight Time –
The South Tower of the World Trade Center collapses, 56 minutes after the impact of Flight 175. The media begins broadcasting the cloud of gray dust and debris billowing through the streets of Manhattan and people running to escape it.

Kim came into the living room behind me, and together, she, my mother and I watched – along with most of the world – as the South World Trade Center Tower disappeared into a cloud of smoke and dust.

We were discussing what would make the South Tower collapse when the North Tower, which had been hit first, hadn't. Of course, so were the newscasters and dozens of people who were interviewed. None of us moved from the television for the next half hour, until the next wave of news.

> **1028 Eastern Daylight Time – The North Tower of the World Trade Center, the first struck by a passenger jet, also collapses.**
>
> **1041 Eastern Daylight Time – NBC confirms that a passenger jet has gone down in Somerset, Pennsylvania. In audio between the air traffic controllers, one reports that Flight 93 is down. Another requests confirmation, "He's landed?" and the reply, "No, he's down."**

We still sat motionless, helpless, speechless until the news confirmed that a fourth jet had crashed into a field in Pennsylvania.
How many jets have been hijacked? Will this stop?

CHAPTER 14
JULIE

September 11, 2001, 11:30 Mountain Daylight Time

Although I could have taken Dagmar to her PT appointment, the three of us sat dazed at the devastation playing out on live television instead. I guessed no one there would be exercising today. The therapists would be as dumbstruck as we were.

An hour later, Zach called. "Julie, they've grounded all aviation in the U.S. and Canada," he said, though the news had already covered the closure of American airspace. "No commercial or private flights for who knows how long," he continued. "I can't get to Amber any way except driving."

"Now what?" I asked, feeling even more helpless. To him. To Amber. To all of New York City.

Watching the buildings collapse had been nauseating for me, and it had upset Mom, who knew nothing of Amber's situation yet. She might not be Amber's grandmother by blood, but the bond had been just as strong. I would have to tell her soon.

"It will take me at least three days to drive across the country," he said. "I'm trying to reach Del and Kenny so they can look after the horses."

Through the panic came a solution. "I have an idea if it will work." No need to lower my voice – Mom and Kimberley were glued to the television at a volume that vibrated through the house. "Maybe Gerald can go – that's almost two days sooner than you could drive. If he can find her, then you can meet them back in Michigan."

"Dr. Katz? Sure," he said, not sounding convinced. "Call him. I'm packing to go, either way. I'll be on the road in another hour. Let me know what you find out."

We disconnected, and I turned to watch the other two women, a generation between them. Strangers who had become friends because of their respective medical issues, helping each other, now holding hands as the newscasters repeated the same information with new suppositions.

I walked back into the kitchen to put water in the kettle for tea and placed it on the stove before dialing Gerald Katz.

"Julie," he said, sounding distracted and breathless. "Is everything all right?"

"If you mean Kim, yes. She's fine."

"No, not her," he said, then corrected himself. "Not just her, everything. Are you watching the news?"

"Yes, and it's beyond comprehension."

"Exactly." He seemed to focus more on the call.

"I need to ask you a huge favor, Gerald." I explained Amber's situation in New York.

"Of course, Julie, anything I can do to help."

"I hate to ask, but could you go try to find her?"

"While I would do so without question, Julie, I should not," he said. "I had cataract surgery yesterday and am not supposed to drive."

The idea sank in my gut.

"Just a second," he said, covering the mouthpiece of his phone for a short time. "Let me check something. I'll call you right back." He hung up without waiting for an agreement.

His return call couldn't be soon enough, but I hoped Amber could get through to me, too.

Ten long minutes later, after I'd made and served tea to Mom, my phone rang.

"I was hoping Kayleigh and Reese could go, but he can't get away from the hospital with this panic going on. But I have another, maybe better alternative. Brandan Callaghan said he would go. He has connections in the city that might help. Is that okay?" Gerald asked.

"Really? That's better than okay. I could kiss you!" A tear ran down my cheek in relief.

"He said he had to stop by the HR department to let them know, but he will be home in half an hour and call you then." He hesitated. "Is Kim all right?"

"She's doing great, Gerald. She and my mother are so good for each other. Bringing her here was the right decision for everyone."

"I trusted you could help her," he said. "I wish I could repay you by getting Amber."

"You couldn't, and I understand. But you gave me an alternative."

I peeked into the den and asked Kim if she would like to talk to her father, and she took my phone and went to the kitchen so she could hear better. I took her seat by my mother.

"Is Amber okay?" Mom asked in a whisper.

"How'd –" I started to say, then pointed to the television. "She's safe, but she's in Manhattan somewhere. How'd you know?"

"I'm a mother, dear."

"Zach is driving to New York, and a friend of mine from Michigan is going there to help," I said. "We'll get her out of there as soon as we can find her."

Kim brought my phone back and sat beside me. "Thanks," she leaned over and took my hand.

Long after I expected, or maybe it seemed long because my sense of timing was off-kilter, my phone rang again.

"Julie, it's Brandan. Sorry for the delay. I'm on my way home to grab a few things. What can you tell me?"

"First, thank you," I said, taking my cup and going to my bedroom for some quiet. "I haven't been able to contact her again since her first call, but she said she is in Manhattan in a high-rise hotel, facing the Towers. She told me she saw the impact of the first plane. She had trouble getting a connection. We were talking when the call went dead. When the second airliner struck."

"She called from her cell phone?" he noted. "I'm sure every phone in New York is in use. It'd be easier to find her if she'd use the hotel phone. Location, get that first if she calls again."

"I've been trying to reach her, calling and sending texts."

"Texting, hmmm. My phone doesn't do that."

"I don't know how much cash she has, but I'll call the credit card company and make sure she can use it." I took a moment to sip the tea and think. "She doesn't know her way around the city, so unless they evacuate the hotel, I hope she has the wits to stay put."

"I'll pack a bag and hit the road in a few minutes," he said, "and I'll call in a few hours to check in."

"I'll pay for everything, I promise," I said, feeling the dread settle a bit in my stomach. "Zach will be on his way east within the hour from Washington, so you two can work out details to meet later. He'll be glad to hear about the help."

I ended the call and sat slumped on the bed I hadn't taken the time to make today. Crawling back in and hiding under the covers seemed enticing.

"Julie," Kim whispered from beside the door, startling me from my worries. "This all this is too much for Dagmar. She's crying."

She stood in the doorway, a hand resting on her pregnant and ballooning belly. Without realizing it, I suspected.

"What can we do to help?" Kim asked.

"Her or the rest of the world," I replied, shaking my head. "Let's go see if one of our famous brunches will help us all."

Zach didn't call again until he had been on the road several hours, but he was glad to hear that Brandan was already on his way to New York to help us locate and retrieve Amber.

"He knows someone in the police department there," I said, hoping his contacts were still alive, given the mayhem shown on television. "He's been in the city several times, so he knows his way around better than she does."

I'd never been there so trying to find my way around during a disaster the likes of which we saw on television would be insane.

"You spent a little time in New York City, didn't you?" I asked, the thought occurred to me.

"Don't you remember the cup I bought for you from the Metropolitan Museum of Art?"

"You told me about the Nolan Ryan signed baseball in the cup, but not why you bought the cup. What were you doing there?" I asked, again without response.

Zach didn't expound on the reason.

"Will it help you find Amber?" I prompted. If he didn't want to discuss it now, I didn't want to ask why but whether it would be useful experience.

"It might."

The news launched another recap, putting all four airliner crashes into a timeline, showing the footage over and over. I was sick of it.

"I've gotta move," I said to Zach. "Hang on a sec'." I had to escape, leaving Mom and Kim to the television. I poured myself a drink and went outside to sit at the patio table in the sunshine and fresh air. Today felt more like a black and white silent movie, making me wish for something stronger than iced tea. I watched condensation form on the glass and roll to the table.

My attention came back to the phone. "Millions of people across the country must be saying the same things I am. I can't believe this is happening. Is that all? Am I safe where I am? Is it safe anywhere?"

"And millions of them are hearing the same answer," Zach answered. "We don't know."

"Brandan told me to get her specific location first if I reach Amber. What else should I tell her? Should she try to get out of the city or stay where she is? What if she already left the hotel and we can't find her?" My heart rate began ramping up again. "I already paid the credit card balance we gave her for emergencies, but what if she runs out of insulin or –"

"It'll be all right, Julie," he said, with barely enough enthusiasm to convince me he believed it either. "I'll lose signal for a while. You stay put, stay safe. Tell her the same thing when she calls. We'll find her. I love you and I'll . . ." he was saying when the connection dropped.

So many more questions tumbled through my head. I wanted to do something, go locate Amber, go dig through rubble with so many others working to find survivors, and or in what I understood would turn into days of rescue and weeks of searching for the dead.

How wrong was I about that?

I couldn't remember feeling this helpless since my father was killed, but that was a dark cave I didn't want to enter again.

Damn you, Anthony Bock!

Standing up from the deck chair, I wanted to scream.

The scream I heard came from inside my mother's house.

CHAPTER 15
JULIE

September 11, 2001, 12:10 p.m.
I tore through the back door to find Kim and Mom tangled in a heap on the oatmeal-colored carpeting, blood coming from somewhere I couldn't see.

Neither of them answered me, but they were both breathing.

I dialed 9-1-1 on the phone I was surprised to find in my hand, grateful there was a connection.

The dispatcher must have gotten enough information from me, but I don't remember saying anything except that I needed two ambulances. A few minutes before EMS and the Albuquerque Fire Department Rescue arrived, Kim came to her senses enough to tell me she had felt a horrible pain in her lower abdomen and stood. My mother may have recognized Kim's obstetrical emergency and tried to stand to help or to come get me or something, but she stumbled, and Kim tried to catch her.

Within what seemed like an hour but was less than six minutes, the house was wall to wall with paramedics assessing the two women, starting oxygen and IVs, EKGs, and packaging for transport.

Trying to keep out of the way, I provided history for one then the other teams. Someone asked me to gather Mrs. Madigan's medicines for them, and I did. Swept them all into a paper bag I'd found under the sink. Kim didn't have any except her vitamins.

I answered someone's question about hospital choice, saying they both needed to go to the University of New Mexico Hospital.

In the chaos, someone else came through the front door, taking up space in my visual field but not in my brain processing. I didn't recognize that this person didn't join the medical efforts on the floor, but I couldn't look away from the medics to see who it was.

"Julie?"

The voice was persistent enough I almost pulled my attention from the medics, one pair getting ready to put Kim on a gurney. I wanted to go to the door and tell her I'd be there soon, but I couldn't move.

"Julie." The voice shimmered on the periphery of my focus. "Julie!"

I finally looked up to find a face whose name wasn't available to my brain. I blinked.

"We're almost ready, too. Can you let UNMH know we're inbound hot with two?" someone asked the person who had spoken my name.

She nodded, lifted a portable radio to change channels, and spoke into it in a calm, professional manner.

I hated that she could be so collected and calm when I was standing on a knife-edge between hysteria and whatever might be worse.

She stepped around the medic knelt by my mother, coming toward me, saying my name again.

"Taylor?" I blurted, although I had no idea how my brain had found the name.

"Yes. Julie, come on. You can ride with me," she said, putting a hand on my shoulder. "Where are your house keys?"

I must have made a vague motion toward the hooks beside the front door.

"Let's let them go out first," she said.

With that, I recalled what I'd admired most about Taylor Healy – the way she could take the most out-of-control scene and in just a few calm words, control it like a conductor of an orchestra.

I sat, my eyes still on my mother, what little of her I could see.

The second gurney was brought into the living room by two firefighters. It was lowered, and my mother and the equipment strapped down, then rolled out.

I stood.

"Julie," she said, putting her arms around me when I broke like a steel pipe, gushing tears and panic.

Didn't take long to run out of either. I pulled away.

"What are you doing in Albuquerque?" I asked, wiping my face on my sleeve. "I thought you moved to –" I shrugged. "Somewhere."

"They made me an offer here I couldn't refuse, so I stayed," she said. "What are *you* doing here? I know this is your mom's house. Is Kim your daughter?"

The questions seemed so difficult to explain, I didn't know where to start.

"We had gone to Michigan for my boss's retirement party and his younger daughter's wedding in July. Kim is the older daughter. She'd been in trouble and was pregnant, so when Mom had a stroke and I needed to come back, I brought Kim with me."

Taylor helped me gather clothes for Mom and Kimberley and lock the house.

I saw an EMS Supervisor's SUV parked across the street, which explained why she had shown up. "I'm happy to see you."

"What happened today?" she asked, unlocking the door for me.

I shook my head. "What hasn't happened?"

She gave me her famous half-smile. "Isn't that the truth."

On the way, I called Vera, but she didn't answer.

"She's working today," Taylor said after I left a message. "I'll find her. What do you mean back to Michigan? I thought that's where you lived."

"I've, well, we've lived in Washington for five or six years now," I said, the story jumbling in my head. "Before that, there was this big serial murder in Michigan – wait. Do you know about Jeremy?"

"I haven't seen him in a long time. Not since he asked if he should go see you while you were in the hospital here, but I told him not to." She parked near the emergency department. "I didn't think you'd want to see him. I hope I wasn't wrong."

"No, you were right. There's so much more, Taylor, but not now," I said, wishing my voice didn't sound so whiney.

"Absolutely not now." She pulled out a business card, scribbled on the back, and pushed it into a pocket of my bag. "Whenever things are better. Let's go find your family."

• • • • •

Kim had gone straight to Labor and Delivery. Mom was in the ED, headed for a CAT scan as soon as it was available for the next patient.

I stood beside her, holding her hand.

She did not open her eyes, even when I spoke to her.

The heart rate was a little low. Blood pressure was high again. Way high.

A doctor entered the room, snapped something at a nurse who was hurrying by, then stepped closer and introduced himself.

"It's most likely she had another stroke, so we're going over to radiology and wait for the next slot," he said. "I saw her last time. This seems much more serious."

Yeah, no shit. Last time she was conscious and responsive, wasn't she?

"She's had every single dose of medicine since she came home," I said, wishing he was wrong. "We hadn't missed a single physical therapy until this morning, but she was fine when she woke up, and we had a light breakfast. I was outside, but when she thought Kim was in trouble, she tried to stand to help her, but I don't know what happened in those few moments."

Nurses came to unhook my mother from telemetry and blood pressure cuff and such, ready to roll away to have a CAT scan when the first seizure began.

I had a good idea of what would happen in the next thirty minutes. I glanced at the doctor and said, "Do what you can, I've got to go to OB."

When I spun around to go down the hall, Vera almost ran over me.

"They paged me to come to the ED. Is it Dag?" she asked, out of breath.

I nodded. "She's had another stroke, and Kimberly is upstairs now, too. Can you stay with her? I have to check on Kim."

"Of course," she said, leaning back to view the commotion in Mom's room.

"They're going to intubate her."

She nodded. "I'll call when she returns from CT."

I took the stairs. I was less apt to run into anyone I knew, and I needed to burn off the adrenaline spike that was making my heart race.

After calling Dr. Katz, which went better than I expected, I tried half a dozen times to reach Zach, who I really wanted to talk to. I'd given up when my phone buzzed in my hands, clenched so tight that it hurt to pry them open to answer a call.

I'd only taken a breath to say hello.

"Julie! Oh my God, I've been trying and trying to call!"

"Amber! Where are you? Are you still at the hotel? Stay there if you can. Do you have enough insulin and supplies?"

"For a few days. There's a pharmacy across the street," she said. "I still haven't heard from Ethan."

"Tell me where you are —"

The connection went dead before I could ask for the information I needed most or tell her who was coming to find her.

I wouldn't have told her I couldn't care less that she hadn't made contact with Ethan, but it is true.

September 11, 2001, 2:28 p.m. Mountain Daylight Time
"I'm in Idaho, past Boise," Zach said. "Have you heard anything?"

I started crying again. "I got another call from Amber. I was only able to tell her to stay at the hotel before we were cut off again."

I could tell Zach pulled over to talk to me.

"Julie, what's wrong?"

"Mom had another stroke, and Kim is pre-eclamptic with premature contractions and light bleeding, so I'm at the hospital with both of them."

"Should I come there instead?" The offer was genuine.

What should have been a simple answer was anything but. I wanted him to be here with me, to be the rock I needed more than any other time in my adult life. But Amber needed him, too.

"No, go find Amber. She needs you to do that."

"Are you sure?"

"Yes," I said, trying to sound confident. "Your mother is here to help me."

"She's been trying to call me, too. I guess I know why now." He paused. "Is Dagmar, I mean, how is she doing?"

"Zach, she's on a ventilator and has had several seizures. The CT scan shows a large hemorrhagic stroke, not like the one prior. This is near the base of the brain. I don't think she will recover."

"You're not going to have to . . ." He didn't finish the sentence.

Take her off the vent?

"I'm her only living relative, so the decisions that have to be made are mine to make," I said. Tears spilled down my cheeks again.

"Look, I figure the airlines will be back in service in a few days. Brandan will probably get to New York and find her and be back in Michigan before I can get there. I'll coordinate with him about getting Amber on a plane to New Mexico," he said, working out a plan in his mind. "I don't want you to have to go through this alone, Julie."

"I appreciate that, but you take care of her first, okay? I'll be all right."

Not fine, by any measure, but maybe all right.

Who was I trying to convince?

"Keep me posted on her. What about Kim?"

"They have her contractions stopped, but her blood pressure is elevated. She'll be here several days at least, if everything returns to normal. If she has more contractions, the goal will be to delay delivery as long as possible. Every day makes a big difference." I sighed. "She thinks Mom's stroke is her fault."

"Oh no," he replied. "I'm so sorry."

"I haven't told her the prognosis for Mom for fear it could make her blood pressure go higher."

"How long will you wait for any signs of improvement with Dagmar?"

Before I pull the plug? If he can't say it, can I really do it?

"I don't know. A few days, maybe."

"I should be there with you."

"Zach, if not for a dozen other crises in the world that have a higher priority, you would be." I wiped my eyes. "I appreciate your unending support, but Amber needs you to be her dad more than I need you to be my husband. What will you say to her?"

"About going to New York? I don't know. What was she thinking?"

"Perhaps she wanted to help him find his roots and not something like she was falling in love."

I heard the truck start.

"You know, I'd forgotten about him since she went off to college," he said. "He'd better hope I don't run into him anytime soon."

CHAPTER 16
JULIE

September 11, 2001, 11:38 p.m.

Sleeping wasn't a possibility in ICU. I wasn't supposed to be in Mom's room, but the nurses let me be.

Activity in the ICU cubicle was nonstop, with ventilator alarms, pumps beeping for dozens of reasons, and her ongoing seizures. Once I had dozed off, sleep had given my brain access to horrible dreams sound-tracked with the cacophony of noises I'd heard in my own hospitalizations, leading to jerking awake when a nurse came in to change an IV bag.

She apologized for startling me, but I took it as a sign I should go check on Kim.

Standing outside her door, I heard her talking, but couldn't hear the other person speak. I didn't want to interrupt if she were on the phone to anyone except the boyfriend who got her into this mess. I'd raised my hand to open the door when I heard her say, "Kayleigh, I'm scared," followed by more silence.

I knocked and peeked around the door as I opened it.

Kim waved at me to come on inside.

Even with the lights low, Kim's room was much cheerier than the drab grays of ICU. The TV played soft music. Noises from the hall were softer, less harried.

"Julie's here. Want to say hi?" she asked into the phone, then handed it to me.

"Hello?" I said, not wanting to give away that I already knew who it was, letting her tell me. "Hi, Kayleigh! How are you?"

"I'm okay, I suppose, but I'm worried about Kim."

"She's in good hands."

"How's your mother?" she asked.

I didn't want to let on the dismal prognosis for her in front of Kim, so I replied that there was little change so far.

"I understand, Julie, and I appreciate you protecting her," she whispered.

"How's your dad?"

"He's doing okay," she said. "He told us about Amber. Have you heard from her?"

"I talked to her this afternoon for a minute, and I told her to stay put until Brandan gets there."

"This is all so crazy. I'm glad she's okay. I wish we could have gone to get her for you."

"Thank you, Kayleigh, but I'm glad your father thought about Brandan." I'd run out of semi-cheery topics and was about to hand the phone back to Kim when she spoke again.

"We're pretty freaked out over the attacks this morning. It's nauseating."

"All that and more. It's almost unreal." I was at a loss of vocabulary to describe what had happened. I was too tired to think of more to say when I heard my cellphone chirping in my pocket. "It's Zach, so I need to go. I love you. Here's Kim," I said, handing her the phone and digging in my jacket. I opened the phone, waved to Kim I'd be back in a minute, and went out the door.

"I'm in the hospital, Z," I whispered, "hang on a second so I can walk to the waiting room."

"Okay," the voice replied, sounding as wrung out as I did.

I made it into the empty waiting room and collapsed into a chair. "How's the drive going?" I asked.

"Crazy. Drivers are courteous. It's weird." He must have changed hands. "How are you?"

"No change. Kim's awake. She was chatting with Kayleigh on the phone when I stopped in a few minutes ago."

"I asked how you are, Julie." His voice was soft, caring.

"I'm exhausted, emotionally and physically."

"I can still come to New Mexico if you need me."

"You need to go –"

"I will not leave you there alone if you need me," he interrupted me. "We've agreed Brandan is closer and is the best chance to find Amber. I won't make it to New York in time."

"Zach, as much as I want you with me, what if Brandan needs help and you should have gone on to New York to help find her?"

"That's not likely to happen, and I could fly to New York from Albuquerque if he needs me. Otherwise, he can put her on a plane at the closest airport for a flight to Albuquerque or back to Seattle when air travel re-opens," he said. "That's all I'd do. She needs to get back to school."

"Crap, I didn't consider where she needed to go after you find her." I wiped my eyes. "It's been hard to make priorities for anything today."

September 12, 2001, 3:51 a.m. Mountain Daylight Time
I must have fallen asleep in the waiting room, because I woke to someone in scrubs, touching my arm.

"Mrs. Samualson," he said, "I'm sorry to wake you, but you need to come to ICU, please."

"Is it my mother?" I asked, checking my watch. "Sorry, dumb question."

"Yes, but I only know I was asked to find you and bring you to the unit."

I checked the man's nametag, which read Larry, Nursing Supervisor.

I took a moment to yawn and stretch before standing, suspecting it would be bad news if Larry didn't tell me. Excusing myself to the restroom in the waiting area, he waited without rushing me, giving me a chance to wash my face and wake up.

The face looking back at me looked better than I felt.

We walked through halls, taking an elevator, then into the intensive care unit. In ICU, I saw several people in the room where my mother was.

Larry veered off when he saw I knew where I was going.

I stood behind one nurse, watching, until she sensed someone close and turned to me.

"Oh, please," she said, stepping out of my way.

I recognized Dr. Morgan, mom's neurologist, and another doctor. When he saw me, he motioned me closer, introduced me to the cardiologist, Dr. Naeem Khan.

"It looks like she's having a myocardial infarction now," he said, taking the EKG from the physician I did not know and handing it to me. "Nurses began seeing changes an hour ago. The second labs are not back yet. The question is, do we take her to the cath lab, or wait for the next labs?"

"You waited an hour to ask me that?" I blurted. "Cath her, please."

The two physicians exchanged glances.

"Yes, I am very aware this stroke is hemorrhagic, and that a catheterization and angioplasty could very well be fatal," I said. "But having an evolving myocardial infarction you can stop with stenting trumps the stroke, so she might have a chance, albeit fractional, of recovery. With both, she has no chance at all. Where do I sign?"

He nodded at the other doctor, who also nodded then left the room.

The nurses began new tasks, including bringing me a consent form to sign, and I stepped back while they worked until I could move close enough to take Mom's hand.

"I know you can hear me, Mom. I love you. We're all fighting for you."

Her bed was rolled out of the room, the effort taking seven people, including one manually ventilating Mom.

With the room empty, I wilted into the only chair, letting tears fall down my cheeks again.

Not yet 24 hours since a national tragedy had overshadowed my own. Three women close to my heart were in jeopardy in three enormously different situations. I wanted to be strong for them all. I was trying. But I wasn't sure at that moment I could keep straight what I wished to be the outcome in the next 24 hours for them.

I wanted Amber to get back to school in Seattle, but finding her could take several days.

I hoped Kim's labor and the pregnancy-related high blood pressure were under control, and that she wouldn't have to stay in the hospital until delivery.

That left my mother. I wished she would recover back to at least this time yesterday, but deep in my heart, I knew that wouldn't happen. The neurologist had told me the second stroke had been larger than the first seven weeks ago. Worse, this one had been hemorrhagic, not ischemic like the first, meaning she had bleeding in her brain instead of having a blockage.

This may or may not have been a side effect of the medications she had been taking to prevent another stroke. Crazy as it seems, prevention of one type increases the threat of the other type. Mom and I had discussed this, and she agreed to take the medicines, understanding the risks.

The brain damage that had already occurred, we both knew, was irreparable. Recovery had been an attempt to reroute signals through her brain. She had lost little of her recent or remote memory, but she had lost almost full muscle control and sensation to the left side of her body. Before she'd come home, she'd told me that, although her nursing career was finished, she would work hard to recover what function was possible because she wanted to remain independent. But she'd also confessed she did not want to go through losing more, and she made me promise that if something else happened, I was to not chase miracles that would leave her alive but with no ability to live.

"Chasing miracles," I said, "which is exactly what I'm doing, isn't it?" Pulling my knees to my chest, I rested my head on them. "I don't think I can do this alone, Zach. I wish you were here with me," I said, more tears stinging my eyes.

"All you had to do is ask," his voice said from the doorway.

CHAPTER 17
JULIE

September 12, 2001, 5:48 a.m. Mountain Daylight Time
I jumped up from the chair and rushed into his arms.

"You should be halfway across the country to find Amber," I whined, pounding on his chest softly with my fist before burying my face in his shirt. "But I'm so glad you are here."

The strong arms around me did not budge, and I soon found they were holding me upright while I sobbed.

Tears soaked into his shirt. Tears of frustration, my worries, my fears. Tears because I knew my mother was at the end of her life, and yet Kim was nearing the time of bringing into the world a new life. Tears that I didn't find any of this fair.

Finally, all my tears were cried out.

"What about Amber?" I said, wiping my face on an offered handkerchief.

"I talked to Brandan, explained the situation. He told me I needed to be with you," Zach told me. "I agreed."

We stepped out of the way when three nurses rolled Mom's bed back into the room, with a fourth who continued ventilating her by hand until the machine was hooked up.

"The doctor will be in to speak with you in about ten minutes, if you would like to go into the quiet room to wait," a nurse with a long black braid said as she hooked Mom to the heart monitor. "It's just out the door, second door on the right."

I nodded, and we went to wait in a room with pale soft décor. I knew hundreds of family members had received awful news inside these walls.

Tears threatened to fall again.

"I'm here to support you, Julie, no matter what," Zach said, taking my hand while we sat in chairs that, in true hospital fashion, hadn't been comfortable in decades.

I gave him the latest update on my mother and Kim.

"You got here really fast," I said. "How was your drive?"

"Really fast," Zach said, leaving me to my own calculations.

What should have taken nearly 22 hours he had accomplished in, I looked at my watch, less than 18 hours?

"Any tickets?" I asked with a weak smile.

"Stopped twice, explained the situation, and was let go with a good-luck and be-careful warning both times. I knew I had to be here and that it was time-critical."

"And again, you should be halfway to New York by now, but thanks," I said. "Other than fast, how was the drive?"

"I'm sick of the media. The radio broadcasted nothing but hundreds of speculations on who was responsible, how many people had died, and the endless politics. Witnesses who saw the airliners hit the buildings, even if I didn't see it the first time," he said, shaking his head. "It's hard to wrap my head around, but then thinking of Amber being there, exposed to all of that makes me furious."

Which was why Zach shouldn't have diverted his trip for me, but I was thankful he came to Albuquerque.

"I haven't seen a television except in waiting rooms, but I'm glad. I made Kimberley turn it off."

"Tell me what happened," he said, holding my hand.

"I'm not sure. I had been outside while we were on the phone, then after we hung up, I heard Kim yell. When I got inside, they were both on the floor. Mom didn't speak but she squeezed my hand." I meant to finish the story when the doctor came into the quiet room.

Zach introduced himself. "Could you start at the beginning? I just got here."

Dr. Khan began his calm, rational explanation that my mother had suffered a second stroke, this one hemorrhagic – meaning vessels and tissue were damaged by bleeding rather than an obstruction, he explained to Zach – and that the EKG changes seen early this morning indicated a heart attack.

"In the cath lab, her blood pressure kept falling, making attempts to access the occluded coronary artery difficult and ballooning it open dangerous, but we couldn't chance using an anticoagulant," he said. "We did balloon the vessel open and place a stent, but it hasn't seemed to make much difference. The damage that occurred to the heart was irreparable."

"But she's alive," Zach countered.

"Yes, for now. Medications are keeping her heart rate and blood pressure stable, but this is only temporary and won't be effective long. A day or so at the most," Dr. Khan answered. "Probably less, honestly. The question now is, how much more do you want us to do?" he said, turning to me.

"I'm her only blood relative and durable power of attorney, I'm sure you know." I sighed.

He knew I understood his question was whether I wanted heroic measures performed, knowing they wouldn't save her life or correct the medical problems she was dying of.

And he knew that making the decision was painful, no matter how long a family had known it was coming.

He waited for me, striking a patient, quiet pose. Ready to offer more information if requested.

I didn't need more.

"Make sure she's comfortable," I answered. "No more heroic efforts. When her heart stops, it stops."

"Are you sure?" Zach asked me.

"No, damn it! I'm not sure!" I snapped at him, then hung my head. "Zach, my mother died this morning at her house. Her body hasn't given up yet."

The physician nodded. "I'll let the charge nurse know your wishes."

"I would like to stay with her and leave her on the ventilator, at least for a while," I said, my voice tinny.

"I'll ask if they can move her to a room further from the commotion at the desk."

Telling the doctor I wanted to let my mother go when her heart stopped was the hardest thing I'd ever said out loud. But the medical background tucked away in my head understood it was the right decision.

My mother, a nurse for decades, did not wish to be on life support or to be a prisoner of a useless body. She'd told me so while recovering from her first stroke.

Had her first stroke not happened at work, she might have fallen at home and not been found for hours or days, lying on the floor until muscle tissue began to break down and clog her kidneys and then her coronary arteries.

Her life could have ended that way, I know. Instead, I'd had time to be with her. Now, she was dying because her brain was severely damaged a second time.

I had to be strong enough to let her go.

An hour later, Vera Samualson dropped by the room where they had moved Mom. I knew they had been friends since we moved to New Mexico from Seattle when I was a kid, so she was grieving, too.

By 9 a.m., Mom's heart rate was in the 40s.

When Dr. Khan came by to check, I asked that the ventilator be turned off.

I wasn't ready for her to die, but then, I didn't figure I'd ever be ready. Zach and I had talked and held hands and hugged and cried on and off through the night. After the ventilator was disconnected, I spent an hour alone talking to my mother, telling her how much I loved her, how proud I was of everything she had accomplished, and that thanks to her, Kimberley was doing okay and out of danger.

"I hope you're looking forward to seeing Dad again soon. Give him a big hug for me, but don't tell him about Bock," I said. "Don't ever think of that monster again. If it's time for you to go, I understand. We will all be okay, though we'll miss you, and I love you very much."

The three of us sat at Mom's bedside for another hour, listening to her breathe. A nurse came in to mute the alarms as her heart slowed.

The EKG showed changes to the shape of the complexes, indicating the infarction – the death of the heart muscle – was worsening.

Over the next ten minutes, while both Vera and I held her hands, Mom's heart slowed to zero.

The nurse turned off the remaining machines without a word, letting us settle into a world without Dagmar Madigan.

Watching her body stop was like watching the sunset. Not the dramatic crash I'd feared, mostly because I'd been strong enough to state that no further attempts to save her body should be made. Her death was peaceful because my mother's soul had already escaped and gone.

Gone where? My lack of religious belief exploded the question in my chest.

Zach and Vera may have felt the peace that my mother's death was a miracle to transition to a perfect forever home, but I'd never had to consider such a possibility in the death of others.

Not as though no one I cared about has ever died. That list was long, starting with my father and ending most recently with Mary Anne Katz. I'd faced the death, albeit fake, of Zach. Yet in all that, religious belief had not affected my way of seeing death.

Zach put his arm around me and said, "The decision only seems like it's yours. You told me long ago that as a paramedic, if a patient were to die, nothing you did would change the outcome; but if he were to live, nothing you did wrong would change that, either."

And remembering that, I was sure my mother was gone.

CHAPTER 18
JULIE

September 12, 2001, 10:14 a.m. Mountain Daylight Time

"I can go with you now to find Amber," I argued after my next long cry. "We can go –"

"No, you need to stay here to make funeral arrangements and to be with Kim," he replied with a look that I was not to interrupt him, "and I will stay here with you."

"Amber needs –" I began my debate again only to be hushed with a finger to my lips.

"Not negotiable, Julie. Brandan is there and will be more effective at finding her than either – or both – of us would be if we were there right now. He knows the city, and he has contacts. He can't get into Manhattan yet, and neither could we. We have things to do until we hear from Amber, and nothing we do will change what's happening in New York."

With Zach's and Vera's support, I made initial funeral arrangements for her to be buried next to my father.

Selfish as it was, I found it unfair that my world had changed today in the shadow of the enormous losses that had changed the world within hours two days ago.

Like the loss of a child's beach sandcastle compared to the wave of the tsunami that destroys it.

News coverage of the attacks in New York, Washington D.C., and Pennsylvania continued to be a social priority everywhere we went, but I silently and selfishly wanted my grief, my loss to be just as meaningful. My world had stopped turning. However, the fact my mother had died on September 12, 2001, made me feel my grief hadn't been lost in the thousands of others who would be remembered forever.

• • • • •

Although I'd been in and out of Kim's room throughout the morning, I didn't have the heart to tell her about my mother's stroke. By noon, though, it was time to have the discussion I'd dreaded. Because she felt responsible for causing Mom's fall, I feared the possibility Kim might think she'd caused Mom's stroke and later her death, which could cause her blood pressure to spike.

However, she was scheduled to be discharged, so I didn't want to wait to tell her, in case she had another physical reaction needing further care, considering the pregnancy complications she'd faced so far.

Zach joined me, walking through the hospital halls. I hoped I had prepared myself well enough for the task.

I stopped outside Kim's room, steeling myself once more.

"She will be okay, just like you, Julie."

All I could do is nod, then I turned to knock and go on inside.

"I'm almost ready to go," Kim announced. "Oh hey, Zach. What are you doing here . . ." Her eyes jumped back and forth between us. "Oh, no. Please tell me she's okay."

I went to her bedside. "No, Kim. She passed away this morning. I wanted to make sure you were okay before I told you."

"That's not fair, Julie! I didn't get to see her!" she yelled, pounding a fist onto her bed.

"She had another massive stroke yesterday, Kim. She didn't regain consciousness. Then early this morning, she had a heart attack."

"I still should have said goodbye, just like you told us to keep talking to Mom!" Tears trailed over her bright red cheeks. She meant I'd told them when Mary Anne got to the end of a hard fight against breast cancer, that she could hear them even after she was unconscious, that they should keep talking to her.

"You're right, Kim. I'm sorry," I said. "I was wrong not to let you see her, but I'm worried about you and the baby."

Zach took a breath to speak, but Kim beat him.

"No, Julie, I'm sorry. I know what losing my mother meant to me, and I don't want this to be about me. I'm sorry she's gone."

We hugged and cried.

I looked up to see Vera had come into the room and was hugging her son.

We wiped away tears and greeted each other.

"Mom agrees we need to go on to New York to help find Amber," Zach said.

"I'm taking time off, so I'd be glad to have Kim stay with me," Vera added.

"Being so far out of town might not be a good idea," I said, "but you're welcomed to stay at Mom's house instead."

Do people freak out being in a house after the resident has died?

"That's a great idea. What do you think, Kim?"

She nodded.

"What about funeral services?" I asked. "Should we wait and do a memorial later?"

"That would be the right thing to do, too," Vera said. "A memorial when you return with Amber."

• • • • •

Brandan called a short time later. "They're limiting access into Manhattan," he said. "Although I might get there on foot by ferry, I'd rather have my vehicle. I took a nap, waiting on a contact with NYPD to call me back. I'm in a holding pattern for now, parked near the New Jersey Turnpike."

"Let us know when you're cleared to enter," Zach told him, holding the phone so we could both hear. "We haven't heard from Amber again, but I'll start trying more often."

"I got out and talked with a few people who'd come from Manhattan on ferries through the evening. The haze over the city, the fear in people's eyes – it's indescribable. Some had escaped the collapses with minutes to spare," he said, "and many just look like, I don't know, zombies. That thousand-yard stare and one foot in front of the other, without a clear sense of where to go because they can't go back home."

"That's what it looked like on the news. Radio makes it sound even worse," Zach responded. "I can be on my way as soon as the airlines are up or I'll be on the road again soon."

"Don't bother trying to fly. How's Julie's mom?" he asked.

Zach looked at me before answering. "It's a good thing I came this way. She passed away this morning."

"Damn, tell Julie I'm so sorry."

"Thanks, Brandan," I spoke so he could hear. "It was only a matter of time. Thanks for sending Zach here. I'll get him on the road."

• • • • •

We got Kimberley discharged and back to my mother's … I guess I'd have to say my house from now on. It had taken me five years to stop calling it my *parents'* house after my dad died.

Anyway, we got her home and settled, with a reiteration of the doctor's instructions – no lifting, no straining, no shopping or walking any distance, etc. for a few days. She wasn't on strict bed rest but was to be on minimal exertion, nonetheless. We arranged it so she could stay in the master bedroom where the television was, on the absolute promise she wouldn't watch the endless media coverage of 9/11 running 24 hours a day.

"It makes me sick, worse than morning sickness sick," she said. "I mean, I'm sorry it happened, but I can't do anything to change it. You two need to go find Amber. She must feel so lost by herself."

"I hope she isn't alone," Zach told her. "As angry as I am that Ethan lured her to New York, I hope he's with her now."

I left keys, phone numbers, anything I could think of to help Vera with Kim. I also gave her a credit card, which she refused to take.

"Nothing is going on here that I can't take care of," she said with her hand on her hip. "Go. Call when you can, when you find out anything about Amber. Be careful. We'll be praying for good news."

• • • • •

We loaded my bag, little more than a couple changes of clothes and a few toiletries, and a cooler of drinks, then Zach headed to I-40 Eastbound.

I was checking out a U.S. road atlas when Zach told me to check in the glovebox.

Inside, I found my duty pistol, three rolls of quarters, and a handful of pictures.

"You have a new filly," he announced as though we were just having morning coffee. "I had Julaquinte bred again last fall, intended it to be a surprise when we got home in July, but things didn't work out that way."

Flipping through the photos, I admired the princess air the foal had, as though she knew she was special and spoiled.

"You have to pick another musical name for her."

"I'll work on it," I said. "Why, by the way, are you driving my truck?"

"Registration matches to a Washington State law enforcement officer," he stated, "which might have a little bit of pull along the way. I made sure to grab your badge and creds, too. They're in the console."

"Glad to know you didn't have me reinstated to the New Mexico State Police again," I muttered.

"Thought about it."

I looked over in time to catch his just-kidding snark.

I think he's kidding.

"Your truck gets better gas mileage, and it will be a little easier to drive in New York City than mine," he said.

"See? That wasn't so hard to say, was it?" I kidded back. "Glad you brought it. I don't like yours."

• • • • •

The September sun was blinding us both in the mirrors as we neared the Texas border. It occurred to me that six years ago this month, I'd been in a Michigan hospital. Nine years ago, I'd driven here while recuperating from David's attack.

I must have dozed off, because I woke to find us parked at a barbeque place in Amarillo, Texas.

"This okay?" he asked.

"Absolutely!" I replied. "They have fantastic ribs." I didn't explain that I'd driven to Amarillo back when driving was part of my getting away from Albuquerque while I healed from David's assault. "I love the fried jalapeños."

"Those I liked, too," he said, shrugging when I looked at him in surprise. "Another place I followed you."

Though I didn't know he had, it wasn't a surprise, knowing he'd even flown to Seattle on one of my escape trips.

I was turning to step out of the truck when my phone rang.

It was Amber.

Pushing the button, I began talking without a greeting. "Are you okay? Where are you?"

The call crackled in heavy static, " –the hotel . . . Ethan has my. . . and I have to –" The connection popped and went dead.

I dialed Amber's number, got voicemail, repeated half a dozen times with no answer.

Repeating back her exact words aloud, I tried to interpret what I heard. "Something about Ethan, the hotel, I don't know," I said, cursing under my breath. "I *told* her to stay in the hotel, damn it!"

"Freebie," he said. "But a milder choice of profanity than what's going through my head. If she leaves, it makes locating her twice as hard. I hope she takes her phone with her and can keep it charged."

"Why? So we can keep trying to call her?"

"No, if we need to track her, I can call in a favor."

We headed inside the restaurant and were led to our table, but he had not yet explained what he meant. I excused myself to the restroom to give him a minute to think about this favor, whatever it was. Returning to the table, I wanted him to tell me. I thought I could wait him out, but when he started talking about how much farther we might make it before dark, I shook my head.

"No, Zach. What favor? From whom?" I demanded, barely containing aggravation.

"Someone with our cell phone company who has a bit of an unadvertised skillset, so I've been told."

"Why are we not using that now?" I climbed levels of more flabbergasted by the minute. Any tool we had should be in play, I thought.

"Tracking her phone doesn't benefit us right now, and I don't know if he can or will do it twice, so let's wait until it would provide the best information to help us when we can use it."

The answer was so vague, I wanted to shake him.

Zach went back to his laminated U.S. map, asking me if I thought we should go northeast at Oklahoma City or stay on I-40.

I leaned over to look and offered my opinion that going through Tulsa and St. Louis made the most sense, on to Indianapolis.

"I agree, maybe we can spend the night in Indy. Can you drive to OKC, then we will switch? It's 24 hours from here to New York City. We can go all the way if we keep switching."

That made sense. Four to six hours per shift behind the wheel and a bit of sleep, it was a decent plan.

The server brought us heaping plates of ribs, roasted pork loin, potato salad, beans, Coleslaw, and the cornmeal-breaded fried jalapeños we both loved, fried the way Zach's mom fixed okra.

From prior experience, I suspected the jalapeños wouldn't be as pleasant in 12 hours.

"What brought you to Amarillo when you came here," Zach asked between bites of a thick beef rib, which left barbeque sauce on his cheek.

I pondered the question. "Nothing particular thing here, although I'd have certainly come back for these," I said, swiping a fried jalapeño ring through a spicy buttermilk dressing and popping it in my mouth to chew before speaking again. "It was just another destination to drive to and turn around. A direction on the freeway."

"You drove a lot, but I never understood why."

"Because driving felt like the only thing I could do where I had full command. How far to go. Which direction. When to stop. I hated not having control of the memories that wouldn't go away. Closing my eyes to sleep equaled nightmares. Although I didn't want to really be anywhere different, it was the idea of going somewhere different."

He nodded and kept chewing.

"How many times that I left Albuquerque did you follow me? And why? Surely you had a job to do that didn't include chasing some lost soul."

"The job was never so important I wouldn't have tried to be around to save you."

"Why did you think you should save me?"

He put his rib bone on an empty plate, wiped his mouth and the barbeque sauce on his cheek. "Remember, I'd seen the look in your eyes. You didn't want to be saved any more than you wanted to be loved, but that doesn't mean you didn't need someone to do it." He stirred the dressing with an onion ring, folding it in half to fit into his mouth, and chewed. "Follow you? Dozens of times." He grabbed another rib and took a bite.

"That wouldn't be so creepy if you were average." I never understood how I didn't realize someone was following me, much less someone who stands six feet six inches, but he can just blend into the walls when he wants to.

"You weren't looking for me. I was never sure what you were looking for. But after your trip to Seattle, I knew it wasn't me."

I took a sip of sweet tea. "I don't recall exactly." I wished it were a cold beer, given the discussion.

"And I won't ever ask you to remember, Julie. How's the pork?"

CHAPTER 19
AMBER

September 12, 2001, 8:02 p.m. Eastern Daylight Time
I'm freaking lost!

Granted I was pissed when I'd walked out of the hotel at noon without knowing what I should do or where to go, but I kept walking until I was hopelessly lost. The sky wasn't much of a clue what time it was, and the lights don't go off. I've probably walked in one big circle. Where could I find Ethan, and did I even want to?

Leaving his phone could have been an accident. Going to an appointment that was toward the World Trade Center and then not returning could be due to being hurt – or killed – during the attacks. I wanted to believe he didn't dump me here.

At least I hope not.

I was carrying my backpack, but it was stuffed and heavy enough to throw off my balance, making my back hurt.

After I'd walked several hours, I realized I didn't know which direction I ought to go. It didn't make sense to go toward the World Trade Center area, given what I'd seen on television. As far away as I was now, there was a thin blanket of gray powder on everything.

I decided my first goal would be to dump out my backpack and make it a more manageable load to carry.

I walked past an alley, I guess you'd call it, but I couldn't make myself go into it, even the few steps it would take to make it to a dumpster.

Safety had never been a concern, but I'd never been alone like this in Albuquerque or rural Washington. My stomach fluttered at the thought of entering a drab dead-end passage, so I kept walking.

Near the next corner, I found a trash receptacle. I stepped back against the building into a slightly recessed doorway secured from the outside with a large rusty padlock. Here I was able to squat and dig through my pack and take out stuff to get rid of.

The weather had been clear, but I couldn't count on that lasting, so I kept my windbreaker, a clean sweatshirt and pair of jeans, three pairs of socks and a sports bra, my Walkman and headphones, and all my diabetes supplies. I kept my phone and Ethan's, and the charger. While the rest didn't seem to be much, it was bulky and heavy. I hoped I wouldn't need the frilly sweater, dress shoes, the tiny purse I hadn't used. Only because it didn't take up any room, I kept the necklace Ethan had given me the first night I was here. A silver chain with a black obsidian crystal pendant.

Damn, that seems like a week ago!

What an idiot I was to have left my wallet in his jacket after we'd gone out to eat the night before because the damned purse I brought was too small for my wallet and phone together. Ethan had offered to carry my wallet, that way I could get to my phone if it rang, you know, if Dad called or something. I couldn't imagine he would take it on purpose. But he also left his phone at the hotel before —

Before the world fell off its axis.

The little nook I'd tucked into offered a ledge to sit on out of the wind and out of the way of crowds of people on the sidewalk, so I stayed there, trying to think through my predicament.

Dad is coming to get me; I know he will. But how will he find me?

I pulled my cell phone from my pocket and checked. Battery power had decreased to half. I doubted I could make a connection anyway, so I turned the phone off. I'd check it again in three hours, I decided, to see if someone had left a message.

My stomach grumbled. I didn't eat lunch before they threw me out of the hotel. Where could I find something to eat?

Without money.

My eyes wandered the street opposite my cubby hole until I saw the answer — a church with a line of people.

They didn't all look homeless. A couple wearing blue uniforms, cops maybe, and other people in business clothes that weren't pristine, like they had been unable to get home to change.

After the towers fell, perhaps the church was feeding anyone affected by the disaster, and I could ask for something to eat.

I hoped I could explain my problem and one of the cops could make a call to Dad. Surely they would help me once I explained my situation.

I got to my feet and slung the pack over one shoulder, appreciating how much lighter it felt as I crossed the street.

CHAPTER 20
JULIE

September 12, 2001, 9:24 Central Daylight Time

Since those days of my recovery, I've liked driving at night less and less, yet I took the shift driving east out of Amarillo. The interstate led into the darkness between small towns.

An hour and a half later, I took a quick exit to the McDonald's in Shamrock for a bathroom break and coffee. Zach probably knew exactly what I was doing, but he didn't stir when I stopped the truck. Didn't look like he'd so much as twitched when I returned, yet he reached for the cup I'd bought for him without opening his eyes as I pulled onto the interstate again.

"You're scary sometimes, you know that?"

He smiled, took a drink without looking, best I could tell in the dark.

"I have a job offer," he said, then frowned.

"Really?" I said, surprised. "Didn't know you were looking."

"*I* wasn't looking. *You* just have wildly persistent colleagues."

"The sheriff?"

"Not Wade, though I might have taken him up on a job," he said. "It was Nolan Forrester."

"No, not the FBI!"

"I didn't say I was taking it," he replied. "Although now I sorta wished I had. Would make this trip a lot faster."

"Are you implying I'm driving too slow?" I waved around to the random lights on the horizon. "It's almost deer season, and I do not want a new truck, a hospital stay, or any other delay."

"No, I just figured a federal agent could catch one of the first flights tomorrow when aviation is ungrounded."

I shrugged. "What kind of position? It's not like you live in a thriving metropolis now."

"Something about training at Quantico, and I wouldn't want to live there." He took another sip of coffee. "This is awful, by the way. So no, I won't take the job." He put the cup back in the holder, fluffed his makeshift pillow against the door.

"But do you want to?"

I saw him shake his head in the dash lights. Next time I glanced over, he was asleep.

I wish I could drop to sleep like that.

I drove, following one highway stripe after another. At least tonight my mood wasn't quite as black as the darkness beyond my headlights.

From Albuquerque, I'd driven thousands of miles over the Southwest – California, Arizona, Texas, Oklahoma, Colorado, and Wyoming. I'd flown once to Seattle, spent a few days. Found a little trouble along the way. But all this time later, I'm not sure exactly why I drove.

Alone time, yes.

Music up loud, crying where no one could see. Not necessarily prowling, just covering miles.

Pretending it was an escape.

I discovered I could leave anything but my memories.

Driving any direction on an interstate highway from Albuquerque leads to wide open spaces. Sunsets. Sunrises. Bright sun. Starry nights., I'm sure all those things were present and appreciable, but I didn't recall having seen much of it.

I tried not to think any more about my drives at night. I didn't want to think about Amber's predicament. I absolutely didn't want to think about my mother, knowing I had many more tears before I could settle into a more solid acceptance of her death and move on.

As I drove through the dark, I wondered how my grief would differ if the 9/11 attacks hadn't occurred. My emotions, as monumental as they were to me, seemed trivial in comparison, and I hated feeling that way. As though my mother's death was insignificant in the world. That my grief didn't matter.

Her death may seem inconsequential to everyone except me, but it's the greatest loss in my life.

I understood the enormity of lost lives on the East Coast, parents, sons and daughters, friends, co-workers who were either the victims or the survivors of an unimaginable tragedy. An emergency services worker myself, I was heartbroken for those who gave their lives to save others.

Selfish that I grieved for them yet felt slighted they didn't grieve for me, dumb as that sounds.

The radio, when we'd listened, spouted hour upon hour of either the ongoing news or lack thereof. No music to be found. The station I caught coming into Oklahoma City echoed the news in the voices of those who survived the April 1995 bombing. A reprieve from the conspiracy theories and unproven speculations.

So much remained in the chaos after the September 11 attacks. I couldn't fathom the fear of those in the airliners, of those who were trapped in the World Trade Center Towers. The desperation of those who were trapped above the impacts, and the fire that made some choose to jump.

I pulled in for gas east of Oklahoma City, expecting Zach to wake slowly and take his time getting ready to drive.

When I pulled the nozzle from the pump and turned, he stood there by the Yukon. I jumped, and he smiled like a two-year-old who just missed getting caught eating chocolate cake but wearing the evidence all over his face and hands.

I stomped my foot. "It's bad enough you do that so well. You don't have to act like it's fun."

He leaned to kiss my nose. "I do. And it is." He turned and walked away with too much spring in his step for a man who had been asleep in a moving vehicle for several hours just minutes ago.

I'd been awake and was achy and stiff. I was looking forward to crashing for a few hours and to waking up for breakfast in Joplin, if I recalled the route correctly.

While I was pumping gas, I tried to count how many times I'd driven through Missouri traveling between Albuquerque to Traverse City. Twice a year or so. What I'd enjoyed most about traveling that far was getting an audiobook long enough to last most of the trip each direction.

Reading was always a favorite pastime, so I found that when reading wasn't possible, listening was a nice distraction during hundreds of miles of driving.

I'd wondered several times how difficult it must be for narrators to read out loud for hours. How hard it would be to catch an author's intended inflections or maintain the characters' voices throughout the story.

Fueling completed. Zach wasn't back yet, so I climbed in and pulled the truck forward into a parking slot, grabbed my oversized tote bag and slid back out. As I walked to the door, I saw Zach pacing an aisle with his phone against his ear, in an animated conversation that I desperately hoped was with Amber.

Suddenly he yanked it away from his head to look at the screen, then made a stomping motion much like the one I'd made after he'd scared me.

Then he turned directly toward me, shook his head once.

I rushed inside to him. "What? Who was it?"

"Brandan," he said, pausing to take a breath and calm down. "The hotel manager where she was staying was very informative but . . ."

"But what?" I snapped.

"Grab snacks, bathroom, whatever you need. I'll tell you once we're on the road again."

Damn it if I didn't hear Willy Nelson singing in my head now.

Knowing arguing would be pointless, we split to shop. I grabbed a six-pack of soft drinks, chips, chocolate, and a bag of snowflake-shaped white-chocolate-covered pretzels I did not intend to share.

Zach set his selections next to mine on the counter, ending with a can of sardines.

Oh, hell no! Not in my truck.

The look on my face was probably loud enough for him. It should have blown his hair back.

He winked and paid for our junk food binge.

Back in the truck, he got the driver's seat and mirrors adjusted for his size before we took off again.

"What's the story?" I asked, having waited as long as I could stand it. My patience had evaporated.

"Remember when Amber called, the second time?"

I nodded, not following.

"She called you from the hotel phone, not her cellular," he said, waiting for me to catch on to the clue. "I gave the hotel number to Brandan before we left Amarillo and –"

I shook my head to clear cobwebs, I guess. "How do you know where she called from?"

"Amber called again when we stopped at the restaurant in Amarillo, right? While you were in the restroom, my idea of tracing the next call rattled around my head, so I looked at your phone. I realized you'd had a call from a 212 area code, which is New York."

I thumped my forehead with my palm.

He continued, "I gave the number to Brandan to call or whatever he thought would be best. He got into Manhattan an hour ago, so he went straight to that hotel."

Determined to wait for him to continue, I had to bite my lower lip. Eventually, I decided if he'd had good news, he wouldn't have reacted as he did on the phone. And if it were important, he would tell me. I reclined my seat and grabbed a pillow and blanket from the back, with the obvious intention of curling up to sleep.

The ploy worked.

"The manager had told her she had to leave when the room reservation was up," he said in a growl so low I barely heard. "He made her go, even though she offered to keep paying for the room, but she couldn't produce a credit card or ID. Another clerk told Brandan that Amber claimed Ethan had taken it by accident, but the room was reserved and paid for with a credit card in a different name, one she didn't recognize. Without any way to pay to stay, she had to leave."

"Whose name?"

"Sean Smith. Ring any bells?"

"No. When did she get kicked out?"

"Today around one. Brandan said she left without a fight. If she doesn't have any money or identification, where would she go?" He glanced over at me, his frown illuminated by the dash. "Where would you go? You're good at this."

I sighed. "Okay, so I have never been to New York before either, but I've lived in large cities. Under most circumstances, I might seek out a hospital for social services. But with the towers collapsing, I suspect the hospitals are full and chaotic." I stopped to think. "I wouldn't, but Amber might try to find help at a Catholic church."

"Yeah, I like that idea." He shifted in the seat. "What else?"

"If she had money, she would go to a zoo for me to look for her. However, she wouldn't waste what little money she might have to get there," I said, hoping her priority would be finding somewhere to eat. "She said she had a few days of insulin supplies, but if she runs out, she may end up in a hospital. That might be beneficial. She'd be getting meals and medication."

"There's roughly sixty hospitals in Manhattan, but it's manageable to call them all if necessary. A few are specialty facilities we could eliminate."

"How do you know these things?" I asked, astonished.

"Trivial Pursuit," he answered in sharp sarcasm.

"Amazing. Where would she go?"

"Honestly, right now I can't get past her eviction from the hotel." He muttered a lengthy string of profanity involving the manager's species and genetic history that was unfit for an everyday conversation.

"Good thing we're still in Oklahoma," I muttered. "You might calm down before we arrive and someone gets hurt, but the list of potentials keeps getting longer."

"Good night, Julie," he said, dismissing my observation.

CHAPTER 21
JULIE

September 13, 2001, 7:51 a.m. Central Daylight Time
When I woke next, Zach was exiting the freeway in some little town in Missouri, well northeast of Joplin. A bright sunbeam passed over me as he turned toward a restaurant for breakfast, I hoped.

"I slept harder than I thought I could in a moving car. I'm kinda out of practice at it," I said, stretching. A yawn came next.

A yawn Zach did not repeat, nor did he answer me. He parked, and I thought he was waiting on me to put my shoes on and whatever else, but when I looked over, he had leaned back against the headrest, eyes closed.

I was almost afraid he had gone to sleep until I saw his lips move in one single word: Amen.

We both wobbled getting out of the truck and straightening the stiff angles of the seats, coming together and taking hands as we walked to the entrance. But once we stepped out of the traffic lane of the parking lot, Zach stopped and whirled me around into a hug we held for a long time.

When he released me, he smoothed my sleep-mussed hair and then kissed my forehead. "I'm glad you are with me."

• • • • •

The place wasn't quite full, and we were seated without waiting.

Coffee arrived in a carafe with two cups, which was a welcome beginning. We ordered what sounded like a lot of food.

"I'm starving," I said.

Zach nodded but looked like he was a thousand miles away.

After seeing the prayer this morning, he probably was.

I excused myself to the restroom for much needed morning tasks, ending with a long face and arm wash followed by a dab of cream I had stashed in my purse while I'd been in Albuquerque to keep from feeling like a prickly pear cactus had attacked me. I finger-combed my hair into submission but not style. My reflection had looked far worse, I told her.

Back at the table, Zach took his turn to go to the restroom, and of course, the meal was served while he was away.

I started without him with a slice of toast I'd smeared red jam on, wondering how far today would take us.

He came back and slid into the booth opposite me, picked up his coffee cup and drained it. His face was pink, so I surmised he had done a similar wash-up. "Brandan called again early this morning. He'd walked in a spiral around her hotel, asking people about her."

"No success?" I asked, refilling his cup from the carafe.

"Maybe," Zach said, ignoring the cup and picking up a slice of bacon he didn't put in his mouth. "He says there is a church soup kitchen across the street from the trash can where he found clothes that could be hers, but nobody remembers seeing her inside yesterday."

"Has he checked shelters and –" I started, only to be interrupted by the server, checking on our meal.

Zach asked her for Tabasco Sauce, and she zoomed away again. He took a bite without really considering what it was. "Julie, he said no one serving remembered her. He'll go back again today. And yes, he's checked every hospital, shelter, restaurant, fire station, and soup kitchen within the radius he's covered. He's gone to his car to sleep."

"Why didn't he get a hotel?" I asked, cutting my eggs and taking a bite.

"I asked but he said he just needed a nap."

"Someone said the airlines are flying again. Maybe you should catch a flight in St. Louis?" I suggested.

The server brought a bottle of hot sauce and slid it a few inches across the table as she whizzed on past, carrying a full tray above her head.

Zach dumped a quarter of the bottle on his eggs and hash browns. "No, we'll be there by midnight tonight, and I don't want to have three people and three vehicles wandering the city."

"But if we split up, we can cover –"

"No."

" – more ground," I finished. "Why not?"

"You've never been to New York City, so I would rather you stay with me." Not a demand, and sweet in a way, but not very efficient.

We finished our breakfast, took a quick walk to loosen crampy muscles and wake up, bought gas and more soft drinks, then headed northeast again, hoping not to hit an audacious traffic jam going through St. Louis.

I drove, and Zach read the map.

We didn't discuss looking for Amber again until we were on I-70 and out of the sprawl of the city.

Zach's phone rang fifteen minutes later. "Brandan, get any sleep?"

I could barely make out Brandan's reply.

"Okay, looks like it will be after midnight when we get near." Zach paused, listening. "No, don't stay up. It makes more sense to look in daylight. Yeah? Which one? Let me grab a pen." He took the one I held out, wrote something Brandan told him, which happened to be an address and phone number. "Sounds good, man. You be careful. I'll call around ten o'clock. We're aiming for Liberty Park from I-78 after midnight. Okay." He pushed the end button.

"Liberty Park?" I asked.

"Good parking for a nap," he replied. "Or it was until a few days ago."

CHAPTER 22
AMBER

September 13, 2001, 10:19 a.m. Eastern Daylight Time
I'd had a meal here last night. It wasn't great, but it was filling. When I told them what had happened, one lady offered me a place to sleep in their shelter, though they were already full, telling me at least it would be safer than sleeping anywhere else. But we all had to get out of the building before the food preparation began, so I was wandering up and down the block when I saw two men in police-type uniforms in a shelter food line.

Instead of city police officers, though, they worked for a security company. Still, if I explained my predicament, they might help me, but by the time I got to the line, they were being served, and a dozen people were behind them. After I went through the food line, they were already gone.

At least I had something to eat.

The makeshift dining area was almost full, a single seat here and there. I found a chair between two men near the double door exit, squeezed into a place at a table so small I had to hang my pack on the back of the chair.

Conversation was solely about the World Trade Center catastrophe, with gossip I hadn't heard — that it was all a conspiracy orchestrated by the United States, that the jets had bombs on board, or the Pentagon hadn't been hit by a jet but by a US missile. It sounded spastic crazy to me, but someone asked me a question and got me involved in the discussion.

My attention had been diverted long enough I almost missed a glimpse of my bright green backpack slung over the shoulder of a man with stringy dark hair, just as he was squeezing out the door and to the left.

I scrambled out of the tight space, knocking over both my chair and someone passing behind me, taking off after him, trying to weave my way through the throng of people in line for food.

Once outside, the thief might have thought he was free until I whipped around the door and yelled. He took off at a hard run, and I fell in behind him by twenty yards or so.

I wasn't wearing sneakers, but after closing the distance by the second intersection, I was sure I could catch him in the next block if he kept —

CHAPTER 23
JULIE

September 13, 2001, 2:19 Central Daylight Time
While I drove, Zach called his mom for an update on Kim and put his phone on speaker so I could listen.

"She's resting like the doctor told her. We took a short walk outside before lunch for a little sunshine," Vera explained. "She talked to her father last night. He asked how she felt about him coming to see her. She said yes and asked if he could stay with us while he was here. Is that okay, Julie?"

"If she wants to see him, it's an excellent idea," I replied. "The third bedroom really has a bed, but it's neck-deep in Mom's horse stuff."

"I'll move in there, and he can have the guestroom."

"You're the boss, Vera. Whatever works for you," I said.

"Any word on Amber?"

Zach explained Amber had been kicked out of the hotel.

Vera said a few of the same words Zach had.

"Julie's deputy friend from Michigan is already in New York looking," he said, "and we'll be there by midnight."

They chatted a few minutes more and then Kim took the phone to ask me again if it was okay that her dad came to visit.

"Of course. He's been worried about you."

"Thanks, Julie. For everything. I'd probably be in jail if you hadn't offered to help me."

"I offered. You accepted, which was the hard part," I said. "It was your first choice."

"I'm in good hands. Go find your daughter. She needs your help now," she said.

Zach said the goodbyes and disconnected.

I wiped away a tear.

"Are you okay?" he asked, taking my hand.

"No, not really," I said.

"We will find her, Julie. She has the three best cops you know trying to find her."

"Three that I *know*?"

"Brandan, me, and Nolan."

"Bloody hell, Zach! When did he get involved in this?"

"I'd made it into Idaho yesterday," he said. "He was still trying to recruit me when I told him about Amber."

"He is in Michigan, right? What is he doing?"

"I didn't ask. He's been helpful. He's tracking Amber's credit card and phone call activity."

"If she doesn't have her wallet, how useful is that?"

"If Ethan took it by accident, he wouldn't try to use it. One the other hand," he said, "if someone uses it, the information could help find her."

"Or it might not."

"Plus, by the time we arrive, cellular service may be back to stable levels, so he has been sending a text message with a toll-free number every four hours. If we haven't found her by tomorrow, he can have the company ping it for location."

"He's your friend with secret cellular talents?"

"No, not him."

"I give, who?"

Zach explained to me he had worked with an officer in Houston. One of Harper's high school friends worked for the same cellular company we used.

"It's not a widely known fact that cell phones can be tracked so accurately, but this guy is one of those who can do more than just ping a phone for its location in the network."

"I don't know exactly what that means, but it's quite all right," I said. "You have some cool contacts, too."

CHAPTER 24
AMBER

September 13, 5:18 p.m. Eastern Daylight Time

I dreamed I was in a hospital, I think. It didn't make any sense.

And I hurt. Everywhere. Even my tongue hurt.

Then I puked. Everywhere.

"I'll get you some medicine," a thin woman in blue scrubs told me. "You have a concussion."

That sounded familiar, but I didn't understand why.

"Can you tell me your name?" she asked.

Of course, I thought. I opened my mouth, but I couldn't remember.

Everything in my head seemed jumbled.

I said the only name that came to me – Julie.

CHAPTER 25
JULIE

September 13, 2001, 4:16 p.m. Central Daylight Time
We stopped for a late lunch, though we'd been snacking. I drove an expedient seven hours from Joplin to Indy while Zach slept. When we reached Indianapolis, we both needed a meal out of the truck. I picked a chain restaurant in hopes of having a menu we'd be familiar with and not have to wonder if we'd like what we chose, but he wasn't very talkative.

Somehow, we weren't as far as he thought we should have been.

"I'm driving a reasonable speed over the limit," I said. " Traffic was horrible in St. Louis, and the speed limit in Illinois and Indiana is 70. I'm trying not to get thrown in jail for speeding."

He apologized. "It's not your fault, Julie. I don't mean to complain. I'm hungry and achy."

We ordered, conferred with the map again while we waited.

Less than an hour later, we were back on the road.

He spoke to Brandan to get an update once we were outside the city and traffic had smoothed out, but there was no news.

"What are some attractions in New York you would deem not to be missed?" I asked, tired of the silence. "If we were vacationing."

He thought for a moment. "A professional sports game of the season – baseball, basketball, hockey, et cetera. There are hundreds of restaurants and little shops. You'd hate Fifth Avenue, but you might like parts of Central Park. There's a dozen incomparable museums in addition to the Met," he said, "and the Intrepid Sea, Air and Space Museum."

"Really?"

"Well, I'm not a Yankees fan, but . . . "

"That's not what I mean!"

"My degree is in art history," he said. "Why does it surprise you I like museums?"

"Not that either. Why would you be interested in a ship?"

"Because it makes you crazy that I say things like that," he said with a mischievous grin. "I'm not hot on boats or airplanes, personally."

I slugged his arm.

"If we didn't have a reason to go to New York, I wouldn't go again. Ever."

"Never been," I said. "Never going back."

"Agreed," he said, raising his plastic bottle of water in a toast.

I clinked my glass bottle of iced tea against it.

"Are you okay with not getting a room for the night?" he finally asked.

"Of course, although I'm worried about you driving if I go to sleep."

"You drove all day while I slept. I'll be okay."

"But if we're late getting into New York, you'll want to go looking for Amber. You haven't had a lot of decent sleep in days."

"No, I won't, Julie. We need to meet with Brandan," he said, stifling a yawn. "I'll make it through this, then once we're home, I'll sleep for a week. Speaking of which, are you bringing Kim back to Washington with you now when you come home?"

"We'll see," I admitted. "Gerald is flying to Albuquerque, so it may depend on how long she goes before delivery. She's all set on New Mexico Medicaid, so I'd encourage her to stay, if my opinion counts."

Planning what to do with Kim now stunned me, but at this point, I had too many options and not enough information to decide. Nor was it a priority.

Instead, I fluffed a pillow and reclined the seat to a more comfortable position.

Zach's new estimated time of arrival in New York was closer to sunrise, so unless he woke me for conversation, navigation, or fueling, I might be able to get six hours of sleep before we arrived.

Oh, how I wish I was in my own bed.

He turned the radio on, found a station playing music finally – we were both mentally exhausted from hearing news that was now old.

In a way, I wanted to stay awake to listen for a while to celebrate a bit of normalcy, and perhaps that's why I faded to sleep so easily.

I must not have woken when Zach stopped for gas, or he can be as quiet doing that as he can other things, I thought when he touched my arm gently to wake me.

"I thought you'd want to see this," he said, handing me a bottle of water.

The truck sat facing east, showing us a brilliant sunrise on the right, and the Statue of Liberty on the left with New York City's skyline behind. Minus the World Trade Center Towers.

• • • • •

September 14, 2001, Sunrise over New York City
The only thing that came out of my mouth was, "Wow." My mental thesaurus hadn't stirred yet, waiting on coffee.

The cloud of dust that had hung over Lower Manhattan had dissipated, but the iconic skyline had been forever altered.

My brain skipped to the idea that probably hundreds of movies had included scenes with those two skyscrapers. Would I ever see another without thinking of the last few days?

"Incredible," I said, managing four syllables this time.

Zach only nodded.

I wondered what was on his mind.

Finally, the sun rose above the horizon and the spell broke.

"We're going across to meet Brandan for breakfast and discuss our plans," he told me, starting the truck. "For the record, I still want to break Ethan's right arm."

"If not for him, we wouldn't have seen that sunrise," I replied. "I'm ambivalent at the moment."

That feeling didn't last long as we drove north.

"Doesn't the Holland Tunnel go to Manhattan?" I asked, seeing the signs and struggling to read the map as we moved.

He continued past, explaining that we'd have to enter from the Lincoln Tunnel as the Holland Tunnel remained closed to civilian traffic due to proximity to the attacks.

Two lanes of the tunnel going each direction, he explained. Although the approach had confused my sense of direction, and not considering an outrageous $12 toll, the sheer quantity and movement of traffic freaked me out. Being inside a tube under a body of water, with thousands – okay, maybe just hundreds, who knows – of cars, I seriously wondered if a person could hyperventilate and vomit at the same time.

I concentrated on the first to prevent the second, but I had my finger on the window button, just to be safe.

Trying calm my anxiety, Zach continued telling me trivia about the tunnel. "Even though the targets were the World Trade Center Towers," he said, trying to engage my attention, "traffic through the Lincoln Tunnel made it what was once thought to be one of the highest risk terrorist marks."

That piece of information didn't help my apprehension, so I changed the topic slightly. "All four planes hit East Coast targets. Where else might be a target if they weren't limited by airplanes?" I asked. "Would only political targets of high value would be chosen?"

"Plenty of other targets where destruction would not only disrupt the financial status of this country but the social status," he said, which took my mind off the reflected lights in the tunnel and my blossoming claustrophobia. "Two symbols of power were targets if the Shanksville plane was headed to the White House or Capitol like the media speculates. But that doesn't directly threaten the average person like the Twin Towers did. If that's the goal, why not Disney World or Mall of America, or maybe the Super Bowl?"

I cringed. "That's pretty average American."

"With a fairly high body count and children. That always steels people's anger. Terrorism isn't necessarily creating a high body count. It's instilling fear that the act could happen again, making the target population become a danger to itself in the pursuit of safety. I'd say we've reached that level quickly," he stated. "And now back to daylight."

"Thanks, but I'm not sure which was darker, the tunnel or the conversation," I said. "Which borough are we coming into?"

"We're in Manhattan, but you mean which neighborhood, like Tribeca or Hell's Kitchen. Boroughs are the big divisions of the city, like Queens, Long Island, the Bronx," he said, making a dozen turns that again had me lost.

"Uh, I guess so."

"Our hotel is near Madison Square Garden."

"Explains everything." It really didn't.

"Brandan will meet us there and we'll have breakfast, make plans," he said, as calmly as though this were any other law enforcement task and not about his missing daughter or the boyfriend who summoned her to New York and abandoned her in a hotel amid a national disaster.

CHAPTER 26
JULIE

September 14, 2001, 9:04 a.m. Eastern Daylight Time

In a tall building housing not only a hotel but other businesses, we checked in and went to a room on the sixth floor. We each carried a medium bag, but I also had a laptop with a charger in mine. We took turns in the bathroom, Zach first, then I took a quick shower and washed my hair.

I was out and drying off when Zach knocked and said Brandan would be there in ten minutes. That gave me time to dry my hair and rub lotion into my dry skin.

Brandan knocked just as I came out of the bathroom, so I opened the door to a man I knew well but hardly recognized. Since I last saw him last two months ago, he'd lost weight, let his hair and beard grow out. But I hugged him anyway.

We grabbed our stuff and went downstairs and across the street for breakfast and briefing. We ordered, then Brandan spread out his map.

"Here's the hotel where she left," he said, spinning the map for us to see and pointing to a location in the center of lower Manhattan from what I could tell. "The one desk clerk says she went left when she went out the front doors, or northeast. I've walked that path in an expanding circle both days. It's redundant, but it seems to be the most logical route to follow. Maybe you should walk it today and I'll go north or more west."

"Where could she obtain diabetic supplies nearby," I said. "She said there was a pharmacy across the street. I'm concerned that she didn't have more than another day's supply or so with her."

"Good point," Brandan said. "I did check with that pharmacy, but no one recalls seeing her."

"If she didn't have money, she probably wouldn't bother with a big-name pharmacy, but maybe a smaller one where she could explain her circumstances and get it without paying," Zach added. "There is a lot of goodwill right now."

"She could become confused and ill quickly after running out of insulin, or if she takes it but hasn't been eating," I said. "We need to hope she is with or is found by someone who calls 9-1-1."

"We should start calling hospitals in the lower and middle part of Manhattan," Brandan said. "I haven't talked to Blair, yet."

"I don't want to jinx anyone, but is he someone who would have been at the Towers?" Zach asked.

What had been a serious discussion changed when Brandan laughed. "It's not what you're thinking," he said, "Blair is my sister."

"Same question, no problem being at ground zero?" I asked, not knowing that soon the description would become the proper noun to describe the hole.

"I doubt it. She's an English professor at a college in Queens. She should have been in class on 9/11."

That's nice, but Amber was supposed to be a freshman in a Seattle college classroom, too, and yet here we are.

"I haven't spoken to her in a month or so," he continued, "but she was teaching this fall."

"Could she help us?" I asked.

"Haven't called her yet. I was hoping to crash at her place, but once I checked out where it was, I knew I wouldn't want to drive that far every morning. But she probably knows people who could help, too. Her ex-husband is NYPD."

"Do you know him well?"

"Only met him twice, and I thought he was an arrogant ass," Brandan said, smiling. "But he could still be useful. They got married when I was working out in California, then I visited briefly before I moved to Michigan."

"How do we proceed?" Zach asked.

Food came, interrupting the planning, and we ate without speaking more of our search.

I kept looking up, peeking out the window at every honking horn, siren. Sounds began to overwhelm me, and a migraine threatened to knock me on my butt. Being out of commission was the last thing I wanted, but my drugs were back in the room. I poured myself another cup of coffee just for the caffeine.

Plates cleaned, we moved them to the side and unfolded the map again.

"I recommend splitting up to go north and south on Eighth Avenue for ten or fifteen blocks, then one block away from the center and back thirty blocks the other way, zigzagging."

Doing the math in my head, I almost choked. "Over a hundred blocks? What are we looking for?"

My feet already hurt thinking about it.

"It's roughly twelve miles," Brandan told me. "Pretty level walking, lots of traffic. I recommend checking any fast food places, clinics."

"And churches, especially with food services," I added. "She's Catholic."

Brandan nodded.

"Should we call hospitals, too?" Zach asked. He shrugged. "Never worked a missing person case."

No, Dear, you were the missing person several times.

"We're at the point it wouldn't hurt," Brandan said, turning to pull out several pages of printouts of Manhattan hospitals out of his bag.

"Time to call in my favor to track her cell phone," Zach said, explaining to Brandan. "I know a cop who is friends with someone who works for our cell company. Harper tells me this guy can theoretically do more than ping a phone for a general location, but that would be a start. Theoretically more would be phenomenal."

"Why don't you two go back to the hotel and start on those tasks, I'll go back to what I've been doing," Brandan offered. "You can walk later or take subways from one stop to another on the ACE. Someone mentioned that hiding in them could offer her protection from the weather." He traced colored lines on the map for Zach. They were meaningless to me.

Are we supposed to huddle and break?

At least I could go back to the hotel and take medicine for my headache.

Brandan pulled out his wallet, but Zach stopped him.

"Hey, not only do you not get to buy meals for us, I owe you a lot of cash for your –" Zach started to say.

"And we can work out those details later," Brandan replied, standing and zipping up the lightweight jacket he wore to cover a shoulder holster.

Thank you, New York, we're keeping our guns.

• • • • •

"Headache?" Zach asked me as we entered the elevator at the hotel.

"That noticeable?"

"Like a flashing neon sign on a moonless summer night."

"Smashing. I have medicine," I said. "I'll be fine in an hour or so."

After two tablets and a bottle of water, I picked up the list of hospitals to call in search of Amber.

My vision had a pair of scintillating zig-zag lines of light crossing a dark smudge in the center.

I blinked several times, but it didn't help.

Zach dialed to talk to the contact he'd vaguely mentioned, ended up leaving a message.

"I'll ask Harper to call his friend and ask whether he can help us now," Zach said as I browsed the list to start making phone calls.

All I could do is nod.

"Julie, go to bed. Everything we can do is being done. I'll go walking and wait for a call back."

"I need to help," I said, just before my breakfast made its way back up.

• • • • •

Zach had pulled back the covers on the bed for me, gone to the vending machine for something to drink and put it in the little refrigerator in the room, and dug in my bag for my nausea medicine. All while I was puking.

Then he tucked me in, turned the air conditioning to its "snowstorm" setting, plugged in my cell phone to charge and left it next to the bed.

"Anything else?" he asked.

"Curtains."

"Ah yes," he said, pulling the blackout shades closed and the sheers back over them.

"Wow, you are fabulous," I said as he kissed my forehead. "I believe I'll keep you."

"You don't have a choice. Call if you need anything," he told me, "and when you wake up."

With that, he left to wander the streets of Manhattan, and I drifted off to sleep.

I'd had two severe attacks like this in the past five years we'd been together. What I didn't tell Zach was how the drug-induced sleep was fraught with nightmares I didn't otherwise have anymore. But waking in a strange place sometimes made the dreams worse.

I fought sleep as long as I could, repeating to myself that I was safe, that I needed a nap, that everything was okay. My brain's other side saw right through the lies and cued all the tumultuous emotions I'd felt in the last few days to play back.

CHAPTER 27
AMBER

September 14, 2001, 9:10 a.m. Eastern Daylight Time
My vision was fuzzy, but I could hear all these beeps and alarms.

I woke in a hospital room again. I mean, it smelled like a hospital, and I was in some weird contraption pulling on my right leg, and something built over the bed like a cage.

Really, I just woke up and couldn't come up with any of those big words. My right leg hurt. That I was sure of.

"Hello?" I yelled. "Somebody?"

A woman pulled back a curtain and said good morning to me.

I didn't know what time it was, but I repeated the greeting.

"My name is Carla. Do you remember what happened to you?" she asked, doing stuff around the room, like filling a water glass, fluffing my pillow.

"Um..." *Last thing I remember was... no... oh shit, I don't remember...* "No."

"Can you tell me your name?" She sounded casual.

I tried to mimic that confidence while I thought, then shook my head in spiraling anxiety. "No. My head hurts," I said. "Is something wrong? What happened to me?"

"I'll get you something for the pain," she said, touching my hand, pressing my fingernails. "You were hit by a car yesterday. Does your arm hurt?"

I nodded, which made my head swimmy.

She listened to my chest, belly. Checked my toes, asked me to move them.

"Moving them hurts my right leg a little," I said.

"You were admitted yesterday after orthopedic surgery for a badly broken thigh bone."

"What happened to me?"

"You were hit by a car, so you have quite a concussion and a few broken bones. They did surgery on your leg overnight."

"Car?" I asked. She was talking too fast and it sounded funny. "What city am I in?"

"You're in Manhattan, Sweetie."

That didn't feel right. I wouldn't want to live in New York, so why was I here?

"I don't live here, do I? What happened to me?"

She told me that I'd been hit by a car and had a concussion that might cause my memory to be mixed up. That I had a badly broken femur – thigh bone – that required surgery last night.

"Will my memory come back?"

"Of course," she replied. "It's just a combination of the drugs and the concussion."

"Do you guys know my name?" I asked.

"I only know that you told the paramedics your name was Julie."

CHAPTER 28
JULIE

September 14, 2001, 2:29 p.m. Eastern Daylight Time

I rolled over and opened my eyes, looking at my watch to find out it was after noon, which made me happy until I threw back the covers and checked the room clock, realizing my watch was set for two time zones earlier.

The nausea was gone, and the headache was a whisper of its previous roar. I got up and went to the bathroom, taking my phone with me in case Amber called.

Sure enough, just sitting down on the toilet, it rang.

I looked, but the caller ID was from my mother's home number. When I was done and had washed up a little, I called back. Gerald Katz answered.

"Everything is okay here," he said, trying to prevent any panic. "We're wondering if you'd had any more contact with Amber."

"Zach and I arrived early this morning, and we had breakfast with Brandan, and they planned their day. Then I had a migraine after we ate, so the guys went on a walk-about through a thousand city blocks. I'll start calling hospitals to see if she's a patient somewhere in Manhattan," I replied.

"That's good, but what if she is a patient but isn't coherent," he suggested. "A patient in diabetic ketoacidosis might not be awake and oriented enough to know her own identity."

The idea rocked me back in the chair like I'd been slapped. "Of course! What if she's a Jane Doe because she ran out of insulin. She doesn't have her wallet." I forgot the lingering headache. "Thanks, Gerald. I've gotta get on this. Tell the ladies I said hello."

We hung up.

I pulled out the list Zach and I had looked at just a couple hours before. I'd have to call hospitals in this neighborhood or borough, whatever it was.

First, I dialed Zach for an update. He answered on the second ring.

"How are you feeling?" he asked after trading hellos.

"Better. Did you talk to your friend's friend about Amber's phone?"

"Yeah, and it was good news and bad," he said. "The phone was powered off and on several times. Two days ago, it completely disconnected from the system abruptly, its battery dead or removed on purpose. Somehow the system knows the difference. He was able to give us a location radius of eight blocks of its last known location, so we're searching for it now."

"Gerald reminded me that asking if Amber Samualson is a patient might be a mistake when calling the hospitals," I said.

"Yeah, she doesn't use Hennessy anymore."

"What if she's having diabetes problems and isn't able to remember her name?" I prompted. "We need to ask about unidentified young females."

"True," he said, then moved the phone away from his mouth. "I'll be right over." Then back to me. "Brandan found something. I'll call you right back." And he hung up.

Dang it, Zach. You can walk to another place and not have to disconnect the call on a cell phone.

He did call back within a few minutes. "We found Amber's phone," he said, a bit winded. "It was wedged in a drainage grate. It's dead and damaged, but I'm sure it's hers."

"How do you know? You said it was damaged." I said, confused.

"I made her put a four-digit code under the battery, so she could identify it if it got lost."

"What four numbers, may I ask?"

"Zero, five, six, seven," he said.

"Your birth month and year, how clever."

"I thought so," he said, sounding proud of himself.

"I suppose you'd say that AVBD2D wouldn't have fit," I asked.

"Exactly," he said, laughing. "You call around, start with the hospitals closest to the hotel, Brandan suggested. It's the first page. We'll talk with the regulars in this block and see if they saw anything."

Sounded like the best plan, so we hung up and got to work.

• • • • •

September 14, 2001, 8:29 p.m. Eastern Daylight Time

Zach arrived back to the hotel around seven, when it should have been dark, though so much light came through the windows when I opened the curtains, it was hard to tell.

"We're hungry," he said. "If you're feeling up to it, Brandan found a good restaurant a couple of blocks away."

I was awake, dressed, eager to escape the hotel room, and hopeful they had better news than I did.

Brandan's room was on the same floor as ours but in a different wing. He was waiting on us by the elevators.

"Calling hospitals to ask about Jane Doe's takes a lot more time," I explained. "There are quite a few unconscious patients who haven't been identified admitted after 9/11, so general information doesn't know how many of them look like Amber. I'm getting transferred from unit to unit."

"No luck, eh?" Brandan asked as we went out the front of the hotel and turned right.

"Not yet."

"We sort have a lead," Zach said, squeezing my hand as I walked between the two of them. "One of the storekeepers on the corner where we found the phone told us there had been some thefts this week from people who are not usually on the streets, like those suddenly without a job or the volunteers who've come from all over the country to help at the Tower sites."

Brandan continued. "Thieves typically do not want cell phones, so they just dump them as they go, waiting for the street scrubbers to wash them down the drains."

"Did you call the police? Maybe Amber filed a report if it was stolen," I suggested.

"Without her phone or identification, she might not have been able," Zach said. "Brandan checked, and the NYPD doesn't show a report was made."

"Have they made any arrests on other thefts?" I asked, astonished how finding her phone had been of so little use.

"Not yet," Brandan said, laughing. "We're going to help a little with that."

"What's that supposed to mean?" I demanded.

"We're gonna do a little undercover work tomorrow," Zach explained as we turned to enter the restaurant. "Well, Brandan is. I'm his wingman."

Our discussion was interrupted as we were seated at a table, ordered drinks, and browsed the menu.

When the server returned, Brandan started to order, but Zach shook his hand and ordered steak and lobster for three. "Your only choice is how you want your steak cooked," he said. "But if you say well done, we are no longer friends."

Brandan smiled and handed the server his menu. "Medium, please, then. Baked, loaded, and salad, Italian."

I repeated the medium request for my own as well as the baked potato and salad, and Zach gave his usual rare cooking instructions, which I always kidded him is ten degrees above uncooked.

"I bought clothes today at a second-hand shop, and a cool backpack," Brandan said. "I like shopping with him. He bought me anything I wanted."

I rolled my eyes.

"The goal is not filthy or homeless-looking, but like a displaced and unemployed after the World Trade Center collapse, just enough so to attract a thief."

"The store owner told us there's a church soup kitchen and shelter a block away. Even if we don't catch the right thief, we might catch one who will talk," Zach concluded.

"You guys are scary," I said, sipping my water. "And that is a crazy idea. Why does Brandan get to be the bait?"

They both looked at me like I'd gone nuts.

"Who would steal *his* backpack and risk being pummeled by a giant?" Brandan said.

Good point.

"What am I supposed to do while you are out trolling for thieves?"

"Keep calling hospitals. If she's not on the street, she is most likely a patient somewhere," Zach said in a much more serious tone. "Because if she isn't, I don't want to think of other possibilities."

"Couldn't she have turned her phone off to save the battery and dropped it without knowing, then it went dead?" I asked.

"Sure, but no matter what, why hasn't she found another way to contact us?" he replied. "I'm trying to remain positive, but," he said, lowering his voice, "there's a lot of weird people out there."

I nodded.

"Let's get some rest," Brandan suggested, "and start toward the church at 5:30. Should put us there twenty minutes after they start serving."

"Oh joy, oatmeal," Zach groaned.

"Hey, you don't get to eat, remember?" Brandan said, beaming. "Besides, tomorrow's creamed wheat."

He and I laughed.

Zach reached for the dessert menu to pick something he could have for breakfast.

• • • • •

We returned to our rooms, and Zach took a shower that I had to intrude.

"Took you long enough," he said. "I miss this."

Strong arms wrapped around me, steam billowed around us, and the world was right again for a little while. After turning off the water and drying each other, Zach carried me to the bed.

Very right.

CHAPTER 29
JULIE

September 15, 2001, 5:17 a.m. Eastern Daylight Time
With little else to do but eat his carrot cake and get dressed, he did so with intentional silence as not to disturb me, but I woke to the sound of him brushing his teeth.

Knowing he was distracted, I tiptoed from the bed to just around the corner from the bathroom and waited.

He finished, spit in the sink and reached for a towel, saying, "Did you need in here?"

Dang it! He has superpower hearing, too.

"Yeah, I didn't want to scare you."

He laughed. "Julie, check out what the mirrors reflect from here."

Right back to the bed where I'd been laying.

"You thought you'd be all sneaky and stuff, didn't you?" he said, throwing me over his shoulder and whacking me solidly on the butt, then dropping me onto the bed. "I'll have to finish this later. But I won't forget where I left off."

I tilted my head inquisitively. "Zach, how is this –" I waved my hand toward the window, "how does the fact your daughter is missing not stop you from being, I don't know, so you. So affectionate."

"Baby, the fact that you are helping me is the only thing holding my head together. One long hug, one brief touch. It's those moments of sanity and encouragement that keep me going." He touched my face with both hands. "Besides, I don't know how else to be around you."

Leaving me with a mind-blowing kiss, he went to meet Brandan on their stakeout/sting operation, so I went back to calling hospitals again, asking about a young female adult who might be a Jane Doe.

At one hospital, my call was transferred to a nurse who was downright rude. After half a dozen and no luck, I decided to have breakfast in the hotel lobby.

I turned on the television while I dressed, half-listening to the latest on the rescue-turning-recovery at Ground Zero, which indeed was now its media name. The footage of the second impact and the subsequent collapses of both Towers were played again, twice, along with the picture of the crater and dozens of men visible in the picture.

The attacks had been initially named the responsibility of al-Qaeda, and now all sorts of politicians were diving into the discussions about retaliation, proof, and such.

After only a few days, the news began predicting numbers of lives lost, especially in fire departments.

No way could I conceive how a body count would ever be completely accurate in what had to be thousands of tons of debris — only a person reported missing would be determined a fatality, I presumed.

Wait, I thought, would someone be presumed dead just because he was reported missing in Manhattan during this?

• • • • •

"Can't talk," he whispered.

"I know how to –" I started, but the connection went dead.

Not one single time could I remember Zach hanging up on me.

What the heck, I thought, so I called our cellular phone company and asked for the call records for Amber's phone to find Ethan's number. When I stressed the enormity of the emergency, those records were faxed to the front desk for me within the hour. I retrieved them and grabbed a candy car and soft drink, then back in our room. Scanning Amber's phone records, I found Ethan's number in less than five seconds. And I dialed it on my phone.

The number made a connection and rang, to my surprise. Twice. Then it went to voice mail. That seemed weird, so I dialed again. Straight to voice mail this time.

How did Zach say the technician had explained Amber's phone — that it was turned off then had no power. I'd always thought they were the same thing. Was this what I heard when I called Ethan's, that it was on then the battery died?

Could Zach's friend's friend do the same location on this phone?

My phone rang – Zach, breathing hard.

"Sorry, we were chasing someone."

"Really? Is it the right guy?"

"I'll ask him when he regains consciousness," Zach said, panting. "I'm getting too old for this shit. We're waiting for a patrolman."

"He took Brandan's pack?"

"No, but he grabbed a bag of a young lady sitting near Brandan."

"Tell me about her," I said.

"Here, you ask her what you want to know," he replied, handing the phone to this woman.

"Hi, my name is Julie Samualson. We're looking for our daughter. Can I ask you a few questions?"

"I guess," the female said. "I don't know how I can help."

"What did the bag that was stolen look like?"

"It's jus' a large knock-off tote, fake leather. Nothin' fancy."

"Did you notice anyone watching you in line, while you were eating?"

"Nah, I maybe shoulda paid more attention, but not really."

"I don't mean this to be insulting, but are you a displaced worker from the Towers or residences nearby or are you homeless?"

She laughed. "This week, Honey, I'm all of those. No car, no paycheck, no job, and can't go back to my apartment. I spent the last three nights in shelters."

"Wow, I'm sorry. Is there anything we can do to help?"

"No, that's okay, but I 'preciate it."

I meant to thank her but thought of one more question. "Have you heard of anyone else having a bag ripped off?"

"No, but I've been walking north from the Financial District, staying in a different place each night."

I thanked her, and she must have given the phone back to my husband.

"You called. Find out anything important?"

"Important but I'm not certain it's helpful," I said. "I had our cell carrier fax me our call records and found where Amber and Ethan had talked, repeatedly I might add, during the last few months. It was in a 313 area code."

"Wow," he said. "Good thinking."

"I called, and it rang twice then went to a mailbox that wasn't set up. I called again, but it went straight to voicemail, like it had been powered off. Can your friend ask his friend to trace another phone?"

"I doubt it. It was an all-favors-owed one-time-only deal," he said. "Any luck with the hospitals so far?"

"No, but I'll ask about Amber and Ethan from now on."

"You think they were back together somehow?"

"Maybe."

"And maybe I can't wait to wrap my hands around that little shithead's neck for getting my daughter to skip out of college to end up in this –"

"Whoa, Cowboy," I said, trying to defuse the issue. "Ethan may have invited her, but she made a choice to come, and neither one of them knew what would happen."

"She wouldn't have come to New York if he hadn't *invited her*." The sarcasm in his voice was harsh. He cleared his throat. "I'm sorry. I'm afraid we won't . . . that we won't find her."

"We're doing everything we can, Z'."

"I pray it's enough." He hesitated, and I could hear background voices. "Cops are here. I gotta go, but I'll call Harper again when I'm done. Can't hurt to ask."

I went back to calling hospitals, scribbling notes of who I talked to and what time, making a whole new list, four hospitals per page to leave room for notes.

Brandan's list had been random, but I wanted it to be alphabetical, or by specialty. I tried the phone book.

Amber or Ethan, I said to myself as I waited for the phone to be answered at each of those facilities and as I wrote second and third and fourth numbers to call.

Honestly, after looking at yellow pages advertising describing the sizes of these hospital facilities, they had to employ more staff than the number of residents in the county where we lived – nearly a thousand beds plus nurses, doctors, housekeepers, administrators, record managers and IT, kitchen staff, and many others.

A nursing supervisor at a smaller hospital dialed various departments while I waited on hold, letting me know between each which unit she had called and the obvious result. As time-consuming as it had to be, she called a dozen individual units that had unidentified patients, asking if there was a young blonde woman or a wavy brown-haired young man. None were remotely close to Amber's or Ethan's descriptions.

I thanked her for taking her time to personally check for me.

"I have a teenage daughter, too," she said. "She's a pain in my ass some days, but I'd be out of my mind if she were missing and thankful for someone to help me. Hope you find her, Julie."

• • • • •

Checking the clock, my back was not as surprised as the rest of me to see I'd been sitting for two hours. On my way to the bathroom, I stretched my arms above my head and twisted, letting my back creak into a loud pop.

I needed snacks so went to the vending machine at the end of the hall for a bottle of water, which cost me four bucks! Back in the room, I slid it across the desk, paused to look out the window.

From the sixth floor, the view was mostly of similar-sized buildings across the street, with taller high rises in the distance. My stomach tightened at how much the city made me feel closed in, suffocated. I'd noticed the night before how loud and dirty New York seemed compared to where I'd lived all my life.

I was ready to go back to calling when Zach knocked and waited for me to open the door.

"What was that for?" I asked.

"I didn't want you to shoot me when I came in," he said, as if his explanation shouldn't make as much sense as it did when I thought about it more. "I brought us lunch."

He set out half-pound burgers and fries for three, I noted, while I explained my new focus on calling hospitals and the help I'd received at one.

"Brandan will be here in a minute. He had to go change shirts," Zach said, pulling out a chair to sit. "Bloody nose."

"Sounds like a rough morning," I mused. "I'm just a bit jealous I wasn't there."

Zach laughed. "No, you aren't."

"No, not a bit," I confirmed. "I have concluded I do not like New York City. Not a single thing so far."

"Didn't think you would," he said, kissing my forehead. "Attitudes on the streets are different now than last time I was here. More patriotic, more unity, but not tranquil or friendly like Albuquerque or Traverse City."

"You've never told me why you came here before." I hoped my hint sounded casual.

"Nor do I intend to tell you anytime in the near future," he said.

"Really?" I said, puzzled. "You've never not shared something with me when I asked."

He wrapped his arms around me, pulling me close to his warm body. "You know almost everything in my past, Julie. I don't keep secrets just for me. It's important, though. Please trust me that I can't and shouldn't. Not now."

"I understand," I said, but part of me did not. I didn't mean to pout, but I must have.

"One day, I promise."

Brandan knocked and broke the spell and Zach's embrace.

Over better burgers than any franchise could make, we chatted about their setup this morning.

Brandan had stood in line with a couple of dozen people, waiting to be served the hot breakfast cereal of the day and a few slices of bacon, finally edging inside then getting a plate. The only open seats were toward the back of the room, which wouldn't make him a tempting target, so he ate standing so he could be closer to the door.

"No question in my mind who the kid was when he started scoping out the crowd. This girl, Talisha – you ever heard that name before? – she had a chair facing away from the door but near it." He took a bite, so Zach continued.

"I saw this guy, like Brandan said, standing across the street to start with, then went the end to cross at the light. He hesitated a few doorways down, looked at his phone, then tucked it into his pocket and made for this gal's bag. She took off after him. Brandan took off after him." Then Zach took a bite, giving the story back to Brandan.

"I didn't get out of the building fast enough, but Z' took him out several doors down."

"What happened?" I asked when neither of them continued. I looked back and forth, then laughed. "You guys were scammed! They made you as cops, so one swiped the girl's bag as a test to see if you'd chase. She's part of it."

They both looked a little ashamed, especially because I figured it out so fast.

"I told you she'd know," Zach said swiping a couple of fries through mustard instead of ketchup. "The cops couldn't do anything since she wouldn't press charges, on him or us. Can you believe they asked her that? We tried appealing to the scammers to see if they recognized Amber. No dice. I'm fairly sure the guy recognized the green backpack, but he wasn't talking to us."

"That stinks," I said. "I'll keep calling. Anything else you heard on the streets that might have been helpful?"

"Not really. My sister suggested visiting EMS stations to see if anyone recognized her," Brandan said, then plopped the last bite of his burger in his mouth and chewed, brushing his hands together.

"That's a sound idea, but there's no telling how many crew members would have been on duty since she left the hotel," I countered. "If she needed an ambulance, she might not have been recognized as the pretty young woman she is."

"I'll go to the stations for the Lower East Side and Kip's Bay. Not likely any other station would have responded into this area unless they've moved units since 9/11," Zach said. "You want to go out with me this afternoon?"

"Oh, hell no," I said. "I've never had anxiety attacks, but just walking around last night gave me chest pain."

While Brandan sipped from his straw, he held out his hand and wiggled his fingers at Zach, who pulled out his wallet and handed over a handful of twenty dollar bills.

"You *bet on me?*" I squealed, looking from Brandan to Zach. "And *you lost?*" I threw my napkin on the desk we were using as a table and leaned back in the chair.

They laughed again.

"I could shoot you both and ask the paramedics who come to get you where they'd . . . "

The idea snapped in my head like a dead branch over my knee.

Trauma.

All along she would most probably have been admitted for a diabetic issue, but what if she'd been injured?

I pulled out a map from Zach's bag and unfolded it, trying to find where the hotel was in relation to the World Trade Center, then looking for the area I assumed Zach and Brandan had been this morning. The three closest trauma centers were Mount Sinai Beth Israel, NYU Langone – which turns out is a large group of hospitals, I'd found out from browsing the yellow pages – and Bellevue.

"Call the EMS director and ask him where a trauma patient or a diabetic medical patient found in this part of the city would be taken if unconscious or confused," I said.

"Whew," Brandan said. "I thought she was really thinking of shooting one of us."

I turned and gave him my happy innocent smile. "Not just one of you, my dear," followed by my *I might not shoot you, but I could* laugh.

"God, I miss your wicked sense of humor, Julie," Brandan said. "Let's start calling. The first one to find her doesn't have to drive."

That was a bet I could make. I had the list.

They both started on the EMS angle. I called Bellevue.

I can't say that finding her first made me a winner, but I didn't drive.

CHAPTER 30
AMBER

September 15, 2001, 1:32 p.m. Eastern Daylight Time

"Julie?" It was familiar, but I knew that wasn't right, yet I didn't know what my name was.

I wish my memory would come back soon!

A nurse peeked in the door. "The doctor says you're doing well enough to transfer to the surgical floor today!"

My spirits should have been brighter regarding the move, but at least I knew the staff here. I didn't want to start all over. I hated being the kid who didn't know who she was.

I also didn't want to cry, but I did after she left the room. Like I couldn't help it.

Closed into a room with a window overlooking something if I could get up and look through the smudged glass, but it was probably just more dirty buildings, and the thought of it was depressing. I doubted I'd recognize any landmarks to help me remember who I was or why I was there, although I was still positive I wouldn't have chosen to live in New York.

Lunch had been delivered, but it was as yucky as my mood, so I covered it up and closed my eyes instead.

Sometime later, the same nurse came back in.

I figured it was time to was moved to another room, another floor, another bed. I wasn't looking forward to it.

Instead, she came over and took my hand. "I want you to close your eyes and count the number of people I mention in a story."

"Why?" I asked, not wanting to play another silly game.

"Humor me."

I sighed and closed my eyes.

The story she began sounded like a conversation one might have with a friend over a casual lunch, talking about other friends.

"I was out the other night with Susan and Tina to see a movie. We ran into Paula and Stephanie, so we invited them."

I had to use my fingers to keep track, even though she spoke slowly.

"Along the way, I saw Brenda and Darlene going into a coffee shop, so we went in. The server was a friend of Carla's, so we ordered. Amber brought me a latte with . . . "

My eyes shot open. "Say the last two names again."

"Carla and Amber."

"My name is Amber!" I yelled with joy. "I remember!"

And around the doorway peeked a familiar face. "Dad!"

The nurse, whose name was Carla, winked at me and let in Dad, Julie and Brandan, the deputy from Michigan.

Wait. What's he doing here?

CHAPTER 31
JULIE

September 15, 2001

Although finding Amber was a huge burden lifted off our shoulders, we discovered getting her home would not be as simple as buying an airline ticket back to Washington.

Zach and Brandan had been on the right track about the bag thieves. Amber's bag had been stolen while she was eating at a shelter near where the guys were working. In her attempt to get it back, she ran after the thief. Crossing through the second or third intersection, she'd been hit by a vehicle that hadn't stopped. EMS picked her up and brought her to Bellevue Hospital.

She had been admitted with multiple injuries including the concussion and a broken arm, as well as a badly fractured femur for which she'd undergone surgery. Capping that, they found out she was a diabetic with out-of-control glucose levels. This had kept her in ICU. Because she didn't remember her name or ours, much less phone numbers, they couldn't contact anybody.

Once Zach and I showed up, the nurse had names to present to Amber, hoping she recognized one. The technique worked.

"How did you know that story would work," I asked the nurse.

"Often a concussion makes it hard for the brain to look in the right folder for certain information it seeks. It knows the folder exists, but the harder it tries to open it, the harder it locks down. By giving the brain a different task, such as counting people rather than naming them, the folder opens more easily," she explained.

Zach looked at me, then her again. "How would you even know that?"

"Neuro ICU for twelve years," she said with a brilliant smile. "I've seen the neurosurgeons' magic."

Carla and another nurse moved Amber and her new entourage two stories down to a surgical floor now that her diabetes was under control. They wished her the best on their way out, and a new nurse and tech her settled her into the private room, brought an extra chair, and finally left us.

Amber's head fell back, taking a big breath in relief.

She looked like I had at times, with a large bruise on her face, a cast on her right arm past the elbow, abrasions on her hands and left elbow. Her leg was not immobilized, but she moved as though it hurt.

"I was so scared I'd never remember anything and be left to wander this forsaken city all by myself," she told us. "How did you find me?"

We took turns explaining parts of the search, leaving out my mother and Kim for now. I would tell her, but not in front of Brandan, because I knew she would cry, and that her reaction might embarrass her.

"Did you find Ethan?" she asked. "I mean, I didn't expect you to look for him, but that he'd contacted you or something."

Zach took a breath to answer, but I spoke first. "No, we haven't heard anything about him."

"Do you have any idea where he was going that morning? A name of a lawyer, street location, anything?" Brandan asked.

Amber shook her head. "I don't want to believe he's dead, but what else could have happened? He wouldn't have abandoned me, I'm sure of it."

Zach's nostrils flared in anger at the idea.

"No one identified him when I was calling hospitals to find you, but there was no match for him by name or description," I told her. "I'm sorry."

When we'd talked ourselves out, Zach stood and said he needed to take Brandan back to his car and on the road back to work.

"I don't want you guys to leave me," she whined.

"Amber, I'm not going. I'll be right here," I told her. "The nurse said you didn't eat your lunch. Can Zach bring you something back?"

She pouted but thought for a few seconds. "Know somewhere I can get a grilled chicken salad?"

"Honey, it's New York City," Zach said, kissing her forehead. "I can find anything here."

She laughed. "Probably not good Mexican food," she challenged.

"Or Texas barbeque," I added.

"Okay, but it's New York City. I can find a damned salad," he relented.

"Five bucks," Amber said.

Brandan said goodbye and kissed her cheek. "Try getting lost in Hawaii next time?"

"Thank you for coming to help find me," she said, almost like a real adult, and hugged him with her unbroken arm.

After the guys left, she sighed. "You don't have any good news, do you?"

"We found you, which is spectacular," I replied. "But there is bad news, too."

I explained what had happened to my mom, which left us both in tears.

"I'm sorry for all the trouble I've caused. I thought I'd only be here two nights and go back to school," she said, wiping her eyes. "I didn't mean for Grandmom Dagmar to have another stroke."

"Amber, her stroke was not your fault."

"But if I hadn't come," she started again.

"If airliners hadn't been flown into buildings, if you hadn't come here, if we hadn't gone to Michigan during the summer where you met Ethan. . . There is no end to the if's we can't undo or change. Things happened, and we go forward."

"How can you say that?" she asked in astonishment.

I tried to hide the smile, remembering a similar conversation we had when her mother had been killed.

"Did I have a choice that Mom died? Could I have done anything to stop her from having a stroke?" I asked. "The answer is no. Could we have stopped you from coming to New York? Probably not. Look, I'd like to change all of those things, but the only option I have is to go on."

"I'm sorry I missed her funeral."

"You didn't. We'll have a memorial service when you're well. Vera is staying with Kim at Mom's house, so it might be crowded for a few days when we return."

"Why?" she asked with a frown. "What else is wrong?"

"Kim had an episode of premature labor, so Vera is staying with her in town in case it happens again."

"But she's okay, right?"

"Yes," I said. "Gerald flew in to see her, too, so that's better, too."

"Why was Brandan here?"

"Shortly after you called me on the 11th, all flights were grounded. Knowing it would take Zach three days to get here, I called to ask Gerald, but he'd had cataract surgery and wasn't supposed to drive. He asked Brandan, whose sister lives nearby. He was happy to come help. Zach detoured through Albuquerque to get me, then we drove to New York, too."

Then it occurred to me that we'd already told Amber why Brandan was here.

"I need something to drink," I said as an excuse. "Can I get you something?"

She declined, and I went to the nurse's desk.

"Will her doctor make rounds again today?" I asked.

The nurse shook her head. "He saw her in ICU this morning."

"I'm concerned that although she remembers her name and us, she's still forgetting things we told her an hour ago."

The nurse taking care of her was summoned for me to talk to, and I repeated my worry.

"I can't tell you anything about her due to the privacy laws," the woman in gray scrubs told me, turning away from me.

"I'm aware of HIPAA, which was enacted in August 1996 to provide *accountability* for the privacy of patients. Let's try this again. I'm positive she was not competent to make medical decisions or to legally consent to treatment on her own behalf if she only remembered her name today, and furthermore, no one in this hospital can accurately determine that she is who she says now. But it hardly makes sense that someone who intends to pay the six-figure medical bill for care no one was competent to consent for would do so with the sole intention of intruding on her privacy."

The nurse huffed air out her nose like a horse. "The doctor really ought to explain her diagnoses and treatment plans," she said, "but the ICU nurse told me she had noted a few short-term memories did not seem to stick, but others did. Like she knows she didn't have lunch in ICU, but she's not sure what day it is."

Time to ratchet down the antagonism, Julie.

"When you are in the hospital, it's hard enough to keep track of days without having a head injury," I said, easing off on my bitchiness a little. "Sometimes even the night nurses don't know for sure."

She smiled in agreement. "She does have a small subdural hematoma, but the doctors elected to wait and see how it does. She's on a heparin injection twice a day."

"What about the surgery on her leg?" I asked. "What did they do? And I do speak medicalese pretty well."

"The chart says they had to do an open reduction and internal fixation, a rod through the femur. As soon as she's ready, we're to get her up and moving, which will not be easy with the fractured arm."

"And her arm?"

"Closed comminuted radius fracture, distally," she said, pointing at her arm to demonstrate. "No fixation hardware or surgery needed."

"Repeat head CT?"

"Yesterday. Right temporal subdural hematoma, originally 3 cm by 2 cm, has decreased in size."

I nodded. "Is she scheduled for PT and OT?"

"She has been seeing PT twice a day. She will see Occupational Therapy today for a full evaluation, including memory and other higher brain functions. She came in unconscious, so I have no doubts she has a traumatic brain injury that will require work."

"What time is her OT visit?"

She checked the chart. "Three o'clock."

"Do we need to register her now and provide insurance information?"

"I'd appreciate it, now that she knows her name."

See, that wasn't so damned hard, was it?

"We live in Washington State, so what's the timetable for her to be moved home?"

"She won't be cleared to travel for weeks yet, I'm sure, especially walking around in a commercial airport."

"No, private medical charter," I said.

"Oh, that would be expensive," she said in a snarky, sarcastic patronizing tone. "I'm guessing $5,000 or more."

Oh, it would be considerably more.

"As opposed to staying in New York for a month or more, it's a real bargain," I replied.

While I didn't have that much money in my purse, getting it wouldn't be a problem, even if Amber was ready to be discharged tomorrow. On the other hand, I wondered if she'd been treated like a homeless person and thus someone without insurance. Adequate but maybe not exceptional medical care.

I went back to the room, finding Amber asleep, so I cuddled up best I could in a chair

Flying her back to Portland, Oregon, left us other logistics to figure out. If we all flew to Oregon, what would we do about my truck? If Amber and I flew back to Albuquerque, getting her to and from PT would be easier, and Zach could drive back home to Washington..

Figuring it out must have overwhelmed my brain into sleep.

I startled awake when someone came into the room for Amber, but Zach was sitting in a chair at the end of the bed, watching her.

Amber woke easily, and we excused ourselves from her room while the assessment began.

Out in the waiting room, I dropped into a worn chair, and Zach sat next to me, leaning forward, elbows resting on his thighs.

"Another damned waiting room. I'm tired of these."

"At least we found her," I said, wrapping my arm around his back. "Everything else has to get easier from here."

He dropped his head. "Yeah, we found her. Brandan is spending a few days with his sister, by the way. Said there was no sense in passing up the opportunity."

"Good for him. I spoke with the nurse about Amber. The therapist with her now is to help assess any deficits after her head injury. She has some short-term memory loss, like not remembering what we'd said about how we found her, but it seems to be improving."

"Great," he said, but his voice was choked.

"I can take her back to Albuquerque for a month or so for rehab, then home for the holiday break," I suggested. "She ought to be ready to go back to school in January."

"We're supposed to trust her to go back to college?" he growled.

"I know you're angry, Zach, but sticking her in a box will not change what has happened. If this had gone as she planned, we might not have known about it for weeks," I said, though I wasn't sure I was defending Amber or defusing her father. "Tell me you didn't do anything so, I don't know, dumb when you were her age."

He shook his head. "No comment. Yeah, kids are kids. But I'd still like to string Mr. Wenzler from a tree by his ankles and . . . "

I coughed politely to interrupt him. "We'd have to find him first. Since we're stuck here for a few days at least, shall we work on locating him?" I asked. "Your daughter would think you were a hero."

He sighed hard enough the magazine covers rustled on the table in front of him. "I don't know where to start."

"Do we contact his parents? I doubt they know he's here. We should have found out if he flew or drove, and if he drove, where's the car?"

More logistics. Seemed like a reasonable start to ask Amber.

CHAPTER 32
JULIE

September 15, 2001

Perhaps a little afraid of her father's reaction, Amber took a little prompting to tell us what Ethan's plans had been once they were here.

"We went to dinner the first night, and then he was going to see the attorney the next morning and be done, so we'd have the rest of the day free to sightsee. I wanted to go to the top of the Empire State Building, see Fifth Avenue and Times Square. He said he had tickets to a Broadway show that night. I had a flight back to Seattle the next day."

"He flew?" I asked. "What day?"

"The day before, from Detroit. I assumed he flew. I'm pretty sure he was leaving the same day I was."

"Do you have phone numbers or any information about his adoptive parents so we can call and see if they've talked to him?"

"I did, but it was all in my phone."

"We found it, but you won't be getting phone numbers," Zach said. "It was smashed and half an inch from being washed down a sewer grate."

"Ethan's phone went to voice mail after ringing the first time I called it," I said. "But you said he didn't take his phone with him that morning, right?"

"It was in my pack when it was stolen."

"We can request a call history from Ethan's phone carrier and identify a number for his family," Zach told her. "Did it ring any time after he left for his appointment?"

She squinted for a second. "I don't think so. I didn't turn it off, but I don't know if the battery had died before my bag was stolen."

Zach looked back at me.

Her eyes filled with tears again. "I'm so sorry, Dad, Julie. I didn't mean for everyone to have to go through all this looking for me."

"Lots of people haven't been found, no matter how many are looking for them. We're glad you aren't one of them. What if you'd gone with Ethan that morning? Something horrible might have happened to you, too, and we wouldn't know." Zach stood and bent to hug her. "You're still grounded until your thirtieth birthday."

"Dad!" She let go and punched him in the arm.

He moved away and leaned against the ledge at the window.

The mood lightened again, so we kept shuffling the virtual puzzle pieces about her and Ethan's trip.

"You need to call for the favor this time, Julie," Zach said. "Nolan should probably obtain Ethan's phone records."

I made a note on a pad I'd borrowed from the nurse's desk. "Do you know why Ethan came to New York? Something more specific? A will, perhaps? Letter from his real mother or father?"

"No. I wished I'd asked more questions."

"Did he ever tell you that he knew who his father is?"

"Not that I remember, but he kept asking questions about his mom, like I was supposed to know or telling me I should ask you."

"Like what?"

"Sorry, Julie, the harder I think, the fuzzier it gets in my head."

I understood how disconcerting it was to realize things feel fuzzy, like facts were supposed to be lights in my brain, but everything was dim and shadowy with occasional flashes. I hoped it improved for her.

I also understood how difficult it was to sit with a patient in a hospital bed, having been that patient or family member way too many times. Zach was getting antsy, I could tell.

He wasn't built for sitting quietly in a hospital room.

"You need to rest," I told her, but she started crying again.

"We'll check out of our hotel room and move closer to the hospital," Zach explained, though I wasn't sure being closer was his entire reason.

"I'm afraid I'll go to sleep and when I wake up, you will be a dream and won't come back."

"We aren't a dream, and we'll be back this evening. I promise." Zach took a permanent marker from his pocket and wrote his phone number on her cast, along with, "*We love you. That will always be real.*"

"Thanks, Dad."

• • • • •

We did what Zach said, packing and moving to a closer hotel.

Once in the new room, I called Nolan.

In the background, raucous children were laughing.

There were two boys, ten and two, and a five-year-old girl, last I heard.

"Julie! Hang on a minute," he yelled, hoping to be heard. The sound lessened and a door closed. "Whew, that's better. How're you doing?"

"You know me, Nolan. Always one catastrophe or another or I'd have stopped to see you guys in June."

"Brandan said your mom had an emergency," he said. "I understand."

"That was weeks ago. This last week has been difficult," I started. "First, the whole 9/11 attacks, then Mom had another stroke and did not survive. She passed away without regaining consciousness a week ago. A week? Hell, I don't even remember what day it is."

"I'm so sorry, Julie. Can we do anything?"

"Actually, yes, you can, but it's not about Mom. On the tenth, Amber secretly flew from Seattle to New York City to spend a couple of days with a guy she'd met in Michigan when we were there." I let that sink in a moment before continuing. "She was here, watching the World Trade Center attacks happen out her hotel window, but Ethan had left that morning to go to a meeting with a lawyer."

"You're in New York, too?"

Suddenly I couldn't go on, so I handed the phone to Zach.

"Hey, Nolan," he said with intermittent pauses. "Yeah, doing okay, considering. We are really here. This is a convoluted story on top of Dagmar's death." He touched my cheek and went on talking. "Amber tried calling to let us know she was here in New York City right after the first plane hit, but cell service was scarcely existent. When I couldn't fly, I drove to Albuquerque to be with Julie. Brandan Callaghan drove to NYC and started searching."

I walked to the bathroom, leaving them to talk without me listening. I'd hoped for a tub, but there was only a walk-in shower, which would have to do. Peeling off my clothes, I found a sample bottle of my favorite shampoo in my toiletry bag, then stripped to soak, soap, and breathe out the stress that had accumulated in my shoulders for weeks.

Maybe the concierge could find me a masseuse. One who could work on my back for three hours straight, then just let me sleep where I lay.

I'd finished washing my hair and was just letting the water run down my face when I heard the bathroom door open and Zach came in.

"Can I share your steam?" he asked, already naked.

"Of course. You're always welcome in the shower with me when there's room."

"I like it just as much when there's not enough," he said, opening the door and inching up behind me. "Maybe even more."

I'd been in the hot water for at least fifteen minutes, yet his body was warmer than mine when he enveloped me in his arms from behind as completely as the steam.

He made a low throaty sound as he nuzzled my neck, and the rest of the world and its problems washed away like the water down the drain.

• • • • •

"Nolan will do his FBI thing for us," he said as he dried me off with a fluffy towel worthy of his efforts. "He'll try to get records, but it might be a day or so."

"We aren't going anywhere anytime soon," I said, taking the towel from him and returning the favor.

"Then perhaps we can take advantage of the New York City tourism," he suggested.

"Like what? A trip to the top of the World Trade Center? No, wait. Can't ever do that again," I said with sad sarcasm. Not as though I'd ever wanted to, but now I wouldn't ever be able to go.

"There's a few other things worth seeing," he said. "This evening, we could go to the Met for the rooftop wine tasting. Great views. Or we could walk across Brooklyn Bridge and take a ferry back after sunset."

"Let's go to the Met," I said. "You can tell me all about it."

• • • • •

We visited Amber again late in the afternoon, then took a cab to the Metropolitan Museum of Art and enjoyed a city sunset from the rooftop.

"This is nice," I said, taking a sip of a Shiraz resembling a glass of garnets in the dusk. "Nothing beats a sunset on a wide-open horizon like Albuquerque."

"Yeah, New Mexico has some great skyscape," he admitted.

As we rode back to the hospital in the cab, I confessed that our outing had been more enjoyable than I'd thought.

That sent the driver off on a travel tangent, asking where we were from, what we'd seen so far, and making more suggestions. Although it was supposed to be a conversation, he did most of the talking but added a couple more ideas to the list of possibilities that Zach seemed to recognize.

We got out at the hospital and walked what felt like another four miles to Amber's room through halls with wafting uncomfortable but familiar odors. By now, I was sure I could identify hospital departments by smell alone.

"Mr. and Mrs. Samualson?" a voice called as we passed the nurses' station.

We turned to see a different nurse than I'd discussed Amber's health with earlier.

"I wanted to let you know the occupational therapist reports Amber's doing better, and he is very hopeful her memory losses will resolve by the time she is ready for discharge," she said. "Physical therapy had her up on her feet for a few minutes this afternoon, too. Toe-touch only, but vertical."

"That's progress, thanks," I said, "but how did you know who we are?"

She glanced from me up to Zach and laughed. "Carla told me I couldn't miss him."

I whacked him in the chest backhanded. "What did I tell you about being big in public?"

We entered Amber's room, and she set off describing her day like they'd served her two cups of coffee with dinner until finally, Zach had to rein her in like a wild horse.

"Let me see if I can recap all that," he said. "The occupational therapist says your memory is better today, and you recalled more of what happened before the car hit you. Then the physical therapist had you taking a few steps with a walker. Right so far?"

"Yeah, so I'm hoping I can go back to college in a few weeks," she concluded.

"Amber, going back this semester isn't a realistic possibility. You've already missed a week and haven't even been discharged yet," he said.

Her bottom lip pushed out.

"You can't drive, and it's very unlikely you'll be able to attend classes while you're doing physical therapy," I said. "We should get you withdrawn, then you can start again in the spring."

"I don't want to wait for spring! I'm already up on my feet, so I can walk around. You tell her, Dad."

"You were on your feet for five minutes and a few steps. Let's give it a week of rehab, then we'll see," he said, trying to avoid the building explosion. "It's not up to us, though. We'll have to get it cleared with a physician for you to leave, as well as his limitations for activity and orders for PT, then we have to transport you home."

"Which brings to mind several questions about how to accomplish getting you somewhere, getting me back to Albuquerque, getting my truck and Zach home, and so on."

"Dad and I get on an airline and –"

"Amber, you want to jump out of that bed tomorrow and go back to your life, and it's not going to happen. Your femur was broken so badly they had to use a rod to hold it together. Getting back on your feet will take rehab to – "

That did it.

She broke out sobbing. "I don't want rehab. I just want to be normal again!"

No sense talking to her like this, I thought.

Sobs gave way to sniffles in time.

"If you want to be normal again, you need to do what the doctors and therapists tell you, here and back home," I said. "It might be better for you to go with me to Albuquerque so we can take you to physical therapy without driving to Portland and back every day."

I could see we were getting nowhere with this.

Zach tried as well, but it pushed Amber closer to tears again. When he opened his mouth to start another round, I push my hand on his knee to stop him.

"Let's see how PT goes tomorrow, Amber," I said, not arguing her intentions to be normal or go back to classes. As well as her physical injuries, I also understood that her high-strung emotional reactions could be due to her head injury, which would also take time to heal.

We spent another half hour with her, avoiding discussion of her future recovery, the death of my mother, or any mention of having fun in New York after she had another head-spinning devil-speaking emotional meltdown that we had not been staying with her day and night.

She'd have made Linda Blair proud.

When we finally got outside, Zach let loose with a similar string of expletives, and I let him vent until a cab stopped for us.

"What on earth is she thinking?" he demanded as he opened the door for me to scoot inside.

"Z', you have to understand – she isn't thinking clearly," I said, hoping to calm him. "It's emotion, not logic. The head injury is scrambling her reasoning."

"Geez, I hope it clears up soon," he said. "I can't handle much more of that."

He gave the cabbie the destination, then returned to our conversation. We both probably were hoping not to be bombarded with more intrusion by the driver.

"Remember when she was first diagnosed with diabetes," I reminded him. "It was overwhelming for all of us, and it was permanent. Amber felt like she was a freak to her friends."

"That was different."

"Really? How so?" I challenged.

He didn't answer right away, and I let him work it out.

"Most of the time, her friends couldn't see what was wrong with her," he finally offered. "Now, people can see the results of her injuries, and a slight jig to her memory might be acceptable, but that out-of-control emotional bomb would be pretty freaky to them. Does she even know it's weird?"

"I doubt it, but I believe it's temporary."

We both leaned against the force of the cab making a hard whipping maneuver to avoid a bus, which I found aggravating, much like a lot of other New York normals.

"We still need to figure out where to go and how to get out of here with her," I said. "Does she go back to Washington or to New Mexico? Do we fly or drive?"

"Honestly, I'm too wired to think about any of that."

"Let's have a good night's sleep and start fresh tomorrow," I said.

He grinned, raised one eyebrow, and leaned toward me and whispered, "I said I didn't want to think about medical stuff, not that my plans included sleep."

September 16, 2001

We had both predicted the next twelve hours correctly. Wrapped together much later, we slept soundly and way past Zach's usual internal alarm. That alone was a pleasant surprise because I usually woke up in an empty bed, and he was out feeding the horses.

It's three hours earlier. No West Coast human should be awake at this hour.

We cuddled a bit together, then his morning started with a shower. While it was my turn, he went out for breakfast.

I must admit, there's no shortage of fabulous food in New York.

Zach brought back two cups of real coffee, two toasted bagels with my favorite toppings, a couple of frittatas, and a handful of donut holes.

He'd also brought in a copy of *USA Today* to browse for more actual news than we'd gleaned from the television. While it was nice President Bush had visited Ground Zero to talk to the people working, I could only imagine how disruptive it was to have put a President into a locale like that due to the security concerns.

"What's your idea about getting her home?" he asked me. "I kinda need to get back to the livestock."

I frowned. "Since when are four horses livestock?"

"An expression," he said, not lying very well. "And it's five now, remember?"

"Not convincing, Zach. Try again."

"I fenced off the lower half of the property for thirty head of steers."

"I see. Another surprise?"

"Was it?" he asked hopefully.

His phone rang, interrupting our discussion.

"Nolan, how's it going?" Zach said in a cheery voice, then listened mostly, with an occasional *uhhuh* or *really*. Then his face changed.

"Hang on," he said. "I'm putting you on speaker. I hate to ask you to repeat . . ."

Nolan said it was no problem, said hello to me, then started talking again.

His news included two facts: Ethan Wenzler did not exist. No birth certificate in Michigan. No driver's license in any state. The cellular phone number I'd given Nolan to trace was a burner, meaning its account couldn't be obtained for a history of phone numbers or texts. If it had GPS, which was unlikely, the phone was completely powered off.

One of these facts alone might be an explanation, but not all of them.

If I felt anger, it was nothing like the fluorescent red on Zach's face.

"Bringing her here and dumping her, while a lot of distasteful things, is not criminal. I suspected that he disappeared, but not on purpose. I can't believe he knew about the attacks on the World Trade Center, but it was a perfect disaster to be lost in. Should we bother looking for him?" I asked.

Amber liked Ethan, and I so wanted this whole thing to be benign for her sake.

"His first contact was to ask for information regarding Penny Daniels, according to Brandan, right?" Nolan asked. "What did he want to know?"

I tried to think. "He said she is his biological mother, but he just wanted to know more about her. Penny's husband wasn't helpful."

"I doubt Daniels wanted the intrusion," Zach offered. "Might be hard to discuss a spouse with something from her past."

"Something?" I asked.

"An illegitimate child." He shrugged at my stern look at the insult.

"Amber doesn't remember any contact information. She said it was on her phone, which we found, dead and smashed on the street. No idea who or where his adopted parents are," Zach continued, frowning. "But he told us he was in his second year at MSU in criminal justice."

"Those are things I can check," Nolan replied.

"Amber believes he flew from Michigan, so maybe the airlines will have an identity on him," I added.

"Amber flew, too, right? Did she buy her own ticket?" Nolan asked.

"Yes," I said, giving him the credit card numbers.

Another glare from Zach.

"Why am I getting the bad vibes?" I asked him. "I'm not the one responsible for this."

Facial apologies and air kiss.

"I paid off the balance so she'd have money available, but that was before we found out the hotel manager had kicked her out." I slapped my head. "I ought to cancel her card now since it's missing."

"Before you do, let's see if someone uses it," Nolan suggested. "Give me the number and I'll set it up. I'll also *suggest* they refund the return flight since no one could fly."

"One other thing," Zach said, interrupting the goodbyes. "When Amber was kicked out of the hotel, it was because the reservation was in the name of Sean Smith. Can't be but forty-two thousand of those, but could you check?"

"Databases-R-us," he quipped.

CHAPTER 33
JULIE

September 17 – 22, 2001

We spent the week working with therapists and Amber to learn how to help her transfer, stand and move with a walker.

"Let's talk about options for discharge," Carla said, sitting beside a physical therapist named Tally at a cafeteria table Thursday morning. "Amber will be ready to go home in a few days. Time to do discharge planning. Where will her PT be set up, and how will you be getting her there?"

"We live in a rural area, and though there are plenty of facilities for PT in Portland, they're several hours of driving a day. I think she'll do better in Albuquerque," I explained. "The question is whether we need to fly charter or if she can go commercial in a wheelchair."

"She's quite determined not to let this keep her down long," Tally said. "I wouldn't normally agree to it, but she could probably do a commercial flight with an adult escort, so long as the doctor agrees."

Amber's memory had improved, although we spent another hour a day helping her with mental exercises as well as physical ones. She was making at least one more lap around the floor each time we walked, although she wasn't fast.

"Zach went to see if he could find out anything about Ethan this morning," I told her on Friday as we walked. "Do you remember anything that could help us find him or his parents?"

I had agreed with Zach the night before that we shouldn't bring up that we'd asked Nolan to help us identify Ethan.

"One of the things he asked me several times was what happened to his grandmother's or his mother's journals," she said, taking slow, deliberate steps, supported mostly by the walker.

How did he find out about Penny's journals? Was he just fishing or did he know they existed?

I didn't know. Why did he think I did? Did Mark Daniels tell him?

"I told him you'd never mentioned any of this to me, but he seemed a little pushy that you knew and wouldn't tell him." She stopped to make me look at her. "Do you know about them?"

"I told him in July, Penny found her mother's journals. But she also told us Bock had killed himself," I said, trying to remember the order of things. "She'd found them and showed me a few passages. The DA had told Brandan she could take them with her to Phoenix, but then she backed out. I offered to make copies and then send her the books."

Did we ship them?

For the love of green, I couldn't remember anything except for Penny's mom's words about her sister, Angela, and Robert Bock, the man she married after she was pregnant. A man who eventually cut her throat, an act witnessed by a child who grew up and reenacted it, repeatedly.

"Penny found her mother's journals. Could she have found her own, which might have entries from when she got pregnant?" Amber asked.

Were any of her own in the box? I never looked. Had Penny only found her mother's books or were hers in the box, too? Did she take hers with her when she flew home?

• • • • •

September 21, 2001

Checking on flights, Zach and I decided he should fly with Amber on Sunday, a lower demand day. His logic was that he could supply the muscle to keep her safe, if needed. I would drive to Albuquerque, then he could take my truck back to Washington.

Amber was discharged late Saturday afternoon, much to her relief.

"I'm sick of those walls. I just want a decent meal," she said from the front seat of the taxi. "Even a burger."

"Zach has a place in mind. But you have to keep your blood sugar well controlled to help you heal."

"I know," she said. "You picked up my insulin and stuff, right?"

"Got it all," Zach told her. "Everything is at the hotel."

Not a clue where we were or where we were going, I did recognize that we'd been driving longer than it usually took to reach our hotel.

Amber was fascinated with the sites, and Zach's goal had been to let her see a bit of the city.

The cabbie gave her quite a tour around Mid-Manhattan before stopping in front of a restaurant with a line of more than thirty people waiting outside. A doorman came to offer me a hand while Zach retrieved Amber's walker and helped her to her feet. We were escorted straight to the entrance past those waiting.

As we approached, one man near the door whirled wildly as Amber moved behind him; Zach stepped between them and lifted him off his feet by his collar to keep him from knocking Amber over.

The guy's head whipped around to confront his assailant, only to realize that he hung several inches off the ground and was still less than collar-high in comparison to the man who had picked him up. What might have been a fight changed suddenly to a gracious apology before his feet touched the ground again.

Inside, we were seated at a table off to the side away from the most traffic, and Amber's walker was folded and tucked behind her chair, leaving her facing the entire room of people, including a few celebrities.

"Dad," she whispered, "how did you ever get us in here?"

"I know people," he said.

I have so many more questions about that, Zach Samualson.

No menu was brought, but the waiter in a tuxedo asked Zach if the selections made were acceptable, and he made a simple nod. The waiter seemed to vanish.

"I don't even get to pick my food?" Amber said in a pout.

"Trust me, it's much better than a burger, and you will love it, I promise," he answered, patting her hand.

Amber looked around, seeing that she had not only the best seat at the table to view the restaurant, but possibly had the best table in the restaurant.

Moments later, an elegant woman in bright white head to toe, came to the table and shook hands with Zach, who introduced us to Señora Maria Eduarda Rosa del Fuego, the owner and chef.

Or at least I think that's what she said – it rolled on her tongue like spiced honey.

"Please, call me Edie," she said in a thick accent. "Your filet mignon as you like it, of course, but I also have exquisite lamb chops with a garlic lemon sauce tonight."

Zach looked at Amber, whose eyes were wide and round.

"While lamb sounds fantastic, Edie, we shall have beef all around, please, and closer to medium for them. I'll have the grilled bacon-wrapped asparagus and baked potato. For Julie, the creamed spinach and mushrooms and lobster macaroni. And for our daughter," he said, as if this particular fact would be a surprise to Edie, "asparagus and the lobster mac."

"My pleasure," she said, then stepped aside for a server to present a bottle of wine to Zach. "My compliments, Señor Zach."

I blinked and she was gone, but a crystal plate and saucer along with a full silver setting had arrived between being seated and Edie's arrival, so smoothly placed as to have gone unnoticed.

Or by magic.

The sommelier had vanished after pouring a glass of wine for each of us, and I blinked away the slow-motion mode in time to see Zach lift his glass in a toast.

Amber had a glass of wine as well, although she was under the legal drinking age.

I opened my mouth to object, but Zach made a slight tilt of his head to stop me, and he congratulated us on a successful reunion. We touched crystal glasses that rang in unison, then sipped.

"Non-alcoholic, Julie," he explained.

"How do you know the chef, Dad?" Amber asked, mostly because I hadn't regained my voice yet after meeting the chef.

I've known Zach a long time, and I don't recall ever being so jealous of a woman standing next to him. It wasn't logical, but I felt it just the same.

Zach's eyes met mine. "We met when I was a cop in Houston," he said. "But it's not a suitable story for public or dinner table discussion."

I realized he may have said all he ever intended to about who this woman was or how he knew her, and I would have to accept his decision. Jealous or not.

Amber's focus on the story disappeared as quickly as the staff, and she began to look around the room, recognizing several celebrities.

"Isn't that –?" she asked, not daring to say a name out loud. "You know, from that movie last year?"

That description could have encompassed any of a thousand actors or actresses. Brad Pitt, Julia Roberts, Matt Damon, anyone out of whichever *Star Wars* episode was most recently released.

Neither of us turned to look, but her excitement hummed.

I thought for a minute she would simply implode, try as she did to remain mature and restrained.

Fortunately, our first course was brought by three servers who presented plates to us in unison, then in keeping with the theme, promptly disappeared. Another beamed in to make sure all was to our satisfaction.

He refilled our wine glasses and then also vanished.

Amber waited to see what Zach did before picking up a utensil.

"The easiest way to remember it," he told her, "is to select from the outside in toward the plate. I promise no one will snatch away your food if you use the wrong fork."

She seemed as relieved about the information as I was.

Although my meals have never been formal, way too many of them have been from a sack with fries, I thought and dabbed my lips daintily with a pressed linen napkin.

"Why wasn't a salad first?" she asked.

"Because Edie believes people don't come to her restaurant to eat lettuce. Now try the appetizer."

Amber selected a fork and cut open what appeared to be a fried ravioli.

She and I took a bite at the same time. Not an Italian breaded and fried ravioli, but a delicately crunchy pasta filled with a spicy white cream sauce or maybe cheese with mushroom pieces.

Zach cut open one of his two ravioli bites, finding it was stuffed with guacamole and chicken, so I tried my second as well. I found them interesting, but not something I wanted a dozen more of as a meal.

Appetizer plates removed, and steaks were presented, again in a choreographic dance of foodservice. The sides were plated on separate dishes.

With a nod from Zach, the three men again disappeared.

I picked up a fork and sharp knife that wasn't necessary to cut through the filet with a twisted piece of Canadian bacon around it and put a small slice in my mouth.

Chewing was hardly more necessary than the steak knife. The beef almost melted on my tongue. I savored the taste, until I realized it was familiar.

"Who taught whom to grill?" I demanded.

Zach touched his chest as if he were offended.

I raised an eyebrow, and then took a bite of the creamed spinach.

Soothed by exquisite food, I gave up trying to be angry with Zach.

When he ordered dessert for each of us, I realized I could enjoy it because I hadn't eaten so much I was miserable already.

Amber received Crème brûlée that was caramelized at tableside in a flashy demonstration. I had chocolate mousse that tasted like clouds. And Zach chose Key Lime pie on a crushed pretzel crust.

Those we shared, despite the formality of our environment, and none of us cared one iota if others thought our behavior was crass.

Screw 'em. No one understands what we've been through, and damn it, we deserve every dreamy bite.

After a fabulous meal and dessert, we headed to our hotel. I'd left it up to Zach to make room arrangements to include Amber, so I wasn't surprised to find we had been moved to a suite.

I was stunned that he'd reserved us a penthouse suite with a view to the south and west.

Once Amber was settled in for the night, Zach and I went to sit on the balcony overlooking the lights reaching to the horizon.

"More people you know, huh?" I said, marveling at how different New York City looked from fifteen stories. "I'm beginning to think I don't want to know why you were here before."

"I'm quite sure you don't, actually."

No clues. His expression was utterly neutral.

I had asked and been refused an answer a couple of times, and while I found this out of character for him, I honored his decision to not tell me. But I was curious why a man who'd never kept secrets from me about anything else was so perfectly discreet concerning this.

The breeze was cool, and I had put on a jacket. And of course, Zach sat in short sleeves.

"You're still okay with driving back to New Mexico?" he asked.

"Yes," I said with a yawn. "I could use a break to be alone for a few days."

"I think you could, too." He stretched his arms over his head and yawned in echo of my own. "Please be careful."

"I will. I'll be on the road as soon as you leave for the airport tomorrow."

"You can stay longer if you wish," he offered. "You can sell the truck and fly back to Albuquerque if you'd rather."

"I finally got that truck broken in!" I argued. "Nope, I'll drive."

He reached and took my hand. "Thank you for everything you've done to help me find Amber and get her back."

"Of course, Zach. Why wouldn't I have helped?"

"Didn't say you wouldn't have helped, just that I appreciate you doing it with me."

"I appreciate you making your way to New Mexico when you had this to do."

We sat, looking out over the lights of Manhattan, nearly daylight-bright when compared to our little home back in Washington. Or at least that's what was on my mind.

When Zach led me inside to bed, I had no question what he had been thinking.

CHAPTER 34
JULIE

September 23, 2001

I escaped New York City without being in an accident or losing my sanity, but it had been a close call for both on numerous occasions. If I'd thought NYC drivers were crazy, I'm sure they thought the same of me. A few had communicated their sentiments to me by several voice and hand signals.

Once on an interstate away from bumper-to-bumper traffic, I relaxed, found a CD of light rock as the soundtrack in the background of my scattered thoughts, and I just drove with little else on my mind than the peace of being out of the chaos.

After stopping for the first tank of gasoline, travel food and drinks, and a squooshy pillow to rest my arm on, I decided it was time to have the conversation I'd been avoiding with myself.

Sure, Julie, which one?

I had promised Zach I'd stop at night and sleep, so perhaps later I could make a list of those things to keep my mind occupied for the next thousand miles.

Right now, I had Albuquerque on my mind. Kim and her baby, Amber and her fractures, me without my mother. I had to make it through these thoughts without crying.

While Mom was recuperating, she and I had discussed tasks I needed to take care of, such as house chores and maintenance, banking and bills, and her final wishes. Neither of us had taken that part too seriously, other than recording some of her choices, such as which funeral home or cemetery she'd chosen, the music she wanted to be played.

At least Zach and I don't need to have that discussion.
Yes, you do, Julie.
I'd already planned Zach's funeral once.
Your mother helped you with it or the plans wouldn't have been made.
I could do it again.

Doubtful. But what about him?

The two voices in my head laughed hysterically at each other. I found it a tad unnerving.

Now I had to plan Mom's memorial, get the girls healthy, and decide whether and when to sell the house and her car, the horses, all her belongings.

I imagined having a garage sale, her equestrian gear covering the front lawn.

However, memories of Mom were still so raw I was on the verge of bawling.

Next subject.

I needed to go back to my job, too, although Wade Fordham had assured me that my patrol car and desk would be waiting when I returned.

Few people had jobs like mine, and I was thankful to have a tolerant boss. He wasn't paying me while I was gone, and I suspected he didn't want to find anyone else with my skillset to replace me. Nonetheless, I was looking forward to getting back to work.

One subject down – work.

Next, Kim. She had approximately six weeks until her due date. At least in New Mexico, she and her baby had not been exposed to the significant problems she'd faced in Michigan. Her blood pressure and swelling had stayed under control after a day in the hospital, and she hadn't had any seizure activity indicating eclampsia.

The ultrasound done several weeks before her hospitalization had demonstrated the baby was a normal development and size, if not perhaps a few weeks large, making gestational age slightly uncertain. Gender was noted, but she told the doctor she didn't want to know.

I remember my mother approving of the decision. "Gender was a surprise for thousands of years."

Had Kim decided to keep the baby or to give it up for adoption? Would she go back to Michigan? I didn't know the answers, but I hoped she and Vera had been able to discuss options and she had decided.

Vera had been helpful beyond words, first when she had to call and tell me about my mom, then in keeping everything running without hiccups since I'd arrived with Kim.

While she didn't have any strong connection to Kim, Vera took her in and provided what Kim needed the very most – motherly affection and acceptance.

I wasn't sure, but I had a feeling Vera would be giving me the same nurturing. Thinking of losing my mom made me want to curl up in a lap and be rocked like a young child while I cried, and I had no doubts Vera was just the woman to do it.

Damn, I need much longer topics to think about if I want to stay focused for 2000 more miles.

I checked the clock, wondering if Zach and Amber had made it to Dallas by now.

He said he'd call when they reached the next departure gate. Maybe they had lunch already. But I probably had the time zone thing wrong. I couldn't remember when the clocks changed, though not in September, I was fairly sure. If not for the "spring ahead and fall back" mantra, I'd have to look it up twice a year when and which direction to change my clocks.

Security at the airport had been crazy when we went to the departure lanes by cab, but considering the hijackings two weeks ago, I thought it wasn't out of reason.

Every reaction to the hijackings had been over-the-top. Security seemed to make most people more comfortable, but I was skeptical.

Perfect safety is the delusion of those who expect others to provide it.

Getting Amber and her luggage out of the taxi had taken more than the two minutes allowed for "load and unloading only," the announcements blasted, deafening and constant.

One police officer had come along on foot and banged the driver's side of the car to get the cab to leave until Zach stood up to his full six and a half feet plus boots and yelled back, "I'm not finished unloading our luggage and her walker yet, if you don't mind!"

I'd handed Zach one more bag from inside the car, kissed him, hugged Amber, and slid back into the cab, all while the officer stood, waiting impatiently.

"Geez, it's a little frightening out there," I'd mumbled when the taxi had pulled away from the curb.

"Try being Egyptian," the cabbie'd retorted. "Nothing personal, but suddenly Americans suspect that anyone with dark skin and an accent is a terrorist."

"I'm sorry you have to go through that."

He was right, though. Suddenly groups were divided, based on their skin, clothes, religious beliefs, and speech.

Oh, brother, this is going to get ugly.

Driving west out of the metropolis into rural America, I saw signs of patriotism and religion grow more prominent than in NYC. Radio stations had played music to support the patriotic atmosphere, by Lee Greenwood, Billy Ray Cyrus, and others. Talk-show media was stuck on week-old facts and unending suppositions regarding the attacks. Today's big news was that Anthrax spores were being sent through the mail, mostly to politicians and media companies.

Beware the plain white envelope.

Just two days ago, in racial tensions, a group of Muslims was reported to have attacked and killed a man in England. George W. Bush had declared a "War on Terror" only the day before.

When will this senseless killing end?

When indeed, but is it senseless? Are the reasons we hear or presume the reasons why someone designed such devastation? Has the world ever gone a year without a war somewhere?

Wars have been fought over land, over religion, over policies for thousands of years. I wasn't convinced yet the media knew or was telling us the whole truth of what this fight was really about.

I've seldom kept up with global or national political situations. I'm a skeptic when media coverage is overblown on one event. Makes me question what the attention of Americans is being diverted away from by the hype. While the attacks on 9/11 weren't planned or executed by the U.S. government, it didn't mean the catastrophe wasn't being exploited to cover up other news.

For example, on September 10th, hadn't U.S Secretary of Defense Donald Rumsfeld given a speech regarding more than $2 trillion in Pentagon spending that couldn't be accounted for? More media hype? A smokescreen? Bullshit?

No further mention of it. Ever, I bet.

I shook my head. That's why I've always hated politics. Not often was an event as important as it was portrayed. Seldom were the really important events investigated.

Skeptical was probably a weak description.

In less than two weeks, rumors of grandiose conspiracies flourished. Things like whether planes had been flown into the Towers, though most of America had witnessed the second crash live on television, or whether the jets carried bombs that caused the structural damage, triggering the buildings to collapse.

I recalled the conversation Zach and I had – what other targets might be at the top of a terrorist's list. High financial value? Extreme body count? Symbolic significance?

This subject kept me occupied almost a hundred miles farther down the highway, mostly talking to myself.

My phone rang, so I answered it and hit the speaker function, knowing it was Zach.

"I remember now why I hate flying. Our trip to Michigan should have been a stern lesson," he grumbled. "Hope your drive is going better."

"Despite highway patrolmen who think talking to myself is a crime," I teased, "so far, so good."

"You got stopped already?" he asked, and I could hear Amber in the background, saying *I told you so!*

"No, I wasn't stopped."

I heard him shush Amber. "Boarding is in half an hour. Need anything from the airport in Dallas?"

"Don't need a thing."

"No Dallas Cowboy paraphernalia? Eight-dollar beer?"

"Nothing unless you find a place with those pillows with the little beads in them."

"I'll look. Where are you now?" he asked.

We both knew he wouldn't.

"Not quite to Allentown, but I'm taking I-76 to I-70 to Columbus, then I-71 through Cincinnati to Louisville," I repeated from memory. I hoped I didn't get too lost along the way. "I'm not stopping until you call me from Albuquerque."

"Well, aren't *we* all defiant now?" he jabbed at my alternate driving plans.

"I was that way when you found me, I believe."

"No, you were stubborn and defiant." He hesitated. "Wait, was it defiant or deviant? One simple letter. I always get them confused when I think of you." His voice lowered in timbre but not in volume.

"Very funny."

"Defiant. I may just have to –"

"Would you two stop?" Amber interrupted in a loud voice. "It's embarrassing."

"We'll have to continue this in person," he said, back in his professional voice. "Don't forget you promised to stop and sleep."

"Three days to get to New Mexico, at least."

"That doesn't mean you should drive straight through to Amarillo and sleep there for three days, either," he warned me.

"I hadn't thought of that," I complained. "I promise to stop and sleep."

"At night. In a hotel room."

"You take the fun out of being bad."

"See? Back to stubborn and defiant."

In the background, I heard a final boarding call for some flight.

"I'll see you in a few days," I said. "Then we'll see who is stubborn and defiant."

"Or deviant," he suggested in a whisper. "I'll have a hotel room waiting."

We disconnected after the be-careful's and love-you's.

So many of our quirky little conversations were full of flirty innuendo and anticipation. We'd always done it, since the early days when he showed up to terrorize me, making the fear a part of our game.

Looking back, I hated that I'd wasted a lot of time hiding from wanting to feel love or be loved in the wake of what my now-dead husband had done to me.

Years later, I still felt the twitch in my arm that would trigger the muscles needed to tug my collar up over the scar across my neck.

I wondered, why can't I call David Wesley an ex-husband and be done without the explanation of him being dead? I heard few condolences for David's death, mostly from people who didn't comprehend that I had been the one to put those two bullets in his chest. I mean, he *had* cut my throat, so it was justified. The whole story seemed too sordid to explain to anyone, so I didn't bother with it anymore.

If people felt sorry for me being a widow, they weren't close enough to already know the truth or for me to waste time explaining it.

I also hadn't discussed details I'd suppressed about David's assault and Anthony Bock's inspirational contribution with anyone except Zach and the psychiatrist I'd eventually had to see several years ago. Most of it my mother didn't realize, and I was grateful.

Wouldn't ever, now.

My eyes blurred with tears I tried to blink away.

I had things to take care of regarding her death, which put me back at the beginning of my thought train, and I didn't want to deal with it while driving.

I mentally flipped through things to contemplate.

Brandan's vacuum-sealed body came next.

He hadn't mentioned it while we were in New York, so it was possible it was solved, but it was a tolerable mental diversion, nonetheless. The questions added up as the miles rolled by.

What happens to a human body when it's vacuum-packed? Whole, besides the entire logistics of having a machine big enough to do it, could also depend on how much vacuum is pulled. Does it matter? It should. What about cutting up the body. Would it decompose slower or at all? How soon after death would it have to be packed to prevent decomp? Although there are bacteria through the GI tract, could that be isolated until the last to prevent contamination? What about the bacteria on the skin? Could it be pre-treated with an antibacterial? What if you froze the body first?

I entertained myself with the self-conversation until it was time to stop again for fuel, which surprised me.

Zach tolerated my wandering attention and lost track of time a lot when I was working. I could bury my nose and be lost in a book for research or a computer searching records for hours.

He never seemed to mind it any more than Laser did after I adopted him. The dog had served with the Grand Traverse County Sheriff Department with Matthew until his death.

Not wanting to hear the next statement in my head, unfortunately, I couldn't prevent the voice defiantly pointing out that I had been the one to kill Matt.

Laser became my dog because the sheriff asked me. He did a little law enforcement work with me, but he became a beloved guard dog to me and then a best friend to Amber.

Amber. What would we do about Amber after this escapade?

She was old enough for college, old enough to make choices like flying across the country to see a young man.

Old enough to have sex with him.

I guessed that unless Zach found out that had happened, he'd moved past grounding her till she was thirty. Maybe just twenty.

I hope she didn't.

First, we had to get her on her feet and back to school. I wished I had an idea how long her recuperation might take.

Amber, however, thought she should be able to stand up once day and take off at a full gallop again the next. While I admired her youthful determination, I was more of an orthopedic realist after having broken my ankle and requiring surgery.

Getting old sucks. Rehab sucks.

Trying to slow her down, what would she want to do in the meantime, I wondered.

Would she try to find out why Ethan had left her alone in New York City?

Her father definitely wants an answer to that question.

What had Amber said, that Ethan insistently asked whether I knew anything else about his mother or her journals?

That idea niggled my brain, but I couldn't grasp it.

The detectives working on her brother's murder had invited Penny to Michigan. I remembered that she wanted to look in the attic of her childhood home for her mother's journals. We located them, and she had browsed them before she left Michigan, looking for more information about her aunt, which turned out to be a crazy disaster involving Anthony Bock.

Who, I found out, was my half-brother.

With so much windshield time ahead of me, Bock was not what I wanted to ponder.

Why not?

Nope. Not going there. Never again, given a choice.

I would be happier to devote all my mental capacity to counting highway stripes from here to New Mexico than that.

Though not nearly enough years had passed since Bock had died in Zach's hospital room in Florida to forget, pondering him shouldn't infuriate or nauseate me, but it did.

I'd consider the reasons why another time.

If I really must.

And I didn't question that I would.

CHAPTER 35
AMBER

September 23, 2001

"I hate flying," I told my dad as we finally got off the jet in Albuquerque. My body ached from being cramped and not being able to get up and walk due to the bumpy flight from Dallas.

When I said it, I figured he'd say something sarcastic or mean like, "You flew to New York and got us all into this mess."

He didn't.

"Me, too," he said, trying to rearrange our carryon bags over his shoulder.

"You can hang that one across my walker," I suggested, pointing. "I'm okay now with both arms." Oh, had I been happy the cast on my right arm had been removed and a wrist splint placed instead.

"I'll carry. You concentrate on walking without getting knocked over or tripping."

Except for the one time I'd gotten the back leg of the walker stuck between the jetway and fuselage of the jet the first time we boarded, I hadn't even stumbled.

Cushy first-class seats didn't hurt, so I could stretch out my leg. Dad probably thought so, too.

The difference in security between my flight to New York and this one leaving was so huge. Cops and police dogs and security people were everywhere in the airports, and suddenly no one could come behind the checkpoints like before, so Grandmom Vera didn't drive to the pickup lane and its stupid two-minute warnings until we'd collected our luggage and Dad had called her.

I was so glad to see her, but then I realized I'd never see Grandmom Dagmar again, and I couldn't help but cry.

If I hadn't been so stupid and let Ethan talk me into meeting him, I could have flown to Albuquerque to see her before she died.

Grandmom Vera let go of me and wiped my tears, seeming to read my mind. "No, dear, she was already gone as soon as she had the second stroke. Her body might not have died then, but she was gone."

"How did you know why I'm crying?" I asked her as she helped me into the back seat of her car.

"I was hoping you weren't crying because of me," she said with a wink and closed my door.

She let Zach drive to Grandmom Dagmar's house and helped Zach unload my bags.

Kim and Dr. Katz came outside to meet us.

I must have been staring at Kim's belly, which was huge.

"Five more weeks to go," she said, putting both hands on the bulge. "November 3, the doctor says. I can't wait till there isn't a basketball bouncing on my bladder, kicking me in the ribs."

We went inside, and I collapsed into a broad chair. "And I'm tired of having six legs."

Zach took my stuff down the hall to a bedroom, and I noticed Grandmom Vera went with him.

Gerald and Kim sat across from me and wanted to know all about seeing live in New York what they'd watched on television, so I was describing that when Dad and Grandmom came back.

He looked a little green, like being airsick had caught up with him, but eventually, he came and sat with us.

Maybe some of the stuff I'd remembered Dad hadn't heard, and he explained a little of what he and Detective Callaghan had gone through to find me because I'd lost my phone when my bag was stolen.

"I had help from someone who works for the cellular company, who gave us its location before it died, which narrowed Manhattan down to about eight city blocks."

"You *found* her phone?" Kim asked. "That's like finding a fish in the Great Lakes."

"No way!" I exclaimed, because this was news to me, too. "You mean if I'd had my phone with me, you could have found me?"

Dad made a half nod and shrug together. "Would certainly have improved our chances. Julie got Ethan's number from our bills."

"Wait, I'm confused," Kim interrupted Zach. "You found Amber's phone after it had been stolen because you tracked it, but you didn't look for Ethan's phone after you got the number?"

"Ethan didn't have his phone," Dad explained. "And what my friend's contact did is not something we could ask for a second time."

"I'd left my wallet in Ethan's jacket pocket the night before because it didn't fit in my dainty little purse when we went out to dinner, so I didn't have any money or identification or anything," I said, adding to the story, "but he left his phone at the hotel that morning."

"On purpose?" Kim asked. "Why would he do that?"

"I don't think he meant to."

"When was the last time you went anywhere without knowing you had your phone with you?" she replied. "What if it was intentional? Devil's advocate."

I shrugged, unable to know for sure. "You'd make a great detective," I said. "Those are super questions."

She blushed a little, then winced. "If you never heard from him after he left that morning, is he, I mean, was he was where the buildings collapsed?"

"Like, do I think he's dead?" I said, suddenly very aware of my growing animosity. "I hope so."

Anger stirred in my stomach, as I considered possibilities I hadn't examined closely in the last week or so.

Being kicked out of the hotel was embarrassing and frustrating. On the streets with nowhere to go, not knowing where to seek help without money or identification, I'd felt like a child lost from his parents on Halloween night, alone in a world of monsters and make-believe. But waking in the hospital without any memories of how I got there or what my name was had been terrifying.

To think that someone I'd liked, a lot, could be responsible for putting me in such a dire situation made me hate him.

CHAPTER 36
JULIE

September 23, 2001, 7 p.m.

Headlights streamed in the oncoming lanes and blinded me from behind occasionally though few vehicles dared to pass me. I was speeding, after all.

I watched for signs for hotels, feeling a weariness crackle in my joints. My eyes were dry, making each blink a risk that my lids wouldn't lift again. I yawned and opened my window for fresh air.

Before I reached an exit to find a hotel, my phone chirped.

"Hey, Babe," he said. "We made it safe to, um, Dagmar's."

I heard the hesitation. "It's always going to be her house to me," I said, hoping to relieve him of the struggle of what to call it. "How was your flight?"

"Dismal," he replied. "I'm thrilled to be on the ground and to know I'll get to drive back to Washington."

"Sorry. I'm looking for a hotel somewhere in Ohio," I said, yawning again.

"Good. I'm on my way out to the ranch."

"Why? Surely there's enough room in town?"

"Not exactly. Seems I have several things to tell you."

Oh, great. That never seems to end well.

"Sounds as though I need to devote more attention to it than possible when I'm driving," I said. "Let me check in somewhere, and I'll call you back."

Fortunately, hotels were available at the next exit, so I went through the routine of parking, checking in, and unloading a couple of small bags to carry to my room, juggling key card and luggage inside, then hurrying to the bathroom, then finally I collapsed onto the bed to catch my breath.

Five minutes. Close my eyes for five minutes.

Which, of course, led to me waking four hours later with a crick in my neck and a chill.

Too late to call Zach now, although he wouldn't complain if I did most nights. He had to be as tired as me.

I gave in to the urge to strip and crawl between the soft cool sheets on the other side of the bed. No checking my email, my phone messages or charging status, barely taking time to flip the light switch on the bedside lamp before sleep zapped me.

Without turning over, I must have melted into a dreamless lump right there, which is where I woke to the sound of someone beating on the door the next morning.

• • • • •

September 24, 2001, 12:35 p.m.
Not morning, it was past noon!

Intentions to hop out of bed to answer housekeeping through the door were altered by poorly responsive, stiff muscles and joints.

"I'm staying another night!" I yelled through the door. "I'll call the front desk." Which I did, and as much as I hadn't planned on it, I fell back into the mess of sheets and fluffy comforter without cratering into another sleep abyss, trying to start a slow waking process after hearing my stomach rumbling as loud as the housekeeper's knock.

I finally stretched and got up in a more suitably leisurely manner, digging through my tote for a candy bar or something to tide me over till I could find real food. However, my cell phone was dead, and the charger was in the truck.

Getting dressed and going out might as well include food, so I cleaned up a little and headed out in hopes of finding a breakfast-all-day place.

Four blocks, easy parking, quick seating, and fresh coffee.

I might have sounded a little unstable when I ordered a mega-meal that included three eggs over easy, double bacon, hash browns with onions, French toast, and a bowl of fruit. With the biggest glass of milk she had. And another refill on the coffee, please?

While I waited, I browsed a newspaper, still nearly cover to cover with fact and theory on 9/11. Keeping truth separated from fiction had become difficult, and media was not clarifying any of it.

I skipped the sports, classifieds, obits, and business sections of the Cincinnati paper, which left me with enough to be finished when the food was delivered.

I tried not to scarf it down, pondering what news Zach had wanted to tell me last night. And I also wondered if sleeping alone in a quiet place without early morning chores that had to be done might have prompted him to sleep late, too.

With that, my plates were empty.

I felt a little ashamed I hadn't enjoyed it.

You didn't even taste it, Julie.

After paying for the meal and returning to the hotel, I considered leaving anyway, but the whirlpool tub in the room looked inviting, so I turned on the hot water to fill it.

Sure, the hotel had an indoor swimming pool and hot tub, but ever since Jeremy McNeeley had identified the waterborne amoeba used to kill Penny and her daughter, I was one drop shy of being unable to use public facilities. I realized the absurdity of such a phobia since well-kept pools and spas should not have such nasty organisms, but plain running tap water might.

I turned off the water and picked up my phone to check the battery level after charging for an hour, but it was still too low to power on.

Great, I was in nearly the same situation Amber had been in, with a phone full of numbers I didn't remember, now useless.

Time to shop for a battery or a whole new phone.

I checked on the water in the tub, then opened drawers to find a telephone book to locate a store where I could replace my phone. Though finding an address then necessitated using a map, I found a retailer nearby and made a note of the address and directions.

After I turned off the whirlpool water again, checking its steaming temperature, I decided I needed to talk to Zach before I did anything else.

I dialed from the room phone.

One ring.

"Julie? Oh my God, I've been worried about you!" he said instead of a reasonable "hello."

"I'm sorry," I began, "I must have fallen asleep as soon as I sat down last night and scarcely moved again until noon. I was going to call but I realized I hadn't charged my phone, so I plugged it in and went to breakfast. An hour later, now, I've discovered it's plain dead."

"I've been trying to call, and your phone kept going straight to voice mail as Amber's had, and I was afraid something had happened to you." He inhaled and blew out hard. "I was trying not to panic, but. . . "

"I'm sorry, Zach. I didn't mean to upset you."

"I know. I'm just a little sensitive today."

I asked him to call me back at the hotel so I wouldn't run up an exorbitant and unnecessary long-distance bill, and he made me promise I'd answer, only half joking.

The phone on the desk, however, had a speaker function. Although I couldn't run the jets and hear the conversation, soaking and talking could be possible, so I undressed while I waited for his return call. The timing was perfect.

We exchanged apologies again, and the speaker worked great, so I slipped into the tub and sunk to my neck in the water.

"What was it you were going to tell me last night?" I asked.

"Oh, where does the list begin?" he asked in syrupy sarcasm.

"That bad? You said the flight was horrible."

"It was, and yet arrival has revealed other things that are so much worse. Like my mother. Apparently hosting Dr. Katz has become a pleasant and personal endeavor of hers."

"You mean they are . . . " I didn't finish my sentence before the laughter blurted out of my chest in fits I tried to disguise as coughing.

"Yes! That's exactly what I mean!" he explained. "My mother and your previous boss!"

His footsteps echoed on the hardwood floor as he paced, which told me he was at his mother's house at the ranch.

"Zach, Sweetie," I tried to say in a calm, supportive voice that cracked into laughter I couldn't cover anymore.

"It's not funny!"

Oh, but it is! And the fact that this is the most significant piece of bad news you have makes this even more hysterical.

"Are you drunk?" he demanded.

I was finally able to gain control of the raucous hilarity that had threatened to submerge me if I belly-rolled.

"No, I am perfectly sober, Zach," I replied, wiping a tear from my eye and attempting to be serious. "Why is it you believe Vera and Gerald shouldn't be interested in each other? They share a medical background. They've both lost a spouse."

"But she's my mother!" he exclaimed again, almost pushing me back into uncontrollable giggles.

"Zach, how long had we been sleeping together before we told either of our moms we'd been seeing each other?"

"That's different."

"How do you think you were conceived?" I asked, flustered but still very amused. "She was having sex long before and, I suspect, long after you and Zoe came along. Who knows if she was having sex with anyone after your father died."

"Don't say that."

"Doesn't she deserve to have a male companion after all these years?"

"Well, yeah, but . . . but . . ." he stammered and then chuckled. "I guess it's kinda dumb to think she wouldn't, um, you know. But Dr. Katz?"

"You just didn't want to know about it or who she was doing it with. I understand. Though a little surprising it's Gerald, he's a smart and kind man," I said. "Keep in mind that he could be your stepfather if this –"

"See? You had to go and say it, didn't you!"

"Hey, at least he's not a serial killer like Bock," I countered.

He sighed. "Fair enough." He paused a moment. "Where are you?"

"Still east of Columbus, Ohio."

"No, I mean it sounds hollow."

"Oh, it's the speakerphone," I said, hesitating, "so I can sit in the whirlpool while we talk. I'm not leaving today, but I'll go buy a new phone in a bit."

"Wow, you must be tired," he mused.

"Feeling much better after a ginormous breakfast," I said, "but this hot water is splendiferous."

"I see your vocabulary hasn't woken up yet."

"What else?" I asked, wishing for hotter water.

"On the flight back, Amber asked me to sketch a portrait of Ethan, to help find him in that mess, maybe, I don't know," he said, referring to the collapsed World Trade Center Towers. "We'd both seen him, so it wasn't hard to do. She noted that he'd let his hair grow out a little."

"You have, too," I noted.

"Irrelevant. When we got in yesterday, after Mom waylaid me with the news about Gerald, the girls were discussing how Amber ended up with Ethan's phone and without her wallet. Kim questioned her pretty hard on whether she thought he did that by accident or on purpose."

"Wow, that's deep." I shivered.

I really want more hot water, even if my skin is turning red.

"I told them how we'd located her phone but not his," he continued. "After Kim questioned his intention to take her ID and leave his phone, Amber began to wonder if he set her up. She's completely changed her mind about wanting to find him."

"Understandable, I suppose."

"It gets way worse. Amber showed the drawing I did of Ethan to Kim. The guy we know as Ethan Wenzler is also Kim's baby's father, Sean Smith. Which is the name of the person who paid for the hotel room in New York, right? I'll see if Nolan found anything on him. An age range could help narrow down the search."

"This keeps getting more convoluted each time I hear his name."

"I faxed a copy of the drawing to Nolan, but Amber was pissed."

I hesitated, trying to clear my head. "Do you have any good news, Zach?"

"No, but that was everything. But with the happy couple in one bedroom and the respective daughter and granddaughter each in the other bedrooms, I chose not to sleep on the sofa-bed."

"Eww, yeah, I've had a night or two on it and do not recommend it if you want to be able to walk the next day."

"Changing subjects slightly, is there anything Mom or I can do to help arrange a memorial for Dagmar while you're on the road?" he asked.

"Ah crap!" I said, splashing. "All my contacts were on my phone, so I don't have them."

"On your laptop?"

"Umm," I said, trying to remember if I'd kept last year's Christmas labels. "Yeah, that might work."

"Why don't you email me the contacts you do have, and I'll start making calls to people," he suggested. "The girls want to help. I'll buy Amber another phone today."

"I don't remember the priest's name at Mom's church, but surely he's already heard. She would want it to be there."

"Mom already called and talked to him, and it's fine any day we want to plan it, he said. What sort of service do you want? A regular funeral or an informal memorial and reception?"

"I want a brief service where he speaks a little about her, then a simple gathering with snacks, if that's okay."

"Will do."

"Everyone doing okay?"

"They were when I left last night. I've been waiting for you to call before I went to town."

"I'm really sorry. On second thought, I don't want to spend another night here though," I said, feeling guilty enough wasting time. I decided to check out, buy a replacement phone, and hopefully make St. Louis or further today.

"I'm glad you got some rest."

"Did you?"

"Not really," he said. "I was awake for a long time, flipping channels on the TV. How can we have eight hundred channels and still not have anything worthwhile to watch?"

"Eight, eight thousand. You're too smart for most of them."

"I don't like stupid, either. That eliminated 796 of them."

"That's probably why we have four horses."

"Five."

"Oh, dang it, I keep forgetting. Filly, you said, right?" I rubbed my cheeks, feeling the water start to cool, at least in my imagination. "I'll work on a name. Is she a registered, um, dang it, you know, the breed?"

"A Friesian," he provided. "Of course she's registered."

"As if Friesian studs are bred all over Washington."

"Several are, actually, but we only needed one." He must have stretched his back – I heard a pop. "I should get going. I'll let you soak in peace. We can talk again later."

We said our long-distance goodbyes, and I hoped the desk phone would disconnect after he did, so I wouldn't have to get out of the water.

After draining and refilling the tub with a few more inches of hot water, I felt much like a boiling noodle, the tight muscles finally began to relax. I had one more bout of giggles about Vera and Gerald and Zach's reaction to their relationship.

I wouldn't have thought they would make a couple, but as I told Zach, they did have things in common.

Having not met Zach's dad, it was difficult to understand what had freaked him out about Gerald, although I suspected it was the typical belief that your parent or parents didn't have a personal and private life after we learn about sex ourselves.

I didn't ask and never wanted to know details of my mother's relationship with the man Anthony Bock pretended to be with her. He killed so many people for little more than genetics and jealousy, blaming his behavior on a background that eradicated his ability to separate right and wrong.

I'm glad he's dead, too.

Heart pounding in my chest. Pulse increasing higher than the heated water had caused.

Years ago, I liked that feeling – the tingly muscles and racing heart, a sprinter at the blocks, waiting on the gun.

Deep breath.

Another.

I hadn't felt the adrenaline-spiked jazzed-up sensation since before Zach and I got married.

I don't, like it.

Yes, you do, Julie. You just don't like that you like it.

When did my inner voices begin to include my mother?

Not your mother, dear.

Climbing out of the tub, I grabbed a towel, thinking of anything except the white elephants peeking out of the closet.

Yes, hitting the road would be acceptable, because here I was unlikely to reflect on anything except Bock and other dead people.

I dressed and stuffed my dirty clothes into the bag, made sure I had my chargers and toiletries, and hurried out the door in hopes of trapping the elephants behind me for a while.

CHAPTER 37
JULIE

September 24, 2001, 5:40 p.m.

Once I'd obtained a new phone and chargers, because God knows they can't redevelop a new device using a previous cord system, I pointed the front bumper westward.

City traffic past and cruise control set, I dialed Zach to update my travel plans. He didn't answer, so I left a message.

Radio was boring, and I didn't want to dig for something new to play.

Back to thoughts.

The previous night was the first time in a long time that I had dreamed of David. It wasn't memory as I sometimes still had, but fictional dreams of being back in a restless marriage smothered by the knowledge I didn't want to stay, but I had no way to escape. He had crowded into my profession as a paramedic, making my life more desperate. Calling the cops didn't work. Seeking the help of others did nothing to extricate me from what I knew was coming eventually. When we fought, I bit him, but I couldn't make it hurt – my teeth just wouldn't break the skin. As the dream went along, I recruited Zach to help me drown David and get rid of the body.

I hadn't yet met the grown-up Zach when I was married to David.

Next subject.

I scanned through a dozen radio stations with the continued bits of news and commentary, occasional music.

Mostly cloudy all afternoon, it was almost six o'clock when I pulled into a roadside park on the west side of Indianapolis, having driven through rush-hour traffic. I took a brief walk, then decided to take a break and set up the new phone since it reached full charge. Thankfully I was able to keep the same number. After a few minutes, though, I gave up and tossed it into the passenger seat, bored with the necessary work it would take.

Not having to drive into the late day sun, I pulled onto the freeway again, listening to nothing more than the noises of the wind and pavement for another hour.

Reaching for my phone to call Zach, I realized the ring tone was different when it chirped in my hand. None of my contacts were identified, but I recognized Zach's number, and I pushed the green button to answer.

• • • • •

September 24, 2001, 5:14 p.m. Central Daylight Time

"It's Kim," he said, his voice hoarse. "Mom brought her and Amber and Gerald out to the ranch this afternoon before I left, just to get out of the city for a few hours. Amber wanted to show her the rest of the horses even though Kim had seen Kalimar." He had to pause. "They'd been down at the barn and were coming along the east fence toward the house. Purgatory came trotting toward them, so they stopped at the fence to offer him a carrot, too." He paused again, blowing out a breath hard. "Purgatory went nuts, charged the fence and swung and kicked them both before I could get out to them."

"Oh my God," I gasped. *No no no.* "Are they okay?"

"Amber got knocked off her feet, but he kicked Kim straight in the belly."

"Are they okay?" I repeated.

His voice broke, the sort of hitch that happened just before he broke down and cried.

"I drove as fast as I could, and an ambulance met us at the edge of town to take Kim," he said. "Mom and Gerald went with her. I drove in with Amber to get her checked out."

I didn't know what to say, afraid to make any guesses.

"Amber's all right. Landed on her bottom, she said, but it must have jolted her hard. She wanted to get x-rays."

"Zach. . ."

He did not reply.

My heart trilled a second in my chest, followed by an ache. I didn't want to hear the words when he couldn't speak them.

"Kim? The baby?" I asked, though my voice almost too weak to make out.

"No."

His silence made me pull over at the next exit and park on the shoulder of the road.

"Do I need to . . . I don't know. What should I do?" I asked more to myself than to him.

"It's my fault," he whispered. "I shouldn't have let them go out there to see the horses alone. Amber didn't know about Purgatory being bat-shit crazy."

"No, Zach, it's not your fault. You couldn't have known something like that would happen," I replied.

"But I should have!" His voice had changed to a harsh, throat-ripping sound. "Purgatory hates strangers. He's. . . he . . . well, he won't be a threat to anyone ever again."

Zach swallowed hard, and I knew he meant he'd put the horse down.

He believed it was the right thing to do to euthanize an animal that had intentionally hurt someone and could no longer be trusted. Purgatory had a traumatic history that made him unable to tolerate trailering, but I didn't know he didn't like strangers.

I'd only ever seen him from across a pasture.

No way could I make it to New Mexico in time to help.

Who are you fooling, Julie? You can't help.

My eyes spilled tears.

"You could drive on to Traverse City," he told me after regaining a bit of emotional control. "Meet Gerald there for the funeral, I guess. He hasn't set up anything yet."

"What about Mom's service?" I asked, wiping my eyes with my hands.

How selfish. But the services for her were as much for me as anyone else, weren't they?

"Where are you now?"

"West of Indy, maybe an hour or so."

"You can go back to the airport, fly here for Dagmar's service, then we'll fly you to Michigan for Kim's," he suggested, although it sounded like it took all his energy to put together such an idea.

I'd agreed with Zach's descriptions of flying long before the recent changes. Security made it miserable now, from what I'd seen, so flying was not something I wanted to do.

Whose funeral services do I go to? Gerald would understand, I'm sure, but it was my fault Kim was in New Mexico in the first place. On the other hand, I was entitled to go to my own mother's services.

"I don't know what I should do, Zach. I want to . . . "

I wanted to just scream and scream. I wanted to go home and sleep in my own bed beside my husband for the first time since July.

"Let me talk to Mom and see what we can do. I know Gerald wanted to attend Dagmar's service. Maybe she can ask him to delay services for Kim a day or so."

"That's not fair to him or Kayleigh," I said, wiping my nose. "I want to be there, but I need to have Mom's, too."

"None of this is fair to anybody, and you have to do what is right for you."

"And you?"

"I'm screwed up about all of this, Julie. Messed up. But I'll be beside you, wherever you are."

"Let me know what you find out. I'll keep driving. If we decide I should fly, I'll stop in St. Louis. If not, Traverse City is roughly ten driving hours from there."

We hung up after more comforting words were exchanged.

Who was comforting whom?

I meant them, but I had an empty feeling, not so much short-circuited but hollow, as if my chest had been scooped out like a Halloween pumpkin.

Not needing fuel but in dire need of a bathroom break, I put the truck back into drive and continued along the exit toward the cross-street. Going either direction from there would lead to gas stations and restaurants. In the rearview mirror, a car with flashing lights approached.

Oh, for crying out loud, not now.

I was stopped at the intersection. Hoping he'd go around didn't happen, of course. However, stopping where I was would block the turn lane on the exit, so I put on my flashers and made the right turn and proceeded to a safer place to stop.

When the officer or trooper or deputy, whatever he was, walked up to my truck, I noted he approached cautiously, one hand resting on his holster, trying to appear casual.

Out of state plates, probably.

I'd already rolled down my window, turned on the cabin lights, and put my hands at 10 and 2 on the steering wheel in plain view.

"Good evening, Ma'am. We received a call for a vehicle stopped on the side of the exit. Was that you?"

"Yes, sir."

"Is everything okay?"

"Yes, I was talking to my husband about a young girl I'd be taking care of."

Putnam County Deputy, F. Hughes, I noted, bent further to look into the truck, head tilted in confusion.

Maybe he thinks you're transporting drugs and sampling the load.

"Oh, if I only knew where to start that story to make it believable," I mumbled, "and you had an hour to waste."

"Try me," he challenged.

"I'm on my way back from New York City. My stepdaughter was there on 9/11, then her friend disappeared with her wallet and license and she was kicked out of the hotel. Then she was hit by a car and in a hospital with a head injury, so she couldn't call us. We had to drive to pick her up due to the grounding of all flights. Since July, I'd been in Albuquerque with my mother, who had a stroke, then she had another on 9/11 and died the next day. . ." I looked out at him, realizing how unbelievable I must have sounded, but he motioned for me to continue. "Her dad flew back with her to Albuquerque, but then my ex-boss's daughter, who was pregnant and staying there with me and my mother in New Mexico was kicked by a horse and killed this afternoon."

Fresh young clean-shaven face, bright eyes, totally disbelieving or just trying to make sense of what he'd been told, though I wasn't sure I could repeat it or clarify it.

Hell, I'm not sure I even comprehend it.

"It doesn't matter. I was upset, so I pulled over."

"Yes, ma'am, that's understandable and appreciated. Just making sure you didn't need any help."

The last law enforcement officer to check on me on the side of the road probably still has nightmares.

"Do you need to see my credentials?" I asked. "I'm a Washington State deputy, and I do have my firearm. They're both in my console."

His young face lost its freshness in a lopsided frown.

Indiana isn't the most gun-friendly state.

"Left hand, promise," I tried to reassure him, waiting for his approval to reach. He finally nodded.

Awkward as it was, I twisted far enough to open the console and flip it open, then groped around for my wallet and badge.

When nothing I touched was what I wanted, panic rose in my throat.

What if . . .

I blinked and remembered I'd put my wallet, badge, and gun into my tote, which I'd carried to my room last night then back out when I left today.

"Um, as embarrassing as this is, I believe everything you want to see is in the bag on the other seat."

I hope it's in the bag on the other seat!

"I see," he said, now smiling. "No one could make up what you just told me. If you can tell me the name of the owner of this vehicle, I'll let you go on your way, if you promise to slow down a little. You know," he winked, "in case you've been driving over the speed limit."

"Julie Ann Madigan," I said, almost slapping my hand over my mouth for the mistake. "Samualson, I mean."

Geez, I've only been married for five years!

"Good enough," he said. "Be careful, Ma'am."

He tipped his hat and retreated to his patrol car, leaving me alone with the ghosts of Anthony Bock and his victims, a list that had continued growing. Despite his death, I held him responsible for Kim's death, too, since it was Ethan who had involved her. If not for him, she'd be alive.

Probably.

I checked my mirror in time to see the deputy pull around me onto the street before I screamed and pounded on the steering wheel.

Then, I had to look and make sure my creds and gun were safely in my bag, where they belonged.

CHAPTER 38
AMBER

September 24, 2001

The ER was busy, so I had to wait to be seen. Fear had finally subsided, and I'd stopped shaking. Dad sat in the chair beside the gurney, holding my hand. He hadn't wanted to let go when the x-ray person came to take me.

The tech, Andrew, chatted on the way through the halls to Radiology, asking what had happened, and I explained how I'd been knocked down by a horse and how I was worried about my new femur hardware.

"Thanks for the heads up. If Leslie didn't know, it would nuke out the first film."

"Nuke out?" I asked, wondering what the heck he meant.

"The metals white out the image," he said, making an air explosion gesture, laughing.

He would have been very handsome except for a lot of acne scarring on his face.

Once in the radiology department, he was all business, helping the actual radiology tech to position me on the cold hard table and in various positions. After several "hold your breath's" and "now breathe's" from a woman behind a wall I presumed was Leslie, Andrew helped me up and into the wheelchair, rolling me back toward the ED.

"How'd you break your femur," he asked.

"Hit by a car in Manhattan, I'm told. I don't remember it."

"Kansas?" he asked, astonished.

I turned slightly to look at him. "No, New York. Is there one in Kansas?"

"Yeah. Awful about the Towers, huh?"

"I watched it happen out my hotel window!"

"No way!"

I nodded.

He whirled me around a corner and into the ED. "But I'm confused then. Why are you here now?"

Why?

"Because I let a crazy horse kill my new best friend," I said, feeling hot tears on my cheeks when we rolled into the cubicle where Dad sat.

Andrew helped me onto the gurney, said goodbye and left.

"I'm okay, Daddy," I said when he stood up, reaching to pull him close for a hug that I'm not sure which of us needed more.

"I know, Sweetie, but I'm not."

He'd told me Kim had died.

I wanted to cry. Though I was felt like crying, was supposed to cry, I only felt numb.

And we hugged each other and let the tears fall for a long time.

"I heard what you said to the tech, Amber," he finally said, helping me get settled onto the gurney again, pulling his chair closer. "I didn't think Purgatory would be so aggressive. What happened to Kim was not your fault, it's mine."

"No, it's mine. I never should have –"

"I beg to differ with you both," Dr. Katz said from the doorway. He looked, I don't know, like some of his air had leaked out. "All of you and Julie," he said, putting his arm around Grandmom Vera's shoulders, "had done so much for Kim to see that she believed she was worthy of being loved again. She told me how much it meant to her, and I believed her. I'm sad, of course, but I know she was happier with herself than she'd been in several years. And because of that, I was able to spend time with her I wouldn't have had."

The doctor came in and explained that there was no damage to the hardware in my leg, although my back and butt might be sore. Dad signed the discharge papers when the nurse finally brought them, and we went back to Grandmom Dagmar's house.

Dr. Katz offered to go back to the ranch with Grandmom Vera and let Dad and me stay in the house.

"No, I already have my stuff there, and it will take less to move Amber's than yours," Dad countered. "If that's okay."

That seemed acceptable to everyone except me, but I figured Dad had a logical reason why his recommendation would be better, so we got my bag and took Grandmom Vera's truck.

"Are you hungry?" he asked after we left the house. "I didn't find a lot of stuff at Mom's house that doesn't require cooking, and I just don't feel up to it. Let's grab something to take home."

I made a couple of recommendations. We agreed on the easy choice and got burgers, then went back to the ranch.

I was beginning to feel achy, so Dad had to help me up the stairs of the porch. I couldn't have made it by myself with my cane, which was still out by the fence near the barn, but it was too dark to look for it.

After we ate, I melted into the sofa and pulled a pillow to my chest to elevate my arm, the one I'd broken in New York.

"I'm sorry, Dad," I said. "None of this would have happened if I hadn't been so stupid and believed Ethan. Or whatever his name is."

"The hardest part of the lesson is that seldom does a choice to say or do something not affect someone else."

"What if we could find Ethan?" I said. "Not that I want to forgive him or whatever, but what if we did?"

"I don't know that he's committed any real crime unless he uses your credit card. Nolan did some background checking on him, and he isn't a student at MSU like he said, at least not with the names he's used."

"Why would he lie to me about his name?" I was as angry as I was disappointed. "What a bastard."

"Freebie," he said, hoping to cheer me up. "But far nicer than the names I've called him in the past week or so."

"Can we find the journals he kept asking for?"

"What do you mean?"

"Ethan or whatever his name is must think there's something in them he wants bad enough to go to so much trouble," I explained, "but he hasn't found them yet. Maybe if we get them, we can figure this out."

CHAPTER 39
JULIE

September 24, 2001

I almost hugged my bag, grateful to find my stuff.

I've stuck my hand into a drawer and come up without the weapon I expected once before. A missing gun is nauseating. Knowing Amber had lost most of her belongings and then had to survive in New York City still made me a bit queasy.

Before walking out of the house, I'd been in the habit of checking I had my sunglasses, keys, driver's license and wallet, cell phone, and firearm. Sometimes body armor. The last few months of living in Albuquerque upset every routine I had. Then the circumstances involving Amber, my mom, and now Kim . . .

I'm lucky to have found the right vehicle in the parking lot today when I left the hotel.

I glanced at my phone, but I couldn't take any more depressing news.

With a quarter tank, I could drive a hundred miles plus another twenty reserve or so before my next fill-up. It was already dark, but there were no hotels at this exit, and I considered going a little further. Even if the truck didn't need gas, I had liquid exchanges to be made and could use a drink.

Because no other cars were around, I parked by the pump and went inside, taking my tote with intentions of going to the restroom first, getting a handful of snacks and drinks, then getting gas, and getting back on the road.

I washed and dried my face after relieving myself, took a minute to dig in my bag for a tube of lotion for my face and hands, which had begun to itch after the hot water whirlpool earlier.

Better.

Hefting the bag strap over my left shoulder, I walked out of the zig-zag entrance of the restrooms into the main store. I'd turned left toward the coolers and grabbed a bottle of apple juice, when I heard a low gravelly voice, near the counter.

"Empty the register."

I pretended I didn't hear it, hoping it had been a joke or a hallucination on my part.

The next two sounds shattered any hope I had of the situation being benign. "NOW!" the voice yelled, followed by a gunshot.

CHAPTER 40
AMBER

September 24, 2001

"I thought Julie would have called by now," I thought out loud as I finished cleaning the kitchen table. "How late was she going to drive?"

"She was late leaving where she stayed last night, and she had to buy a new phone today," Dad replied. "She's heard a lot of bad news over the phone the last few weeks. I'm sure she's enjoying the quiet. I certainly would be."

"Why did you want to come back to the ranch tonight?"

"I know you feel horrible, too, but I couldn't stand the thought of Gerald coming back to where his daughter was killed."

He sank into an overstuffed leather recliner in the den.

"Yeah, but she didn't die here," I countered.

"Not technically, but there's that connection," he said, thumbing his temple. "I need to bury the horse, too."

"Why did you shoot him?"

Everything had happened so fast, at least to me. The other horses had come to us in the corral, on the north side of the barn, so when we were walking toward the house, past where the steel fence changed to barbed wire, here came Purgatory for carrots, too, I thought. He'd never come up to anyone before that I remembered.

Dad didn't speak.

"When he got to the fence, he just reared and became a blur of hooves and crazy like the cartoon of the Tasmanian Devil. I ended up on my back, but Kim was several feet farther away, curled up and screaming."

"We were sitting on the porch when I heard her," he finally said. "He'd almost kicked his way through the barbed wire, but he was cut up, tangled in one strand, panicked. I'd never have been able to get close enough to help you or him, and he wouldn't have stopped if he'd gotten loose." Dad paused. "You and Kim were already down. I didn't have a choice."

Purgatory had still been rearing and kicking like a rodeo bronc when I heard the gunshots that dropped him onto the ground where he'd been kicking up a cloud of dirt.

"I'm sorry you had to shoot him."

"None of this was your fault." He rubbed his temples.

"This is *all* my fault, Dad! From you and Julie having to come find me to this today. None of it would have happened if I hadn't been such an idiot to meet him in New York! I liked Ethan. I trusted him."

"I trusted Purgatory, but the right set of circumstances showed me that sometimes trust needs to be earned and maintained."

I bit my lip. "I didn't have sex with him."

Dad opened his arms, and I sat on his lap in a big, comforting hug. "I'm glad. That kind of trust should be for someone you know deserves your love."

"Even if you're not married? I mean, what about you and Julie?"

He mirrored my surprised expression that I'd just asked him such a personal question, then nodded his head.

"I won't lie to you, Amber. Julie and I had sex before we were married. It was great before, but getting married has made our whole relationship stronger."

"You guys don't act like other couples, you know."

"I suspect we aren't. In a hundred ways," he said, laughing. "And we are perfectly happy that way."

"Why? I don't get it."

"For the record, you don't have to get it, so long as we do," he said. "You'd have to know a lot more about Julie to understand what she was like when we first started seeing each other. She had nearly been killed by her husband and —"

"She was married before?" I was astonished.

"Yes, he'd thrown her down a flight of stairs after cutting her throat. She almost didn't survive. She shot and killed him, probably just before he was going to finish killing her."

Oh my God!

"So, when we first met, as adults, she didn't want to have anything to do with love."

"Me either, right now," I muttered. "How'd you change her mind?"

"My good looks, fantastic charm, and unyielding persistence."

I punched his arm. "Really!"

"Mostly persistence, really." He pushed to get me off his lap. "You're squashing me."

I made a *Pfffffth* sound and helped him to his feet.

"Let's go call her."

CHAPTER 41
JULIE

September 24, 2001

Ah shit!

I touched my sweatshirt pocket for my phone, realizing I'd left it in the cupholder in the truck.

After a second gunshot and the sound of breaking glass, I decided that having my phone wouldn't be the answer anyway.

Sliding my hand into the tote bag, I wrapped my hand around my pistol in its Kydex holster, thumbed it free and clicked off the safety, trying to decide whether to drop the plastic bottle of orange juice or use it for diversion.

More yelling.

Decision.

Tote hanging from my left arm, orange juice in my left hand, and head down and poking through the bag, pretending to look for my wallet, I turned and walked toward the man facing the clerk at the counter.

In my peripheral vision, I saw the clerk, one hand in the air, pulling currency out of the register.

I was amazed at how easy it was to move so close to him. I dropped the bottle and tote, deployed my weapon, pointing it to the base of the guy's skull, right above where I'd grabbed a handful of shirt collar.

"Drop it, police," I said.

In retrospect, it was much too easy.

Gunshots rang out in quick succession.

Three, maybe four.

One shot.

I fired.

Another shot.

Son of a bitch, my chest hurts!

The shooter in front of me stumbled backward, pulling the trigger just before or maybe as an involuntary response to being hit. I didn't see her get hit, but the clerk fell, too. Under the counter, I could see her on the floor.

Only one person was still standing. One who hadn't been hit in the shooting.

I had dropped my gun, didn't know where to look.

Too afraid to move my hands off my right side. Not sure I could move my right arm.

The person standing, with a Halloween-like ghost mask and a knit cap covering facial features not hidden behind mirrored sunglasses, stood over me.

Leaned over and picked up my gun and my tote, both to my left side above my head, then walked away.

Getting harder to breathe.

I couldn't have imagined anything hurting so badly. My chest burned like fire. I tasted blood, choking on it when I exhaled.

But in that hazy, fiery pain, I wasn't sure if the suspect who had calmly taken my bag and gun hadn't stopped at the door and given me a little wave on his way out.

CHAPTER 42
AMBER

September 24, 2001

"That's weird." Dad pushed a button and dialed again, but Julie didn't answer. "Maybe she's getting gas or something."

This time he waited to leave a voice mail, but the message said it hadn't been set up.

"She got a new phone today."

We chatted a while, and he went downstairs to take a shower, I thought.

I picked a book from Grandmom Vera's chair table. I'd never heard of the author, who was from New Mexico. The book was huge, even in paperback, but it did sound interesting.

Dad wasn't back when his phone rang, so I answered it, figuring it was Julie.

"Hey there!" I said.

A man's voice responded instead of my stepmother. "I'm trying to reach someone who knows Julie Samualson."

"Who is this?" I demanded.

"Ma'am, I'm Deputy Frank Hughes of Putnam County, Indiana. This is the number she gave us when we found Ms. Samualson."

"She's married to my father, Zach Samualson. What do you mean you found her?" I was on my feet, searching through the house for Dad. "Is she okay?"

"Is your father available?"

"Yes! Jesus, I'm looking for him! Give me a minute!" I lowered the phone and yelled.

He stuck his head in from the back porch.

I held the phone out to him, and he took it. I could only make out a few words, but Dad's face got paler as he made sounds of agreement and distress. He finally stopped pacing and kinda melted into a chair before disconnecting.

"What?" I whined, though it bordered on yelling. "What else has happened!"

"Julie was trying to stop an armed robbery in the gas station where she stopped, but she was shot."

Criminy sheep-shit!

"Was?" I said, but my voice squeaked. "Please tell me she's all right, Dad. Please?"

"She's in surgery, but the deputy says she is okay, Sweetie. The bullet hit her in the chest on the right. Punctured a lung." He blinked hard a few times. "The clerk only had a minor wound. Julie shot and killed the first suspect."

"If he's *dead*, he's not a *suspect*!" I stated.

He only nodded. "The other one took her gun, her purse, and her truck. Police found the truck twenty miles away, wrecked, burned."

"Go!" I said. "You've got to go. Grab your bag. I'll call Grandmom to meet us at the airport."

He sat, staring ahead for a few seconds, then nodded again and stood.

I started back for my stuff when he reached for my arm and pulled me into another hug.

CHAPTER 43
JULIE

September 24, 2001

Stay awake.

Stay alive.

I lay on the cold floor, two difficult breaths away from puking, lightheaded, sweaty, or dead.

Not a good sign, Julie.

Another ambulance.

Another emergency department.

More pain.

Lots of activity in the ED. A physician who looked too young for Amber to date. A military-sharp nurse who barked succinct orders around and sometimes over the doctor.

Another doctor, this one a woman.

Harder to breathe. Woozy.

Cold stuff on my chest.

Ouch! Son of a bitch, that hurt!

Chest tube.

Ooh, way easier to breathe.

A dozen questions about my medical history and the scars.

A few questions about the shooting.

I signed my own consent and was finally given something for pain. Off to surgery for wound cleanout and whatever else was necessary.

I suspected I'd be the one with the questions when I woke up.

• • • • •

September 25, 2001

Midnight, give or take, I thought. The noise outside the cubicle was low, lights were dimmed.

Everything was quiet.

Damn it! Not the Q-word, cursed by all who worked in medicine and law enforcement alike.

One never says "quiet," "I'm bored," "I have plans," or "Can I leave early?"

I hoped the gods of chaos didn't hear me.

Maybe being a patient wouldn't count.

Really? How much worse could things get?

Hospital room. Probably intensive care. Again. I could see the reflection of the monitor in the mirror over a sink. IVs in both arms. Oxygen in an irritating rubber-smelling nasal cannula. A lot of pain in my right ribs.

Taking inventory of pains and tubes had gotten old many hospitalizations ago.

I closed my eyes and went back to sleep.

Voices.

My brain woke me when I heard voices outside the cubicle.

A familiar voice.

"The deputy said he'd be here in half an hour," a female said. "Let me see if she's awake."

The cubicle door eased open, and a dark-headed woman in navy scrubs came inside the room.

"I'm Dr. Allison. I took you to surgery last night, but you probably don't remember," she told me, doing a thorough assessment of my lung and heart sounds, bowel sounds, and checked the drainage system for the chest tube. "I hope you got a little rest. We removed a nasty hollow-point bullet from your right lung last night, but there was one fragment I couldn't reach without cracking your chest wide open. Everything was stable where it was, so hopefully, no one has to retrieve it later."

"That explains the chest tube," I said, hoarse and dry, realizing the severity of my condition the night before. "Hurts like hell."

"I bet it does. Maybe this will help." She opened the door and motioned to someone, "You can come in now."

And there stood my forever hero.

• • • • •

Zach sat in the uncomfortable-looking chair next to the bed, holding my hand. Although neither of us knew much, we shared tidbits of information the robbery and shooting, waiting on the deputy to come fill in the details.

"I told you last time we did this that I didn't ever want to see you in an ICU bed again," Zach said, "then I realized one of the alternatives to that wish was not ever seeing you again."

"I didn't mean for any of this to happen," I replied. "When I heard the first gunshot, I just reacted."

"I never thought about having to bring your armored vest with me to New York, either. You're getting to be more than high maintenance."

"How'd you get here so fast?" I hadn't given any thought to how Zach had gotten to – "Wait, where is here?"

"Terre Haute Regional Hospital."

"Wow, I didn't think I'd driven that far."

"You hadn't, but the ambulance brought you."

"Back to my question then, how'd you get here? I mean, how did you know where here was?"

"You had given someone my phone number."

I squeezed his hand.

He went on to explain commercial airline flights would have required at least two connections and hours of sitting in an airport overnight, so he chartered a jet in Albuquerque.

"Have to confess, it's sure nice having the entire plane and a tall blonde flight attendant all to myself," he said with a smile. "The legroom alone was worth the cost."

"Which I don't want to know," I said. "It's worth it that you're with me now."

Here. Déjà vu.

Our discussion was interrupted by a uniformed deputy, Neal Orlando from Putnam County where the robbery took place, and another in a suit, Detective Cade Martin, assisting from Vigo County. Introductions and handshakes all around were made, but they declined a seat.

"Before we provide any details, I'd like to review your statement," the second man said. "Some of what we have is a bit convoluted, even after we got the report from Deputy Hughes, first on the scene."

I tried to explain everything that had happened from the time I exited the freeway and was stopped by the deputy just before.

"I parked at pump four and went straight to the restroom and had been there five or six minutes, washing up a little. I came out and went to the coolers along the wall to the left. I'd opened the door and grabbed a bottle of juice when I heard the first gunshot."

The next sixty seconds seemed to have been a flow chart in my head of yes-and-no decisions that led me up behind the man pointing a gun at the clerk at the counter.

"Honestly, I'm not sure if I heard another gunshot before I reached the suspect at the counter, but I don't know who fired in what order next," I said. "There were four, maybe five shots in all. One shot, then I'm sure I fired the second, then the third, possibly a fourth."

From what the clerk told them, she hadn't been sure if I had been hit before or after a shot had struck her. She had only been grazed on the upper arm.

"The clerk states that after you and the first suspect both fell, she saw the second suspect walk over and pick up your gun and your bag. Surveillance confirms her statement and shows the suspect walking to the door, looking back and sort of waving, getting keys out of your bag. Outside angle shows him getting into and driving your vehicle away."

"He didn't take the money?"

The two men looked at each other.

"It was an armed robbery, right? The clerk had opened the register and was putting cash on the counter when I approached," I pressed.

Martin nodded, letting me make my own conclusion.

"But the second robber didn't take the money," I said, "only my stuff."

"The clerk indicated the money was *stolen*, but she didn't tell the deputy the suspect took it, so that's another matter. However, she was extremely specific when she described the suspect taking your gun and bag."

"I remember seeing that, too. I couldn't reach my weapon – couldn't use my right arm."

"You didn't see the money get taken?" Zach asked me.

"No, but I was kinda busy bleeding on the floor," I replied with a sneer to him, then turned back to the deputies. "The man I shot fell backward and knocked me over, but I'd already been hit. I can see why the suspect might take my gun or my truck, but if he didn't take the money, why not? Did he take the dead suspect's gun?"

"No, still near his hand."

My gun was gone as was the bag I'd been carrying inside the store, which included my wallet, credit cards, cash, keys.

So was my truck, along with my new phone, clothes and stuff.

My credentials – badge and county sheriff's identification.

All gone.

"No clues for either question," one said.

The other added, "There was a vehicle in the parking lot with prints matching the dead suspect, but not any we've found for the second person. We presume they came together, but it's hard to prove."

"I'm guessing you've already found my truck," I said, feeling a sinking sensation in my stomach.

"Looks like they rammed it into a wall then set it on fire. No sign of a gun in the vehicle either. Sorry."

"Any sign of a car waiting nearby?" Zach asked.

Martin shook his head. "Asphalt behind an abandoned warehouse. No notable tracks, no footprints."

"You realize that, besides my wallet and gun, the robber now has my badge along with my creds, right?" I said feeling the sensation in my gut like an anchor falling to a slimy silty lake bottom.

"I fully understand the extraordinary ramifications, Ma'am," Orlando said. "We're running surveillance video from the store and traffic cameras to see if we can make out an identity, but I doubt there's a fair chance."

"How long to find out who the dead guy is?" I asked.

"Nothin' on fingerprints, so could be a week or more for DNA processing, then longer to find a match probably."

"What do you need from me?"

"For now, nothing. We'll get comparisons for the bullets. At least there's one gun left at the scene, and since you didn't shoot yourself, we'll figure it out."

"Really?" Zach asked. "It doesn't make sense that a partner would take one gun but not another used in the crime."

I opened my mouth to ask another question when my chest seemed to freeze, pain ripping through so fast I couldn't inhale.

Like a goldfish out of water.

Zach swallowed hard and reached to hit the blue button on the wall over the head of the bed, then pointed to the door to the deputies as nurses rushed in, almost knocking the men over. Zach took his place in a corner.

I didn't comprehend what was happening. Several medical complications crossed my mind, but I couldn't have named them. An oxygen mask put on my face didn't help because I couldn't inhale enough.

Alarms went off, one by one. Pulse oximetry, meaning my blood wasn't getting oxygen. Heart rate increasing. Anxiety racing.

Dr. Allison came rushing in, snapping orders.

She bared my right upper chest and felt around before making an indention with her fingernail. Then she swiped an iodine swab across under my collarbone and stabbed a large IV catheter and needle into my chest. Yanked out the needle.

I could hear air *whoosh* out, but the next breath I took was easier.

Pleural decompression. Oh wow, that's better.

She then turned her attention to the tube sticking in the side of my chest, tugging a bit, checking the suction settings.

"Sorry, that had to be scary," she said when she finished whatever she'd been doing. "The vacuum system used to keep your lung inflated occluded, probably with a large clot. We'll get a quick x-ray, but it's back to doing its job now. The needle is just temporary, we'll take it out after the film. Good thing the nurse recognized it so quickly."

I shook my head and pointed at Zach.

"Happened so fast, I didn't know what else to do," he said.

"Good job, then," she told him. "No more cops today though."

No arguments.

CHAPTER 44
AMBER

September 25, 2001
Dad called and talked to Grandmom Vera.

I guess I don't have to call her that anymore since Grandmom Dagmar's gone.

He must have given the phone to one of the nurses, who explained something serious that also happened, so I had to wait for her to tell me. But the longer I listened, the worse it sounded. Finally, I could tell Dad was back on the line.

I couldn't stand not knowing anymore, so I held out my hand until Grandmom relented and gave me the phone.

"What happened to Julie?"

"We were talking with the deputies when she had a clot in the chest tube, so she was having trouble breathing. The doctor came and corrected it, so everything is okay now," he told me, probably having to repeat what he'd just said to Grandmom.

"Promise?"

"She's in stable condition, and she ought to be released in a few days."

"What about the funeral for Grandmom Dagmar? And Kim?"

"Sweetie, we can't get to either one."

"No!"

"Amber, Julie doesn't want to miss them, but she –"

"What about me?"

"I don't understand."

"You're there with Julie. Grandmom will go back to Michigan with Dr. Katz. What am I supposed to do? Stay by myself?"

I growled in frustration, handing the phone back to Grandmom.

She went back to her conversation, and I hobbled off to the kitchen, stomping as much as one gimpy leg would let me.

When she was done, she came to the kitchen and sat across the table from me.

"Would you like to go to Michigan with me?" she asked.

The simple yes I wanted to say was replaced by tears. "I don't know what I want."

"Amber, this is hard. It is for all of us. I will not leave you alone."

"Don't you want to go?"

"Of course I do, but making sure you are okay is more important to me than being with Gerald."

"You really like him, don't you?"

"I do," she said, reaching into the fruit bowl for a banana, which she peeled and offered me the top half, which I broke off and took a bite. "I like how smart and funny he is. I like that he understands how living without a spouse feels, though I've done it a lot longer."

"Wasn't it lonely?"

"Sometimes," she said, taking and chewing a bit before continuing. "At first, with two little kids and a fulltime job to keep me busy, meeting someone new took more energy than I could muster. With the ranch, which Kai and I promised each other we'd keep for the kids, I eventually figured out I didn't need a husband, although there were times when I needed a man to help run it."

"Did you think Dad would ever come back and live here?"

"I thought he might until he got on at the DEA, but not now. He has his own dreams with Julie, and I couldn't have picked a more perfect partner for him. She's a lot tougher than you probably realize, and they are so good together. I hope you find someone like that in your life, so don't settle for anything less."

"Like Ethan, or whatever his name is. I liked him, you know? But then he dumped me in New York City." A shiver shook me. "Why would he do such a shitty thing?"

"I don't know. It was a horrible thing to do to someone you call a friend." She tossed the banana peel into the trash.

"Worse, other horrible things have happened," I said. "Things that are my fault."

"You shouldn't take responsibility for anything but your decision to go to New York. There's no way to know whether the other things would have happened or not." She reached across the table and put her hand on mine. "For example, Kim was already here. I'd have taken her to the ranch sometime or another."

"But Julie wouldn't have gotten shot," I countered.

"Maybe not. Or maybe something else would have happened, like a car accident. Something that could have been worse."

She was trying to be positive for me, I could tell.

"Or perhaps she would have taken Kim to the ranch, and that damned horse could have injured them both."

"So, you think our futures are set?"

"No, I believe things happen the way they do for a reason I can't understand."

I wasn't sure I understood any of this.

Dr. Katz came in. He had been to a funeral home to arrange to send Kim's body back to Michigan.

Just thinking about it made me want to bawl.

CHAPTER 45
JULIE

September 26, 2001

I concentrated on being a patient and left the detective work to the deputies and Zach after he threatened to stop giving me any more of the details if I didn't behave.

He did let me pose a few questions that had been on my mind.

"Who was the guy I shot?"

He sighed before speaking, holding up his hands to keep me in the bed. "You didn't shoot the guy who died. You and the dead guy were shot by the same gun. They matched the bullet that hit the clerk to your gun."

"No way!"

"The shot you heard before you approached didn't hit anything but the ceiling. The dead guy fired twice but didn't hit anyone."

"He didn't shoot anyone. I shot the clerk," I reiterated, unhappy at this conclusion. "You mean this guy's partner shot him? And me?"

"Apparently so."

"That doesn't make any sense!" My loud exclamation caused a tug at the incision on my right ribs, though the chest tube had been removed earlier in the morning. I knew if I didn't control myself, I wouldn't have answers until I was discharged or much later.

"No, it doesn't, does it." Not a question. "What does that mean?"

"Unless we find out who the dead guy is, I'd be guessing. You?"

"Nothing so far."

I moved my hand toward my cup from lunch without any hope of reaching it, so Zach scooted it closer. "If he has no criminal history, how will they match him?"

"Probably won't make any difference to us. You're cleared to leave from that perspective."

"What's going on in Albuquerque?"

"Mom has been able to postpone the service for your mother so everyone could go to Traverse City for Kim's funeral first. You okay with that?"

"Of course, but what about Amber?"

"She'll be going with Gerald and Mom. They should be there tomorrow."

"I can't fly, they say," I confessed.

"That's okay, I got another vehicle, but it's used," he said. "I figured it would be better to trade in a used one I didn't like than a new one that would depreciate when I rolled out of the lot."

"Is there something wrong with it?"

"Not really except it's, um, blue." He wrinkled his nose. "Like neon-sign sky blue. They didn't have anything else with options I liked, so this will do."

I laughed. "What if I *wanted* blue this time?"

Zach made a gagging expression.

"Red it is. Ho-hum."

"Not a gray one on the lot," he assured me.

"Damn, and I'd finally figured out how to use everything on the one I had."

CHAPTER 46
AMBER

September 26, 2001

"I'm sick of airlines," I said, dragging my luggage off the carousel in Traverse City.

The suitcase Kim had borrowed when she went to New Mexico, I thought dismally. I'd packed the few meaningful things she'd brought from Michigan to take back to Kayleigh.

Dr. Katz had gone on ahead to meet with her and Dr. Connors, so we could load everything and leave the wild new security of the airport.

Outrageous, seeing so many changes since July. Some of it was absolutely freaking crazy.

"I'll get it," Grandmom told me, taking my rolling bag away from me.

The last thing I'd do is stand between that woman and her mission after I learned how she'd overcome being a widow, ranched her husband's land and raised two kids. Tough was the best word I could think of, but it was a positive tough.

Outside, the crisp, fresh air was invigorating.

Grandmom and I stood back while Dr. Katz and his remaining daughter cried a bit, then we got into Dr. Connors' minivan to go to the Katz's house.

No one spoke during the ride, which was awkward.

Once we arrived and the men carried in the luggage, Kayleigh took me back to a spare bedroom and sat on the bed, patting the space next to her for me to join her.

"I wanted to share with you that Kimmy told me how much you helped her. She thought you were so brave, surviving in New York City alone, but then to help her when you got to Albuquerque."

"I didn't do any of that, really," I argued. "I was the one who wanted her to go see the horses at Grandmom's ranch!"

"Kim loved horses, but I bet she didn't tell you that, did she?" Kayleigh smiled. "She wouldn't have. She thought it would sound dumb to you because she didn't know much more than a mane from a tail."

"Why didn't she tell me? I'da loved to've talked about horses with someone new," I said, tears blurring my vision.

She hugged me tightly. "She told me she'd made a true friend," she said, "and I have, too."

"I thought you'd hate me," I admitted.

"No, Amber," she wrapped her hands around mine. "Someone really smart once told me that losing someone you love isn't fair, and there's no explanation why it's one person rather than another. But it's God's plan, no matter how much it hurts."

CHAPTER 47
JULIE

September 28, 2001

Two more days in the hospital had been dull, but I made it to discharge without any further complications.

We'd stopped in Terra Haute before leaving town to buy me another new phone, for which I had to pay full price after the last brand new one had become charcoal in the fire that destroyed my truck after it was stolen.

"I'm glad I hadn't spent time getting it all set up," I said.

"By the way, the insurance company thinks we're getting too expensive," Zach told me. "I told you you're high maintenance."

From western Indiana, getting to Traverse City meant either going far out of the way east to Indianapolis to stay on interstate, or taking a lot of lesser roads to get to Chicago and around Lake Michigan.

Either way, riding with a broken rib most of the way across the lower portion of Michigan was painful.

Pavement gets rougher going north in direct proportion to the increasing effects of winter weather. Cement highways start with seams every twenty feet or so. Each winter the ice heaves the seam apart, and so the highway department comes along in the summer and cuts out the single seam and pours a replacement segment, producing two seams to thrust apart the next winter. This means the roadways are either torn up by the winter weather or being repaired during the heavy summer tourist traffic.

Subsequently, the highway management style resulted in a jarring rhythm often matching the beat of my heart or vice versa. The bumpy ride was exhausting, with interspersed stretches of new smoother pavement.

I was thrilled to see the Traverse Bay come into view, knowing the ride was nearly over, though the streets near the bay were as bumpy as any of the highways.

Finally facing the bay, Zach turned right to go toward the Old Mission Peninsula, and I was disappointed at how the downtown region had changed so much in the last few years.

"Want to move back?" he asked, the question surprising me.

"No, this doesn't feel like home anymore."

He pulled into the driveway. "You're okay?"

Asking if I was okay had been his consistent question throughout the ride, especially when the road got really rough, and I had pulled a small pillow to my ribs for support.

"I'm okay." I reached over and squeezed his hand. "And you?"

"Other than not wanting to be here for this, everything's gravy. I wish I could turn back the clock to when we landed in July."

I understood what he meant. So many things I wished hadn't happened led to us sitting in this driveway today.

Oh, how I'd rather be sitting on the deck at home, listening to the wind in the trees.

Zach laced his fingers with mine. "I love you."

Three words I never tired of hearing.

• • • • •

September 29, 2001

Kim's service was only a memorial as burial had already taken place. Only her family and close friends knew the services included Kim's unborn baby.

Funerals, in my memory, always take place on cold, windy, or even rainy days. The Traverse City afternoon, however, was a beautiful, warm and sunny expression of the best of Kim's personality.

Kayleigh spoke through her tears, reading the last letter she'd received from Kim just days before she died.

"Since our mother died, I've been so unhappy without her love, without realizing how much I had from you and Dad. I understand now that I can't control who leaves our lives, only that we should love those who remain even more. I will spend the rest of my life making up the lost time when I didn't love you back."

I hadn't cried before that, not really. Tears and watery eyes, but not until I heard her reconciliation to her sister and father did I bawl.

Gerald had seemed calm during most of the day, shedding tears at the church when he stood to speak about his older daughter. Vera sat next to him, held his arm when they walked by a wreath of flowers and photograph one last time as he sobbed.

After the service, there was a family gathering at their church hall.

Having only met them briefly at her wedding, Kayleigh introduced me to Reese's parents and a younger brother. I sat with them and chatted a bit.

They seemed like nice people, except I noticed neither had much to say to Amber as she sat with us for a short while, which I thought was a bit haughty, until the over-accessorized Mrs. Connors told me in a hushed whisper that Kim had been *pregnant*, as if I hadn't known.

As if it were ghastly and an inexcusable, unforgivable indignation her older son had *married* the sister of such a girl.

My indignation barely in check, I leaned forward toward her as if to share the secret. "You will find Kayleigh is considerably different from her sister," I said, dabbing my mouth daintily with the paper napkin, then scooting back the metal folding chair as I stood, letting it screech loudly. "Hopefully she can live up to your high standards and the outrageous expectations you have for Reese now that her dead sister and a baby aren't around to spoil your self-righteous opinions."

Kayleigh, who had already left their table, did not hear my nasty outburst.

Zach, who had been doing his vanishing-into-the-walls trick, met me by the punchbowl after my conversation with Adrienne Connors.

"Wipe the smug off your face, Julie," he leaned closer to whisper in my ear. "That was a beautiful razor-sharp insult you shouldn't share with anyone else."

I looked up at him in amazement. "Not only are you a ghost, you also have incredible hearing."

"No, I don't, but the look on her face after you left was pure angry loathing that she'd not only been snubbed but that she didn't have the last word," he said. "I caught the slight smirk on Mr. Connors' face that you made a slam dunk with such eloquence."

I couldn't help but smile again.

"I suspect Kayleigh doesn't have much more respect for Mrs. Connors than you do," he said, taking the cup from me and sipping. "Rich people can be so snooty, don't you think?"

"Wonder if they know of Reese's idea to move to Africa?" I said, with a chuckle. "Bet they won't be inconvenienced to visit him there."

• • • • •

While I didn't want to check into yet another hotel, I certainly had no intention of staying in a house with them, but the Connors also excused themselves to go home.

Probably for the very same reason I didn't want to be around them.

"Julie, it's okay," Kayleigh encouraged. "If she wants, Amber can stay with us, and Dad has plenty of room for you and Zach."

I found it to be funny, that she would choose Amber over her in-laws, but it seemed to be a perfect solution.

Finally, everyone had left but us, Vera, and Gerald. He had lit a fire and poured us each a drink.

Vera had been busy, keeping the hospitality organized and supporting Gerald. Now the couple sat in recliners side by side.

They looked handsome together.

"I've been waiting to talk to you both until we had some quiet time," she said, focusing on Zach. "I've kept the ranch all these years because of your father. I'm getting too old to keep it running the way it should be."

Zach's legs tensed beside me though he only nodded.

She turned to me. "I'm sure Zach's told you about Gerald and me."

Not a question, so I didn't answer. Zach nodded again.

"I won't sell it, but I'm giving it to you. That way you can do with it whatever you see fit," she said. "You've already paid for most of it anyway."

I asked, though I could have guessed her answer. "What will you do, Vera?"

"Without any other ties to New Mexico, I'm considering retiring and moving here with Gerald."

"Or I might move down there, but we'd buy a place in the city," he added. "It's a beautiful area with a lot less snow shoveling."

He's never been there in a windstorm or wildfire.

"I like Michigan, too," she offered. "Maybe we'll do both. The point is, I'd like to get the legal stuff out of the way before the end of the year. Before Thanksgiving, if possible."

"Vera," I asked, since Zach had said nothing so far. "Are you sure?"

"Yes, Julie. I'm very sure. I'd considered doing this when Dagmar had her first stroke, moving to town where we could both live if things worked out. I wish it had, of course, but I've wanted to be free of the ranch for a while. I worry if someone I'm paying is doing what is supposed to be done while I'm away."

I looked back at Zach, waiting for him to speak.

"Julie and I will have to discuss the options, Mom," he finally said. "I want you to be happy, and I appreciate that keeping the ranch has been a burden for you for a long time."

"From the time you could saddle your own horse, I knew you could take care of it, but Zoe never had any interest in either the animals or the land."

Muscles in his jaw twitched. "No, she didn't."

In all the time I'd known them, I'd never heard them mention Zoe's name in a conversation together.

I knew Zach felt responsible for her death, but so many of the details surrounding her murder had been kept from Vera. On the other hand, I wondered if Vera secretly held Zach responsible for Zoe's death.

The silence between them was thunderous in a room with only the sound of the wood crackling in the fireplace.

"I'll let you know," Zach said, getting up and leaving the den.

The door to our bedroom slammed shut hard.

"Julie," she said in a softer voice. "I don't know what to say to him about Zoe. I understood what happened to her, in general at least, and I've never wanted to know more. Does he think I don't care?"

"It's the most painful event in his life. He believes no one can understand how he feels because they were so close," I offered. "He's tried to protect you from the hurt, but it's something the two of you need to discuss without me."

She looked down at her lap. "I don't think we can do that."

"Vera, I suspect neither of you has ever opened up about how big the hole is she left. I'll talk to him, but one of you needs to make the first move."

I excused myself, taking both our empty glasses to the kitchen on my way to the bedroom where Zach had gone.

He was stretched out on the bed on top of the covers.

"Don't say it," he told me. "Not right now, anyway. I need to –" He sat up. "I need to think about it."

"Not a word," I replied. I kicked off my shoes and sat on the bed beside him. "But I do need you to unzip my blouse."

"That?" he said, "That I can do."

CHAPTER 48
JULIE

October 2, 2001

Although we hadn't planned on being in Traverse City more than a few days before going back to Albuquerque and doing yet another memorial service, the tension between Zach and Vera grew until I just couldn't stand watching it anymore.

"I understand I'm not involved in any of this, but the rest of us are bystanders catching flak from your problem, so you two need to get this out in the open and fix it or it's gonna destroy us all," I announced after lunch. "Both of you, out to the car."

Vera appeared bewildered at being spoken to like an errant child.

On the other hand, Zach looked angry and defiant, knowing what my lecture was going to be about.

I picked up the truck keys and told them to follow me, leaving an equally bewildered Amber and Gerald behind.

No one spoke for half an hour, as I drove from the Old Mission Peninsula into Traverse City then east and again northward, headed to neutral ground. The apprehension between them felt like a low boil on the kettle. Finally, near Elk Rapids, I found a place to park.

"Now, both of you have things to say about Zoe's life and death," I announced. "I don't know if it's doubt or regret or blame of the other, or just lack of understanding. I don't care. But you need to talk about it. Now."

Two second graders couldn't have looked more uncomfortable being in the principal's office for some miscreant activity.

"Shall I start, then?" I asked, looking back and forth. "Because I've certainly got a lot on my mind on the subject."

Vera spoke, but she did not look at her son. "I've always known you tried to protect me from the ugly details of Zoe's death. At first, I needed you to hide them. Losing Kai was losing a friend, a partner. You and Zoe were closer to being a part of me than my own mother, and losing a child is the worst thing a mother can ever feel. Eventually, I began to want to know, needed to know, but you wouldn't talk to me about her."

"Mom, I couldn't possibly have told you how Zoe died. I still can't. You say we're a part of you. There will never be anyone closer to me than she was, and I didn't just want to protect you from knowing what happened to her, I still don't know the words to describe how her death affects me. You —" He looked hard at me then back. "*She* was stabbed and killed, but *I feel* that pain every single day," he said, his voice twisting in agony. "I don't know how to explain that to you or anyone else."

"Zach, I wanted to be able to console you. I didn't understand how two kids could be so close. Seeing you after losing her made me think of a character in a book where the little boy lost his shadow. I didn't know how to make it better for you. But still, I'd lost my sunshine, so I needed you to help me, too."

I understand a little more how my mother felt when my father died.

"Help you? Mom, I did the only thing I knew how to do to help you." And then he stopped.

Whatever the next sentence in his head might have been, he was not saying it aloud. Ever.

Not even to me. Or perhaps, especially not to me.

Vera resumed talking to him, but as I watched him, I was positive he didn't hear another word she said.

• • • • •

When we got back to Gerald's, I called Brandan and asked if he could find out where the copies of Penny Tucker-Daniels' journals were, and whether I could take them with me when we left Michigan. After a little searching for the answer, he called to tell me the copies had been in evidence but destroyed, but the originals were never shipped.

"Ethan said that Mark Daniels told him he'd discarded all of the journals," I told him.

"Interesting. He told me that she left her mother's but brought home her own journals from that box, and he's kept them for their daughter."

"I'm willing to pay for him to make copies if he doesn't want to send them."

"He's agreed to send them directly to you, but he does not want them to be involved in another criminal investigation."

"That's great," I said, "for me at least."

"I asked him to send them to you in care of the Skamania County Court House Building, but not the sheriff's office. You can come get the older books here and send them all back to him when you're done."

CHAPTER 49
AMBER

Not like I'd had much else to do on the drive, first to New Mexico, then on to Washington, but reading Sally Tucker's diaries about Penny in her mid-teenage years was boring, watching-cow-crap-dry boring. I decided to discuss it instead.

"Julie, did you read any of this?" I asked.

"Just the parts where Anthony's mom was killed so he went to live with Penny's family."

"I thought diaries were for third-grade girls who imagined their worlds were important enough to document and need locks," I chided. "I didn't have a diary."

"You should keep a journal," she recommended. "Not those imaginary life secrets of a child, but the memories and emotions about the things since your mom died. Like when you found out you are diabetic."

"Sounds boring, worse than this stuff," I said. "Why would I do that?"

Julie said she'd been encouraged to write in a journal after her dad was killed, then again after her previous husband tried to kill her. "Writing helped me, being able to slow down and think about words to describe how I was feeling when I didn't want to talk about it. I had a lot of anger and depression I couldn't say out loud to anyone."

Dad and Julie exchanged this look that reminded me of the arc of electricity I'd seen in photos of Tesla's bolts of lightning.

While the whole diary thing from Sally was boring, I could tell Dad knew all about the things Julie was telling me and more.

We spent hours during the drive, discussing those events, she said, because she thought it was time I understood more about her and how her life was changed by Anthony Bock – Penny's cousin. Julie also talked a little about the day Bock killed her father, and how she was in the building at the same time. When she tried to stop the bleeding, her father made her run.

"I can't imagine leaving Dad if he were shot and bleeding to death," I said. "After we were on the search a few years ago, I know he wouldn't leave me if I were hurt. But he'd tell me to go if he thought I'd be in danger."

"That same man who killed my father was also in the house when David almost killed me. And then he continued murdering, including Penny and her daughter," she said then paused, looking out the window. "That's why dealing with all this makes me grumpy."

"Ethan's uncle did all that? No wonder you're a little pissed off."

Julie hadn't told me many details about what happened to her until our trip home from New Mexico, and although it seemed weird to hear it from her now, the story explained a lot about her.

"Your life seems more like the head-on collision of two high-speed freight trains than mine does," I told her.

"I always thought of it more like a mid-air collision between supersonic jets," Dad said to me as if Julie couldn't hear him. "Glad I'm not the only one." And he smiled, finally.

"Tell me more about your journals. Do you still write?" I asked.

"No, once we got married, I burned them," she said. "I no longer wanted to keep the hatred and anger. Physically destroying them was liberating."

"Made a good campfire, too," he added.

"Dad, did you know all this about Julie?" I asked.

"Most of it," he said. "Not about her journals or what was in them at first, but I knew what had happened to her dad. Mom took us to the funeral. Later, while Julie was in the hospital, Mom had told me what David had done, but that was a year or so before we began seeing each other. I wasn't around for a lot of what Bock was doing because of work."

"He got his share of Bock, too, though," Julie added. "Bock had gone to Florida to kill him, but Dr. McNeeley arrived there first and warned him."

"So, what happened?"

Dad shook his head, so Julie answered.

"Bock came into the hospital room where Z' and his partners and Dr. McNeeley were, and your father ended up killing Bock, once and for all."

"Wait, what were you in the hospital for?" I interrupted.

"I'd been injured on the job," he replied without further explanation, so I didn't offer any either, but I had a flash memory of hearing him get shot on the beach.

"Wow, I bet you're glad he's dead and it's over," I said, suspecting he hadn't told me the whole truth.

They looked at each other in this weird, electrical current way again, then Dad just laughed.

"Amber," Julie said when he finally got the laughter under control, "I'm not sure that even being dead will stop the repercussions of what that bastard did."

I didn't understand.

"You're nose-deep in diaries about his family, still nursing injuries you suffered after getting to know his cousin's son, and you don't believe there's an echo of the evil Bock in everything?" Julie asked me.

I thought about our discussions for a while.

"Do you really think he had that kind of effect on everyone around him?"

"You figure this out and let me know your decision," Julie said.

"I'm trying to find out what happened to Ethan, er, Whatever-His-Name-Is," I argued. "What does Bock have to do with him?"

"Penny was lacking in maturity, both getting pregnant and dealing with the consequences, so I don't know what the connection might be."

Although Sally Tucker's diaries certainly went back way before Penny's birth, I initially felt no need to dig that far, but hearing Julie talk about Anthony Bock, I thought that would be a good place to start.

Sure enough, as I read her diaries, there wasn't a lot about when Anthony came to live with them, but Sally Tucker did write about her sister.

October 12, 1960 – I can't believe what's happening! The Detroit police called to tell me Angela had been killed by her husband. Murdered! Why? I don't understand. They say she's dead, but that's all they'll say other than it was her husband. Bob Bock was a bastard to Ang' but I never believed she was in danger. The police want to know if we can come get Anthony. Not tonite. I can't drive now. My hands shake so bad I can hardly write, but I have to do something or else I'll scream and scream. Nick isn't home yet with the car anyway. I said I'd come tomorrow. I finally got my nerves settled enough to call Momma in Florida. She said the police called them, too, but she didn't know any more than I did. I heard Pa bellowing in the background, yelling that Angie got her throat slit like a pig, and it was a shame that bastard son of hers wasn't home to get it, too. As much as my heart aches, I told Mom I'd said my last words to my father for being such an arrogant selfish bastard, that it was all his fault this happened to Angela in the first place – he gave her no choice but to marry Robert Bock. Mom didn't argue. She didn't say a thing – just hung up. Only one of them is dead, but tonight, I lost everyone else in my family with one phone call.

I read the passage out loud to Julie.

"If you look closely, you'll see where her tears smudged the ink in a few places," she replied. "I remember when Penny showed me that entry."

"How did these women get pregnant?" I asked.

"Sex," Dad said, turning to look at Julie and then said in a mock whisper, "Do we need to have that talk with her again?"

"Dad!"

"Very likely the same way Kim got pregnant," Julie said.

"Yeah, sex," he repeated. "Do I need to explain that to *both* of you?"

Julie smacked his arm.

"They didn't even have a real funeral for her sister!"

Neither of them replied, and I kept reading.

Sally wrote a lot about how her nephew fit into the family.

"Mrs. Tucker doesn't write much about her other kids. Wouldn't she mention who Penny might have been going with?" I asked.

"I probably wouldn't spend a lot of time writing about Cody Randall and you because I couldn't see it being a permanent relationship," Julie said.

"I understand, but she'd write about her only daughter getting pregnant, wouldn't she? Like, I've completely missed it."

"I get the impression that Sally Tucker didn't chronicle her life in day-to-day fashion, so you may still find something."

CHAPTER 50
JULIE

Driving to Albuquerque took a long two days, even switching with Zach to drive. He was quite emphatic Amber couldn't take a turn, even on the boring stretches of interstate, though he wasn't thrilled that I relieve him, either.

Amber had bought a book of interesting things to see on the way, but no one wanted to draw out the trip any longer than it already was to stop for touristy things. We'd stayed in a hotel southwest of St. Louis, which had meant Zach drove through the city at night.

Having taken the same roads many times, I knew he meant to miss the morning traffic. However, once we hit the I-44 to Oklahoma City then I-40 west into Albuquerque, it was a monotonous drive. I wondered if Amber had changed her mind and wished she'd flown back with Vera.

Still, we saw patriotic banners and billboards weeks after 9/11. We listened to one NPR program on the aftermath so far and the changes in the American psyche. Each of us had a different perspective of that day. I can't imagine how disturbing it was that Amber watched it happen.

"No one who saw the media coverage that day will ever forget it," Zach said. "There is a wild sense of unity, patriotism right now, but I suspect it won't last."

"I had nightmares about it a couple of times," Amber confessed. "Not now, but the first few weeks."

"This terrorist attack is the sort of psychological event most people never experience except in war," the person on the show related. "Some people are unable to cope with this and will suffer anxiety, whether they live in New York or Washington, D.C."

When the program ended, Zach had one more illuminating observation: "9/11 isn't just about the loss of life, but the loss of our interpretation of freedom."

• • • • •

Once in Albuquerque, I considered not having a service for my mother. In the wake of 9/11 and other catastrophes since she'd died, it seemed lame to have a memorial for her death.

Vera changed my mind. "A memorial isn't about her death now, Julie, but to celebrate her life of such beautiful kindness. She touched so many people at the hospital, patients and co-workers alike. Several parents of newborns she cared for have asked me to let them know when a memorial service would be."

That seemed like a lovely tribute.

"The loss of one is neither greater nor less than the losses of the many," Zach added. "Let's celebrate what a fantastic lady she was."

Amber talked me into having a dozen of Mom's photos enlarged and to make them available to those who attended if they wished to take one. That, I thought, was the best honor of all. I chose two dozen, including the last one I'd taken of her and Kalimar together, which I had enlarged to 24 inches.

"Amber, what would you like to do?" he asked. "What reminds you of her that you'd want to share?"

She thought a minute. "No, it's dumb."

"What you feel is never dumb," Vera encouraged.

"I'd never heard of Hermits, but she made them when Dad and I were here," she said. "I loved them."

"Splendid!" Zach said. "Let's make a couple of batches for the memorial. What a wonderful way to share something special you loved about Dagmar!"

They seemed excited about the idea.

"Wait! *My* mother knew you were alive, too?" I asked, putting my fists on my hips. "And what is a Hermit?"

Turns out, she had known Zach was alive.

And Amber explained about Hermits. "They're a soft, chewy sugar and molasses cookie with crushed raisins, clove, and nutmeg. They originated in the New England area in the 1880s in a New York church cookbook. She showed me her recipe. It's in the red cookbook on the pastry shelf."

Come to find out, I'd forgotten that I love them, too.

We planned a memorial ceremony to give people a chance to speak. While it wasn't a traditional funeral, it was good closure for me to meet so many of the friends she'd made at work and with her horses over the years. Still grieving but with a sense of acceptance, I met a lot of families in whose lives she'd made a difference in the nursery.

That, I thought when I got ready for bed that evening, is how a funeral should be for the family. Time to remember and gather without the fiery shock and anger and sadness of a death.

• • • • •

Until I saw an ambulance go hot through an intersection on our way home from lunch, I'd forgotten I'd seen Taylor Healy when Mom had her stroke.

I can't deny it. Lights and sirens still give me a tingly feeling in my chest.

After searching my jacket pockets and bag, a new tote Amber had picked out since my last one was probably part of the ashes in my burned-out truck in Indiana, I couldn't find the business card Taylor had given me with her cell number on it. When we got home, I called the ambulance service directly and asked for her. Two transfers later, she picked up the phone.

"I'm so sorry I didn't get back with you sooner," I said. "You wouldn't believe the long string of catastrophes we've been through since I saw you."

"Knowing you, I might not, but I'll try. Can you swing dinner tonight without the family?"

"You know about Zach and Amber?"

"Vera filled me in. That's quite a story itself. We could all go if you want, but I thought it would be good to catch up without an audience. They'd just be bored."

"Let's do it, then. Shall we meet somewhere?"

We'd agreed to meet at one of Albuquerque's best New Mexican food restaurants at 5:30 that evening, I announced to Zach.

"That's excellent," he told me. "You need an evening away from us. But without bleeding."

I scowled.

"Hey, I'm no longer the last one who got shot," he observed.

"Who is Taylor?" Amber chimed into the conversation.

"A paramedic I rode with during paramedic school. We're going out for dinner tonight to catch up."

"Why does Julie get to go to dinner with some guy from her past. That seems a little suspicious," she noted.

Before I could reply, Zach stated in a low voice. "Taylor is a woman, though it wouldn't matter."

After starting with a huge basket of chips and a salsa that would melt steel, we raised our Grande Margarita Especiales to salute a long-overdue get-together.

"Tell me everything," she said, dipping a chip.

"Too ambitious, even for you. I don't have that much time or voice," I replied. "Let me start with Jeremy, though. You know I was at UNMH because David almost killed me, and Jeremy asked you if he should come to see me, right?"

She nodded and scooped more salsa onto another chip.

"He took your advice and didn't come, which was the right thing at the time. I didn't see him again until late 1995, when I was working at a Michigan Medical Examiner's office. He was an epidemiologist for the CDC, and he came to Traverse City when we queried a parasite sample."

"Jeremy went to Michigan to see you?" she asked, astonished. "What about his –" She stopped when I held up my hand.

"He was able to contribute to our murder case and another, but after a short reconciliation in our relationship, I discovered he was married with a daughter, which infuriated me. He left Michigan, but somehow he ended up following the killer to Florida, where he went to warn Zach – my husband now – when this monster came into the hospital room to start a firefight." I hesitated, wondering how much more there was to the story, sipped the drink. "Jeremy was also shot and killed."

"Oh, Julie, I'm so sorry. I knew Jeremy'd gotten married, but I hadn't heard from him in several years – six, maybe seven."

"Not the way you probably wanted to hear he died, huh?"

"There is no good way," she said, dismissing that subject and moving on. "When your mother was in the hospital the first time, Vera told me about you and Zach," she said with a sly smile. "You married him, huh? Wow."

"Says a lot about his mental state," I said. "Or mine. It's been five years."

"And the daughter?" she prompted. "Not your child by birth."

"No, Zach's from his teen years. Her mother died, and Amber has lived with us ever since. She started college in August, with a major bump along the way. She was in Manhattan on 9/11, which is another endless story."

"Really! I can't imagine you with a teenager, Julie," she said with a hearty laugh.

"Every day has been a challenge." I had more chips and salsa.

Taylor described her intentions of going back to Bayfront Hospital in Florida in 1997, but that she had been offered an enticing package to stay, so she did. "It wasn't just money, but that alone blew Bayfront's offer off the planet."

"Good for you."

"And the man who made me glad I took the offer is now the father of our bouncy two-year-old daughter." She pulled out her wallet to show me.

"But your name didn't change," I stated.

"No, he said it didn't make a lot of sense for women to change their names for the licenses and stuff. He retired from the fire department when Chelsea was born, and he's the home parent now."

"Someone I knew?"

"Remember the guy we called Peaches?"

Yes, I did.

We laughed, ate more chips, and finally ordered food.

"I'm so sorry about your mom, Julie. She was a great nurse. And the girl who was staying with you at your mom's? She's due now, right?"

I swallowed hard. "She was killed by a horse a few weeks ago."

"Oh no, that was her? I heard the call. Did she get bucked off or what?"

I explained the sequence of events and the horrible conclusion. "I was on my way back from New York City, in Indiana."

"What on Earth were you doing there?"

"Again with where to start," I said with a sigh. "Amber had met a young man when we were in Michigan in July. She went off to college while I was here with Mom. He invited her to New York for a few days and then abandoned her on 9/11."

"Not much of a friend, I'd say."

"No, not much." I explained a few points about the trip back, skipping the shooting and the rest of the story about Ethan because I just didn't want to discuss it anymore, so I turned it back to stories of her family and goings-on in New Mexico.

What I'd hoped to be a happy catching-up evening had begun to weigh heavily on my heart, and it seemed I only had bad news to share.

CHAPTER 51
JULIE

Home.

I've never been so happy to be anywhere in my life as when Zach turned into the driveway to our cabin in Washington.

The cross-country drive from Michigan to New Mexico and then home was painful because of the one rib fractured by the bullet. However, the drive had kept us from facing the craziness of airports and jets, the still-new-and-growing security, and snotty-nosed passengers.

I wanted to go back to work, but not for another week or so.

Relieved when Zach and I had gotten past the head-butting over my insistence he and his mother discuss the rock wall between them, he had confessed to me on our last night in Albuquerque that he appreciated me interceding.

Lying in his downstairs king-sized bed at the ranch, in the dark in a shamble of sheets, he whispered a portion of his New York secret.

"I've told you before that Zoe and I were sharing an apartment, and after she was attacked, how she changed," he started.

Curled up beside him, my head on his shoulder, I nodded.

"Remember when I told you the men who attacked her paid for their crimes?" he said. "Maybe when we were in Hawaii."

"No, we were at the cabin in Washington and you'd taken me riding on Del's horses."

Didn't matter.

"I knew you'd remember. Like you probably remember I said they didn't go to jail."

Don't like where this is going.

"Zoe didn't know who had raped her, but when she wasn't all bat-shit crazy, she managed to find out. She trolled the streets and found one of them. She made friends with the guy's sister, Yolanda, who was trying to dig her way out of the gang herself. When Zoe was attacked and killed by several members of the gang, this girl, still a teenager at the time, came to me," he said, then paused. "With her help, we put a stop to the gang."

That's very vague.

"She helped police set up a bust during one of their crime sprees," he said. "During the takedown, those two were shot for resisting arrest."

Ohhh, I see. How sad. Not.

"Yolanda went into a witness protection program to get out of Houston, including into the school of her choice," he said. "I wasn't supposed to hear from her again, but she contacted my mother at the hospital, asked that she give me a message."

I waited.

"She asked me to come to New York a year or so later and help her with a problem, so I did. You've met her as Eduarda, Edie. She now has her own restaurant."

"That trip to NYC is what you don't want to tell me," I concluded.

He must have thought hard before nodding. "I did something there that needed to be done to protect her, and we vowed we would not ever discuss what happened."

"Then I respect your secret, Zach. I won't ask again."

"Actually, she called on our way home and told me she liked you, and that if I ever felt the need to tell you, she approved."

"I appreciate it, but I'll leave that decision up to you."

He nodded, "I'll tell you, someday."

And knowing he did something to protect her made the secret he kept simply fine.

CHAPTER 52
AMBER

I was exhausted when we finally got home, but I carried as much of my stuff up the stairs to my bare room as I could manage, which wasn't much given the cane and wrist splint.

Dad said he'd bring up my bags in a while.

Tired of sitting, I changed clothes and headed for the barn. I'd missed the horses a lot, although I felt bad about Purgatory. I understood how his behavior was based on past trauma and how it could be dangerous.

Thoughts of the journals I'd read in the truck began to feel a little like the dull, crummy feeling you have a day or so before you come down with a cold.

Years of Sally Tucker's scrawling about their farm and family was mostly dreary. Arguments with her husband, late freezes messing up their cherry crop, a few childhood accidents. She did have a few stories I found funny, but most were tearful, like including her sister's murder and getting her nephew, but not much about Penny.

Sally's daughter may have been a good kid, or maybe she was simply less of a stress-inducing child than the boys.

Dad and Julie were sitting out on the deck when I headed to the barn, walking carefully on the ground with my cane.

Cool but sunny instead of the rain I sometimes felt would never end. I could hear birds in the barn and the trees. From beyond the barn, I heard an occasional nicker and smelled alfalfa hay. All this clean, country sense came back into my head hard, making me realize how much I'd missed it.

Going around the left side of the barn, the horses came trotting over toward the pipe fence of the corrals.

I hoped Dad wasn't watching, but I kinda stumbled back when they rushed toward me, a flash of fear I'd get kicked again.

Denali, Rainier, and Waldo were in one section, eager to be the first for nuzzles. In the adjacent paddock came Julaquinte, followed by a fuzzy shadow I had to look twice to make sure I saw.

A colt! Or a filly, I couldn't tell.

Curious enough to peek around its mother at me.

I went into the barn and grabbed half a dozen apples from the bucket and went back out to treat the horses. With a little coaxing, Julaquinte approached and the filly, I finally saw, came for a little snack, too.

CHAPTER 53
JULIE

Finally home, it wasn't long before Amber took her cane and limped out to the barn to see the horses. From the sounds we could hear as I relaxed on the deck, the reunion was joyful.

Zach opened the hot tub cover and measured the chemistry balances and the water temperature before starting the jets.

I tried to hide the disappointment I couldn't just go drop into it for a long soak.

"Give it a few hours," he told me, obviously aware of what I'd been thinking as clearly as if I'd said it aloud.

"I've missed that."

"What, that I know what's on your mind?" he said, pointing to the tub. "You were drooling, it wasn't hard."

Smartass.

He looked to see Amber was occupied at the barn.

"Feels like I've been gone for a year," he said, swiping a test strip into the water and waiting to read it. "You must be delighted to be home."

"Absolutely. All the talk of Penny and her family made my head hurt, but I understand Amber wants to solve the mystery."

"She's still devastated about Kim, but she doesn't want you to see that," he said, dumping a spoonful of a chemical into the swirling water then pulling the cover back in place. "While I'm spilling secrets, Brandan asked me not to tell you or more specifically Amber that his wife filed for divorce while he was in New York."

"Oh no," I moaned. "Why?"

"She accused him of living a too-risky lifestyle."

"Because he's a cop or because he's gay?"

"He's gay?" Zach's voice cracked in a falsetto that said he wasn't really surprised. "No, he said she was finally past hiding her life, and she accused him of being a health risk to the kids."

"Health risk? That's crap."

"He had hepatitis a year or so ago. He even moved out while he was sick so he wouldn't expose them. She said he got it from a partner."

"Did he?"

Zach gave me a look that clearly said he didn't ask.

"What kind of hepatitis, did he say?" I asked.

"I don't know one from another. Would he have been a health risk to her or the kids?" he asked, coming over to sit in the deck chair next to me.

"Not likely if he had been reasonably cautious."

Zach nodded, then closed his eyes. "Sounds to me like she wants to drag him through court with a trumped-up reason to make her point."

"Would she do that?" Anger stirred in my chest.

"I don't know, Julie. I never met her."

I hadn't either, though I'd seen her on the news. I didn't recall her name offhand, though she had not taken his last name due to her newscast career. I did remember when Brandan had told Jeremy about the twin boys, who would be in junior high school now if I figured right.

"Witch." I leaned my head back and closed my eyes.

"Even when he was telling me the news, he never had an unkind word to say about her. He's heartbroken she wants to take the kids out of state." He saw Amber was on her way back from the barn. "He didn't want Amber to find out and worry that his problem is her fault, too."

I nodded, nothing to add. If Brandan wasn't mad, I shouldn't be.

"Dad?" Amber yelled from halfway between. "Did you know there's a new filly?"

"Wait till she finds out there are steers, too." He smiled and waved. "We should wait till after supper to tell her, though."

"I'm missing something," I said. "Why should she be excited about cows?"

"Not cows, steers."

"Whatever their gender and reproductive status. We'll never need that much beef."

"Not for stocking the freezer, Julie. They're for roping and penning practice. She'll also find a new roping arena on the north side of those trees," he said, pointing northwest vaguely. "Kenny and I built it after she left for school."

"Weren't you a busy guy while we were gone," I marveled. "But she can't ride right now."

"Think of it as motivation to finish her physical therapy. The doctor said she should be set to ride six weeks after the surgery. She's getting close."

Once Amber had returned to the deck where we sat, she had all sorts of horse yacking to do with Zach, which I happily tuned out and closed my eyes.

The topic of conversation added to the fresh air and lack of motion caught up with me, nudging me into a nap I didn't fight.

• • • • •

Zach touched my arm and woke me as Kenny Underwood walked toward the house.

One of them had tucked a light blanket over my shoulders as the day cooled.

"Mr. Zach, Mrs. Zach," Kenny said in his respectful greeting. "I'm glad you are finally back."

"Not nearly as happy as we are to be home," Zach told him. "You'll never know how much we appreciate you taking care of the place."

"I was happy to help you, Mr. Zach."

I wasn't offended that Kenny did not acknowledge how his efforts had benefitted me, too.

"No, Kenny, you went way beyond helping. You kept the place running," he said, getting up. "I'll write you a check tomorrow, if that's okay, but I also have a proposition to discuss with you now."

They headed toward the barn, mostly because Kenny wouldn't speak freely in front of me, Zach and I both knew.

Zach's proposition to Kenny was one we had agreed on in a previous discussion. While we would provide cash for him for his work, Zach's idea was to buy him a vehicle.

Kenny had spent most of his adult life around Skamania County, hiding from people who were afraid of him because he was schizophrenic, sometimes with paranoia, and often homeless. He had been accused and socially convicted of the heinous murder of his parents, but he was never charged with the crime due to his mental illness. However, two years ago, his brother had been convicted of the murder of his wife's new boyfriend, which had gone a long way to calming the suspicions of Kenny killing his parents.

They were almost to the barn when I heard Kenny give a loud "Whoopy!" that I took as positive feedback to the offer.

He knew how to drive. His dilemma came from the choice to pay for a car or pay for medications, but he seldom could do both, so he made the rational decision that driving would be dangerous without his meds, which I thought was far more self-aware than others with such a similar decision.

However, in the last few years, Zach had helped him with enough odd jobs to keep him fed and medicated, then they built a small house – a shed really because Kenny insisted he needed nothing more – tucked away in the northeast corner of our property. All that had gone a long way to keeping Kenny's life stable, and neither of us thought he would be unsuitable to drive now.

I chuckled a bit at Kenny's formality with me and his wide berth of Amber. Zach had once explained how Kenny wanted to be sure there was no possible hint of impropriety with a female or child.

No doubts regarding his mental illness, he was much more responsible for his decisions and actions than many so-called mentally healthy people I knew.

I like Kenny, but even on his best days, he is a tad different, and some people can't deal with that.

Amber came out to the deck after Zach and Kenny disappeared behind the barn to check out the horses, I supposed.

"Was that Kenny I heard?" she asked, sitting but eyeing the hot tub as I had.

Her incisions have healed enough to soak for a short time. Not as long as I hoped to be chin-deep in hot water, though.

"Yes. Zach went to pay him for keeping tabs on the place while we were gone."

"No, just you and Dad. I wasn't supposed to be here," she said, making a sideways frown. "I'm sorry, again."

"You do not have to keep apologizing, Amber," I told her.

"It's not like I can do anything to make everything all right again."

"You made a decision leading to bad consequences. Learn from that and move on. You can't go back in time to undo anything that happened," I said. "Like what I told you about Bock still having threads of his evil weaving through my life, it's consequences. I doubt he planned that. I don't want it to keep happening. But there it is."

"Doesn't that make you angry?"

"Being angry at a dead man doesn't do anything for me, so I try not to be. Forgiving him or David is something I probably should have done years ago, but I'll never forget."

"When I was talking to Dad about Ethan, he said that hating someone is like drinking poison yourself but waiting for the other person to die."

"That's a good way to look at it."

"It's okay to not forgive Ethan?"

I smiled. "I told Jeremy's wife I was okay if she hated me for what happened with him, but she shouldn't let her anger ruin her or her daughter's lives." I reached and brushed back the hair on her shoulder. "Figure out what you want to, but don't become obsessed with him or his story. He's not worth that."

"What about someone you love?" she asked. "Like you love Dad?"

"I love Zach, and love is everything. But same advice: Don't let love be an obsession."

CHAPTER 54
AMBER

Dad had whipped up a batch of chili and fresh tortillas for supper.

"Why chili? You always fix it for colder weather, but it's been warm today."

"Comfort food. Celebration food. Aren't you glad to be home?" he asked as I sat at the table.

"Yesss," I said in a drawn-out word. "Happy to see the horses, too. Did you hear them?"

Julie nodded. "They missed you a lot. No one spoils them like you do."

"When was the foal born, Dad? It's not Waldo's, is it?" I said, sorta thinking how gross that was. "That would be, like, incest, right?"

"It wouldn't be good practice, no," he told me, passing the tortillas. "She's almost two months old now. I took Julaquinte to a breeder near Burns, Oregon. We have a gentleman's agreement I will take Waldo down to breed two of his mares next year."

"That's super, Dad!" I said, then spooned into the gooey cheesy chili then folded my tortilla into quarters and took a bite.

"How long till you can ride?" he asked, sounding intentionally casual.

"A few weeks or so. I don't think it'll be easy."

"Good. We can start with some slow practice," he suggested. "Get back to penning first, then roping."

I shrugged. "Not like I have much else to do till January."

He nodded like it was a done deal, but he still didn't mention the steers or the new arena.

"Does it ever bother you to ride since you got hurt?" I asked him, referring to the gunshot wound that had cost him a kidney.

"Not really."

I turned to Julie. "Any idea when Penny's journals will get to the sheriff's office?"

"They could already be there," she said. "Didn't sound like Mr. Daniels would put it off."

I was looking forward to reading Penny's journals because nothing in her mother's had led me to Ethan.

Dad and Julie wouldn't think it was right, but I hoped there was a crazy but horribly painful reason Ethan had abandoned me in New York. Kidnapped by aliens and probed to death. Crushed by falling debris at the World Trade Center. Or smashed like a bug on the grill of a high-speed truck.

Oh wait, that was me.

Part of me felt a little guilty because I wanted something horrible to have happened to him, and part of me was glad he hadn't shown up with a stupid lame excuse for leaving me stranded. I'd initially thought he left the hotel with my wallet in his coat and without his phone as an accident, forgetful in his eagerness to meet with the lawyer.

But after a conversation with Kimberley Katz, she left me with little doubt that he'd done everything on purpose.

What was *everything*?

What was the goal of doing some or all of it intentionally?

He couldn't have planned on the jets being flown into the World Trade Towers and their subsequent collapse, so why was he so insistent I fly to meet him in New York? And then why did he ditch me?

CHAPTER 55
JULIE

"Why didn't you tell her about the steers?" I asked Zach as we cleared the table.

"I didn't want to taunt her if she doesn't think she's ready to ride. She'd have been on one today if she did," he said.

"She'll figure it out though. She is a smart girl."

"That's the truth," he said, then looked a little sad. "She went to the barn to see them, but when they came running toward her, it spooked her. I'm worried what happened with Purgatory will make her reluctant to get on."

"I never considered that."

"Are you going back to work tomorrow?" he asked.

"I'll go check in with Wade tomorrow and let him know I'm back in town, but I'm not ready for more than office duty for a few days." Considering the idea, I tucked my right arm against my ribs and found them to still be tender. Perhaps a day or so without a thousand car miles would help.

Zach nodded absently.

"Something wrong?"

"Nothing," he said, lying. "It's kinda weird to have you and Amber back after what seems like eons."

"Needing a vacation from us already?" I jibed.

"Not at all, but I can't go wandering around in my underwear now."

"When did you ever do that before?" I asked.

Naked, yes. Underwear, no.

"Just saying that I can't do it now, not that I ever did."

"Which is like announcing that after my ribs heal, I can play golf," I retorted, "because I never could before."

"We could take it up," he offered.

"Golf? You?" I laughed.

"I've played golf. You could take lessons."

"Really played golf or played undercover golf?"

He sniffled instead of answering, like I'd hurt his feelings.

"Besides, you'll be too busy tending the *livestock*," I said with sarcastic emphasis, "to be out knocking a ball around a pasture with a stick, trying to hit it into a gopher hole."

"Golf, my dear, is more than that. We could make friends and play foursomes, socialize, walk and enjoy the great outdoors, and –"

"And drink," I interrupted.

We both drank, but golf wasn't necessary for a glass of wine or beer. A cold beer was refreshing after a hot afternoon chore. And a glass of wine was appropriate most any time later than breakfast.

"I need to either take up golf or quit drinking, or at least go back to things I need to do here," Zach said. "I gained six pounds this fall with you two being gone."

I nodded. I couldn't see it on him, but I knew the lack of daily activity had put a few pounds on me as well.

"I'm not ready to ride yet," I admitted. "Maybe a walk to see the *livestock*?"

"Would you quit saying that like you own a feedlot?" he complained.

I shrugged. "Okay, let's go see the new arena."

Activity accepted, I changed to hiking boots, then we started our walk.

"This thing with Bock is bothering you, isn't it?" he asked, taking my hand.

Bock had ruined so damned much in my life, starting with the death of my father and ending with . . . Jeez, had it *ever* ended? Not just killing, which he enjoyed, he destroyed the lives of people he didn't kill, like Kim Katz. And me. How much mental anguish could one man cause so long after he was dead?

"What if Bock was Ethan's father?" he continued.

Lunch we'd just eaten rolled in my stomach. "No. Just no. I can't deal with that."

Would I ever be free of him?

"I know, J'. He hurt a lot of people. But, for the sake of discussion, what if?"

"You mean, is there a way to be sure? I doubt it. Suppose Penny did name the father of her baby in her diaries?" I asked, stepping through tall grass. "She could say it was Bock and be lying to get even with him. Or she could say it was someone else. Either way, without scientific evidence, we can't be positive."

"Not to sound insensitive, but would it matter to the questions Amber has been trying to answer?" he asked, swinging an arm around my shoulders. "She is looking to hang his ass on a nail in the barn, sure. But would having the answer make a difference to you?"

"I don't know."

"Let's assume, only for the sake of discussion, that Ethan's biological father was Bock. What are the implications?"

I stared out to the trees beyond the horses for a while. "For one thing, it would mean that I'm related to him."

"Okay."

"It would make him a half-nephew."

Which makes me want to throw up.

"And Ethan was also the father of Kim's baby, right?" he said. "She did tell us she knew him as Sean Smith."

"I respect her confession, but that's not proven, either."

"Then does anything change if Amber finds out who Ethan is if he is Penny's son?"

"Not to me, I suppose," I said. "As long as he isn't related to me."

That makes me feel better.

We walked on through tall autumn grass.

"Out of curiosity, if you wanted to determine whether Penny was his mother and if Bock was his father, what kind of evidence would you need?" he asked with genuine interest.

"While DNA matching is the only way to prove it, the closest full DNA donor linking us would have been my father."

"So, regardless of any DNA link, what difference would it make to Amber?"

"Shouldn't have any effect on what Amber is hoping to find."

"Lawyers never ask a question if they don't already know the answer, someone once told me," he said, smiling. "But I don't know this one. What is it Amber's trying to prove with all this research?"

"She wants to find out who he really is, since we've learned he isn't Ethan Wenzler, isn't a student at MSU, and abandoned her during a major tragedy," I said, carefully wording the next thought. "I'm sure she liked him, and he hurt her. Sometimes you find out about the monster, so you know how to kill it." I smiled. "Figuratively speaking, of course."

"Part of the answer is whether or not he's Penny Tucker's son," he said, nodding. "But for the record, she doesn't want to *literally* pound on the monster more than I do."

"I should have let you kick him out when he came to the hotel the first time."

"Yeah, perhaps." He reached and touched my nose. "But, if I'd known then what I know now, I wouldn't have just kicked him out, and being in jail for *literally* ripping his head off would have ruined our trip."

"How considerate." I grinned. "But think of how much other trouble the rest of us could have avoided afterward if you had."

• • • • •

Zach took a shower before coming to bed.

Something had been on his mind all evening, but it didn't involve me in his shower, I could tell.

I had been staring at the letters on a page of a novel from my bedside table, not even making sentences of the words while I waited for him.

"I've been thinking about the ranch in Albuquerque," he said, settling into a reclining position, reinforcing my assumption he wanted to talk.

"Okay," I said, not voicing the snarky rebuttal that I knew which ranch he meant.

"I love it here. I built this place with the thought of you in every detail. We've created great memories."

"But you have connections back to New Mexico, right?"

He nodded.

"Emotions aside, let's consider logistics. Do you want to move back into your mother's house if she relocates?"

A moment passed, then he smiled.

"I do have some pretty fantastic memories there, too, you know."

"Logistics, Zach."

"Nothing's wrong with the house unless you just didn't like it. It's clumsy. We could build a new one if you'd like."

"The bad memories?" I suggested, referring to what had happened with Kim and Purgatory.

"You said no emotions," he replied. "When I brought you to this cabin the first time, you told me it's not a place's fault what happens there."

"True. And Amber?"

"She'll go back to college, call home for money occasionally, earn her degree and a great job, find a guy I can approve of. I doubt any decision we make will affect her for long."

I tilted my head. "You don't think she considers this her home? Where we brought her to rescue her. Where she could feel safe again?"

"You mean we have to make her feelings a priority in this decision?" he asked.

"No, I'm saying we should *consider* her feelings, not that we have to be limited by them. What's in your heart, Zach? I'm happy being with you."

"I don't want me to be the reason you're happy."

"Not what I said, Cowboy. I said I'm happy being with you, not that you are the only thing that makes me happy."

"Would you consider selling this and moving back to New Mexico?"

"Well, I'd miss the trees and the rain."

"Would it make you sad to go back if your mom's not there anymore?"

"I'm sad she's gone, no matter where I live. Changing addresses won't make me miss her any more than I do."

"Living in New Mexico won't make you dream of David Wesley?" he asked, although he seldom mentioned him by name.

"Moving to Alamogordo might, but not Albuquerque," I pointed out.

"Where would you work? Or more realistically, would you work?"

"I don't know. Maybe I'd go back to school or something. Go back to selling books at the mall. Write a novel."

"Bookstore. Sounds boring."

"Some days, boring sounds fantastic. Books don't demand you work overtime because one of them gets killed. They don't bleed or get sick. Never had one shoot at me. No lawsuits. Worst a book can do is keep me awake at night if I like it. Sounds okay to me."

"You don't care if we go back?" he said, turning to face me, pulling the pillow behind him under his elbow. "Honest?"

"I don't have any objections to going back." I smiled. "But now you have livestock to move, too."

"United Van Lines doesn't haul cattle?"

Funny guy.

"I'd like you to consider one other thing, then," he said, his voice serious again. "I'd like to offer Kenny a chance to come with us and work on the ranch."

"Really." I let that ping around in my head a moment. "He's loyal to you."

"He knows I understand his mental illness and its implications, and that I trust he's stable when he takes his medications. In turn, he trusts me to help him afford and stay on those meds. And he really jammed on the idea of getting a vehicle."

"Then that option is accepted as well. Should we start packing?" I asked.

"Let's wait until Amber's ready to go back to school. I don't want her to worry that our decision is affected by her situation, whether it speeds up or slows down our plans. I'd rather it not involve her until we're ready to do it."

"So she shouldn't have any input into it? What about Rainier?"

"We'll figure out what to do with the horses. She has so much ahead of her, including the horses, and I don't want her to think she should come with us instead of going to college, or that we didn't want her to come if she isn't ready yet to go back."

"Good point." I put the book on the bedside table.

"Nor should she change her career decision because UNM doesn't offer what she wants. But what if she has second thoughts?" he asked, maybe because he was having them.

"Then we should discuss it like adults, but she needs to make those decisions without following us out of guilt."

"You're so smart," he said, touching my nose. "That's one of the hundred reasons I love you."

"Show me the other 99?" I asked, snapping off the light.

CHAPTER 56
AMBER

October 16, 2001

Julie made a trip to town for groceries and brought home the box of books shipped by Penny Tucker's widowed husband, too.

"I can't wait to dig into them," I said, reaching for the box.

"Rules," she said. "You are not to discuss this with anyone who does not reside in this household or is not involved in the investigation. You may not take them outside this house. When you go back to school, the box goes back to Mr. Daniels."

"Julie!" I whined. "I don't even know what I'm looking for."

"You are searching exclusively for information related to Penny being Ethan's mother."

"There's more to this than when she got pregnant," I argued. "Who was his father? That's something Sally Tucker's journals don't tell."

"Those are the rules. Follow them or don't open the box," she said. "If you find other important information, then we'll see where to go from there."

I wanted to scream, but I also realized I could easily fall into this hole and not see daylight for a long time. Worse, I understood there were facets to this family's stories that had caused Julie a lot of pain, mental and physical.

However, just because I wasn't looking for stories about Anthony Bock didn't mean I might not learn more than Julie had told me.

I took the knife she offered me and cut the tape. The box wasn't huge like I'd hoped, but I pulled out eleven books, seven looked old and four appeared newer. All were older than me.

From Sally's accounts, I'd read that Angela's husband, Robert Bock was not Anthony's real father. In fact, Anthony's biological father had been Andrew Madigan, Julie's father. Robert had murdered Angela, which is how Anthony came to live with the Tuckers in Traverse City.

We'd discussed this in detail, Julie and me.

During the multiple murder investigation in 1995 in Michigan, Julie had talked with the first policemen on the scene of Robert Bock's murder of Angela, which had provided an entirely different perspective to Robert's death after a decade in prison and parole, which was likely Anthony's first solo murder.

"You mean he'd killed before?" I asked.

"Penny helped locate another body on the Tucker's cherry farm," she'd explained on our trip to New Mexico. "It's doubtful the victim would have ever been found, but she described how Anthony and her brother killed the old man."

"How old was he then?"

"Fourteen, maybe fifteen," she said. "Besides the old man and his mother's husband, I counted fourteen victims."

All the violence seemed incredibly unreal. Like some movie that goes way overboard on killing, like *Halloween* or *Friday the 13th*.

According to Sally, Anthony was withdrawn, shy, polite. She tried hard to protect him from any social pressures regarding his parents.

Until Julie told me about Anthony's killing spree, I couldn't have realized what a monster Anthony was.

Penny described him as having no boundaries to her private life, having teased her when no one was watching, so even her mother wouldn't believe her. He pushed her down the stairs in the house at least twice. The first time, her mother almost believed the story he'd pushed her when Penny told on him. The next time he shoved her, Sally wouldn't possibly question his alibi when he came running inside right after the fall, even though Penny wrote that he had pushed her then shimmied out his bedroom window and off the porch, coming inside at just the right moment to prove he couldn't have done it.

I remembered Sally's journal entry of her daughter's broken arm and how the girl kept insisting Anthony had done it. "I know I pay more attention to him than to my own kids, but he's been through so much. I'm angry at Penny for trying to blame him when I'm sure he was outside playing in the yard. Maybe having a cast on her arm for six weeks will teach her not to do things to herself and accuse him of hurting her."

Wow, that seemed harsh, I thought.

Penny's brother J.P. caught on to the harassment and began participating in the torment.

I remember having friends in junior high who always complained of being tortured by older siblings, but none of their stories seemed as severe as what Penny wrote having to endure.

Taking notes as I read, I brought them to lunch and discussed my findings with Julie and Dad, although he had little input.

"Penny didn't mention Anthony doing anything of the sort when I talked to her," she said, stopping for a sip of milk.

"But you said she thought he was dead when you met her, right? And the questions you asked were about her brother, so if Anthony had been a problem to her as a child, she might not have wanted to discuss it," I said. "Like, I don't want to think about some of my past."

I meant it as a challenge to see if she would tell me anything else about Bock.

"That is a valid point. Does Penny write anything positive about him?"

She didn't take the bait.

"Not much. She stops writing much at all for a year after she broke her arm."

"I wouldn't bother writing about a problem if no one believed me," Dad said. He took another handful of tortilla chips to go with his sandwich. "What about friends, school, a job?"

"Not much. Working at home, you know, doing dishes and laundry and stuff." I took a bite of my sandwich, made of roast beef and grilled onions left over from last night, chewed while I thought. "She has only mentioned one friend, Hannah, who stayed overnight a few times after Anthony came to live with them. She said this friend thought he was so creepy, she didn't want to come back."

"Oh, he was all that and a bag of chips. He watched his father – his stepfather," Julie corrected, "kill his mother. He took the knife from the kitchen and hid it at the Tucker house, then took it with him when he left."

"The knife that was used on your dad?" I pressed.

She nodded.

"And when your husband cut your throat?"

She tugged her shirt collar up on her neck, but I'd only seen her do it when she was uncomfortable.

"That's enough, Amber," Dad tried to interrupt.

"But I don't understand. Why would Bock want you dead?" I asked, truly perplexed.

"He wasn't trying to kill me," she hissed. Her face turned a greenish-gray, and she got up from the table and took a few steps toward the patio door, then stopped and turned to me with an expression of hurt before escaping.

The slamming of the door left an eerie silence.

"Wow," Dad muttered, then hung his head a moment before responding in a soft monotone. "What do you think you're doing? Bock was an evil bastard. He never intended to kill her. He wanted her to learn to enjoy killing like he did. And what happened to Julie has nothing to do with you trying to find out who Ethan is."

"I'm sorry," I started to argue. "This is connected somehow. I need to know –"

"No," he said, pushing his plate away and raising his voice. "You don't *need* to know anything else about this. You *want* to know if anything Ethan said to you is true, and I suspect little of it is, but none of that is worth the cost of disrespecting Julie."

CHAPTER 57
JULIE

I've run away from that bastard for years, I thought. I finally got my life together. Thought I'd escaped that monster.

And now Amber intends to bulldoze into my past for her own amusement? I want to just scream!

Amber had read and discussed Sally's writings on our ride back to Washington, and I'd provided information about their family to help with context.

Sally might not have written much about her nephew's family after Angela was killed, and although Robert Bock had been convicted of her sister's murder, she may not have known he was paroled within a decade, nor that he was then killed, too.

I'm probably the only person alive who presumed Robert's death was at the hands of his teenage son Anthony.

Everyone involved is dead. It doesn't matter anymore.

Tension knotted in my shoulders as I walked toward the barn to escape Amber's interrogation.

Blaming my emotional turmoil on Amber wasn't fair, but her questions pushed me toward the corners I'd been in at those other points in my life, and I refused to back up another single freaking step.

I opened the gate to the corral and stepped inside, waiting for Julaquinte and the filly to assess whether I was to be graced with their presence.

The slick black mare sauntered my direction, then stopped, head up and ears perked, smelling the anger.

I took a couple of deep breaths to calm myself, which apparently satisfied her.

The filly, yet unnamed I'd been reminded several times, finally trotted up beside her mother to see if I had treats or something.

I'd done a little research into the names in the breeder's pattern of antique musical terms. Names had been divided into types of words, from tempo or other characteristics of the music such as Adagio or A Capella, and modes, which I didn't understand at all but liked the words, such as Aeolian, Lydian, and Ionian.

Julaquinte and Waldaquinte were names of organ stops in some of the oldest pipe organs built. I didn't have a clue what stops or registers or any of the other information meant.

In my research, I'd found a few terms that I liked the way they sounded when I said them aloud, but I thought perhaps I should meet the little girl who would carry the name before I tacked it on.

The filly was shy, delicate-looking with an expressive face but already muscular with a glorious jet-black coat, though the flowing mane and tail, and prancing feathers on her forelocks hadn't grown out yet.

One of the musical terms came to mind, and I said it aloud, "Unda Maris."

The filly took a few steps toward me and stretcher her slender high-set neck to touch my outstretched hand, sniffed and then sort of *boing'ed* back a step and danced like a happy baby goat.

"That's your name, Sweetie. You've been dubbed Unda Maris, which means *wave under the sea*."

"That sounds perfect," Zach said from behind me, causing me and the two horses to freak out just a bit.

I let loose a string of cuss words under my breath.

"Not a freebie," he noted. "That's at least twenty dollars' worth of profanity, most of which I will pretend I don't take personally."

"If you'd stop scaring the hell out of me regularly, I wouldn't owe the profanity jaw a thousand dollars or however much and wouldn't disparage your genetic history." My heart finally stopped galloping with only a few stumbles along the way.

"Sorry, and that's another five."

"I don't think you really are sorry, or you wouldn't laugh every time you do it."

The filly came to the fence and let Zach scratch her neck.

"Being a horse whisperer doesn't make it any better," I said, pointing to the two of them.

"Friesians are very complicated horses," he said, ignoring my barb. "They were bred to be war horses, able to carry men in armor. In the movie *LadyHawke*, the warrior rode a 19-year-old stallion named Othello. He was a magnificent character in the story." He made *oogly* noises at the filly. "Their popularity has done to them what it's done to so many other species like the German Shepard or Cocker Spaniel."

"Really? What?" I marveled, trying to remember I was mad at him.

"Over-breeding and in-breeding to enhance certain traits or eliminate others have led to genetic errors like dwarfism."

I wrinkled my upper lip.

"My point is, sometimes no matter how strong and invincible an animal is, those characteristics can be overused and become weak eventually. A horse trained to jump may develop weak bones if overworked." He turned to me. "Sorta like you."

"Me?"

"You have stood tall under tremendous adversity for years, Julie," he said, reaching over to pick a piece of straw from my hair. "But a rock's ability to withstand a single raindrop is what also allows wind and water to erode it." He silenced my mounting rebuttal with a finger to my lips. "None of the analogies fit, I guess. I wanted to say that it's okay to let others help you."

I nodded, not exactly sure if I was supposed to answer.

"I've put a stop to Amber dogging you about Bock for now," Zach said, reaching over to place a kiss on my forehead. "Your boss called, which is why I came out here," he said. "I think you have a case to solve."

The thought of going back to work made me happy.

Until Wade Fordham told me what it was.

CHAPTER 58
JULIE

To escape the tension at the house with Amber, I drove to the sheriff's department and parked behind the building in the employee lot, thinking how glad I was to be going back to work.

My first obstacle was the touchpad/card reader lock on the back door. I didn't have a badge or ID, and the override codes didn't work, and no one answered when I banged on the metal door. Accepting I'd been away *that* long, I walked around to the front entrance.

"Julie!" Georgia Adams exclaimed, jumping up from her chair. "I thought you'd never come home!" She let me in the security door and then hugged me hard. "We heard about your mother, and I'm so sorry."

Wade must have heard the commotion, and he came out of his office to the dispatch suite and repeated the hug and condolences.

"Gosh, I didn't realize you all missed me so much," I said, blushing. "Zach says you have something for me to work on."

Wade motioned me to his office, and Geo went back to answer a ringing phone.

"Paramedics dropped by a house in the southeastern part of the county this morning and initiated the law enforcement response. Leesa Bowman and her partner Seth Taber were unofficially doing a welfare check on Leesa's grandparents. Her mom calls to check on them several times a week, but because she was out of town, she missed a few days. Leesa called, but no one answered this morning. When she arrived, no one answered the door, so she used her key. The house was," he inhaled and blew air out his nose, which made a soft whistle, "well, there was no question a murder had been committed."

Then I won't ask the question, letting imagination suffice.

"The crew backed out and called us. Richard Langston responded and found what he thinks is the couple buried in the backyard. The hole wasn't deep enough to even conceal the bodies."

"Thinks?" I sat, waiting for the rest of the story. A buried body case, while not common to this part of Washington, wasn't something I particularly had to be assigned to.

Surely he's not just celebrating my return with a double murder investigation.

"The bodies were," he hesitated and flared his nose in an expression of distaste. "They were dismembered and put into vacuum-sealed bags. Doc' Bishop says the time of death could be anywhere from one to three days ago."

My ears got hot, and the nausea that accompanies the sensation of fainting wiggled in my guts.

"Are you okay?" he asked, afraid he'd found something capable of making me sick to my stomach.

He had, but it wasn't the murder itself.

I'd never heard of vacuum-packed bodies until a few months ago in Michigan when Brandan Callaghan had called and asked me about a body found in the trunk of a car.

I tried to swallow, but my mouth was dry, and the sound was loud in my ears.

"Has Dr. Bishop done an autopsy yet?" I asked.

"Well, no. Boyd believed it would be better to turn the whole thing over to the Portland medical examiners' office."

I nodded, waiting for more bad news, but he didn't speak. "Wade, why'd you call me for this?"

"You are the only person I thought of with the experience to investigate or research this."

"Trust me, I don't have enough, Wade."

"It's over my head," he said, almost apologetically. "Unless you object, I'd like you and Langston to transport the, um, bags to Portland today."

"Yeah, I can do that," I said, leaning back in the chair and rubbing my eyes with the heels of my hands. "But there's a bigger problem we should discuss first."

"You're okay to work, right? I mean, you'd been shot, right?" he stammered. "You looked a little sick for a moment."

"Getting shot is not the issue." I tried to find words into that would sound, I don't know, *sane*? "Remember when I left for Michigan in June, before any of this disaster started?"

He nodded.

"One of the deputies there asked me if I'd ever seen," I was able to swallow this time, "a dismembered body in vacuum packing, because they'd discovered one in the trunk of a car."

I could picture Wade's face getting paler with each word.

"This is a unique signature or whatever it's called. I can't fathom how I would be on the periphery of it twice in less than six months, most of the way across the country, by accident."

Wade muttered something I didn't bother to try to decipher.

Worth twenty bucks in the Profanity Jar.

"The question isn't just what happened to this couple and who killed them, but why is the point to involve me."

"What's the answer?"

"I'm afraid to find out, sir."

• • • • •

I rode in near silence with Richard to Portland with the remains packed on ice in coolers in the backseat.

On the way back, he seemed relieved enough for conversation.

"The medical examiner didn't seem any more enthused to receive *that* than I did transporting it," he said, trying to shake it off his shoulders in a quiver I felt.

"First time, and hopefully the last time, either of us ever does this."

"Did I hear you telling the sheriff this isn't your first experience with, um, bodies in bags." The grimace on his face twitched to a smile, then a chuckle. "My mother would never have believed this, I mean, you know, the woman who raised me."

"Neither does the man who raised her, Richard. I didn't see the first bagged body, much less transport it," I said, "but it's time I call Detective Callaghan and compare notes." The thought made me pause while I tried to fit mental jigsaw puzzle pieces together.

I felt a mental snap of connection.

"Oh hell, of course!"

My outburst startled Langston.

The idea didn't quite form in my head, but I knew I was on to something.

"You're doing that scary thing again, Julie," he said, only partially kidding. "Riding with you is like going to an investigative séance."

I made a face at him while I was digging my cell phone out of my pocket. I selected a phone number and hit the dial button, put the phone to my ear and waited.

A woman's voice announced I'd reached the voice mailbox of whatever number I'd dialed, inviting me to leave a message. I did, then disconnected.

I turned to Richard. "Make sense of this. Police found the car in a public lot because two underage people were sitting on the hood, drinking. The plates come back showing the car was stolen, so the cop keeps looking. Finds the keys in it as if it had been left running and died when it ran out of gas; battery dead."

Langston nodded.

"The owner is a young woman, who coincidentally has been missing for, I don't remember, three months. The cop pops the trunk and finds a body, like these, in vacuum-sealed packing. Victim was male, not the car owner. Which could mean there is another body if she was a prior victim."

His eyes had widened behind his aviator glasses. "The only thing in common so far is you."

I hadn't exactly thought of that.

"True," I replied, but the point I was going to make vanished from my thoughts. "The boyfriend was ticketed for public intox. He was the father of Kim's baby, my previous boss's daughter. But when we arrived in Michigan, he turned up and made friends with Amber. He's the one who invited her to New York, then disappeared, abandoning her there on 9/11, which led to this overwhelming mess of the last three months."

Langston cringed a little.

"What's that got to do with the bodies in plastic?" Langston asked, derailing my bullet-train of thought completely.

I mentally went through the sequence that connected my thoughts again.

Pregnant girl and boy.

Car and body in Michigan.

Same boy asks me about a dead woman who had helped law enforcement during a murder in Michigan.

Same boy asks my daughter to go to NYC.

Another two bodies in Washington, with a similar signature. Is Ethan alive?

The string didn't pass straight through all those events. I needed more data.

Kim had said her boyfriend's name was Sean Smith. That name was also on the credit card used to pay for the room in New York City. But was it his *real* name? Probably not.

Maybe Traverse City police could identify the suspect, knowing he used at least two aliases.

Who do they think he was?

I shuddered.

"That kid, who told me he was Ethan Wenzler, wanted information from me about his biological mother, Penny Tucker-Daniels, who I knew from a murder investigation in Michigan. He never asked me about his biological father, but was that because he knew I wouldn't know or because he already did?" I said, talking to myself out loud. Although I couldn't imagine what he thought of it, Langston let me continue.

"Penny mentioned her brother had molested her when she was younger. Had she meant Anthony instead, or had I misunderstood? Or was it both? Penny told us that Bock had been dead since she was a teenager. He most certainly was not."

CHAPTER 59
AMBER

October 17, 2001

Julie came home from her trip to Portland in a foul mood, from what I could hear down the stairs. I didn't come out of my room.

The next morning, however, I knew it was time to make amends.

"What's up?" I asked, walking up to her in the barn where she sat on a bale of hay. "I came to apologize. I was way out of line yesterday."

"Apology accepted. I'm sorry this makes me so crabby. You may be the only one to know the answer to what's kicking my ass about all this," she said, patting the spot beside her.

I sat.

Sitting on the bale of hay wasn't comfortable to my leg but not painful either.

"You've read through all of Penny's diaries?"

"Not yet."

"Any mention of her getting pregnant?" she asked. "Are you to the right age?"

I shook my head, unsure where she was going with this.

"Can you skim ahead to then?" She plucked a piece of straw from the bale she leaned on, stuck it in the corner of her mouth. "We need to know who the father of her baby was, unless Ethan might have indicated that he already knew."

I squinted in thought. "He never said."

"Just curious because he didn't ask you if I knew, did he?"

Waldo nickered outside, and I figured it was Dad.

"I don't mean to keep asking – we've been through it," she said, "but I was hoping you might have remembered if his appointment in New York was about his birth parents or just his adoption?"

"I thought he was there for something related to the adoption," I said. "Other than questions about Penny, I don't recall him mentioning his father, but I'll keep looking."

I went back to the journals to find information regarding Penny's pregnancy and the adoption.

Penny was only five years old when Anthony Bock moved into her life. Her first diary started when she was nine, but during those early years, it was truly a child's writing about her life. Ethan said he thought his mom had been fifteen or so when she had him.

I thumbed through several books in the stack of Penny's journals, looking for a time closer to when she got pregnant.

Teenage anger and isolation she wrote about, and I understood. My mother had to work all the time to make sure she had enough clients to keep her business going and make a living for us, but it didn't mean I didn't hate being at home alone after school and every Saturday because of her job.

I'd finished reading Sally Tucker's diaries before we got home from New Mexico. I didn't understand how a mother could fail to dump out her feelings regarding her daughter's illegitimate pregnancy when she had no problem writing about the boys – her son and her nephew.

Understanding they lived in the age of whispers of "that girl," who would more than likely have been sent away to "live with an aunt" or go to "boarding school" for a while, I wondered when the social acceptance of illegitimate pregnancy began. When did premarital sex come out of the taboo closet? Obviously, it was going on long before any of this, which is how Anthony Bock came to be, but Angela's parents had tried to normalize it by demanding she marry Robert Bock.

How'd that work out . . .

No one seemed to be freaked out that Kim was pregnant, except for Mrs. Connors, who had been shut down in high style when she blabbed her disgust to Julie, I'd heard. Dad said it was a perfect retort.

Dad and Julie had sex before they were married; he had told me so.

I'd thought I might with Ethan on our New York adventure, but September 11 had become more of a nightmare than me having sex and even getting pregnant might have been.

Probably not. Boy, wouldn't Dad have been looking for him if I had!

But I'm glad I didn't, given the way he dumped me and disappeared.

CHAPTER 60
JULIE

Wade put me back on patrol on my official return to duty. No doubt in my mind I wasn't ready to wrestle a prisoner to the ground; nonetheless, back to work I went.

The bodies in bags, albeit a personal tragedy for the paramedic, were a case without any leads. The scene had been photographed and fingerprinted; tracks likely to be identifiable in the yard were casted for imprints; and all the neighbors were interviewed in hopes of finding a witness or home surveillance camera footage of anything suspicious.

Nothing.

The report back from Portland regarding the bodies and bags described the dismemberment had occurred without freezing. The plastic was from a packaging machine company that made its own commercial-grade film for it, but the sample came from a vacuum film out of production five years, according to the company. Based on the identification, the machine was 24 inches wide. It was portable, albeit still quite large.

Not your typical department store home-use machine.

When I checked back with Brandan about the body in similar packaging in Michigan, he gave me the same details except one.

The body discovered in Michigan had been frozen, but he didn't know for sure whether it was frozen before or after it was packed. Nor had it had been identified.

The bodies here in Washington had not been frozen. Cause of death had been a single 9 mm Luger gunshot wound to the heart of each victim.

"Why would the killer freeze a body here but not there?" he asked me.

"Freezing isn't unheard of, but cutting up a frozen body would take significant effort or machinery. It makes your case slightly different from ours, but the question is why is it different? I'm betting the ability to freeze was something available in Michigan but not here."

"Makes sense, but it's scary you are the one making sense of it," he said. "Matthew once told me that you think like the criminals."

"Ahh, aren't you so sweet," I said in a gooey fake Southern accent, then made a retching sound, at which he laughed. "Look for any warehouses or plants in the area that used both freezers and vacuum packing. Meat, probably, but also pre-packaged items such as cheese, dried fruits. Maybe someplace still in business, with a stash of old equipment somewhere, or defunct one with abandoned equipment."

"Now on my list of things to find out."

"Call me if you learn anything," I said, ready to dismiss our conversation.

"Um, Julie?" he said in a softer tone. "I wanted to thank you for asking me to go to New York. I got to see my little sister and her kiddos, and that means a lot to me."

"Thank you for going. We would have been lost and out of our heads trying to find Amber without you," I replied. "Zach covered all your expenses, right?"

"Oh, sure. It's not that. Kathryn, my sister, her ex-husband was killed on 9/11, probably when the Towers collapsed. Me being there was good, like it was all part of a bigger plan. But thanks."

"I'm so sorry, Brandan," I said, wishing I had other words of sympathy.

After I shot David, I didn't receive many condolences. Those offered after Zach supposedly died were either empty words, "Is there anything I can do?" or stupid, painful phrases like, "You'll marry again, you're young."

Of course, he wasn't really dead, was he? How many of those condolences were from people who knew he was alive?

"I hope having her brother around helped made it a smidgen easier," I said. However, I imagined dealing with everyone else's catastrophes had made coming home to divorce papers even harder. "And Zach told me that Molly had filed for divorce. I'm sorry."

"Yeah, I'm trying to be a good parent." He sighed. "I'm angry she wants to take Riley and Vinny to California. I know I work a lot, but I thought we were pretty tight. I always knew this was a possibility."

"Doesn't make it easier."

We chatted a bit more about less painful things, then disconnected.

Disconnected. Cell phones were supposed to make us closer, but I don't see that happening.

• • • • •

All morning, I'd felt like a dark gray cloud was tethered to my collar with a short rope.

Whoever the killer was, I feared, was creating a scene to draw me in, to connect me to the case there. Or maybe my unexpected departure from Traverse City had changed the killer's plans. Nevertheless, the murder there had occurred before I arrived.

Could someone have determined how long before I got there? Is that why the body was frozen?

The murders here were committed after I'd arrived home finally.

Another ominous thought: Had a body been found in vacuum-sealed bags in Albuquerque during my stay? I certainly wouldn't have known, but it was almost more ominous if there wasn't such a crime signature. If not, I had to ask, why not? Why so much time between if I were to have finally arrived in Washington to face a new murder?

No way could I believe the murderer would have been empathetic to my situation with my mother. That made no sense at all.

Why, then, was there a break?

I logged in to the computer and pulled up a search to find a phone number for the detective division of the Albuquerque Police Department.

Either way, I've got to know.

A connection and several transfers later, I was speaking to Detective Hector Salazar.

I began my spiel again with an introduction including my maiden name that was interrupted.

"I've heard of you. My father, Manuel Salazar – Manny? He was the detective who worked with you on the Darci Pierce kidnapping and murder in the '80s."

Although I never wanted to hear her name again either, we had to swap details for a while before I could revert to my main question.

"I'm now with the Skamania County Sheriff's Department in Washington. There were murders in Michigan and here in Washington with an unusual signature – the bodies were dismembered and packaged in vacuum-sealed bags."

I almost heard the profanity running through his head, hoping it had no implications to my sanity.

"I'm wondering if anything similar occurred in Albuquerque in the last few months?" I asked.

"Something like vacuum packing would stand out," he said, "but these days, there's some mighty creepy people roaming wild. I don't recall anything like that, but let me ask around. I'll call you back. Gimme a few days."

I gave him my contact information, and we hung up.

Creepy people, indeed.

CHAPTER 61
AMBER

October 19, 2001

Penny was pregnant in late 1974. That made Whaz-his-name 27 years old, not 21 like he'd told me.

Now I understand why he seemed so mature compared to guys my age.

Reading about her delivery, she'd written in a much sloppier scrawl that she'd heard the nurses say her baby was a girl.

Wait, Penny had a girl?

I reread from her entry about finding out she was pregnant through the rest of that book before I was sure.

Totally sure.

"Julie, I found what we were looking for in Penny's diary," I said, finding her on the deck with her feet up, catching the weak sunshine. "But it's not what we thought."

She sat up. "What is it?"

I opened the book to my first marker and read aloud, from one relevant entry to the next.

September 17, 1974 – No! I can't be!! Ethan and I only did it once, and he promised me I couldn't get pregnant! My father is going to kill me!

"Dad would kill me, too, I bet," I said with a laugh.

"Oh, honey, you can't even imagine how slowly," Julie said with a wry smile.

October 2, 1974 – I told Hannah that I'm pregnant, but so is she! What, is it in the water?? Would like to laugh but have cried myself to sleep for a week. She wouldn't tell me who she did it with.

November 13, 1974 – My mother! That bitch told me she's known I was pregnant for three months now!! I guess she and Hannah's mother discussed it and they're going to send both of us to a *"boarding school for unwed mothers" in Grand Rapids. At least we won't be all alone. She said she's not going to tell Father until I'm gone.*

There were a dozen entries or so while she was in the school, but other than the city, she did not name it. Mostly she wrote about the abysmal environment of the school. They attended mandatory classes, ate "healthy" food, and had a modified exercise class. She was right about having a friend there, as it seemed to be the only good thing about going.

April 30, 1975 – I was in labor for almost 16 hours yesterday, and the doctor finally yanked the baby out with some pliers or something I heard him call them. It hurt so damned bad, I was screaming! They tied my hands down, and the nurse kept telling me to shut up! I know I won't ever find out anything else, but at least I heard them say it's a girl. Another nurse demanded that I tell them who the father really was for the birth certificate. I won't. After the way people have treated me, I'm not making this easier for no one.

Hannah had her baby this morning. They had to take her to surgery, I heard one of the nurses say, because it wouldn't come out. But it was a boy. Stubborn like her, obviously. But they haven't brought Hannah back to the room.

May 5, 1975 – Not like I wanted to stay, but the headmaster just kicked me out, called my parents and told them to come get me. No one will tell me about Hannah.

May 9, 1975 – I'm back home. That word doesn't even mean someplace warm or safe anymore. My parents just treat me like the nurses did, barely speaking to me other than giving me lists of chores to do. I asked my mother if she knew what happened to Hannah, why no one will tell me. Her answer was to mind my own business! What the hell?

"She wrote that the baby's father's name was Ethan, but it was a girl," I repeated. "None of this makes any sense."

Julie took the book and flipped back and forth a couple of times, then slammed the cover shut.

"Wow, Amber. That's some twist. If who we thought is Ethan was searching for his real mother, has he found out it wasn't Penny?"

"But if he didn't know," I countered, "what are the chances he'd accidentally pick a fake name the same as the guy Penny identifies as the father of her baby?"

"Not a coincidence, I'd bet," she said. "Take the next step. Does she ever mention this Ethan's last name?"

I shook my head. "Not in this book."

"Find the name of the place she and Hannah were sent to boarding school? Or anything else about Hannah?"

"Hannah didn't go home when Penny did, and she didn't mention her again through the rest of this book, In fact, Penny didn't write much for the next year or so. An occasional entry describing events in the family, but nothing about Hannah, this Ethan person or the baby."

"Where would you look now?" Julie asked me. "This is a real live research project now. What's next?"

I thought a minute. "I'd locate birth and adoption records in Michigan for this particular year. The 'home of unwed mothers,' she called it later, it's in Grand Rapids. Search school records around Traverse City to find an Ethan – it's not a terribly common name."

She nodded. "How can I help?"

"Authority," I said, standing up straight. "I've got none."

"I'd bet the sheriff would put you on as a consulting research intern," she replied. "That should get you started."

"That's spectabulous!" I bent down to hug her.

Dad came around from the garage in time to hear me say that. "Julie, are you teaching her more jumbled words?"

"You two talk or flirt or whatever you do all the time," I said, then wrinkled my nose at him. "I'm going back to the diaries," I announced, standing and using the cane – my last week using it per the physical therapist – to walk into the house.

I really wanted to go ride Rainier.

CHAPTER 62
JULIE

October 19, 2001

Another day of no news about the murders.

Wade had even joked that Skamania County never had so many murders until I came to work.

Funny, Wade. Very funny.

But unfortunately, true, too.

The dark cloud I'd thought was following me in the figurative sense dumped a literal hard cold rain down my collar yesterday while I was at the scene of a car accident. No serious injuries, but it took a while for traffic to start moving again, and I was soaked to my socks.

The rain stopped an hour after I got into a dry uniform. Of course.

Today the weather was all sunshine and unicorn sparkles, but I'd been stuck inside most of my shift giving station tours to the grade-schoolers.

Once, the grumbly side of me considered telling a particularly rowdy group of third graders about bloody murders, complete with crime scene photos and . . . I didn't.

I guess I would like to keep my job another day or so.

• • • • •

After work, I'd parked my still-baby-blue Yukon in the garage and I gathered my bag to go inside, but I was tired of walls.

I stood and stretched, then dumped everything back into the seat and walked to the barn.

Finding Zach there wasn't a surprise. I didn't always know what he was doing, only that he spent a lot of time in or around the barn.

I flopped down on a bale of hay, feeling as lifeless as the alfalfa beneath my butt, thinking of all the ordeals in my life recently.

Bodies in bags.

An imposter who connived my stepdaughter.

My rib aching more today than recently, for who knows what reason other than a sneeze portending a coming cold.

Amber was looking for more answers, as was Brandan and Nolan, but I was frightened of what we might learn. Worse, I was scared that the truth could be bad news for us all.

Like holding thousands of not-quite-identical black jigsaw puzzle pieces. I don't even know if they all go to the same puzzle.

"Something's bothering you, J'. Wanna talk?" Zach asked me, reaching to take my hand and help me stand. Then he wrapped his warm arms around me and swayed to whatever music was in his head.

"I'm standing in quicksand in a bottomless rabbit hole, and I'm afraid," I said, moving with him, my face buried in his shirt.

He smelled good. Like fresh air and cut grass and horses.

"And I have a long rope to pull you out. Tell me so I can help."

I didn't let go of him, and I fought tears that hadn't begun to fall.

He pulled away and cradled my face, placed his lips on mine in a possessive, protective kiss the likes of which we hadn't shared in years.

"Now talk to me or I'm gonna saddle us a couple of horses for a long ride to jiggle it out of you."

"Let's go," I said. "I need a ride."

Though slightly surprised at my decision, Zach made it happen in short order. Two horses, two saddles and bridles. Even produced a hat for me and boosted me up.

"Lead the way," he said, mounting easily, like sliding into the hot tub.

Soaking had been my first choice.

At an easy walk, Denali's gait was smooth.

Not a horse person until I met Zach, I'd learned how being on horseback could be a mind-clearing, soul-soothing escape.

He'd once told me that being on a horse put him closer to Heaven and in a better place to pray than inside a church because there was no ceiling.

Not pressing either the pace or the conversation, Zach rode quietly slightly behind me until I was ready to talk.

"I'm finding what I know is far outweighed by what I don't know about this."

Zach said nothing, but Rainier quickly inhaled then puffed a breath out through his nostrils, which made a loud purring sound.

I repeated a summary of the last few days' epiphanies in a semblance of logical order, though fraught with commentary, suspicions and suppositions I couldn't verify. Jumbled news. Questions without answers.

Finally, I stopped Denali and turned.

"None of it makes sense, does it."

"Oh, it makes sense. Although I'm sure she would love to tell you herself, Amber has tracked down evidence and discovered who Ethan is and some other facts. She's knock-down phenomenal at research when someone gives her free rein."

Another horse euphemism?

"That means she has good news?"

He nodded, but our conversation was interrupted by my phone, which I'd stuck in my hip pocket.

The call was from an Indiana area code.

"Mrs. Samualson, this is Detective Martin from Terra Haute. I called to let you know we identified the man who died at the convenience store."

"That's great."

I didn't feel that way, but what was I supposed to say?

"His name is Gregory Edward Rigsby, age 28. Last known address in Michigan. He has a criminal history of petty stuff, one car theft with probation, and one charge for sexual assault, charges dropped. No known associates. Parents are deceased, died in a house fire a couple of years ago. No other family we can find."

"Anything else?"

"No CODIS match for his DNA. No other leads for the other suspect," he said. "We found a bloody smear on the door handle. Not a usable print, but I suspect it's your blood, left when the second suspect went out the door with your bag and gun. Does that seem reasonable?"

"As reasonable as anything else in this damned mess, Detective. Grand Traverse County probably still has a DNA result for me if it would save you having to pay to run it for comparison. I'll give your contact information to Detective Brandan Callaghan."

"I bet he never gets kidded about his name, huh," Martin replied.

"Well he doesn't carry a .44 Mag, so maybe not," I replied, knowing his reference to Harry Callahan in the *Dirty Harry* movies.

I'm sure Brandan has heard them all, too.

We exchanged pleasantries and goodbyes.

I wanted to throw the phone across the meadow.

"The Detective in Indiana," I said, pocketing it. "They've identified the dead guy in the store as Gregory Edward Rigsby."

Zach's not-happy-no-good-news look turned pale, and he mouthed a stream of not-so-nice words.

"What?"

"All these cases and . . . " He dismounted and kicked at the ground, startling Rainier. "Did you ever wonder if these cases were related?"

"Of course not, Zach," I replied, my anxiety skyrocketing high enough that even Denali danced beneath me a few steps. "They can't be."

"Hear me out." He walked over to take Denali's reins. "What if the murders and the damned plastic wrap are connected to the robbery where the kid with the aliases was shot?"

I shook my head as he kept talking.

"The guy arrested with Kim and the father of her baby was Sean Smith. The guy who enticed Amber to New York said he was Ethan Wenzler. The guy who was shot in the convenience store in Indiana was identified as Gregory Rigsby. But it's all the same guy."

"No, Zach," I started to say.

"Amber's been looking for the real identity of the jerk who dumped her, who met her when he came to you to ask about his biological mother. Amber's research of Ethan showed that he was born Gregory Rigsby."

I wanted to speak. Opened my mouth, but nothing came out.

"Rigsby has been involved in all of this, right up to his death. He was involved. But so are you."

Almost voiceless, I swallowed hard and replied, "He may have done all that, including murdering the victim in Michigan. But someone killed him in Indiana, so who killed those two people in White Salmon?"

CHAPTER 63
AMBER

October 20, 2001

By being able to back up my research with the authority of a sheriff, I confirmed Penny had a baby girl, as we'd read in her diary, where she listed the father as "Ethan," but there was no name on the birth certificate. She wrote that her best friend Hannah Tolbert was pregnant at the same time and sent away to the same "boarding school." Hannah's baby was a boy.

The two infants had been adopted by Lowell and Heather Rigsby in Ann Arbor – Gregory and Gretchen.

I kept reading to see if Penny mentioned Hannah again, 'cause I'd certainly hoped that two girls who went through so much together would be friends forever.

I'd hoped to spring the news on Julie that I'd found out Ethan's real name and adoptive family when they returned from their ride, but when they came from the barn, they looked like they did at Grandmom Dagmar's memorial service. Dazed.

"Is something wrong?"

Julie shook her head and slouched in her chair at the dining table.

"Remember you told me you figured out Ethan was not Penny's child?" Dad asked me. "The detectives in Indiana identified the man killed at the convenience store robbery as Gregory Edward Rigsby, also known to us as Ethan Wenzler or to Kim as Sean Smith."

The colors in the room faded to dim grays.

"You mean Julie *shot* him?"

"Sorta missing the point, Amber. Same guy."

"I heard, yeah, Dad. Whoever *he* was, he's dead, right?"

They looked at each other in a silent discussion, then Julie spoke. "The shot I fired didn't hit him."

"Are you sure? Maybe after you'd been shot –"

"Ballistics confirmed that his partner killed him. My bullet hit the clerk. Two shots Rigsby fired were retrieved from the walls. The bullets in him and me came from a third weapon not recovered at the scene."

Dad shrugged. "I don't know what was supposed to happen during the robbery, but it's no coincidence *he* was committing an armed criminal action in the same random place Julie stopped to get gas."

Gathered at the dining room table, we discussed the facts. Julie got out her index cards and took notes, listing everyone involved so far.

Amber Samualson

Julie Samualson

Zach Samualson

~~Anthony Bock~~

~~Penny Tucker~~

~~Ethan (the father)~~

~~Hannah Tolbert~~

~~Kim Katz and baby~~

~~Ethan (son)~~ Wenzler / Gregory Rigsby / Sean Smith

Gretchen Rigsby

Except us, everyone on the list but Gretchen was dead. Julie drew connections between Penny and Anthony, Penny and Ethan the father plus a baby Gretchen, Hannah and a baby boy Gregory, Kim and Sean plus an unborn baby, and lastly Gregory and Gretchen.

I explained that the pregnant girls were sent from Traverse City to Grand Rapids to "boarding school" four to five months into their pregnancies. Being born within hours of each other, Penny's and Hannah's babies were adopted by the same couple, Lowell and Heather Rigsby of Ann Arbor, Michigan. They raised the two infants as twins, Gregory and Gretchen.

From the adoption records I'd had unsealed, I found out Hannah Tolbert died in or shortly after childbirth, which explained why Penny wrote no more about her.

Julie said the report from Indiana on Gregory's fingerprints and history showed his age was 28 and not 21, which matched the year Penny and Hannah gave birth – 1975, based on the diary.

Why didn't any of us realize the age was wrong?

I hadn't given any thought to the infant girl, although now it seemed she might be as important as the baby boy. Accessing the records now that Gregory was dead should be a cinch, I thought.

"Penny's daughter was his sibling by adoption," I said. "Should we find her, let her know about Ethan – I mean Gregory. Show her the pieces of her past she might not have known."

"Not all adopted children want to know about their birth family," Dad warned. "The questions we have involve Gregory. Let's stick with that for now."

I wanted to argue, but Dad was right.

Julie looked at me as if she'd just wiped the daze off her brain. "The Rigsby's are dead. House fire a few years ago."

"Oh," I said, frustrated.

"Another question is, why would this guy use different names? So far, we know of three: Wenzler, Smith, and Rigsby," Zach said, shuffling the cards.

"Julie, are you sure you don't want to take over? This does involve you," I suggested.

"Being involved is all the more reason I should stay out of it," she replied.

CHAPTER 64
AMBER

Julie went back to work, and I decided I needed a day off. I'd been reading journals on and off for what seemed like months. I had two more whole journals of Penny's to go, but these newer books were from her adulthood.

My physical post-injury limitations were up, give or take a day, who was counting.

I needed to climb on a horse!

Dad was already out of the house when I got up, so I took my blood sugar and my insulin, then ate a sugar-free toaster pancake from a batch he'd made yesterday, smeared it with yogurt and frozen blueberries and rolled it up around a banana. Took my insulin. Got dressed, and found an old jean jacket of Julie's, too, since most of my clothes were still in Seattle.

I was so ready for this, I thought, almost skipping to the barn in the early morning cool air.

"Dad!" I yelled as I approached the barn.

The response was a high neigh from the filly. Mara… what was her name? No one in the barn, so I went on around toward the corral.

"What's up?"

"Just messing with the baby, a little human conditioning," he said, finishing the buckle on her new purple halter.

"She wears that like a crown," I said, then laughed. "What's her name again? I can't remember the Latin stuff."

"Unda Maris," he said, patting the filly on the rump, sending her off in a dance of lanky legs and bounce. "I think it's German."

"Whatever. I'm ready to ride today," I said, hoping the idea wouldn't start an argument.

"Mind if I go?" he asked.

So, we saddled up Rainier and Denali and set off on a beautiful morning ride.

"I've been considering what Julie said about writing. Her purpose, expressing emotions that were difficult to describe or that she didn't wish to share, was reasonable," I said. "Did you ever do that? You know, after Zoe died?"

Zoe's life and death had been a tip-toe topic for the whole time I've known Dad. We had discussed it a little on the trip from Michigan to New Mexico, but I still didn't have a clear idea of what had happened to her except that she, too, had been murdered.

I'm surrounded by death!

"No, I didn't write," he said thoughtfully. "I drew."

"Like the pictures of me and Julie?" I asked. "I love the one of me I took to college."

"Kinda like that, yeah."

No details.

I'd learned not to push.

"How do you think journaling would help you? Or would have helped in the past?" he asked.

"When Mom didn't come home that first night, I didn't realize how my whole world was gonna change. Grandmother Aggie called the police, and the nursing home people let me stay with her the first few nights, but she was sick. What I wanted," I said, stopping to consider, "no, what I needed was someone to hold me and let me cry, to show me how to understand, how to grieve. I didn't have that. It wasn't until I got to know Julie that I was able to begin to feel something."

"How could journaling have helped that?"

"Everything that happened was a giga-normous close-encounters-kind of introduction to death in the real world. I was angry. At everyone."

Anger wasn't even a fraction of what I'd felt. I hated Mom and Aggie for leaving me. Hated Zach for sending me away. Hated Julie for letting me stew in my own emotions instead of trying to mute them.

"Are you still angry?" he asked, interrupting my thoughts.

Until she told me she'd would stay with me instead of trying to save Dad, did I understand how much Julie loved me. That she would take care of me because she loved him. But so much made sense after that, because of *that* choice, I felt how much she loved me.

"No, but I am still sad about Mom."

"No reason you shouldn't be."

We rode on in silence for a while until I noticed a tall stack of tree trunks, on the edge of a clearing.

"We don't need firewood," I said. "What's that?"

"Kenny helped me clear a field," he answered without any further details. "The firewood's for him."

In the distance, I heard a low *Mmmmrrrrrr*.

I nudged the horse to a faster gait, but the trot was painful, so I spurred him on to a lope, which was less bumpy, until we came to a wide meadow, with a barbed-wire fence and a vehicle-wide green gate.

Inside were Hereford and Angus cattle.

Beyond them was an arena, built of pipe.

"I've been waiting to show you the new roping arena, complete with thirty steers," he said, smiling broadly. "I wanted you to be sure you were ready to ride first."

"Dad, it's fantastic!"

"There's still a little work to do on the chute," he said. "Would you like to help me finish so we can try it?"

CHAPTER 65
JULIE

October 23, 2001

"Can we get rid of that blue thing in the garage now?" Zach asked over an early breakfast of French toast and bacon.

"Yeah, why did you pick blue, Julie?" Amber asked as she poured sugar-free syrup on hers.

"I'm feeling a little bullied, you guys," I complained. "And your father picked it, not me."

We both turned to him with mock consternation.

"Hey, it was available while we were stuck in Indiana, so I bought it."

"I've been meaning to mention how ugly it is," Amber said. "But I didn't want to hurt Julie's feelings."

"But it's okay to hurt mine?" he asked.

"Sure. Why not?"

"Because I could trade your car in and let you keep the blue Yukon instead," he said.

"Would you?" Her eyes lit up. "That's a great idea!"

I gave Zach the "you've-been-had" look.

"You *want* it?" he asked, surprised.

"Yeah, I could carry a lot more stuff in it than my little car."

"It drinks a lot more gasoline than your little car, too," I cautioned. "The insurance is probably higher, too."

"So long as I don't have to call it ours now," he said, "I'm elated."

"You hate it that much?"

He laughed. "Not from the inside. It would be perfect in black."

"You could've had it repainted anytime," I suggested, knowing it was moot now that Amber had absorbed the idea like water into dry sand.

He looked at me again and shrugged. "Okay with me. You?"

I nodded.

"I hope she won't park it here," he leaned toward me and whispered. "I mean, it's *really* ugly."

• • • • •

With the decision being made, on my next day off, we made a day trip to Seattle to pick up her car and bring it back to our dealer of choice in Vancouver.

"Dad, I know you took care of making sure my dorm room was secured until next semester, but can I go make sure everything is okay while we're there?" Amber asked.

"If you want."

"I'd like to grab some stuff, and I might have food or stuff that needs to be removed, so it doesn't attract mice," she said, jiggling her butt in the driver's seat. "This is so cool."

We'd agreed to let her drive to Seattle to make sure she wanted a larger vehicle.

Meanwhile, in the second-row seats, I flipped through the dealer flyers at the current year's trucks.

"Ooh, this one is nice," I said to neither of them. "I like the tan."

"Gray is a fine color this year, too," Zach told me from the front. "Anything but whatever *this* is. I'm afraid someone I know might see me sitting it in. Heck, I'm afraid strangers will make fun of us as we go by."

I tried to hide the smirk but failed. "At least you're not driving it now."

"I'm still wondering if being physically uncomfortable in the back outweighs being mortified in the front. The back windows are tinted."

"Dad!"

Ignoring her, he continued. "We could get in the back seat and make out, you know, try it out?"

"Would you two stop it?"

• • • • •

The rest of our ride to Seattle University was calmer than the first hour, fortunately. After a stop in Centralia for a stretch and bathroom break, Amber drove into the thick of the Interstate 5 mess and exited on James Avenue like a seasoned professional.

Residential parking, like most university campuses, was nowhere near the dorms, but she wanted to stop at her room first.

The campus was, as advertised, a beautiful place, despite being a short distance from the downtown area of Seattle. Not a lot of students were around, but it was during a normal class time of 10 to 11:30, Amber told us.

Zach had taken care of making sure her room could remain closed up, even if she couldn't make it back this semester as she would be returning in the spring. He never mentioned how he accomplished this, or whether it was a difficult or expensive undertaking, and I never asked.

We offered to stay in the truck while she went to her room, but she invited us, which I surmised might have been a code for "I have things for you to carry."

Somehow in all the hullabaloo in New York, she had not lost her keys, so we followed her up two flights of stairs to her room.

A "Do not disturb" sign hung from the knob with a softball-sized gob of tape over the lock, and dozens of envelopes and flyers taped to the door and frame. Some were get-well notes, others unit decorations or event flyers, best I could tell.

"Girls on this hall were a little social," she told us, as if "social" had a particularly malignant meaning. She began peeling off the tape to reveal the lock and insert her key.

She opened the door to a room that had been wrecked.

Furniture was toppled. The mattress had been slit open a dozen directions. Contents of the closet were strewn across the room.

"What the hell?" she muttered. She took a step forward.

I must have had the same slack-jawed expression as Amber when Zach pulled us back into the hallway by our jackets.

"Stay." He scrolled through the list on his phone, punched a button and waited for an answer to request, and then to demand a security officer be sent immediately to our location for a break-in and vandalism, then disconnected.

"Did you have anything of value in there," he asked her. "Stereo, computer?"

She was slow responding to him but nodded first. "Um, both. The camera Grandmom Dagmar got me for Christmas last year. Books." She took a step forward again, but Zach stopped her. "And my diabetes stuff." In anger, she threw the handful of stuff from the door down, most of it fluttering to land in the hallway.

A small refrigerator that had been in the corner, I presume, now rested on its side in the center of the room, with its door open and contents – a mostly-empty half-gallon plastic juice container, a couple of sugar-free cans of cola, four individual serving cheese sticks, a takeout container of what looked like fried rice – spilled out onto the linoleum tile. The electrical cord had been pulled from the wall, so at least the unit hadn't been running for days or weeks with its door open, yet the spoiled food did not stink so it couldn't have been too long.

Across the room, a drawing Zach had done of Amber on horseback, which she'd had framed, was broken on the floor and slashed. The destruction of that brought her to tears.

While we waited, Amber picked up the pieces of paper she'd thrown on the floor, sorting through and keeping the cards, tossing the junk into a unit garbage can. She stuck a couple in her vest pocket.

In ten minutes that seemed much longer, two men in dark blue uniforms came up the stairs just as we had.

Introductions preceded questions and answers in both directions, followed by a not-so-subtle insinuation that Amber had done this herself, to which Zach's posture expanded like a balloon.

"I personally spoke with the dorm manager to explain that my daughter has been out of this state since September 10, as far away as New York City *on 9/11*, and in the hospital there for almost two more weeks. She has been in our company since then, in Michigan for one of her best friend's funeral and for my wife's mother's funeral in New Mexico, so I will not stand here and have you imply she had anything to do with *that!*" Emphasis made with a pointed finger into the room.

I wanted to applaud, his oration sounded so rehearsed and perfect.

The investigation, lame as it was, continued with dozens more questions, most unrelated to her room or the crime, which Zach arbitrated with the skill of a rabid lawyer, either answering or advising Amber which to answer and which she should ignore.

And sometimes telling the officers their questions were ludicrous.

They had yet to ask if anything was missing.

Getting angrier, she threw down a handful of papers. "I'm done with this. You don't care if you find out who did this, you just want to fill out your damned report."

Whether or not they were finished getting answers from her, she walked away from the three men.

I offered to walk with her to her car, somewhere on campus.

Hope it hasn't been vandalized like her room.

"I need some sugar," she said, stopping to face me, leaning against the wall and sliding to the floor.

Digging in my bag would be futile, I knew. She hadn't brought hers with her from the truck, either.

"Is there any in your dorm room?"

"Bedside table drawer," she offered, looking more wilted by the second.

I stood and headed to the dorm door.

"You can't go in there," the younger security officer told me.

"You should be doing your job instead of obstructing me from taking care of my daughter," I replied, stepping around him and into a room with little floor space visible, looking for a bedside table.

One would think it would be bedside, but the bed is in the middle of the floor...

I found something a dorm room might use beside a bed, set it upright and yanked open its top drawer and began digging. Not exactly sure for what, but something with sugar. Stuffed toward the back, I saw a bag of what I had no doubt was marijuana, and then another with some pills, immediately causing a flash of memory of Zach presenting me with methamphetamine powder.

Damn it, Amber!

Making sure no one was watching me, I grabbed those and stuck them in my jacket pocket, then I picked up a couple of pieces of hard candy and a tube of white cake frosting gel I'd suggested, then waded over the debris to the door again.

As I walked by him, I gave Zach a look that could have peeled thirty layers of paint off the walls around us, walked to where Amber sat.

Crumpled was more like it.

I turned back to Zach and asked him to find her glucometer from the room while I unwound a piece of hard candy from its wrapper.

"I hang it behind the door on the coat hook, so I don't forget it," she mumbled.

Somehow in that mess, he found it and brought it to me.

I stuck her finger and tested the drop of blood.

The result was 418.

That didn't seem right.

Careful that she was still awake enough to swallow, I twisted the seal off the white cake icing gel, squirting a bit under her tongue. Her blood sugar being low was worse than raising it higher if the machine was wrong.

"Ma'am? You got this or do I need to call for an ambulance?" the older officer asked, in quite a less antagonistic tone than before.

Amber groaned and swallowed, then said, "Not another friggin' ambulance, please."

I indicated our situation was under control.

"Is there a vending machine in the building?" I asked. "Orange juice, cola, whatever. Peanut butter crackers, too, or something else, Zach."

The younger officer waved at Zach to follow, and they took off down the steps.

I changed from a squatting pose to sitting cross-legged on the floor when my feet began to tingle.

Amber remained awake but drowsy.

"What is most important to us to find out," I told the officer, G. Wells his nametag read, "is *when* this happened. Could you include that when you talk to the other residents?"

He nodded, wrote something on a memo pad he'd taken from his pocket.

To look like he had something important to do with his hands.

"We're not just freaked out parents," I explained. "I'm a deputy from Skamania County."

"Yes, ma'am. I'll see to it we do our best."

Do you sometimes do your worst? Really?

I hoped my face wasn't revealing what I'd managed to not say.

Amber had bought me a t-shirt that read, "Did I roll my eyes out loud again?" for my birthday. It seemed perfect for the moment.

Zach and the other officer returned with a bottle of orange juice and a soft drink, and a package each of crackers with cheese and peanut butter.

Amber sat up and took the OJ first. "I don't know what that was about. I didn't feel shaky like before when my blood sugar dipped, just really sluggish. Was it low?"

"The machine said it was 418," I replied. "But it could be wrong."

She drained the juice and popped open the Mountain Dew.

For a comparison to hers, I performed the glucometer test on myself, with the same blood sugar reading, which was 418. Before I could ask, Zach stuck his hand down for me to test him as well.

Exactly 418.

"No way that could be accurate for all three of us," I said, turning back to Amber. "Out of curiosity, if you'd come back to this after a class and felt weird, and you got 418 when you tested, what would you have done?"

"If I'd had extra calories at breakfast or lunch, which I might have, like during finals," she said, fearing my reaction, "I'd probably have given myself another dose of insulin, because it was so high."

I nodded. "Hypothetically, really. Go on."

"Then I'd clean it up."

"What if the room wasn't trashed?" Zach asked.

"I'd take more insulin, do something to help lower my sugar. Maybe walk to the library to study. I've found a quiet corner away from everyone."

Looking at Zach, I saw him wince and shake his head.

"Let's go use the glucometer in the truck and test you again," I said, taking Zach's hand to stand.

"What do you want us to do about this?" the younger officer asked.

"Do your fucking job! Find out when that happened and who did it," Zach said, towering over him again, producing a business card. "Here's *her* number. Or you can ask for the sheriff."

CHAPTER 66
AMBER

I got in the backseat without being asked. No way they wanted me to drive now, still feeling weird, sorta like my blood sugar was low, but not exactly. But like Julie had asked, if I'd found out it was over 400, I'd have taken another dose of insulin. I didn't tell her, but I'd missed my morning dose a couple of times here, so I really wouldn't have doubted the numbers.

What would I have done if I'd come back to my room and found that mess? Probably cry.

"I know it's silly, Dad," I begged, "and I don't blame you if you say no, but would you go back and see if my jewelry – it's in a green velvet jewelry box – see if it's there? It should be on the closet shelf toward the right."

He was still seething, jaw muscles clamped. "You're right, I don't want to deal with either of them again. Can it wait?"

"Please? Mom gave me a pair of pearl earrings a long time ago. They mean a lot to me," I said.

He sighed. "Anything else?"

"If they're still there, I'd like to have the camera Grandmom Dagmar gave me and the laptop computer, too," I said. "Please?"

He nodded and turned to go back into the building.

Julie let me stick myself for a new glucose level while she watched.

"After the juice, it's 153," she announced, looking over the machine at the reading. "That makes more sense."

"Why would my other machine be so wrong?" I asked.

"We'll get to that," she said, pulling something else from her pocket. "What is this doing in your room?"

"Geez, Julie!" I said, looking around in a panic. "What is it?"

"Don't act dumb with me."

"I don't know what it is, and I don't know why it was in my room," I said, more defiantly. "But, hello? Someone else has obviously been in my room since I was."

"You promise?"

"Julie? I'm in a criminal justice program at a Jesuit school. Drug possession would be an immediate university discharge and a legal offense that would end a career before it started. Not to mention I've got enough medical problems without crap like that."

"Then we should tell security –"

"No! If they find out, they'll think it's mine and that you were trying to hide it when you took it from my room."

"Amber, if I hadn't found it, they might have. Why should bringing it up to them now –"

"I . . . I don't know, but it doesn't feel right," I said. "Just get rid of it! Throw it in the garbage can over . . . No, wait, your fingerprints are on it now."

"And someone else's might be, too," she retorted. "Your call."

"Can you dump out the drugs and keep the bags so we, I mean you can print them at home?"

She gave me this *look* that said she thought I was out of my mind.

"Or we could say it was in the jewelry box Dad's bringing."

"Way to throw your father under a bus, Amber." She sighed. "What if there is more? Anything else that is yours, like liquor?"

I shook my head. "No. You can test me."

"Amber, no matter what's in your room, you haven't had access to it in six weeks."

"But I did open the door."

We both looked down at my hands.

I opened my mouth to say something when I heard the sirens.

CHAPTER 67
JULIE

Given the circumstances, I should not have been surprised that the ambulance and then a rescue truck pulled to within a few yards of our vehicle in front of the dorm. "Stay here," I demanded. "Stay in the truck and lock the doors."

This, none of this, was what I expected.

I turned to go but a thought stopped me cold. "Your hands. Do not touch anything – especially your face. You hear me? Nothing!" I slammed the door.

Rushing enough to catch up with the medics, I followed them, hoping to find anything but Zach on the floor.

The ambulance crew left their gurney on the ground floor and humped gear up the stairs I'd already climbed once, but I dutifully followed to stay out of their way.

At the top, not far from where Amber had been on the floor, laid Officer G. Wells, skin a pale green, with a puddle of what might have been his breakfast beside him and on his pants.

Couldn't help but wonder if his first name began with an H.

Zach hurried to me as the medics began their assessment.

"He had to open the door again for me, closed it behind us," he said. "We were just standing here, talking, when he got pale and then threw up, then hit the floor and had a seizure."

He pointed to his brown sea bass boots, which were now splattered with what looked like tomato sauce and scrambled eggs.

I pulled him away from the group. "And I'm certain that whatever is on the doorknob is what affected Amber, too," I replied in a harsh whisper.

He nodded. "Police are on their way."

"Something on the doorknob, a malfunctioning glucometer," I said, lowering my voice, "and I found drugs stashed in the bedside table. None of this is a coincidence."

Zach nodded though I wasn't sure he knew what I was talking about with the drugs.

"We need to take Amber to an ED to get checked, and see if they can figure out what this stuff she touched is," I said.

"You go. I'll stay and talk to the cops." He sniffed indignantly. "The city cops."

• • • • •

By the time Amber had been swabbed, poked, and fully examined by the staff at the hospital, we really did need to get her something to eat.

Zach had caught a ride to the hospital with one of the Seattle Police officers who had responded to the scene at the university. He was an athletic man with a receding hairline, sharp nose and narrow chin, who introduced himself as Detective Kelby McGowan. In the emergency department, the four of us had a lengthy conversation about the possible clues floating around our lives for the last few months.

The last few years.

I disclosed to him how and where I'd found the drugs in Amber's dorm room and happily relinquished them to him.

Amber might not have been happy with my decision, but given the other events of our day so far, it seemed prudent.

The officer asked Amber a question I hadn't thought of: "Had you found the drugs in your room, would you have used any of them?"

My eyes opened wide while I waited for her answer.

"Absolutely not! I won't deny I've had alcohol now and then with a few friends, but not that. No way. Like I told Julie, it would end my upcoming career in criminal justice." She looked at me, then added, "I would have called security."

Good to know.

"She yanked a bunch of notes and cards from the door itself, but the knob was covered in tape," Zach said.

"It's a dorm joke," Amber explained. "It's happened to me several other times this semester. And the security officer never touched the papers on the floor or the ones I put in my pocket."

Detective McGowan donned nitrile gloves from a dispenser on the wall and carefully moved the envelopes from her pocket to an evidence envelope.

"But Amber," Zach said. "both times when I entered the room, the security officer unlocked and opened the door for me. The second time, he waited while I was looking for the jewelry box and laptop, he was kinda leaning on the doorknob, and then he used it to pull the door closed when I was finished. I'm guessing it all took 45 to 60 seconds. I would presume he pulled the door shut as hard the first time as the second," Zach explained.

"We swabbed the doorknob."

Zach and Amber sneered at each other.

"We swabbed the metal, and we collected the tape," McGowan repeated. "We've had a few cases of China White being used in the city recently, on shopping carts, to cut other drugs. If that's what we find had been put on your doorknob, you were the clear target," he explained. "Symptoms include pinpoint pupils, decreased consciousness, vomiting and diarrhea, low blood pressure. Anything like how you felt?"

"I felt sleepy, kind of," Amber told him. "Like my blood sugar might be low, but different. What's China White?"

"One of the synthetic drugs hundreds or thousands of times more potent than morphine. Legal American drugs in the category might be fentanyl, carfentanil, sufentanil, or the animal tranquilizer dart medication by the name of Wildnil, which is used for exceptionally large animals such as elephants."

"Remifentanil?" Zach asked, which surprised McGowan. "Retired DEA."

They shook hands like they'd found out they'd been in the same college fraternity.

"I put my money on one of those," McGowan said. "But we'll have results back in a week or so."

"Any chance this exposure was a poison instead of a drug?" I asked.

He started to laugh, then thought better of it. "The only difference between a drug and a poison is dose, Ma'am."

Finally, we got out of the hospital and went to a restaurant where we sat, mostly talked out but with billowing cloud-thought circles above our heads like in the comics.

"Why," Amber said with a sigh, stirring the ice in her water with a straw.

"Million-dollar question."

"Why me?" she clarified.

Before our food arrived, my phone rang.

Although it was an Indiana number, I didn't have the mental energy to answer it.

The way things had gone so far, any news from there would probably be as dismal as the rest of the day.

CHAPTER 68
JULIE

I drove the Yukon, and Amber rode with Zach in her car.

Anything not to be seen in this blue truck.

It gave me time to think.

Do other people have this running monologue with themselves? Actually hear a voice in their heads like I do?

Maybe I'll ask Zach.

But do they have two voices that argue sometimes?

First, the bodies in plastic, one in Michigan, possibly frozen, and two in Skamania County. Same plastic, requiring a machine for the vacuum. Three people, killed, dismembered, loaded in a vacuum packing system.

Why that? Could the FBI tell if it were from the same machine? Doesn't matter, but how big is a machine that could use 24-inch packaging? Would it be difficult to transport – heavy, requiring a van? What's the smallest possible machine available?

How was the first person killed – Brandan hasn't gotten back with me about whether the body had been frozen. Maybe the new medical examiner wouldn't know, but Dr. Katz would have been able to tell.

Amber meets a young man who appears to have much in common with her – career path, etc.

We found out his name – names – his college and his age were all a lie. What else was false?

Amber is invited to NYC from Seattle, then abandoned.

The 9/11 attacks couldn't have been predicted, so did that become part of the plan or cause him to abandon the plan? Why would he go to New York City, and why would he want to get Amber away from her home state? Why lure her there, unless the intent was to entice her far from help, where it would be hard to find her once we realized she wasn't in Seattle? Days, possibly weeks. Did he intend to kill her and hide the body, and if so, why?

Or why hide it at all?

Why Amber?

He told us he was looking for information about Penny Tucker, his biological teenage mother.

That doesn't involve Amber; it involved me. And Amber has since discovered Penny wasn't his mother. Did he already know that or was it a ploy to meet me, or her?

The armed robbery seemed to be in a random location, but I was there. And he was killed by his partner.

None of that was random at all. No coincidence I was in the very store this guy and an accomplice decided to rob. What was the point? Was I supposed to be killed, too? Why would he be killed and not me?

Not complaining, but I would have been quite easy to kill, sprawled on the floor.

Amber's trashed dorm room, and the unknown substance that affected both her and a campus police officer.

Had to be very recent because the food hadn't spoiled enough to stink. I didn't determine if it was still cold, which would indicate the pillage took place within the hours before our visit.

How would anyone know we were going to Seattle to her dorm; it was a decision we made just two days ago, right? Did timing matter? Was the substance poison or just enough of some drug to make Amber feel ill enough to use the glucometer, which had been sabotaged. How do you even do that? McGowan had retrieved it for evaluation. But the potential result would have put Amber into a potentially life-threatening situation. And again, why Amber?

Amber. Me. Not Zach.

Why not Zach? If there is any reason these attacks on me also include Amber, why not Zach?

I checked my phone, remembering I needed to return the call to Indiana I'd ignored earlier. Intending to dial, I looked in my rearview mirror, but Amber's gray Honda Civic wasn't in sight.

But I did see a cloud of dirt a quarter mile behind me.

CHAPTER 69
AMBER

Dad was driving my little car.

I say little, because the Civic was hilariously uncomfortable for him, especially compared to the big truck he usually drove. I watched him squirm and try to push the seat back past its stops when his knees still banged the steering wheel.

I tried not to laugh, really I did. Couldn't control it. Didn't want to.

Even miles down the highway, I broke into giggles watching him twist and fidget, trying to get comfortable.

"Who might do such a thing to your room?" he said. "Someone in your dorm?"

"I don't know, Dad. I've only made friends with a few of the girls in my dorm. One who lives on the third floor is in two of my classes, so we walk to another building together then to lunch sometimes."

"Other classmates? Boyfriend?"

"No boyfriend. I didn't even consider Ethan, or whoever he is, as a real boyfriend. We talked several nights a week," I said, "or I did most of the talking. He seemed a bit shy on the phone compared to in person."

"And the drinking?"

"Not a big deal, dad. A couple of girls in the dorm invited me along to one's house for a weekend, and we were drinking wine, but no one drove – we stayed the night. I only had, like two glasses the whole evening. It was kinda fun, you know, grownup. Like the wine we had in New York the last night."

"Acceptable though not legal, so yes, big deal," he said. "I appreciate you being responsible and not driving."

"Being an adult is harder than I thought."

He smiled. "It's kinda horrible until it becomes awesome," he said. "Perhaps in hindsight, however, it would have been a smidge more grown-up if you'd let us know you were going to New York. If you'd been killed in the collapse of the

Twin Towers or whatever, we might not have known until we got the credit card statement where to look for you, and then would still never be sure probably."

"I know, and I'm sorry. I hope a tragedy like that never coincides with me being stupid again," I said, feeling like Typhoid Mary.

"You are not stupid, Amber. Your decision was unwise. People who love you and want you to be safe – maybe the people who'd drive all the way across the country to find you? – they want to have an idea where you are so they can help you if you need it," he said, touching my hand. "If you went hiking, for example, it's reasonable to let someone know where you are going and when to expect you back."

"You're right, and I said I'm sorry," I replied, feeling even more defensive. "But I didn't wreck my room, and I don't know who –"

Then I felt a pop from the front of the car somewhere.

Dad jerked his hand away from mine and gripped the steering wheel, fought it when it shook hard then spun right.

The car swerved hard to the right to the shoulder.

Decelerated.

Spun in the grass and toward a fence.

My head slammed into the window, which shattered, spraying glass all over me.

Jumbled. Dirt and stuff from the ditch.

What I saw beyond the spidered windshield was upside-down, like my brain was spinning.

"Are you hurt?" Dad asked, then coughed.

I blinked two or three times to clear my head.

"What the hell?" I said. I put my hands up, or down, whichever, on the ceiling of the car. "I think so. You?"

"I guess I'm okay," he said, "but I can't move my legs out from under the dash." This was followed by a string of profanity that made me blush.

Absolute freebies, I thought.

This whole day is a freebie.

"Let me get out and see if I can help," I said. "Is there any better way than just releasing the seatbelt and falling?"

"Not that I know of, but be careful of the glass."

Gravity's a bitch.

I pushed the release button at my left hip, but nothing happened. The strap was also so tight I couldn't get enough slack to crawl out of it.

Panic crawled up my spine, with hopefully irrational fears of the car catching fire or sliding down the hill into the pond.

"Hey? Hello? Are you okay in there?" a woman's voice shouted. "I've called 9-1-1."

Purple nitrile gloved hands appeared at my window.

"Do you have something to cut my seatbelt?" I asked, although she hadn't bent down far enough I could see her face.

"No, I'm a nurse, and you should just stay where you are until the rescue can take you out. Are you bleeding?"

I looked at Dad, whose face looked red and splotchy from being inverted, but I couldn't see any wounds. "No, we're okay except scratches and bruises."

"Any medical problems?"

"I'm an insulin-dependent diabetic," I offered. "I need to get out and help my dad."

"No, let's stay put, eh?" she said as though I were four and wanted to stick my hand into a flame or something. And she made that 'eh' sound that Julie said occasionally. "I should start an IV on you, just in case. I carry a kit because I'm on the road so much. I'll be right back."

Dad looked concerned as he continued to squirm to release his legs smashed under the dash. "Can she do that?"

"You're asking me?"

The woman came back to the car with an orange bag, opened it up, and took out a syringe. She pulled my right arm straight and twisted it so hard it hurt.

I tried to pull my hand out of her grasp, but I couldn't overpower her because of the angle. Instead of the kind of device to start an IV I expected, she stuck the needle into a vein on the inside of my elbow and pushed the plunger, then yanked it back out, letting it bleed.

"What the fuck?" I blurted, grabbing the crook of my arm with the other hand to stop the bleeding.

"That ought to help you, dear," she said, dropping the syringe back into the bag and standing. "I hear the ambulance, so I'll be on my way."

"Wait! Hey!" I yelled, but she was gone. I couldn't see anything from where I hung, but I heard the car start and drive away. And I felt all warm and fuzzy.

"Amber?" I heard Dad say. "Amber!"

My vision began to blur, and then everything went black.

CHAPTER 70
JULIE

The car was upside-down and facing the wrong direction, at the edge of a field that sloped down toward a pond.

"Zach! Oh my God, what happened?" I asked, dropping to my knees to lean into his window, which was gone.

Not really *gone*. Tempered glass sparkled everywhere.

"I'm trapped," he said, grimacing in pain. "Where's the nurse?"

"What nurse?"

"Woman who was talking to —" He coughed and swallowed hard. "She shot Amber."

"Shot Amber?" I shrieked, getting up and running to the other side of the car and peering inside.

I didn't see any gunshot wounds on Amber. Abrasions and small lacerations, including blood on her arms, which dangled above – below? – her head. She didn't open her eyes when I called her name. Or shook her. And she didn't look like she was breathing.

That stupid voice in my head repeated an old CPR mantra, *"Annie, Annie, are you okay? Someone call for help!"*

In the distance, I heard sirens.

After all the time I've spent working in an ambulance, seems like I spend a lot of time waiting on one to show up these days.

Zach reached out his arm to hand me something, but he appeared to be disoriented. I took it – his knife.

"Cut her down, Julie. Just be careful."

"Are you injured?" I asked him as I got ready to cut the seat belt, making sure I cut the ratchet side and not the anchor side. Cutting at the anchor side of the belt means the auto-ratcheting will zing the belt across the body into the housing, causing belt burns.

"No, take care of her."

Sharp as always, the blade zipped right through the webbing. I let it drop so I could help reduce the drop Amber would have. Wasn't much, though I saw that Zach had also helped. At least I was able to protect her head and neck.

I dragged her out of the car.

None of the movement woke her.

Pulse, present.

Breathing, barely.

Pupils, pinpoint.

Mouth-to-mouth, once. Again.

Sirens closer.

Again. Not too fast, two three four five, again.

"Is she okay?" Zach said, his voice strained.

I lied. "Yeah, she's all right. How are you?" *Two three four five again.*

"Stuck in this piece of shit sardine can!" Then he muttered to himself, "At least the fire department can cut it into little recyclable pieces. . . "

"Are you bleeding?" I yelled back. *Two three four five, breath.*

"Not that I can tell. Hard to breathe as tight as the seat belt tensioner pulled."

And that's why you're snug in your seat and not hanging halfway to the ceiling of the car with two broken femurs because your legs are stuck under the dash. Three four five, breath.

"I see the fire truck coming. What did you mean a nurse was here? She left?"

I don't know who had called the accident in, but I was glad.

I used to believe I could keep up rescue breathing for hours, but this was exhausting. *Two three four five, breath.*

The ambulance parked north of the car, and the crew got out, coming toward me. Fire engine parked beyond the car. *Two three four five, breath.*

"Ambu, please," I asked one of the medics, who immediately pulled out the blue bag-valve-mask device and took over ventilations for me; the other went to see about Zach. After a breath or two myself, I began to explain what I knew. "Zach is trapped, legs under the dash. Conscious, oriented, pissed," I said, took another couple of breaths.

"Was she ejected?" the medic asked.

Shaking my head, I continued. "No. Amber, 18, was a restrained passenger who wasn't breathing when I arrived. I cut the belt and pulled her out about two minutes ago and started mouth-to-mouth."

He waved his hand. "We had a nine-minute response time. Dispatch said the caller who initiated the response was on scene."

"I called, but the dispatcher told me she already had units on the way. No one was here when I arrived. I've been here about four minutes now, tops." I looked at his jump kit. "I used to be a medic, mind if I help?"

"Anyone who calls it an Ambu knows what to do with it," he said.

We traded places, and I ventilated her in the same slow rhythm, every five to six seconds.

But I can breathe now, too.

He slipped a cervical collar around her neck, listened to her lungs and nodded. Quick head-to-toe exam revealed no other horrible findings.

"She's a diabetic, but earlier today she was exposed to some drug or poison in Seattle, something at her dorm room —"

"You mean you *know* these two people," he said, surprised. "You didn't just stop to help?"

"Husband and stepdaughter," I replied. "Narcan or an amp of D50."

He shook his head at me with wide eyes. "Your call, which first?"

"Let's try the Narcan. I think Zach meant the nurse who stopped to help them gave her a shot —"

The medic interrupted me again. "Whaddaya mean a shot?"

"That's what Zach said, that he thought the woman 'shot her,' but when she wasn't breathing, I stopped asking questions and extricated her."

"Narcan it is," he said, opening the kit and pulling out a package with a prefilled syringe. "Let's do the IM, then I'll work on an IV for a repeat and the dextrose."

On the far side of the car, I heard Jaws of Life operating, metal screeching and popping, and a lot of cussing, which I assumed was Zach. Followed by a heavy thud.

Which I assumed was Zach.

"I'm just fine," he yelled.

I looked up to see him limping around the car toward us. Making eye contact with me, then nodding in approval that I was working on his daughter.

"Come tell me what you meant about the nurse who stopped," I said. "What you said didn't make sense to me."

He watched the medic stick a needle in Amber's deltoid.

"A woman stopped," he said, sitting on the wet grass beside me, rubbing his thighs. "She never came around to my side of the car, so I didn't see her face. She talked to Amber, said something about starting an IV when Amber told her she was diabetic."

The medic and I exchanged glances of disbelief.

"She went to her car then came back and did whatever she did. I couldn't see." He nodded to Amber, also on the wet grass. "Is she okay?"

I felt her start to breathe, and her eyelids fluttered.

Nodded to him.

Yes, Narcan is working, so it's something opioid-related. I was right.

The medic started the IV and taped it down while his partner, now free of the removal of Zach from the car, began assisting.

"She's responding a little to the Narcan," I said. "Can you test her blood sugar before you give the D50? We've bounced her levels hard today."

Twenty-five grams of dextrose – sugar – wouldn't hurt her, same as this morning. No sense in driving her blood sugar sky-high if she was normal.

Turned out to be 186. Again, okay considering she'd had lunch an hour ago.

And with one big breath, she opened her eyes, rolled to the side, and vomited on Zach's pants.

The Narcan was working fine.

• • • • •

"Okay, that's it," I said, getting to my feet. My pants were soaked through but at least not puked on. I offered a hand to Zach, who took it.

"Back to the hospital with you," I told Amber, who very much did not want to go in the ambulance nor to go to another emergency department. I looked at the medic. "That's twice today. I can't be sure the Narcan won't wear off, so take her. Take him to be checked out, too," I said, pointing at Zach with a no-argument expression. "I need to talk to the deputy," nodding my head toward a patrol car that had just pulled up on the scene.

The deputy got out and began talking to one of the firefighters before coming toward us.

Despite groans from them both, Amber was rolled to the backboard and lifted to the gurney. Zach made a no-thanks gesture to being assessed or strapped to a backboard.

No doubt, they were both mad at me, but he climbed into the ambulance and slumped in the back corner, then stuck his head out.

"Hey, get my knife!"

Priorities. I went to the passenger side and picked up the knife, folded and stuck it in my jacket pocket.

"Deputy Isaacs," he said, not bothering to shake hands or even really looking my direction. "I'm told you have an interesting story."

Leaning on the hood of his vehicle, I explained the events of the crash.

"I was a mile or so further south on the interstate when I realized they weren't behind me. I turned around, came back. The medic said a female called this in, but it wasn't me. Zach said a woman who said she was a nurse stopped."

Still little interest in what I was telling him. Just short of an eye roll, I thought.

"A *nurse* wouldn't stop at the scene of a rollover and give one of the occupants a shot and then leave," I said. "But that's what happened. With my stepdaughter's response to Narcan, she was most likely injected with an opioid. When I arrived, no one else was on scene."

He nodded, still very nonplussed, and I was getting angry.

"Deputy, that makes twice today someone's tried to kill my daughter," I said, feeling a sudden urge to strangle him for his nonchalance.

"I thought you said she was your stepdaughter."

And suddenly, I understood.

CHAPTER 71
JULIE

Driving to Centralia gave me twenty minutes to talk myself through this. I had a clear idea of what was going on when I parked at the hospital where Amber and Zach had been taken.

My phone rang, a caller from Indiana. Same number I'd ignored earlier.

"Cade Martin, Terra Haute," he announced, proceeding before I could exchange any pleasantries.

Not that I have any at the moment.

"First, I have to say I hate this genetic crap because I don't understand it. We got DNA information back on the blood smear I told you about on the doorway of the store. I suspected it was yours, but it's not an identical match to the sample we got from Michigan. However, it *is* a familial match to you of some second- or third-degree relative," he said. "There's also a similar familial match of Rigsby to you, but not the same. But the two suspects' DNA match is much closer to each other, like cousins or something."

"Of course it is."

"Come again?"

"Detective, they are half-siblings. Anthony Bock is their father by different mothers. They were illegitimate newborns who were adopted by the same family, raised as siblings. Bock is also," I swallowed hard, "my illegitimate half-brother by my father."

There it was, an explanation I'd hoped to never have to say again for the rest of my life.

My half-brother's legacy of abuse and crime had been passed down to not one but two children, according to the DNA.

I opened the door of my truck, leaned out, and vomited my lunch.

On my way into the shades-of-brown hospital emergency department area, I stopped in a restroom to clean up a little.

At least no one will probably notice how icky we smell here.

A nurse let me into the patient area and pointed out where I'd find my family. I tried to put on a smile.

"If you didn't like Amber's car, I would have driven it to the dealer," I said, peeking into the emergency department room, teasing my husband who sat beside an empty gurney. "You didn't have to wreck it."

He read my mind. "Bathroom," he said, attempting to stand to kiss me, getting up with a grimace. "Did the deputy tell you why the car flipped?"

"He didn't seem to be so mechanically inclined or intellectually interested," I muttered. "I suspect it was sabotage. I also got a call from Indiana as I parked."

I didn't want any of this to be true. He nodded for me to continue.

"Rigsby and the robbery accomplice are half-siblings. And they are related to me. The only way that can be true is if Anthony Bock was their father, which makes them, um, my niece and nephew. I'm not sure how the half-sibling thing works."

The look on Zach's face mirrored what was in my chest.

"All along, I've been stuck, wondering why the attempts were on Amber, not me. I think I've figured it out."

"Why?"

"Rigsby didn't know that Amber is not my *biological* daughter."

Amber came waddling back into the room barefoot and stopped long enough to hug me.

"Are you both all right?" I asked, pulling a piece of tempered glass from her hair and holding it up as a transparent example. "Besides the nuggets you'll be finding for days."

She scooted onto the gurney and crossed her arms. "I'm okay, but I'm a little mad at you right now," she said with a pout. "Someone wants to hurt you, and I'm the target. Wow. Just wow. So solve the case already. I'm tired of this."

"I'm sorry, Amber." I pulled up a chair and sat next to them. "First, this is speculation, so hang with me. You met with Ethan because he was looking for me, right? He must have liked you, or that first evening could have gone very differently. He probably didn't know you existed before then, but when you met him, he assumed you were our daughter – *my daughter*. Do you remember ever mentioning to him that I am not your biological mother?"

Amber's squinted in a moment of thought then shook her head.

"I was telling Zach –"

"I heard. They're both Bock's malevolent spawn. Go on."

"What if he knew all along who his mother or father were. Maybe the home's staff didn't care whether the teenagers overheard, or if they said the wrong gender intentionally. The family who adopted Penny's also took Hannah's baby, so it's possible the mothers were mistaken for each other somehow. It shouldn't matter now who his mother was.

Silence from them, so I kept talking.

"From the convenience store, DNA collected shows he and the other suspect have a very close match, but also a familial link to me, making it positive that their father was Anthony Bock."

Still no verbal responses, but some uncomfortable fidgeting.

"What if Bock was able to track them down before he died and fed them his lies, asked them to continue his legacy. If so, did he tell them to kill me? Or are they trying to kill Zach for Bock's death in Florida. But the best way to *hurt us* would be by killing you."

Zach shook his head in disbelief as I continued.

"Amber, when he invited you to New York, perhaps the intent was to kill you. Perhaps Ethan refused to do it because he liked you. Or their plans changed after what happened with the World Trade Center, which they couldn't have planned for. Then you were hit by the car –"

"Truck," she corrected.

"Truck, yes, sorry. All of that must have interrupted their plans. When you two flew back to Albuquerque, they followed me out of New York. But she –"

"Gretchen," Amber supplied. "Greg's sister's name was Gretchen."

"Yes, Gretchen had had enough of Greg stalling to kill or hurt you, so she shot him during the robbery. Took my stuff, drove my truck away. I suspect she came directly back here and waited for us," I concluded, "even though we were weeks getting home."

"If she's here, how would she have known we were going to Seattle today?" Zach asked.

"No clue, but I'm certain that was her at the car wreck, that she gave Amber a large dose of some super-potent opioid. Now I'm worried she will beat us back home."

"At least we know what to expect," Amber said.

"I asked the deputy who came to the accident –"

"The on-purpose, Julie," Zach muttered, stretching muscles that were probably starting to get tight enough to hurt. "Definitely an on-purpose."

"The deputy who came to the *crash*," I corrected myself a third time, "will find out about the 9-1-1 caller, if there was an identifier for the cell phone, voice recording, something. He'll coordinate it with Wade. The question now is, do we go home, or find somewhere to hide?"

"She's been able to wait us out for months," Amber replied. "If I have a vote, I say we go find the bitch."

"Freebie," he and I said together.

Zach nodded his agreement. "Let the hunt begin."

CHAPTER 72
JULIE

We needed a plan.

Not a game plan, Amber pointed out, because this was no game.

"A battle strategy," she said.

"You saw her," I prompted. "Description for everyone?"

"She had salt and pepper hair pulled back into a loose bun, but she was probably wearing a wig. With the hair and makeup, she looked 60, not 27. Average weight. Blue eyes. She chews her fingernails."

"You noticed that?" Zach asked.

"She grabbed my arm, Dad, absolutely. Looks like it's a habit, because her cuticles and nails were ragged. She had an infected left thumbnail, inner side."

"Great detail," I said. "You two should work on a drawing when we get off the road. Concentrate on the eyes."

We'd agreed this fight wasn't something we could do alone. It would take all our resources, so armed with her description, Zach and Amber were on their phones most of the trip on to Vancouver.

We stopped for fuel and recounted our successes.

"Wade has alerted the deputies and the surrounding counties to look for a single white woman traveling alone," Amber surmised. "If she is headed to our house, I don't think she'd take I-84. Less chance of being stopped by highway patrol on the Washington side."

"Not now," Zach countered. "I called Chris Bell from Portland. He's coordinating with both Washington and Oregon State Patrols going east from the Willamette past The Dalles. We also agreed that being sneaky might mean going from I-5 east on State Highway 12 to Yakima and then south on 97 to the Columbia River. They'll do a roadblock before the crossing to Interstate 84 or go west onto Highway 14, as well as one on both sides at Cascade Locks. Both are good catch points. Anyone who turns around will be pursued."

That rocks.

"I called Agent Forrester," our darling daughter announced. "He'll see what he can find out about Gretchen, too."

"Aces me," he said. "So, while we were working, what did you do?"

"Me? I'm just driving. Making sure cars around me aren't trying to run us off the road."

"Good job, Mom!" Amber said.

That's the first time she ever called me that.

"Did you make up your mind whether we should go home?" he asked. "I can call Kenny and . . . ah shit!"

"What?" Amber and I asked in unison.

"I know how someone would know we were leaving town," he said, slapping his forehead with both hands. "Kenny told me he's got a girlfriend. I haven't met her. But when I told him we'd like to get him a car, he'd mentioned hoping it would be nice enough he wouldn't be embarrassed for her to ride in it. Said she was a bit younger."

"Call Wade. See if they can find Kenny and take him somewhere safe. If she believes he compromised her identity, she'd kill him in a heartbeat," I said. "And see if they can find out what kind of vehicle she owns. Probably something big enough to carry the vacuum packing machine, like a van or SUV. It's portable, but it's not small."

CHAPTER 73
JULIE

"If we expect her to return to Skamania County, for whatever reason, that's where we need to go," Zach announced.

"Large and in charge," Amber replied with a nod. "Tally ho!"

Off we went, east on Highway 14 from Vancouver.

Zach and Amber were busy discussing possible scenarios about finding and apprehending this woman.

Greg Rigsby's sister Gretchen – regardless of whose mother was Penny Tucker or Hannah Tolbert – had to be involved in the murder and vacuum sealing of victims.

I just couldn't figure out why, except to get me involved.

Sure, it might have been an effective way to delay disposal of a body, except that dismembering a body takes a lot of work and cleanup. If it were meant to be found, all that effort seemed like a waste.

Although I still didn't know what the long-term effect of vacuum-sealing a body in pieces was, I doubted it would stop or significantly delay decomposition. It might reduce the odor until the gases released in decomp ruptured the bag, but then it would certainly smell horrible, which leads to it being found most of the time.

Why commit to such a time-intensive, labor-intensive process?

What would the potential delay profit the killer?

Why older people? Just practice? An experiment to see the effects?

Do they know who the first victim was yet?

What about the woman who owned the car, who was missing?

I nodded to Zach to take my phone. "Call Brandan."

Without questioning me, he scrolled my contacts and selected one to dial. Put the call on speaker.

No answer, four rings then voicemail.

"Call the department. Find someone on the case with the vacuum-packed body," I urged.

Zach repeated his actions without the speaker until he got someone on the phone for me.

Micah Downs. A familiar voice at least.

No pleasantries, I began, "Callaghan was working on a case with the vacuum-packed body found in the trunk of a car. I need to know who the owner of the car is or was. And where's Brandan?"

"He's in court today," he said.

"His divorce?" I asked, knowing Micah wouldn't have volunteered it.

"Yeah." He sounded irritated. "Bitch."

"Ten dollars," I said without thinking.

"Huh?"

"Never mind. I need to know who the car was registered to, information from her driver's license, everything you can find. I know she was presumed dead, but I believe she's the killer."

CHAPTER 74
JULIE

"Her name is Gretchen Alice Smith," Micah told us over the speaker when he called me back. "DL address is in Ann Arbor, but the house is condemned. No one's lived there in a decade according to tax records."

"What else?"

"Her maiden name is Rigsby. Her husband, Sean Smith died three years ago from an apparent heart attack at the age of 28. No children. Parents deceased. She was reported missing by a brother, Greg Rigsby, in late April."

Zach and I exchanged looks, recognizing the husband's name as the name of the hotel credit card holder in New York. As the name of the father of Kim's baby. Neither of which could be a man who died three years ago.

"What's the story?" I asked, afraid to find out more.

"In the report, Rigsby stated she had been living with him for several months in Traverse City after losing her job downstate. She borrowed his kayak and went to Duck Lake for the afternoon but didn't come home. After a pretty extensive search, no body was recovered although the kayak was located on the far shore from where the car was left." He hesitated, still reading. "And like you said, she was presumed dead."

"Okay," I prompted.

"That's odd. Her car was at the lake during the search, but then it came up missing a few days afterward. Rigsby denied having keys."

"Then it reappeared in TC several months later with a body in the trunk, go figure. Got it. Just in case, put out a BOLO on her, would you?" I said. "And leave Brandan a message to call me."

I disconnected.

"That's enough to leave me speechless," Zach said.

I smiled. "Yes, but now we know who we're looking for. Call Chris back and have him access her license and send the picture out to everyone. We've finally caught a break."

"If we're in time," he said.

CHAPTER 75
JULIE

"Julie, we haven't been able to find Kenny Underwood," Wade Fordham announced to all three of us in the truck over the phone speaker.

"Have someone check our place," Zach replied. "He has a little shed on the northeast corner of the property, set off the road 50 feet or so. You'd have to drive to and then to the south side of the barn and around."

"Why does he have a shed there?" the sheriff asked, finding the thought distasteful.

"Wade, he's lived on our property almost two years," I said, "ever since Mitch buried a body there. And he's been welcome."

"All right, I'll swing by there myself shortly. Are you guys on your way home now?"

"Just left Vancouver fifteen minutes ago. I'm not exactly sure where we should go when we get there. Any word from any other agencies?" I asked. "I'd feel much better if she were behind bars."

"Or dead," Zach mumbled.

The answer to both was no.

I explained to him that we had a name now for the woman in question as well as a description and that Micah Downs would be sending the history around to the department as well.

What I didn't want to explain, Zach did.

"Wade, Gretchen Rigsby-Smith is the illegitimate daughter of a multiple murderer from Julie's past. Anthony Bock killed a dozen people or so that they could account for, including both his cousins, his biological father, and he tried to take her life as well as my own. He was shot to death in Florida, but we have no idea if he was able to contact his offspring before he died."

"I see."

I don't think so, Wade. Not the whole huge, sordid, evil, unending picture.

"Bock is Julie's half-brother," Amber chimed in from the back seat. "If that's important. I just got off the phone with Detective Downs in Traverse City. He said that the first victim found in the trunk was Rigsby's adoptive maternal grandfather, Walter John Hough."

"What about Gretchen's parents?" Wade asked. "I mean adoptive parents."

"Died in a house fire several years ago," I replied. "I can't see how that was an accident, but who knows."

"Gretchen's brother by adoption is a half-brother biologically. She shot and killed him in the robbery in Indiana where Julie was injured," Zach added. "But he had contacted us in Michigan in July to ask about his birth mother, also one of Bock's victims. He used one name with us, but a different name – his sister's dead spouse's name – with Kim Katz."

"You guys make this stuff up, right? Sit around on cold evenings with hot chocolate and popcorn, inventing ways a single manhunt can be complicated beyond comprehension," Wade said, not really kidding. "Um, hang on a second."

In the background, I could hear radio traffic I couldn't make out. Then he put us on hold to take another call that took two minutes, then he clicked back to us. "That was Blake. He checked the Underwood's old farm." He paused. "Sorry, but he found Kenny. Looks like he'd been shot several times in the chest."

"Not, um, in . . ." I broke off.

"No, just shot."

Somehow that was acceptable news in comparison to the other possibility. The question was, why not?

She didn't have time, or perhaps dismemberment was a ritual that she thought Kenny unworthy of.

"Looks like she tried to burn the place, too, he said, but the fire didn't take," he added. "Listen, I'd dropped home to grab a sandwich, but I'm headed back to the station. You should stop there when you get to town. We'll get you in the bed and breakfast where no one will look."

I looked at Zach and in the mirror at Amber.

"We'll discuss it, but we will stop and check in."

Zach hit the red button to disconnect.

"I'm sorry, Dad," Amber said, reaching forward to touch his shoulder.

He didn't say anything, but I understood every single word on his mind about the death of a friend.

"We can't go home," he finally said. "We can't trust our vehicles left alone."

"True enough."

"On the other hand, I have to go home and check on the horses," he said.

• • • • •

We saw the glow of the fire from Highway 14, and my heart fluttered a few beats when we got close enough to see it was the sheriff's department building, totally involved.

Wade and Bette Donovan stood beside his patrol car a block away. I stopped next to them and got out.

After a hug, Bette broke down in sobs that she hadn't known.

"Known what?" I asked, confused.

"I knew everyone is looking for this woman, so I didn't think twice about a man who came in and asked if Inky Grissom was working tonight. He went into the restroom in the lobby," she said, wiping her nose with a crumpled tissue. "He was carrying a backpack, but I didn't suspect . . . I'm sure that's how he – I mean she – brought in whatever it was to start the fire."

"When I parked in back, she came running out," Wade said. "However it started, it spread fast. Chief said it was all through the crawl space."

"Our place!" Zach said. "If she did this –"

I knew the rest of the thought was that a fire at the sheriff's department would take up most or all the city's and county's fire service resources. There wouldn't be any left for another fire out in the county.

"Send anyone available to our place," I said. climbing back into the cab.

Wade tossed a portable radio at me as I put the truck in reverse.

Scattering gravel, I accelerated to the end of the block, then headed for the cabin.

"No, this can't be happening," Amber growled from behind me. "How could she slip through the roadblocks?"

"She probably headed here as soon as she left the car crash. Even if she didn't, if you're looking for a single female occupant, a male wouldn't raise a lot of suspicions," Zach told her. "The question now is, where did she go?"

"You both miss the point. The fire we left was a diversion of resources. The fire we're going to is a trap," I said. "She'll be there. We're her main targets."

CHAPTER 76
AMBER

The radio Sheriff Fordham had given Julie was silent.

"Why hasn't he called the other deputies?" I asked. "Fire trucks?"

"He's probably using the phone so it's not a public broadcast," Julie said. "Scanning a particular frequency or a whole band is not difficult. She'd be listening."

"Let me out at the highway," Dad said. "I'll come in past the barn."

"Did you even bring a weapon?" I asked.

"No, honey, I brought two." He leaned over and pulled up his jeans, removed a small revolver, straightened his pants back over his boots, then handed the gun to me. "Sorry, five shots, no extra ammo."

"Your .38?" Julie asked. "Check the glove compartment."

Sure enough, although only five more, it was something.

"Julie?" I asked.

"Just one and a spare mag, 31 rounds total."

"Only takes one," I offered. "Tally ho."

"You should stay in the car," Dad told me, looking over his shoulder. "But I can tell that's not going to happen. Get out with me. You can wrangle the horses. No argument."

Julie was leaning forward, peering hard upward through the windshield. "I don't see a fire, do you? Maybe she hasn't gotten there . . . "

Her voice faded to a hoarse whisper.

Ahead, in the occasional tree breaks, I could see a flicker of reflected light in the clouds.

I began to feel a little queasy about all the things in the house that I would lose in a fire. Worse, what all would be in the barn if the horses couldn't escape the pens.

Julie slowed to a stop within a hundred yards or so of the turnoff to our gate.

"I'll go on to the house, you two go toward the barn. You both have your phones?"

I nodded.

"Yeah. Be careful," Dad told her.

We got out and crossed to the west side of the road, and she drove on toward the cabin.

"You will run directly from the fence to the north side of the barn," he told me as we walked. "None of the horses should be inside. Move them out of the corral."

"Dad, what if . . ." I started to say when a large explosion unquestionably came from Five Aces.

"No what-if's," he replied. "We're trying to save the stock, then the house, then the barn – in that order."

"No, Dad," I said, "We save Julie first. Anything else can be replaced."

He smiled in agreement.

CHAPTER 77
JULIE

I made the left turn from the highway just as a fireball lit up the house, but I continued 200 yards to the gate on the right and entered, then parked facing left, out of the way of any possible fire or police units that might be responding.

For the moment, though, I was on my own.

I know it. So does she. She won't be far.

I hoped I could be wrong this time about bait always dying.

This fight would be against the skills and planning of a woman who had gone to great lengths to hurt me, physically and emotionally. She might even still be on the property, or close by, to make sure the fire and explosion were timed to cause a maximum impact on all three of us.

Seeing the house engulfed, knowing almost everything I owned was being destroyed, sadness was overwhelmed by a sudden rage at one man who had, even after his own death, generated so much torment.

Gretchen, whose father had been the result of a one-night encounter with a shy girl by my father almost five decades ago, wanted to carry on or perhaps just finish the work of my half-brother.

One way or another, the battle ended tonight.

I reached to the small of my back and pulled from its holster the brand-new Springfield XD .45 caliber pistol, purchased in Vancouver on the way back from Portland a week ago when Richard Langston and I transported the vacuum-packed body parts. I tucked it into my right vest pocket, then made sure the extra magazine was in my left pocket for easy access and opened the door.

No sirens audible over the roar of the fire, but I held out hope for more help though more police on scene would only endanger more people.

"It's what they signed up for," I remember hearing one man say that about the police and firefighters who were killed at the World Trade Center on 9/11. I remember verbally blasting him in response, "The decision to help others, knowing the ultimate sacrifice might be required someday, is never made with a casual acceptance of the risks taken every single call. 'Signing up' for those jobs doesn't mean you volunteer to become a victim just because the profession is so dangerous." Zach had pulled me away, but my rant received applause from bystanders on the street.

I focused my rage into that same pinpoint.

Carrying a gun, a fire ax, a defibrillator – none of that exempts you from being mortal, but pledging to protect others, even putting their lives ahead of your own, makes you a human with a great heart.

It makes you a hero.

I stepped out onto the grass, considering whether the fire could burn toward my truck, dismissing the idea.

The insurance company is going to terminate any relationship with us anyway.

Torn whether to stay slightly shielded from the fire by the truck or to make my way on open ground toward the barn, where I knew Zach and Amber would be going. I didn't want to lure her any closer to them than this.

My night vision was obliterated by looking at the fire, but it was hard to look away.

Now what?

I took the few heavy steps necessary to move to the front of my truck, stood there, hands in my vest pockets, head hung, my eyes closed against the inferno.

Waiting.

Time meant nothing. A minute, ten? I had no idea. I just waited.

"Hello, Julie," a voice said behind me, barely audible over the crash of the cabin's roof caving in. "I've waited a long time for this."

I pretended not to hear.

What's the worst that can happen – she shoots me in the back again?

"God damn it, turn around!" she shrieked.

My failure to follow her bidding infuriated her to the brink of sanity.

One could hope. . .

She screamed at me one more time.

Eyes still closed to preserve my night vision, I tilted my head to my left, feigning hearing something over the roar, making sure my grip was set on the pistol as I pulled it from my pocket. I turned around and opened my eyes, pretending to be surprised someone was there. I cupped my left hand to my ear.

"Oh hi! Wait, who are you?" I yelled back, stepping sideways to angle her more toward the fire.

Sure enough, she stood ten feet away, wearing black clothes and gloves. The firearm's barrel reflected the flames, making it visible.

Hopefully, I was silhouetted against the house fire in my dark jacket.

"I'm your worst fucking nightmare!" she said, quoting some movie I couldn't name.

The fire thundered in my bones, and I felt the heat on my ears.

"What? I can't hear you!" I replied, leaning toward her. "You're my neighbor from . . ."

She waved the gun at me, losing her patience. She tried to move back into my shadow, but I matched her step sideways again.

I hoped it looked like I intended to shake hands with her as I pulled the pistol from my pocket and fired once. Twice. A third time before she fell to the ground.

Damn it! I can't believe I missed a shot!

She fell to the grass. Her weapon had dropped from her hand, just as it had mine when she shot me. She might have been able to reach it, except I stepped on her wrist.

"I win. I'm the one who gets to walk away from the last traces of Anthony Bock," I screamed, wanting to kick her repeatedly. "You lose. Greg lost. Anthony Bock died, and no more echoes of his evil will haunt me."

The two shots into her chest reminded me of the ones I'd fired at David Wesley so many years ago. Not immediately fatal, but deadly, nonetheless.

Just to be sure, I kicked her gun away. I couldn't see the bloodstains from the wounds, but I watched as the life faded from her eyes.

Probably unsure if what he'd heard were gunshots, Zach stutter-stepped to a halt behind me, panting, a sheen of sweat on his skin reflecting the fire glow on his right, leaving half his face in shadow. Relieved to find me still standing, he told me later.

A wall of the house, maybe the fireplace, fell into the blaze, sending sparks into the sky.

I heard a siren in the distance, which given the roar of the fire, had to be close. Then I made out a second.

Amber galloped up, bareback on Rainier, who seemed unfazed by the fire. "Horses are all safe. Is she dead?" she asked.

I nodded.

"Really dead?"

"Absolutely," Zach and I said together as he tucked me under his left arm as we watched the house burn. "I guess this means we're moving back to Albuquerque, huh?"

CHAPTER 78
JULIE

I relinquished my weapon to Wade per policy, and I asked that he perhaps find it a good home when he was done with it. Never could I pick it up again without feeling its connection to Gretchen Rigsby. In a few days, I would stand for a formal inquiry to determine the justification of the shoot, but who could argue that it was at the very least self-defense.

Knowing the act was self-defense didn't make it feel all that much better.

For all the weeks and months since Ethan / Gregory had entered our lives, and threatening us, killing Gretchen was anticlimactic. Shooting someone is never as dispassionate as it seems on television. As much evil as Bock and his two genetic descendants had wrought on the world, pulling the trigger wasn't without its consequences. Knowing I'd ended a life was gut-wrenching.

I *knew* she was a criminal who had killed what we estimated to be at least five people: her adopted maternal grandfather, who was the victim found in the trunk of the car in Traverse City; her half-brother/adopted brother Gregory; Mr. and Mrs. Prosser, Lesa Bowman's grandparents; and Kenny Underwood. Although it wouldn't be re-opened, the fire marshal in Ann Arbor, Michigan, agreed the house fire that killed the Rigsby's could have been arson.

A tiny part of me wondered if it had to do with shooting another woman. The "whites of her eyes" sort of thing. Or that for all her threats, she hadn't actually harmed me yet.

Zach and I had to have that discussion alone. No one should hear the doubts a cop has when he shoots a suspect.

• • • • •

October 24, 2001
Standing in the parking lot behind the sheriff's department the next morning, discussing the previous night's activities. The fire chief confirmed our suspicion

that the house and everything inside, including Zach's Suburban in the garage, were destroyed. This was not a surprise, though we had not stayed around to watch the firefighters.

The sheriff's department building was nothing but brick walls, the contents were also a total loss.

"We'll rebuild," Wade told us all as the entire staff and their families stood, watching the wisps of smoke still drifting from the building's ruins. "Time to update the place anyway."

This brought a few chuckles.

Chris Bell had driven from Portland, and it was great to see him.

"None of our attempts to stop Gretchen Smith from getting to Skamania County worked, obviously," he said. "We determined she used your credentials to get past a roadblock at the Dallesport crossing before they were set up – before the sketch had been distributed to them, so we presume she came from the Interstate 84, going past other crossings closer to Skamania County."

"That makes sense," I said. "She had plenty of time while we were at the hospital in Centralia."

"Even if not successful, it was a good exercise for coordination of agencies on both sides of the river." He held up a finger and went back to his car, bringing back a stack of donut boxes. "Lane Sebastian couldn't make it, but he sends his best wishes."

I grabbed a maple-frosted donut and excused myself from the crowd to answer my phone.

"Julie? Brandan, I heard you called yesterday," he said.

I laughed. "Yeah, though it feels more like a year ago," I told him. Knowing a conversation about the events of the last day would take a while, I found a shade tree to sit under as we talked.

"Not that it matters now," he said, "but I found out more pieces to your puzzle. Sean Smith did die of a life-long heart-related illness three years ago. Dr. Katz performed the autopsy, so I asked about it. He suspected but couldn't prove that the patient's condition was worsened by an overdose of digitalis. But when I compared driver license photos of him and Gregory Rigsby, I understood how Rigsby got away with using that identity."

"I wonder if Gretchen chose Smith for that very reason," I said.

"Probably. I also found an abandoned warehouse where fruit was dried and packed a decade ago. According to the manager who agreed to meet me there this morning, there appears to have been a break-in and theft of – surprise – a vacuum packaging machine."

"No kidding. I can send it back if he'd like," I offered. "I have so many other questions that don't require answers anymore. Speaking of answers, how'd your court appearance go yesterday?"

"I lost. Molly's moving them to the Los Angeles area."

"I'm sorry," I replied. "Guess you'll be getting some frequent flyer miles."

"Haven't decided. I might look for something closer to them. I worked in Orange County, remember? That would be convenient."

"Our house was burned to the ground, so we're moving back to Albuquerque."

"I can't imagine how depressing that must feel," he said.

"Yeah, lost everything except the animals and barn. That's dismal. But you're welcomed to stop in New Mexico any time."

"I can see Dr. Katz, too, when he moves to New Mexico. Is he really marrying Zach's mother?" he laughed. "I mean, I hope I wasn't supposed to keep that a secret."

"We haven't heard it formally, but I suspected it would happen," I said, "but last we heard, Vera might move to Traverse City. I haven't had a chance to tell them about the fire, either."

"That secret is safe. Listen, I gotta run. Nolan will want an update, too. Give him a ring when you have a chance."

After our goodbyes, we hung up.

I put calling Nolan on my growing list of things to do. First, I had to decide whether Hannah Tolbert's parents or any other living relatives might want to know anything about her last year alive, and the infant who was fathered by someone who became a killer.

No, that's another secret that should stay buried.

Amber was most devastated that the journals we had borrowed from Mr. Daniels were ashes.

"You promised to send them back," she said. "I hadn't finished reading the last book. What if one of her other kids wants to know about them?"

"Based on our past experiences, I'd suggest you run," I said, kidding. "Nothing I can do to replace them. I'll confess."

I called him and explained the fire.

"I'm sorry to hear you lost your house, but I appreciate you letting me know," he told me when I called. "Marissa would've wanted her mother's stuff. She's been all up in Penny's business since Ethan showed up asking questions."

With his mention of Ethan, I spent half an hour explaining the long story of who Ethan Wenzler was and wasn't, from conception through his and Gretchen's deaths.

"Wow," he said when I was done. "I'm glad I didn't know that about him when he came."

"You saw him?" I asked, surprised. "I assumed he just called to ask you about Penny."

"No, he was here in June. I tried to be civil, but for some reason, I didn't want him in my house. Now I know why."

"Good instincts. I wish I'd listened to Zach's initial gut reaction about him. That would have saved us a lot of trouble."

Months and hundreds of thousands of dollars' worth of trouble.

"I have a confession of my own, though," he told me. "Marissa has been hiding the last journal Penny was working on when she died. She told me after I shipped the others."

"She must hold it in high regard, then."

"She does, but there are a few passages toward the end of Penny's life that you should also read. Marissa let me make copies, and I've mailed them to the same address as the books."

"That's very kind of you both," I said. "I look forward to reading them."

"I'm not so sure about that," he offered. "But it's important you know."

• • • • •

The package was waiting when I went to the courthouse the next morning.

I collected the package, a box the size of a ream of paper, and took it back to the rental cabin where we were staying, hoping to find closure to the events involving Penny's life.

Zach was on the phone to Vera when I came in, and based on the side of the conversation I could hear, they were discussing matters of the ranch. Zach's tone sounded calmer now that they had finally broken the ice on the topic of Zoe.

He motioned to me, sign language for did I want to talk to her, and I shook my head.

"Okay, Mom. I'll let you know when everything is settled here and we head that way," he said, then paused while she spoke. "Yes, I know the weather could turn any time now, but Julie can't leave an open inquiry."

I shrugged at him, indicating I still hadn't heard a definitive decision.

They chatted on for a while.

"I'll tell them. Love you, too, Mom." He punched the button to disconnect.

I leaned down and kissed him.

"She is thoroughly elated we will be moving to the ranch, although as you heard, she is afraid a few snowflakes could change everything," he said.

"After everything we've been through, I'm not afraid of a blizzard."

"What'cha got?" he asked, nodding toward the box.

"Penny's husband, Mark? I had to call and tell him the journals were lost in the house fire. He was as okay with that as possible, I guess, but he told me Marissa had kept back Penny's last journal before she died. He said he'd already mailed me a copy of the last few weeks of the book, that I needed to read it."

"Ominous. That's it?"

I nodded and dropped the small flat box on the table. "I'm a little hesitant to open it, given his gloom and our history."

"Doesn't look like a snowstorm," he observed. "How bad could it be?"

"I don't know." I slid down into a vinyl-covered chair. "Like Pandora's Box, I'm almost sure there's something bad inside, but he said I needed to know what it is." I leaned my head forward and rubbed my neck. "Where's Amber?"

"She decided to stay a few days with the Fordham's rather than here with us, but she'll be back shortly. They went shopping – guess it's a good thing my credit cards didn't burn up in the house so she can melt them at the mall," he said, pretending to complain.

"Even better that I have my own," I said with a grin. "We need clothes, too."

"Also, I don't think I was supposed to have heard anything about a party." He rolled his eyes.

"Have you decided you can trust her to go back to school in January?"

"Do I have a choice? You told me I can't put her in a cage and take her with us." He smiled. "Yeah, we've talked a couple of times. I know she'll make more poor choices, but hopefully, that New York thing was the big one so all else will be average young adult life lessons."

I nodded again and looked over at the package.

"Shall I leave you alone for a while?" he asked. "I could go grab us lunch."

"Maybe that's a good idea."

He stood and I flipped him the keys. "I still hate that we're driving that ugly blue truck. Friday we can go shopping without any drugs or car crashes."

"I'm beginning to like it," I said. "Let's keep it, at least till we get moved, if you think we can live with just one vehicle till then. That way we won't bang up a new one or have to drive separately."

He kissed the top of my head and grabbed his sunglasses on the way out the door, leaving me alone with a package of papers from a woman's journal, written more than five years ago.

I went to the kitchenette for a knife to slit the tape, glad I hadn't done that while Zach was here to see. He complained that I abused his kitchen utensils.

Letting about twenty pages slide out, I sat down and steeled myself for something bad.

September 20, 1995

Back in Phoenix for two days and now I'm sitting in the hospital with Jaralyn, who's been getting worse for the last day, high fever and seizures. The doctors don't know what's wrong with her, so I've been holding her hand and crying and praying for a miracle. I was hoping to think of something else, so here I am, writing in this crazy journal again after all these years. Maybe this will be the confession of my sins from decades ago that will save my baby girl.

I had been so afraid that going back to Michigan would make me think of all the horrible things I'd written in books previous and some that I didn't. Julie Madigan and Brandan Callahan (? spelling) made me feel like I didn't need to judge J.P. Or that I'd known Anthony had not killed himself when we were told that by the Navy. It wouldn't surprise me to hear that Anthony is the one who had done all this, that he killed my brother.

I wish I'd told her that it was Anthony who'd molested me when I was young. Because my mother had never believed me about him then, and because the military had delivered news of his suicide to her already, I knew she would never believe me that he was alive. But I also knew she read my diaries, so I wrote stuff just to make it all – I don't know – ordinary.

Hannah Tolbert and I had walked home one afternoon in August, right after school had started, and we wandered over to the barn to see a litter of new kittens. Mom and Dad were gone to town or somewhere. J.P. showed up, being a jerk as usual. He was taunting Hannah, that she didn't have a date for prom because she was so ugly, which she wasn't, but she was pretty overweight. He offered to take her if she'd let him have sex with her. I'm not sure how it happened from there anymore, but she was actually going to do it when all of the sudden, out dropped Anthony from the loft, saying he was going to do it, instead.

I tried to fight them off, but when I woke up, it was pretty obvious that we had both been raped. I didn't know, and she wouldn't tell me which one had done it, but I always suspected it was Anthony. After that afternoon, he disappeared for good. I finally told my mother it had been Ethan Wenzler who I'd had sex with, only because he had moved away that fall. If this ever caused him any grief, I'm terribly sorry. I heard later that he'd died in a car wreck in Wisconsin.

If you've read any of the journals, and I suspect that someday, someone will want to know what happened, you already know that my mother and Hannah's mother compared notes about us both being pregnant. We were promptly sent to a school for unwed mothers over the Christmas holiday break to await the delivery of our babies, then we were expected to come home afterward after the school year in June of 1975 and never speak of it again.

Maybe that would have been possible, except Hannah died in childbirth. Maybe it was just one of those things, but the doctors and nurses were just plain mean to us, and no one cared if what they were doing hurt. I expect they considered it additional punishment for our sins.

I never told Hannah's parents about what happened. I don't even know if they are still alive now or if hearing that news would just break their hearts. I think I would want to know.

I dropped the pages onto the table and cried softly. Two girls, more victims of Anthony Bock.

The pages only left me with more questions – how did Gregory ever know who Penny had named as his father? The only answer was that Anthony Bock must have somehow read Penny's journals after her death, meaning he had been back in their house again. When? Or had it been Gregory after Mark wouldn't tell him he had the journals? Somehow Bock had to have communicated to Gregory that the journals existed. How else would Gregory know that she had written anything about him or this other kid at school in a single volume out of a dozen? Why didn't he take them instead of finding me, or was finding me part of the plan all along?

Had Mark Daniels put together any of this before I spoke to him – his wife's teenage rape and pregnancy, the death of her friend, or that someone had broken back into his home to find and read her last journal's entries?

I hoped not.

Marissa, I hoped, wouldn't come calling someday to get answers about her mother's other child. She deserves to keep memories of Penny that are unscathed by the evil of Anthony Bock.

Nothing left to read, I decided I would drop the pages into the shred-box as soon as I got to work in the temporary quarters of the sheriff's department in the courthouse. Time to be done with this forever. I'd do it when I handed in my formal resignation, one of the hundreds of things to do before we moved.

We didn't have much to pack, I thought.

Many reminders of memories were gone, though the reminiscences remained. We had survived. We had each other. We had a chance to take the next step, halfway across the country again, but back to familiar land.

I was shoving the pages back into the box, I realized that the box wasn't empty. I put down the copies and lifted a makeshift divider, revealing a padded shipping envelope that had been mailed to Penny's and Mark's son Colby. I couldn't read the postmark, but the package was heavier than paper.

I let the contents slide out onto the paper. Several layers of old newspaper were wrapped around a bundle. Inside the paper was thin cardboard that had been folded in half and taped to protect the blade of a grossly discolored steel-bladed kitchen knife. The wooden handle was unvarnished, badly dented and stained.

One note inside the envelope with it read:

Julie, I found this in the box with the journals I sent to you. I didn't want to believe that it was related to Penny's death or anything since then. I know now that I was mistaken. – Mark

And another note, tucked inside the Detroit newspaper, dated September 24, 1995, read:

Mark, I'm not sure you will find this before, but Gregory will come for my knife someday. Or perhaps Colby will find it first. I bet he already knows what to do with it and you can be his first. Maybe he and my children can carry on my legacy, echo my life's work. I'd like that more than anything.

Oh, and if she's still alive, I promise you'll hear from her, and when you do, tell Julie there will be more. A

I realized I'd been holding my breath, but the exhalation made a soft mewling sound, like an injured animal. Hot tears blurred my vision before dripping off my face and splattering on the ink of Anthony's note.

I heard Zach let himself in. He carried two giant soft drink cups and a white bag, which he placed on the table.

He helped me to my feet, and wrapped his warm, strong, loving arms around me, holding me for a long time while I cried softly.

"It's over," I said. "It's finally all over."

The kiss that followed was mind-blowing, as always.

From the doorway came the insistent voice of our daughter, saying, "Get a room, geez!"

EPILOGUE

Hermits really do exist, and although I'm not a fan, the following recipe is from my husband's great-grandmother, Lena Arnot-Torrey – Nan.

NAN'S HERMITS

3 cups sugar
4 eggs
1 cup butter
1 cup buttermilk
2 cups raisins
1 to 2 cups pecans
5-1/2 cups flour (approx.)
2 tsp baking soda
2 tsp cinnamon
1 tsp ground cloves
2 tsp ground nutmeg
1/2 tsp salt

Grind pecans and raisins together, set aside. Cream together butter, sugar, and eggs. When thoroughly mixed, add ground nuts and raisins into cloves, nutmeg, cinnamon, baking soda, salt, and 3 cups flour. Combine this mixture by slowly adding small amounts of buttermilk, then add as much of the remaining flour as needed for consistency to drop a spoonful onto a greased cookie sheet.

Bake at 375 degrees until lightly brown, about 10 – 12 minutes.

• • • • •

A different recipe for Hermits comes from Fannie Merritt Farmer's "The Boston Cooking-School Cook Book," published in 1918 in Boston by Little, Brown, & Co. reads:

1/3 cup butter
2/3 cup sugar
1/3 cup raisins, stoned and cut in small pieces
1 egg
1 tablespoons milk
2 cups flour
2 teaspoons baking powder
1/2 teaspoon cinnamon
1/4 teaspoon clove
1/4 teaspoon mace
1/4 teaspoon nutmeg

Cream the butter, add sugar gradually, then raisins, egg well beaten, and milk. Mix and sift dry ingredients and add to the first mixture. Roll mixture a little thicker than Vanilla Wafers.
(There is no further directions or information about cooking temperature and time.)

May 2020

I've finished the manuscript and sent to my publisher. Along with the rest of the world, I've watched the spread of a virus, getting closer to me every day. Hopefully, by the time the book is available, this pandemic will be history, but I'd like to offer my perspective, especially as it relates to 9/11. This is my opinion, so please understand what I write today may prove to be wrong. Wrong in some cases would be a pleasant and welcome surprise.

CoViD19, a novel coronavirus, began its media debut in China before we watched it explode globally. Even now, wild conspiracies and speculations are offered as to its creation – from eating exotic animals to an accidental (or intentional) creation and release from a covert biological research facility. I've even heard that the virus was a planned epidemic to reduce the world's population or a political ploy for a new world order (no capitalization on purpose). From where I sit, the conspiracies are epic and endless. I doubt we'll ever be told the truth about its origin or many of the responses, and in the present, I guess it doesn't matter.

The September 11, 2001, attacks on the United States of America caused instant and intense fear in a matter of hours, followed by a huge response of near-global human compassion. So far in 2020, this virus has exploded into a global threat with severe consequences on every level of mankind within a few months, affecting individuals, employers, healthcare systems, and governments. Could the response have been different? Yes, absolutely. It could have been better. It could also have been worse.

In my opinion, too many people believe "someone else" is responsible for ensuring their safety. Safety is an elusive concept, as doing anything has a risk, including doing nothing at all. Ultimately, an individual must assume responsibility for his own safety and risks he takes. Common sense may have become the greatest unsalvageable victim to a virus, gasping its final breaths.

If you have read my series, you've read that facts and truth are not always the same. I believe this concept.

What will matter in this battle with a virus is the outcome, which we do not know today.

My wish is that you and your family stay healthy.

I want to offer my condolences to the victims and families of the September 11, 2001, terrorist attacks, along with an explanation. My intention to use this event within my story was not to exploit the horrific tragedy. I have no sufficient words to honor those who perished in the airliners, the Twin Towers, the Pentagon, and the many others.

I have immeasurable appreciation of the hundreds of emergency services personnel worked to save lives, and later recovering minute remains and effects of those who died. I offer sincere sympathy to the families and friends left behind. As someone who was not there, I cannot comprehend the grief of those who were there; but in writing this book, I researched the effects of 9/11 on others like me, who watched from afar and were still affected by it. If my fiction has caused insult, I offer humble apology. I wanted to describe how the tragedy touched the rest of us who weren't in New York, Washington, or Pennsylvania. We watched this tragedy on television and cried. Like Zach feeling the death of his twin sister, September 11 didn't happen to us, but we still feel it deeply. The world stopped turning on 9/11, Alan Jackson wrote. That is a good description.

In an article published by WebMD in 2002, the authors speak about the effects 9/11, (https://www.webmd.com/balance/features/american-psychepost-911#2) stating:

> "While people in New York City and Washington have been particularly susceptible to the psychological impact of 9/11, men and women in every part of the U.S. have been affected as well. Not only did almost everyone view the televised collapse of the World Trade Center towers, but according to the RTI researchers, a startling *10 million adults* in the U.S. had a friend, family member, or co-worker killed or injured in the attacks. Sept. 11 was a terrible loss—not just in terms of lost life, but in terms of a lost way of life," says Yael Danieli, Ph.D., a New York City clinical psychologist, and a founding director of the International Society for Traumatic Stress Studies. She believes that a "new normality" must be established that incorporates uncertainty, including a greater readiness for "anything." She adds, "It means accepting that nothing will ever be the same again. This may feel bad, but it's realistic."

I wanted to write about how this tragedy impacted the lives of people elsewhere. An individual who faced the death of a loved one during that time might have felt the loss was less significant, diminished by the magnitude of losses on 9/11. I wanted to share the notion that, regardless of the pain of the many, the pain of one was no less.

My story does not mention, nor could words do justice to honor the emergency service workers and rescuers who worked so long at the scenes of Ground Zero, the Pentagon, Pennsylvania. Most of my life has been in medicine of one facet or another, including being a paramedic. I'm in awe of the men and women who responded. Hundreds died in the collapse of the Towers, trying to save others. In the years since, many who spent time at Ground Zero have developed terminal diseases related to their exposures there. I've heard some say that people in emergency services, just like military personnel, sign up for the risks when choosing their jobs, but I disagree.

Every single day, they *choose* to protect, to rescue, to treat. Sometimes this choice means putting their lives at risk for others. They do so, knowing the losses their own family would face on the day comes they don't go home. I daresay those who belittle them for making such a choice to sacrifice for others would not do so themselves.

Those brave men and women who stepped forward the most abnormal event that any of us could ever face outside of war. We owe them all – police, fire, EMS, dispatchers, nurses and medical staff, the paid and the volunteers, the civilian and the military – gratitude for their willingness to sacrifice for us. And they should not have to beg for medical coverage after illnesses force them from their professions. We owe them that. If you disagree, go spend a few days in those boots and see if your admiration doesn't escalate.

ABOUT THE AUTHOR

Being squeamish is not a good characteristic for anyone outside of emergency services. It's not helpful for thriller writers, either, says Val Conrad. She loves being able to blend the reality of the places she has lived with actual history, adding the complexities of medicine, and setting a story against a background and bone-chilling crime and the challenge of solving it.

From paramedic to nurse to teacher, Val most recently took time away from writing to finish her third degree and become a family nurse practitioner. She lives in the Texas Panhandle and shares her life with Bill, her husband of 25 years, and a 65-pound lapdog named Grace.

NOTE FROM THE AUTHOR

Word-of-mouth is crucial for any author to succeed. If you enjoyed *Echoes of Like Souls*, please leave a review online—anywhere you are able. Even if it's just a sentence or two. It would make all the difference and would be very much appreciated.

Thanks!
Val

Thank you so much for reading one of
Val Conrad's *A Julie Madigan Thriller*.
If you enjoyed the experience, please check out
the first book in the series!

Blood of Like Souls by Val Conrad

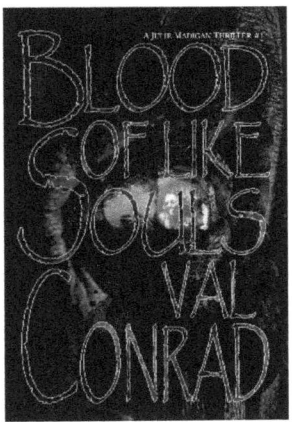

View other Black Rose Writing titles at
www.blackrosewriting.com/books and use promo code
PRINT to receive a **20% discount** when purchasing.

Lightning Source UK Ltd.
Milton Keynes UK
UKHW010655031120
372716UK00001B/23